MANY A TEAR HAS TO FALL

MANY A TEAR HAS TO FALL

June Francis

This first world edition published 2016
in Great Britain and the USA by
SEVERN HOUSE PUBLISHERS LTD of
19 Cedar Road, Sutton, Surrey, England, SM2 5DA.
Trade paperback edition first published
in Great Britain and the USA 2016 by
SEVERN HOUSE PUBLISHERS LTD

British Library Cataloguing in Publication Data
A CIP catalogue record for this title is available from the British Library.

ISBN-13: 978-0-7278-8603-3 (cased)
ISBN-13: 978-1-84751-705-0 (trade paper)
ISBN-13: 978-1-78010-766-0 (e-book)

This is a wo   iously.
are either th   :ribed
Except whe **Rotherham MBC**
for the story
fictitious an
business esta

B54 012 521 6	
Askews & Holts	27-Jul-2016
AF	£20.99
M2	

All Severn H

Severn Hou   M [FSC™],
the leading i AF
All our titles   logo.

Typeset by Palimpsest Book Production Ltd.,
Falkirk, Stirlingshire, Scotland.
Printed and bound in Great Britain by
TJ International, Padstow, Cornwall.

One

'You're not going out in this, are you, dear? You sound a bit rough.'

Maggie Gregory glanced at her landlady and said hoarsely, 'I've no choice, Mrs Cooling. I've had no phone call saying the photoshoot has been cancelled. Anyway, it's indoors and it won't take me long to get there.'

'You wrap up well. You could certainly do with a warmer scarf than that one you're wearing, however pretty it is.' The older woman's eyes brightened. 'I'll tell you what, I'll lend you my mother's old scarf. It's real cashmere and is as soft and warm as anything! You don't want to end up with pneumonia.' She bustled away.

Maggie considered not waiting for Mrs Cooling to return, worried about being late. Her chest hurt when she breathed and she found herself praying that she wouldn't end up with a bad dose of bronchitis like last year. Despite the Clean Air Act becoming law after the Great Smog in 1952, which had killed thousands of people in London, the capital still suffered from peasoupers when cold, damp and a lack of wind combined together. She leaned back against the lobby wall and closed her eyes, promising herself an evening at the theatre as soon as she felt fit. A fellow Liverpudlian, and a student at the Central School of Speech and Drama, had recommended a revue, *Blue Magic*, at the Prince of Wales theatre, starring Tommy Cooper and Shirley Bassey.

'Here you are, dear!'

Maggie opened her eyes at the sound of her landlady's voice and forced a smile. 'You are good to me,' she said.

'Well, I promised my former lodger Liverpool actress Dorothy Wilson, and your brother Jared, that I'd take care of you. Now undo the top buttons of your coat and I'll make sure this scarf is wrapped nice and snug about your chest,' Mrs Cooling said. 'I well remember when I was a little girl my mother rubbing goose grease on my chest in the winter. Not that we had a goose every Christmas, only when Dad had a bonus.' She buttoned up Maggie's coat and patted her shoulder. 'Now you take care. Use your other scarf to cover your mouth so you won't be breathing in so much of that filthy stuff outside – and if you don't mind my saying so, dear, it's time you gave up the ciggies.' She wagged a finger in Maggie's face. 'Not only are they bad for your chest, but smoking ages the skin. You're only nineteen and you don't want to be looking ten years older than you are when you reach thirty.'

Maggie refused to believe that the ciggies would age her skin that swiftly, but thanked her for the advice. She had tried to stop smoking after her older brother, Jared, and sister, Dot, had gone on about it being bad for her health, but her resolve had only lasted a few days. Still, she did appreciate Mrs Cooling's concern.

As Maggie left the boarding house she paused at the top of the steps and eased back her shoulders, recalling her mother saying: *Shoulders back, head high. If you want to be seen to your best advantage, you mustn't slouch!*

Maggie felt a lump in her throat just thinking about her mother but, blinking back tears, she tugged up the silk scarf so that it covered her mouth and breathed shallowly, knowing that if she breathed any deeper it might trigger a coughing bout. She descended the steps and attempted to cheer herself up by telling herself that at least the visibility was not as bad as it had appeared from inside the lodging house. She wasted no time heading towards Gloucester Road Tube station and the Piccadilly line, to catch a train that would take her to the studio in Soho.

'That's a bad cough you've got there,' said Charlie, the photographer, handing Maggie her wrap. 'When you finish here you should go straight home, make yourself a hot toddy and get to bed.'

Maggie felt too weary to say that was what she intended doing, so simply nodded and warmed herself by the two-bar electric fire. Then she went behind a screen and removed the one-piece bathing costume and put on a polka-dot bikini in daffodil yellow and white, draping the matching short, sleeveless wrap with its frilled edging over a shoulder.

She thought of last summer and the lovely russet tweed swagger coat that she had modelled for a winter collection, and how she had sweltered beneath the lights. She wished she was wearing it right now, but that was magazine modelling for you.

'Wow! You look great in that bikini,' said Charlie, his eyes lighting up as she came from behind the screen.

'Thanks, my sister and brother are always saying I could do with more meat on me. They don't understand the modelling business. I just wish I was basking on a sunny beach abroad right now,' she said hoarsely.

'Save your pennies and we could go together,' he suggested.

She drew in a painful breath. 'You know I've got someone, Charlie. Otherwise I'd take you up on your offer,' she said, adopting the pose he had suggested earlier and allowing the wrap to dangle from her fingertips on to the scattering of sand that sat against a backdrop of painted sea, palm trees, and a dazzling sun in a clear blue sky.

'But you hardly ever see him,' protested Charlie. 'Now hold that pose.'

Maggie remained perfectly still, thinking of Norman Marshall, who was a marine engineer and away at sea for months on end. She had not heard from him since the end of November, and that was worrying, especially as Jared's wife, Emma, had written in her Christmas card that Norman's twin brother, Pete, had married his on-off, long-time girlfriend, Peggy McGrath, the week before Christmas. Apparently they were living with the twins' mother, Gertie Marshall, in Bootle. Maggie had tried to convince herself that the all-important Christmas card to her from Norman had gone missing in the post. What with him working on a BP tanker, he sailed thousands of miles to far-distant lands in his job. She had hoped to receive a Valentine card last week, but she had looked in vain for its arrival and could not help but feel hurt and worried. So much so that she had even thought of writing to his twin, Pete.

Last time she had seen Norman had been at the beginning of September, when they had met up in Chatham, Kent. Then he had still been full of the news that his twin, who worked in a shipping office in Liverpool, had not only broken up with Peggy yet again but that she had disappeared. So it had come as something of a shock to hear from Emma that the couple were now married. Did Norman know? He had written twice since last she had seen him, but the letters had been brief and with no mention of his twin. It would have been nice to have a double wedding, just like Maggie's brother and sister had done, but that was definitely out of the question now. She remembered how Norman had kissed her with real passion when they had last parted. She had been convinced he could not bear to let her go and had expected him to ask her to marry him. Although he had never actually said those three little magic words, 'I Love You', to her, she had felt certain that he did.

'Have you gone into a trance?' asked Charlie, interrupting her thoughts. 'This is the third time I've spoken to you.'

'Sorry,' mouthed Maggie, wanting nothing more than to get back to her digs and burrow beneath the bedcovers with a hot-water bottle, a hot toddy and a couple of Aspros.

'D'you want to make us a coffee?' asked Charlie.

She shook her head, thinking he had a nerve asking, knowing she wasn't feeling well. But that was men for you, thinking only of themselves. 'I want to get home before the smog worsens,' she whispered, and went behind the screen.

Her fingers trembled as she got changed, thinking that there were some exceptional men out there; her father, for one. He had cosseted her when she was a little girl and encouraged her to believe that she could do anything if she had enough faith in herself. That was before he had caught the muscle-wasting disease and oh, how he had suffered during the last few years of his life. He had been kind, thoughtful, and so brave. It had been frightening watching him gradually weaken and fade away.

A shaky sigh escaped her as she finished changing into her own clothes. Ten minutes later she re-emerged from behind the screen, muffled up in scarves, hat and coat. 'See you again,' she said, blowing Charlie a kiss as she opened the studio door and went out.

Despite the smog, she was able to find her way to the nearest Tube station and catch a train to Gloucester Road. As she left the station she felt exhausted, and tried to comfort herself with the thought that she did not have far to go. The ringing noise made by her high-heeled boots on a pavement slippery with moisture echoed strangely, and she felt in danger of losing her bearings due to the smog.

She came to a corner. Was this where she turned? She was aware of the shadowy shapes of people passing by; she would have asked directions but they vanished so quickly. She was finding it more difficult to breathe and her chest ached with the cold, despite being well wrapped up. Feeling even more weary than earlier, she stopped and rested against some wrought-iron railings and closed her eyes. She would count to fifty and then move on.

A few moments later she heard a door opening, then footsteps and a clang, as if a latch had been lifted. She caught a whiff of Old Spice aftershave and then heard a match being struck and cigarette smoke tickled her nostrils. Her chest wheezed and she coughed.

'Who's there?' The man's voice was sharp. 'Mrs Sinclair, is that you?'

Maggie wondered if she was imagining that hint of a Liverpool accent as a figure loomed up close by. She decided it was time she moved, but had only taken a couple of steps when her feet slid from beneath her and she fell heavily on to the pavement. As she lay there gasping, she heard hurrying footsteps.

A woman cried out, 'Is that you, laddie? I'm sorry to be late but it's this bloody smog!'

'Stay right where you are, Mrs Sinclair!' ordered the man. 'There's someone on the ground! Be careful you don't trip over them.'

Maggie managed to lift her head. 'Please help me?' she said hoarsely.

A man's face hovered a few inches above her own and blue eyes gazed into hers. 'Are you all right, queen? Here, let me give you a hand up.' Maggie noticed he was wearing a trilby and a checked scarf about his throat. 'Mrs Sinclair, perhaps you could help? You take one side and I'll take the other.'

Between them they managed to hoist Maggie to her feet. 'Don't let me go!' she croaked, clinging on to them as her feet threatened to slide from beneath her again.

'It's all right! We're not going to let you fall,' said the man.

'You don't think she's been drinking, do you?' said Mrs Sinclair.

He sniffed. 'She doesn't smell of it.'

'I haven't!' wheezed Maggie, shivering.

'She doesn't sound well. I think she needs to get warm and have a sit-down,' said the man. 'D'you think you can cope with her, Mrs Sinclair? Make her a cup of tea. I'm a bit behind and I have to get cracking. You know how it is.'

'Indeed, I do. I just hope she hasn't got this flu that's going around. Is the wee laddie asleep?'

'Yeah! Here's the key.'

Maggie felt him remove his hand from her arm and sensed him hand over the key. Then he vanished into the swirling smog.

'Come on, let's get you inside,' said the woman briskly. 'Can you manage the steps? There's four going down.'

Maggie nodded, and somehow she managed to descend the steps to the basement flat without falling. She was aware that Mrs Sinclair turned a key in the lock and pushed open a door. She ushered Maggie inside and closed the door behind them.

A shivering Maggie gazed about her. The room was lit by a single electric bulb hanging from a low ceiling and a fire glowed in a black-leaded grate protected by a fireguard; on the hob stood a blackened kettle.

'You go and sit down while I make us a brew,' said Mrs Sinclair.

Maggie managed to make her way over to a sofa, and only then did she realize that there was a boy covered by an army blanket lying there. His eyes were closed and he was clutching a Dinky car. Cautiously Maggie sat at the foot of the sofa, not wanting to wake him.

'So what's your name?' Mrs Sinclair asked.

Maggie's gaze shifted from the boy's face, to that of the woman who had thrust the kettle on to the fire and was now putting milk in cups.

'Margaret Gregory.' She hesitated. 'That man?'

'What about him?'

'Is he from Liverpool?'

'Recognized the accent, did you? You have a hint of it yourself.'

Maggie grimaced. 'I thought I'd got rid of it after having elocution lessons.'

'I have an ear for accents.' Mrs Sinclair removed the steaming kettle from the fire with a folded cloth and poured water into a teapot.

'So are you on your own in London or did you come with

friends?' asked Mrs Sinclair, lowering herself into a shabby armchair by the fire, still wearing her coat and hat.

'On my own, but there are other Scousers living in this area. I never thought when I came south I'd be glad to hear the accent,' Maggie said hoarsely, drawing her scarf more snugly about her neck. She took another sip of her tea before adding, 'I've heard some say it's an ugly accent, but I don't think it's that bad. Besides, it would be unrealistic to expect every visitor to London to talk BBC English.'

'That's true. I'm from Perth and have lived here for over thirty years, and folk can still tell I'm from over the Border. How long have you been in London, Miss Gregory?'

'Nearly three years.' They had been difficult years at times, Maggie thought to herself, not at all like the life in London she'd imagined. 'I have digs just off Gloucester Road,' she said. 'They were recommended by another Liverpudlian. An actress actually. She's . . . quite well known . . . not only from the stage . . . but also from films and the telly,' she wheezed.

'So what do you do?' asked Mrs Sinclair.

Maggie did not immediately reply, but took a few shaky breaths before answering. 'I'm a model. I was on my way back to my digs . . . from a photoshoot.' She took another mouthful of tea and swallowed.

Mrs Sinclair fixed her with a stare. 'I reckon you need to see a doctor. Pity you couldn't have gone along with the boy's father to the hospital, but no doubt the Outpatients' will be inundated with flu sufferers in this weather. Besides, he has enough on his plate at the moment. His wife is very ill. She could die.'

Maggie flushed. 'I wasn't expecting him to help me any more than he has already,' she said. 'And, as soon as I've finished my tea, I'll be out of your way.'

'If you think you can manage on your own, that'll suit me. The wee laddie has had enough upset, and seeing a strange face might start him off crying again. He misses his mother.'

'What a shame! How old is he?'

'I've been told he'll be five this year.'

'I have a nephew, Owen, who'll be five this year, too. He's my brother, Jared, and his wife, Emma's son.' Maggie drained her cup and, placing a hand on the arm of the sofa, she managed to stand up unaided. She reached for her holdall. 'Thanks for the tea and – and thank the boy's father for his help for me, if you would.'

Still feeling unsteady on her feet, and a mite dizzy, Maggie crossed to the door, opened it, said goodbye and left. As the smog swirled about her, she almost wished herself back inside the basement flat, but she knew she had to get back to her lodgings.

Afterwards, Maggie could never recall that nightmarish journey back to her digs without a feeling of horror. It was such a relief to be welcomed inside the lodging house by her landlady, who hustled Maggie upstairs to her bedsit and helped her undress and into her nightie. She tucked her into bed, saying she would call the doctor.

But it was not until the following day that the doctor was able to visit. He sounded her chest and looked grave and told her she had acute bronchitis and that – although he would like to see her in hospital – she was going to have to stay where she was as the hospitals were full of flu patients. Maggie's agent phoned, but they did not get to speak as Mrs Cooling told her that Maggie was not allowed out of bed.

A fortnight passed before Maggie was allowed up, and during those days she wondered if she had dreamt up the man and woman who had come to her aid and the basement flat with the boy fast asleep on the sofa.

Eventually Maggie did get to speak to her agent, and told her that the doctor was insisting that she visit the nearest hospital for a chest X–ray as soon as possible. Despite her fear that the machine might discover something nasty, Maggie did not argue with him.

As it was, she did have some cause to worry, as the X–ray showed up an old TB scar on her lung. Apparently there was no mention of it in her medical records and that puzzled him. She had no idea how she had come by such a scar and, as her mother was no longer available to consult on the subject, she could only tell the doctor that her mother had avoided doctors and hospitals like the plague, and would dose Maggie with her own remedies, like so many people did before the days of the National Health Service.

The doctor told Maggie that it was a miracle she had survived this latest bout of bronchitis, and that she was going to have to take more care of herself. She must give up smoking, put on some weight, and move out of London to a place where the air was cleaner and fresher.

To say that Maggie was dismayed was an understatement. She had dreamed of a career in modelling since she was a schoolgirl and, although the reality had proved discouraging at times, she had no idea what else she could do. It had been a hard slog gaining experience in her chosen career, and sometimes an employer had considered a free meal or a gift of the clothes one had modelled sufficient payment. Still, Maggie was not ready to quit just yet.

Fortunately her mother, Elsie, had left her some money, which was in a trust fund managed by her brother Jared until she was twenty-one. So she turned to him if she was ever short of the readies to pay the rent. But he was careful with her money and only allowed her so much a month.

If only she could hear from Norman, saying that his ship had docked and he was coming to London to take her out, she would feel so much better. She would be able to discuss her situation with him and, in so doing, learn exactly where she stood with him. Hopefully he would ask her to marry him and, what with him spending so much time at sea, she would be able to carry on with her modelling career for a while.

Filled with hope at the prospect of a more settled life, she wrote to him again, an extremely loving letter. While she waited to hear from him, she decided that she seriously needed to give up smoking. Maybe this time it would not be so difficult, because she knew now that her life really depended on her doing so.

Two

Dear Maggie,

Forgive me for not writing before but I haven't found it easy to tell you my latest news, but hopefully you will understand that these things happen and none of us can foretell the future despite those fortune-tellers with their crystal balls and the horoscope pages in the magazines you sometimes appear in.

Maggie's heart had started to thud as soon as she read the words
'*hopefully you will understand*', but she knew she had no choice
but to read on. The letter had arrived the day after she had posted
hers to Norm, so his could not possibly be in response to the
one she had sent. Her mouth felt dry as her eyes scanned the
lines of scrawling writing; by the time she had reached the end,
she was desperate for a cigarette.

There were none in the flat because she had refrained from
buying any after making the decision to give up smoking. Although
it was only nine in the morning and she had a job to go to, she
poured herself a glass of Wincarnis tonic wine that her landlady
had bought her. Apparently Queen Victoria had enjoyed a glass
in her day. Only after Maggie had drained the glass did she feel
up to reading the second paragraph again.

> *I've met someone else and have asked her to marry me, so we're*
> *getting engaged. We have so many things in common that it's*
> *unbelievable. I'd feel really bad about this if I didn't know your*
> *career in modelling has always been more important to you than*
> *settling down and having a family. I hope we can remain friends.*
> *Wish me well. Norman.*

Maggie swore vehemently and was sorely tempted to smash the
glass in the hearth, only the sensible side of herself told her that
she would have to clear it up and she had no time for that. The
fashion show was due to take place in a couple of hours and her
agent had warned her that she had to turn up at the hotel on
Bayswater Road in plenty of time. She scrunched up Norm's
letter and flung it in the wastepaper bin and burst into tears.

She sobbed for what seemed ages, but eventually there were
no tears left. She scrubbed her cheeks with a tissue and it was
then she caught sight of the clock and gasped, knowing she had
to pull herself together. 'Sod him!' she said loudly. 'There are
more fish in the sea than you, Norman Marshall!'

She went and washed her face and gently patted it dry with
a towel before sitting down and carefully applying make-up. Then
she placed everything she needed in a holdall and headed for the
Tube station. As she was about to pass a corner shop, she hesitated. Then, with a toss of her shoulder-length blonde hair, she

went inside and bought a packet of cigarettes. To salve her conscience she only bought five. On the way out she was so occupied in fumbling for a cigarette that she collided into someone and dropped both the packet and the cigarette. She bent to pick them up, only to bump heads with the man.

'Sorry,' she said, picking up the packet.

'It's all right.' He picked up the cigarette and handed it to her.

'Thanks.' She placed it between her lips with a trembling hand. Then she patted her coat pockets in search of her lighter, only to remember she did not have one with her. 'Damn!' she muttered.

'Want a light?' He struck a match and held it out to her.

Maggie gazed at the man's bearded face and was reminded of the clarinettist, Acker Bilk, with his neat goatee beard. Although this man was dressed casually in a sky-blue Sloppy Joe with the sleeves rolled up and black corduroy trousers. His beard was a bit scrappier than the jazz musician's and tawny in colour instead of black. Also his hair was fair and curled beneath a cloth cap. Definitely not as smartly dressed as Aker, who, with his distinctive striped waistcoat and bowler hat, was a real snappy dresser.

'I really appreciate this,' she said, cupping her hand around his and lighting her cigarette at the match's flame.

'You're welcome.' He blew out the match and handed the box to her. 'You can keep them.'

She took the matches and thanked him. He smiled and vanished inside the shop. She stood a moment, drawing smoke into her lungs. She felt her chest heave but told herself one or even two cigarettes were not going to cause any damage. She thought about the man as she picked up her holdall and walked on, thinking that there was something familiar about him, but perhaps that was because of his resemblance to the famous musician. She hurried along the pavement, thinking about Norm and how he always grew a beard while at sea. She remembered how it had felt when his beard had brushed against her cheek before he shaved it off. Tears filled her eyes as she thought about her ex-boyfriend being with another woman who was now his fiancée.

She finished her cigarette and stubbed the butt out with her heel, grinding it and imagining it was Norm's face. Then she fumbled in her pocket for the packet of cigarettes she had bought and the matches the man had given her. She lit another cigarette and told herself that Norm was not worth crying over. What kind of man was it who finished with a girl by letter? He was a cad!

Maggie decided that if she ever fell in love again it would certainly not be with a sailor. Despite the doctor's warning, she would stay in London and concentrate on her modelling career and become famous. On the heels of the thought, she was gripped by a feeling of impending disaster, and for a moment felt she could not breathe. She had barely smoked the cigarette when she tossed it away and told herself that surely life couldn't get any worse.

As Maggie made for the room set aside as a changing room in the hotel near Hyde Park, she wanted nothing more than to get out of the building. She had a splitting headache and felt sick. Having arrived late at the hotel, she had not only been ticked off but told that she stank of cigarettes. She had blurted out, 'Since when has smoking been a sin?'

Of course, Maggie knew that not only should she have kept her mouth shut, but that she should never have smoked or drunk that single glass of tonic wine on an empty stomach. Her sister, Dot, would have rolled her eyes and demanded to know where her brains were. As for Maggie's cousin, Betty, she would have told her she was an idiot.

One of the reasons Maggie had so wanted to get away from her family was because, being the youngest, the older siblings thought they had the right to tell her what to do – and she had hated it. She had been made up when she'd heard that Betty had married a Yank, Stuart Anderson, and was living in California. She had never thought the day would come when she might miss her cousin.

Distracted by her thoughts, Maggie's elbow caught the shoulder of one of the other models who was wobbling past her on slender high heels.

'Hey, Scouse, look where you're going!' said the girl.

Maggie, whose head felt as if it was going to split in half, snapped, 'Don't call me Scouse!'

She plonked herself down on a chair and wrenched off a black patent-leather shoe and threw it so that it landed in a pile of tissue paper. It was followed seconds later by its mate. A fingernail caught on her stocking which immediately laddered. Her spirits sank even further and she swore. Now she was going to have to use her last spare pair!

The other two women in the room exchanged glances. 'You're in a right mood today,' said one, zipping up the dress of the other.

'Perhaps it's that time of the month,' said her friend.

'I wish it was only that,' Maggie muttered, taking a new packet of nylons from her holdall. She dropped the packet on a chair before stretching an arm over her shoulder and unfastening the zipper of the dress a third of the way down before twisting her other arm about her waist and finishing the job. Wrenching the dress from her shoulders, she eased it down over her slender hips.

'Be careful with that fabric,' warned the designer who had just entered the room. 'You'll spoil it. It needs handling gently. D'you know how much it costs a yard?'

Maggie allowed the dress to pool into a puddle of amber silk on the floor as she struggled with her temper. 'No, but do tell,' she said in the well-modulated tones she had learnt at elocution lessons. 'No doubt the cost to one of your customers would feed a poor family in Liverpool.' Her own words took her by surprise.

'Don't be impertinent,' said the designer coldly. 'Any more of that, Miss Gregory, and you're out on your ear. I don't know what's got into you. First you were late and now—'

'Would you really like to know?' she blurted out.

He stared at her. 'I have no time for this! Get into your next outfit and then you can go. I'll be informing your agent that I won't be using you any more.'

Maggie opened her mouth and then she pressed her lips tightly together. What was the point in telling him about the dreadful time she had been having? Suddenly she longed to feel someone's arms around her, hugging her fondly and telling her not to worry, that everything was going to be all right.

She thought of her mother and how, despite sometimes feeling suffocated by her love, they had shared many a happy hour together. Memories of Saturday mornings when they had taken a bus into Liverpool flooded her with sudden warmth. They would wander round St John's Market and the big departmental stores, such as Lewis's and Blackler's. Maggie had only been a baby when the two stores had been bombed during the war but, according to her mother, they had been rebuilt as good as ever. Sometimes her mother had encouraged her to try on various frocks, but she only ever bought her new dresses for Easter, Whit and Christmas. Even so, her mother would always treat Maggie to something new on those trips into town, be it only a hair slide.

Her sister Dot and cousin Betty had called her a spoilt brat, but her brother, Jared, more often than not, told them it was to be expected that she would be a little bit spoilt. As it was, by the time Maggie was a teenager, the only thing she really wanted – and could not have – was her father alive again.

'Have you gone deaf, Miss Gregory?' snapped the designer. 'Stir yourself and fetch the gown with the butterfly bow or there'll be no wages for you!'

Maggie was conscious of that horrible sensation of imminent disaster. She wanted to run away. Instead, she forced herself to remove the midnight-blue gown from its hanger and turned her back on him. With hands that shook, she managed to put on the dress without any assistance. Carefully she put on her stockings and then, taking several deep breaths, she eased her feet into a pair of cream and navy blue court shoes.

How she managed to reach the catwalk and parade up and down she could never properly recall afterwards.

'Well, you made a right mess of that,' snapped the designer. 'You were staggering about like a drunk. There'll be no wages for you, girl! You can have that dress in lieu of payment. You've been smoking, and no doubt it will stink like an ashtray, much like yourself.'

Despite the rage that filled her due to his insults, Maggie could only stare at him through half-closed eyes. She had a rip-roaring migraine and could only think that she never wanted to do this again. The decision she had made earlier had been completely overturned and there was no doubt in her mind now that this was the end of her modelling career. Word would soon get around that she had been impudent and was unreliable. There were hundreds of would-be models waiting in the wings, believing that the modelling life was glamorous and financially rewarding. They did not realize that one had to work incredibly hard and be outstanding to make a really good living.

Maggie decided not to bother changing out of the gown and

shoes. She put on her coat and dragged a scarlet velour beret over her blonde curls. Grabbing her holdall and ignoring the other girls, she fled the hotel. She had to get out of London without delay! She did not pause to give more thought to her decision, but set out for the nearest Tube station and a train that would take her to Euston. She was going north, back to her family.

Dot would surely never turn her away from her door. So what if her sister's husband, ex-soldier Billy, made her feel that if she stayed at their house it was on sufferance. And if the worst came to the worst, then she could always ask her brother, Jared, and her sister-in-law, Emma, who lived next door to Dot and Billy, if they could put her up. She thought of their son, Owen. He might be a right handful, but Maggie could tolerate him in return for bed and board. After all, she was family.

Three

Maggie drummed her fingernails on the magazine on her lap and willed the train to move. It should have left half an hour ago but it was delayed. She supposed she should be grateful it had not departed on time, otherwise she would have missed it. Perhaps she should have gone to the lodging house first and packed all her clothes. But that would have slowed her down, and Mrs Cooling would have had plenty to say; she might even have persuaded her to change her mind. Maggie decided she would phone her landlady when she arrived in Formby and make her apologies. She had phoned her sister, but their conversation had been brief because Dot and Billy were going away for the weekend. It suddenly occurred to her that the journey was going to be a long one with too much time to think.

Maggie chewed the inside of her lip; she should have made time to phone her sister-in-law, Emma, instead of leaving it to Dot to pass on the news that Maggie was on her way and would like Emma and Jared to put her up. Her sister might forget in her rush to leave with her husband, Billy, for Wales. Of course, she could have stayed in her sister's house on her own, but Dot had told her that Billy's stepbrother, Jimmy Miller, was staying there for a couple of nights before returning to sea.

The carriage door opened and a man appeared in the doorway carrying a couple of suitcases. He had a boy with him whom he nudged into the carriage with his knee. 'Go on, Jerry, get inside. The train will be leaving in a minute.'

The boy was carrying a very small case and hesitated at the sight of Maggie. She thought he seemed vaguely familiar. As for the man, how could she fail to recognize him when they had bumped into each other only that morning? He was dressed more smartly now, in a charcoal suit, the trousers of which had sharp creases. Unfortunately the cut of his jacket was spoilt by the folded newspaper sticking out of a pocket. His shirt was Persil-white and his dark blue and maroon tie she felt certain was silk.

Fancy them seeing each other twice in one day! He nodded in her direction as he lifted the suitcases on to the baggage rack. She watched him remove the trilby from curly fair hair. He placed the hat on top of a suitcase before sitting down on the seat opposite her. Had he recognized her? He didn't appear to have done so, thought Maggie. Suddenly she became aware that the boy was staring at her. She smiled, increasingly convinced that she had seen him before. He was wearing a navy blue woollen coat, unbuttoned to reveal a grey pullover over a blue shirt, grey shorts and knee-length grey socks.

The boy lowered his gaze and placed his small case on the floor between the man's feet, so drawing Maggie's immediate attention to the man's shiny black shoes. She liked polished shoes. Shoes could be so easily neglected, more so than any other item of clothing, in her opinion. Obviously, he was a man wanting to make an impression.

The boy placed his hands on the man's thighs and leaned back against him. Now the look he gave Maggie was a measuring one.

'My mammy's gone to Heaven,' he said.

'Hush, Jerry! The lady doesn't want to hear that,' said the man, closing his eyes wearily.

'I'm sorry about your mother,' she said.

'Why are you wearing a long frock?' asked the boy. 'You look like a princess.'

'Don't be personal, Jerry,' murmured the man, without opening his eyes.

The boy threw back his head and gazed up at him. 'Don't know what that means, Daddy.'

Before his father could reply Maggie said, 'I don't mind answering his question. I'm aware that it's not the kind of dress to wear on a long train journey. Unless it was the Orient Express, of course. But I've been at a fashion show and I didn't have time to change because I was desperate to catch the train to Liverpool.'

The man opened his eyes and stared at her. 'Haven't I seen you before?'

'Yes, this morning. I dropped my cigarettes and you helped me pick them up.'

His expression lightened. 'I remember now. I gave you a light.'

'That's right. Although, to be honest, I had made up my mind to give them up. I've had acute bronchitis, which resulted in my having to stay in bed for a fortnight.'

'That's bad.'

'You can say that again.' She pulled a face. 'But I survived, and so I decided I'd had enough of London and wanted to go home.'

'Home being Liverpool?' he said.

'Near enough. I wanted my family around me. That might prove a mistake, but at least you know where you are with your family.'

'I know what you mean.' He leaned forward. 'Nothing went right for me in London. I wish now I'd taken my chances and stayed in Liverpool, but my wife wanted to start a new life elsewhere. Just the three of us – but it didn't work out.' He sighed, reached out a hand and ruffled his son's hair.

The boy shrugged his hand off. 'Don't do that, Daddy!'

'Touchy!' said his father, leaning back and delving into an inside pocket.

Maggie watched him produce a packet of Player's and a Swan box of matches. She had smoked the last of her cigarettes earlier and vowed no more.

He caught her eye. 'You're welcome to one, but I don't want to tempt you if your aim is to quit.'

She hesitated. 'I'll do without.'

'Sensible girl. Bad for the bronchioles. So, where "near enough" in Liverpool d'you live?'

'I was born in Bootle.'

'Bootle!' He smiled. 'What's a girl from Bootle doing in London?'

There was a note in his voice that caused Maggie to bridle. 'What's wrong with Bootle?'

'Did I say there was anything wrong with it? I spent a bit of time there when I was younger.'

'It was the way you said Bootle.' She folded her arms across her chest. 'I've heard Liverpudlians tell people to go to Bootle. Pretty much as if they were telling them to go to Hell.'

He shifted the cigarette to the side of his mouth with his tongue. 'I wonder why that is? I grew up in a street off Scotty Road, and you'd have a job finding a place as tough to match it. Although, Mam worked hard keeping our house spick and span.' He took his cigarette out of his mouth and gazed at its glowing tip, and then pinched it out and returned it to the packet of Player's.

'Why did you put it out?' she asked.

'Thinking about your chest. Don't want to set you off coughing.'

'That's good of you.'

He changed the subject. 'So what were you doing in London? How long were you there?'

'Been working there for over three years.'

'Doing what? It must have been something posh if the way you're dressed is anything to go by.' His blue eyes met hers. 'You talk nice, too, but there's still a trace of the accent there. I barely noticed it this morning because you didn't say much, but I can hear it now.'

Before she could say anything in response, the carriage jerked sharply, throwing her back against the seat. The magazine slipped from her lap on to the floor and she bent to pick it up. Then the carriage jerked again and she was sent sprawling, and would have landed in his lap if Jerry had not been standing in front of him. The man shot out a hand and grabbed her, managing to hold her away from his son. 'You all right, queen?' he asked.

'Yes,' she said, a mite breathlessly. 'At least we're on our way at last.'

He released her and she sat down on her seat. 'Thanks for preventing me from falling.'

He grinned. 'I seem to be making a habit of helping you out.

This being the second time today. Jerry, pick the lady's magazine up for her.'

Jerry did as instructed and held out the magazine to Maggie. She thanked him and then gazed out of the window as the platform with its notice boards saying Euston slid out of sight and the station was left behind. The train was soon rattling past the backs of tall houses, their windows reflecting the sunlight.

'I wouldn't be surprised if it's dark by the time we get to Liverpool,' said Jerry's father.

'I was hoping it would still be light.' Maggie opened her magazine. 'I'll need to make another phone call when I get to Lime Street.'

'Hoping someone will come and pick you up?' he asked.

'That would be handy, but I only have my holdall with me and I wouldn't expect my brother to come all the way into Liverpool when I can catch the train.'

'Bootle's not that far from Liverpool.'

'I don't live in Bootle now. In fact, I don't have a place I can call home any more.' She sighed.

'Snap! Neither have I. Truth be known, I haven't had a proper home for years.'

There was a long silence.

'So you'll be staying with your brother?' he asked.

She nodded. 'My parents are dead.' To Maggie's dismay her voice quivered.

'Miss them, do you?'

'Yes. Especially my dad! He was the best dad in the world.' Embarrassingly tears filled her eyes.

'Don't cry. Be glad he was a good bloke. I just wish I could say the same about mine. I hated him.'

His words put a stop to her tears. She was shocked. 'Hated! That's a strong word.'

'That's how strongly I felt. To be honest, I despised as well as hated him.' His mouth tightened and his eyes were as hard and unyielding as pebbles. He took the newspaper from his pocket and unfolded it and began to read.

Maggie would have liked to have known why he hated his father and wondered how he felt about his mother. It sounded like his father was dead. Perhaps his mother was dead too, and that was why he had no place to call home in Liverpool. Although it could be that he had a sister or a brother who would provide him and his son with a bed for a few nights until he found a place of his own.

The silence between them stretched and was eventually broken by Jerry sighing and fiddling with the lock on his small case. 'Stop that,' said his father.

The boy ignored him.

'What is it?' asked the man, looking up from his newspaper.

'I want it opened. I want my cars.'

'In a minute. Just let me finish what I'm reading.'

There was a rustling of pages and the sound of Jerry tapping his fingers on the case. 'Bloody hell,' groaned his father. 'Can't you wait for just a few minutes?'

'You said a minute, Daddy,' said the boy. 'And you swored.'

His father folded his newspaper and brought his face down to the boy. 'You would make a saint swear.'

Maggie could not resist a smile.

'What are you smiling at?' said the man, sounding exasperated.

Her smile faded and she almost said 'Nothing', but that would not have been true. 'He's right, isn't he? You did say a minute. But you're not the only parent to make promises and break them. I've heard it said loads of times. My sister-in-law says it to her little boy when she's busy.'

'Alright, smart aleck! I bet you've no kids.'

'No, I haven't! I'm not married. Had a boyfriend . . . but we decided . . . to-to call it a day.'

'Londoner, was he?'

'No! As a matter of fact he's one of us. The trouble was that he became a sailor and I've seen little of him since . . . the . . . then.' Her voice stuttered into silence. She felt that painful ache inside her, just thinking of Norm. She took a deep breath and looked across at Jerry. 'Your little boy is still waiting.'

'All right, queen, I don't need reminding.' He took the case from Jerry and placed it on the seat and unlocked it.

The boy lifted the lid and removed several Dinky cars and began to run them along the seat, making brrrrm-brrrrm noises as he did so.

'Happy now?' asked the man, looking not at his son but at Maggie.

She nodded, her cheeks slightly pink. 'I know enough about kids to realize that it's more peaceful if they're given something to do or what they want. Same with grown-ups really, I suppose.'

'I wouldn't argue. He won't go to sleep without one of his precious cars.' He paused. 'You still haven't told me what your job was in London.'

Maggie thought of saying that he hadn't told her what he did for a living either. At least having a conversation was helping to pass the time. 'I was a model but I got fed up, so I upped and left. Besides, a doctor told me I needed to get out of London for the good of my health.'

He frowned. 'Would you say Liverpool is a healthier place?'

'I'm going to be staying in Formby. My brother has a house out that way. He built it himself. My father was in the building trade, had his own business until he took ill. I was only a kid when he died.' She sighed. 'He was such a good man.'

'So you've told me. You were lucky, queen. And you're still lucky because you've a brother who lives in Formby.' His eyes lit up. 'I always liked going to Formby for a day out. We'd play jumping off the sand hills, but generally we only got halfway down and our legs would be buried in soft sand and we'd end up sliding on our bottoms to the foot of the hill.'

'Did you ever swim in the sea?'

'Yeah, but it was bloody cold.'

Maggie smiled. 'You're nesh!'

'So what?' He smiled slightly. 'What's the point of getting all goose-pimply when you can lie in the sun instead?'

'Oh, I wouldn't argue with that,' said Maggie. 'But I take it you can swim?'

'Course I can swim. Can you?'

'Dad made sure of it because we lived not far from the Liverpool to Leeds canal when we moved to Litherland.'

He looked startled. 'Litherland? I thought you said you came from Bootle.'

'We did, but then we moved to Litherland. I know some people have never heard of it, but it's next to Seaforth. You'll have heard of Seaforth.'

'Of course. There's sands at Seaforth. And I have heard of Litherland. D'you still go back there?'

'Occasionally. I know a family, the Gianellis, who live in Litherland Park. Dad used to worry about us falling in the canal because he remembered a woman drowning near Sandhills Bridge during the war.'

'My dad was found floating in the canal,' he said almost casually, taking out his cigarettes. 'He got drunk, fell in and drowned.'

She was shocked. 'That's terrible.'

'What's terrible? Me changing my mind about having a ciggie?'

'You know I don't mean that. Your father drowning. Couldn't he swim?'

'No idea. He certainly didn't teach me.' He lit a cigarette. 'The water used to be warm at the back of Tate & Lyle's sugar factory. I was thrown in by a bigger boy and managed to doggy-paddle to the side. Someone pulled me out. Me mam had a fit when I came into the house dripping wet.'

Maggie was surprised that he could continue to talk about the canal and near-death experience so casually, after not only telling her about his father's death, but due to his having just lost his wife. She decided to change the subject. 'Do you think there were sand hills at Sandhills Station before the docks were built?'

'Probably. I suppose in the old days it could have looked just like Formby does now. I remember it being a heck of a walk from Formby Station to the beach,' he reminisced. 'It felt like bloody miles.'

Jerry glanced up. 'You swore again, Daddy.'

'So I did, but it's not your place to correct me, son.'

The boy jutted out his lip and his head drooped. After that there was a long silence. The man picked up his newspaper and began reading again. Maggie turned to her magazine, although she had trouble concentrating. She felt sad and aggrieved, knowing that a period in her life had come to an end and she just did not know what she was going to do next.

She closed her magazine, rested her head against the back of the seat and shut her eyes, allowing her mind to drift. Snatches of their conversation came into her head and she was dreaming of the time she had collapsed in the smog. She was roused by the murmur of voices and the carriage door opening. Her neck was aching. She opened her eyes and rolled her head, yawned and stretched.

'You've had a good kip!' said Jerry's father. 'It's a good job I was keeping me eye on you and your holdall. You were completely out of it when a couple of other passengers came in.'

'Thanks.' She stared at him, remnants of her dream still clinging to her. 'I was well away. You know what it's like when reality and dreams get all mixed up?' She paused.

'Go on,' he said.

'You wouldn't remember helping a woman who collapsed the evening of that terrible smog we had a few weeks back? You'd be on your way to the hospital to see your wife who was very ill. An older woman helped you pick me up. I think her name was Mrs—'

'Sinclair!' He stared at her in amazement. 'Was it you? Were you the woman?'

'Yes! You told Mrs Sinclair to take me inside and she did. I remember she made me a cup of tea. I asked, were you from Liverpool, and she told me you were. Your son was asleep on the sofa and he was clutching a Dinky car. Watching him play with his cars before must have triggered the memory. I thought earlier he looked vaguely familiar,' Maggie babbled. 'And your voice, you calling me queen. You called me queen then.'

'Bloody hell, fancy you remembering all that so sudden like!'

'Fancy us meeting on this train. What a coincidence that is!'

They smiled at each other.

And suddenly Maggie felt lost for words because there was such charm in his smile. She waited for him to say something but he seemed lost for words too.

Then he said, 'Next stop Runcorn.'

Maggie could scarcely believe she had slept that long. 'You're joking!'

'No, queen, I'm serious.'

She felt herself relax and moistened her mouth. 'Gosh, I'm thirsty.'

'Here, help yourself.' He handed her a thermos flask.

She unscrewed the top and poured out some of the coffee. It was still hot and sweet and she felt much better after she had drunk a cup. 'Thanks for coming to my rescue yet again,' she said, handing back the cup. 'Do you have a place to stay tonight?'

He barely hesitated. 'Me mam's house. She never did like me marrying Bernie and had a blue fit when we left Liverpool.'

Maggie imagined an over-possessive mother who resented any girl to whom her son took a fancy. 'So is Jerry her only grandchild?'

'Yes, and now Bernie's dead, Mam will welcome us with open arms. It's what I need. Someone to take care of him while I'm working.'

'You've a job to go to?'

'I worked my apprenticeship as a motor mechanic. I'm planning on building up me own business,' he said earnestly. 'I was up in Liverpool the other week having a gander at suitable premises.'

'I wish you luck,' said Maggie.

'Thanks!' He grinned. 'What about you? Will yer be able to get any modelling work up here? It sounds really glamorous.'

'There's really very little glamour about the job,' said Maggie. 'That's why I'm glad to be out of it, although I'm not sure what I'll do next.'

'Have you thought of going on the stage?' he said, leaning forward. 'You've got the looks.'

She smiled. 'Thanks, although I think there's more to acting than just having a pretty face. I know Dorothy Wilson from Liverpool who's an actress and has worked her way up and is now famous.'

'That's the way to do it. Have someone to put a word in for you.' He paused. 'Your boyfriend . . . d'you think you'll ever make things up with him?'

Maggie did not immediately answer and then she said in a hard voice, 'I doubt it. He's engaged to someone else now. They could even be married, unless she's changed her mind about him, because it's no fun having someone who regards the sea as his mistress and is away for months on end.'

'I never fancied living on a ship meself. Confined with a lot of men, having to take orders and every move you make being watched. No, the seafaring life was never for me, although I have seen a bit of the world.'

'Where've you been?' asked Maggie with real interest. 'I have a cousin in California.'

'Been to Australia but then I started feeling homesick.'

'Did you meet your wife when you came back to England?'

He said smoothly, 'That's right. It seems yonks ago now.'

'I know what you mean about time. Sometimes it goes so quickly and at other times it drags.'

He agreed.

They fell silent as the train began to slow down as they approached Runcorn. Soon they had crossed the bridge over the narrow stretch of the Mersey and were on the final part of the journey.

'You know what, queen, I wouldn't mind meeting up again,' he surprised her by saying. 'I'd like to know how you get on.'

Her sore heart lifted. Here was a man who had put himself out for her twice, but what about him only just having lost his wife? And what would his mother say if he told her he was meeting a woman he had met on the train?

'I know it might sound strange to you, me suggesting such a thing, but I'll need to get away from things and life has been tough the last few months. It's not going to be easy for Jerry and me living with Mam.'

Maggie said slowly, 'I do understand how you feel. I know it won't be easy for me either. It can cause difficulties when it's not your own place.'

'So how about it?' he said. 'What about us meeting up? Say in a month's time?'

'All right! Easter will be over by then and the weather should be getting warmer.'

'How about a Saturday evening outside Exchange Station? Would seven thirty suit you?'

'I should imagine so. Is that three weeks this coming Saturday?'

He nodded.

Maggie took a deep breath. 'There's only one thing more I'd like to know and that's your name. Mine's Margaret Gregory.' She held out a hand.

He took it. 'I'm Tim. Timothy Murphy.'

'Pleased to meet you, Tim Murphy.'

They shook hands, and she liked it that his grip was firm but not hand-crushingly so. 'Let's hope we have lots of good news to tell each other by then,' he said.

Four

Maggie wasted no time heading north across the city after parting from Tim Murphy and his son. She had not bothered phoning her brother as there had been queues outside the telephone kiosks. Neither had she taken the time to change in the Ladies toilet at the station. She soon realized that was a mistake, having forgotten just how long the walk was to Tithebarn Street, but she did feel a need to stretch her legs after the long train journey. Last time she had come home she had taken a taxi to Exchange Station, but now she decided she needed to watch her pennies. Not that she was short of a bob or two, but she had been brought up by her mother to make a habit of saving even a little a week.

As Maggie walked across St John's Gardens to the rear of the soot-encrusted walls of the neoclassical St George's Hall, she was aware of the signs of spring about her. She liked flowers and noticed the spears of the daffodils were showing buds. Maybe they would be in flower for Easter. Several beds were planted with tulips and wallflowers. She could almost imagine the heady scent of wallflowers. She and her mother had always made sure of planting them in September so there would be a good display in the garden of the house in Litherland. Emma liked wallflowers, too, and no doubt there would be a border of them in the Formby garden, and maybe also up at the cottage in Whalley which Emma had inherited from her grandfather and was where she had grown up.

Maggie left St John's by the exit opposite the museum on William Brown Street. She remembered one of her old school teachers telling the class that the building had been severely damaged by firebombs during the blitz, and that there were still parts of the museum in the process of renovation. She thought of the museums and art galleries in London that she had not taken the time to visit, and knew that her cousin, Betty, would have thought her crazy not to make the most of her opportunity. Especially when her digs had been within a short walking distance of the V&A and Natural History museums. Maggie hadn't visited a single one, but then she was no culture vulture, unlike her artistic cousin.

As Maggie passed the entrance to the Mersey Tunnel and headed up Dale Street, she found herself wondering, not for the first time, how Betty was managing as a mother. She found it difficult to imagine her cousin balancing motherhood, her beloved painting and being a housewife all at the same time, and in a new country far away from her family.

By the time the Exchange Hotel was in sight, Maggie was limping. She had paused in front of the window of the Wizard's Den, which was filled with a hotchpotch of jokes and tricks, such as itching powder and artificial poo. She thought of her nephew and how this was just the kind of place small boys, and big boys, enjoyed.

As she went through the high arches next to the entrance to the Exchange Hotel, which led to the railway station, she gritted her teeth, suspecting that a blister was forming on her left heel. Why was it that one foot was bigger than the other, so that one shoe was always tighter or looser, instead of an exact same fit? Despite being in pain, she decided to wait until she was on the train before changing into her old comfortable shoes. She would phone Jared when she arrived at Formby Station as there was a bit of a walk to the house.

Maggie was sitting in a carriage inspecting her bloodied heel beneath her torn stocking when a voice said, 'That looks nasty!'

At the sound of the man's voice, Maggie's heart seemed to flip over. She looked up into the familiar handsome face that was so like Norman's that for a moment she felt breathless. Then she noticed the walking stick resting against the wall of the carriage.

'Oh, it's you Pete,' she said huskily, lowering her foot.

He gazed at her intently. 'Are you all right, Maggie?'

She tilted her chin. 'I just thought you were your Norm for a moment. We've split up, you know?'

'No, I didn't know.' He frowned. 'Norm and I aren't as close as we used to be. He hardly ever writes and I don't know where to get in touch with him so I can keep him abreast with what's happening at home.'

'Doesn't he write to your mother?'

'Now and then, but not recently,' Pete said.

'So you don't know that he's got himself engaged to someone else,' Maggie blurted out.

'You're kidding!'

'Would I joke about such a thing?' There was a tremor in her voice. 'He wrote and told me. I received the letter this morning.'

'That's not on,' Pete said angrily. 'What's he playing at?'

She sighed. 'Perhaps I shouldn't have said anything. Maybe he's planning on surprising you by turning up with her out of the blue?'

'Possibly.' Pete stared at Maggie. 'When did he last write to you before the letter this morning?'

'I hadn't heard from him for a while and it's months since I've seen him. I was getting worried.'

'A lousy way of letting you know he's still alive,' Pete said grimly. 'It must have come as a terrible shock.'

'Obviously. Especially as I've been ill.'

'I thought you looked pale. Have you had the flu?'

'No, acute bronchitis,' she replied. 'The doctor told me I needed to get out of London, so I decided to take his advice and come home to recuperate. I've just got off the London train straight from a catwalk job.'

'You must be tired.'

'I am a bit. Anyway, it's good to see you, Pete. I believe congratulations are in order. Emma wrote to me about you and Peggy getting married.'

He smiled. 'I bet you were one of those who thought it would never happen. It might not have, if Peggy hadn't run away and her father died.'

'I heard she'd gone missing. Anyway, I couldn't be happier for the pair of you. I bet your mam was made up.'

'She was over the moon. Even more so as we're living with her until we can find a place of our own.' He eased his lame leg and winced. 'Not easy with the housing situation the way it is. I bought a car last year, but that money would have come in useful for a deposit on a house.'

'I remember your Norm saying you could do with a car.'

His face clouded at the mention of his brother. 'I suppose you're on your way to Formby?'

'I'm staying with Jared and Emma while I decide what I'm

going to do with the rest of my life. No more living in London and no wedding on the horizon.'

Pete looked slightly uncomfortable. 'Did you really want to marry our Norm? I've always thought of you as a career girl, with your heart set on becoming a famous model.'

'Apparently that's what he thought, too.'

They were silent for a while and then Maggie said, 'Tell me – do your mam and Peggy get on all right? I've heard there can be problems when two women share a kitchen.'

He smiled slightly. 'They have their moments, but Irene decided the sensible thing to do would be for the girls to take turns at cooking the evening meal.'

'Irene! What's it to do with her?'

'She has our spare room. You do know her mam died not long after she remarried and moved into her new husband's house, and the children's home was closed down where Irene worked?'

'I think Emma mentioned it in a letter and that Marty had decided to rent the house after Irene and Jimmy's mother moved out. Jimmy had gone back to sea and Irene had been offered a job by Betty in California.'

'That's right. Then Irene's mam took ill while Irene was out there so she came back but had nowhere to live, Jimmy had been putting up at Billy and Dot's when he was home from sea, so Mam offered her our spare room. Our two mams having been great friends for years. Irene's now working at Litherland Nursery. She's not going to be at ours in Bootle much longer. She's hoping to get married this year.' Pete glanced out of the window and took hold of his walking stick and stood up. 'I'd best make a move. This is my stop. See you again, Maggie.'

'See you.' She had been about to ask who Irene was marrying, but decided it could wait until another time. Although no doubt Emma would know the answer.

Several people entered the compartment, and it was only when a woman looked at her askance that Maggie realized she was still in her stocking feet and had her holdall on the seat beside her. She took out her comfy shoes and put them on and placed the high heels in the holdall. Suddenly she could not wait to see Jared, Emma and Owen, although no doubt her nephew would be in bed by the time she arrived at her brother's house.

Maggie was not feeling in the best of moods as she replaced the receiver on its cradle in the booth at Formby Station. Emma had told her Jared was working late, finishing a job, so would not be able to give her a lift. She picked up her holdall and, at the same time, put her shoulder to the door of the telephone box. It scarcely budged so she shoved really hard. She heard a yelp and then the door gave way; she would have fallen to the ground if a man clutching his stomach had not thrust his free arm across the opening.

'Didn't you see me?' he demanded.

Embarrassed, but not wanting to show it, and telling herself that he shouldn't have been standing so close to the door, she said stiffly, 'No, I'm sorry. Could you move your arm?'

He lowered his arm and stepped aside. She brushed past him and set off down the hill towards her destination, wincing at every step she took, despite having changed her shoes, and wishing her brother could have finished work early. She took deep breaths of lovely fresh air. Formby village was surrounded by farms, and was close enough to the sea to catch the occasional blast of salt-laden air when the wind was blowing in the right direction.

Twenty minutes later, she arrived at the house. She realized that Emma must have been watching out for her, because the front door opened almost as soon as Maggie unlatched the gate. Her sister-in-law was brown haired with pleasant features, and possessed a smile that made her look almost beautiful at times. She walked slowly down the path towards Maggie.

'I saw you limping. What have you done to yourself?'

'I should have changed my shoes earlier,' Maggie said. 'I was wearing these gorgeous high heels.'

'Pride comes before a fall,' said Emma, linking her arm through Maggie's. 'But never mind, you're here now and can put your feet up. Jared's on his way. He telephoned a few minutes after you did.'

'I hope you don't mind my coming to stay? I just had to get out of London. I didn't mention it to our Dot but the doctor told me I have a TB scar on one of my lungs!' The full horror at the mention of TB hit her again, and Maggie swallowed the sudden lump in her throat.

'When did you find this out?' asked Emma, sounding shocked.

'A few weeks ago. I had a terrible bout of bronchitis and spent a fortnight in bed. The doctor sent me for a chest X-ray.'

'Your landlady should have let us know,' said Emma, frowning.

'I didn't want her to worry you. In fact, I pretended to myself it didn't really matter about the TB scar because it was in the past, but now – now it scares me.' Maggie followed Emma into the house.

'You mustn't worry,' Emma said firmly. 'Weren't you inoculated against TB when you were at school?'

'Yes, but—'

'No buts. Even if you hadn't been inoculated and it reoccurred, which isn't likely to happen, I'm sure they have drugs to treat it these days.'

'The doctor was concerned because I've had several bouts of bronchitis since living in London. The smog can be really bad.'

'I'm not surprised,' Emma said. 'But now you're here for a little holiday, you'll have plenty of fresh air and soon be back at the job you love. Spring's arrived, and even in London the smog will be a thing of the past.'

Maggie decided not to mention she had no plans to return to London and that they might need to put her up for much longer than a little holiday.

'Maybe you should visit our doctor while you're here,' suggested Emma, leading the way into the kitchen. A few moments later, a tantalizing smell of hotpot assailed Maggie's nostrils as Emma opened the oven. 'I hope you're hungry,' she said.

'Starving,' replied Maggie, remembering she'd had little to eat that day. She shrugged off her coat and hung it on the back of one of the chairs at the Formica-topped table in the centre of the room.

'Well, if you're that hungry, I won't make you wait until Jared comes in,' Emma said, setting plates and cutlery on the table.

Maggie sat down and gazed around at the welcoming home her brother had designed and built. Emma had stressed that the kitchen must be big enough to have their meals there. Although she'd also wanted a dining room for when they entertained guests, and that was situated off the lounge that ran the width of the house, with windows that looked out over the front and rear gardens. One day Maggie would like such a house herself.

Emma removed the lid from the casserole dish, and Maggie was reminded of the times she had travelled further north in Lancashire to stay at Emma's cottage in Whalley. She remembered how she had upset her sister-in-law by eating so little of the good food she had served up. It had been years since Maggie had eaten heartily of any food put in front of her. Always in her thoughts had been the need to remain svelte.

As her sister-in-law ladled out the hotpot, Maggie said, 'I wish I was as good a cook as you, Emma.'

Her sister-in-law looked at her askance. 'There's nothing stopping you from learning. One of Jimmy and Irene's stepsisters, the daughters of their mother's last husband, wants to go to catering college after she leaves school. She has a bit of a way to go before that happens, but it's nice to know that some of the old skills can still come in useful. Not everyone wants their food out of tins, packets or a freezer.'

'But they all come in handy, Emma, when you live in the depths of the country or you're on your own and out working all day,' said Maggie. 'I wouldn't want to cook a meal from scratch in such circumstances. But I have to admit that your cooking is better than any I've tasted from a packet or a tin.'

'The way to a man's heart is through his stomach, so they say,' said Emma in a teasing voice. 'I remember Norman Marshall turning up at the cottage years ago with his older brother, Dougie. It was the weekend, and I'd only just started in the business of offering light meals and teas for hikers and the like. Norm's twin Pete was in hospital and Dougie and Norman had brought their bikes up on the train. They wolfed down everything I put in front of them.'

'Norman and I have broken up,' said Maggie abruptly, reaching for a spoon.

Emma dropped the ladle, splattering gravy on the table. 'Why?'

'He's found someone else.'

'While at sea?'

'Tankers have to dock sometime.'

Emma was silent a moment and then she murmured, 'D'you think he thought you'd want to carry on with your career in modelling after you were married and didn't like the idea?'

Maggie shook her head. 'We never discussed marriage, and we never will now, because he's engaged to this other girl.'

Emma sat down and picked up the ladle. 'Engaged! That's a bit much!'

'That's what I thought when I received his letter.'

'You mean he didn't even tell you face to face?'

'No.'

'But the pair of you have known each other since you were at school!'

'I must admit it came as a terrible shock.' She dipped her spoon into her plate of hotpot. 'I met Pete on the train coming here. Norm hasn't even told him about this other girl, and he's his twin.'

'What about his mother?'

Maggie shook her head and took a mouthful of food.

'Well! I am surprised,' said Emma. 'You're probably best rid of him if he's that bad at communicating with his nearest and dearest.'

'I'll keep telling myself that when I feel like crying,' Maggie said. 'Anyway, Pete did tell me something interesting that no doubt you already know. Irene is hoping to get married this year.'

'Aye, I believe they want to tie the knot as soon as possible, but there's a problem.'

'Do you know who she's marrying?'

'Peggy's brother, Marty.'

'But I thought he was married to someone called Bernie!' Maggie stared at Emma. 'Oh, I see. That's the problem.'

Emma was about to say something more, but at that moment there came the sound of a key in the latch and the next moment Jared entered the kitchen in his shirtsleeves. 'Hiya Mags!' He placed an arm around her shoulders and gave her a squeeze. 'So, to what do we owe the pleasure of this visit?'

'You're not being sarcastic about it being a pleasure, are you?' she asked suspiciously.

'Would I? What is annoying is when you don't arrive when you say you're going to,' said her brother bluntly. 'Like the other Christmas when you let us down and turned up for New Year instead, and we'd gone up to the cottage to see Hester and Ally.'

Maggie flushed, thinking how Emma had first met Hester when the latter had been evacuated to Whalley during the war. They had lost touch when Hester had returned to Liverpool, only to meet each other coincidently having visited Lenny's coffee bar in Liverpool at the same time a few years ago. 'I couldn't help that!'

'I know! You were offered a more exciting way to spend your Christmas than with your family.' Jared kissed his wife. 'Are you all right, love?'

'I'm fine. Don't fuss . . . and stop teasing your sister. She's been having a bad time,' Emma began to heap food on his plate.

Jared shot a look at Maggie. 'What's wrong?'

'Nothing for you to concern yourself about,' she said sniffily. 'I can easily go back to London if having me here is a bother.' She put down her spoon and stood up.

'There's no need to get a weed on. Eat your dinner and don't take everything I say so seriously. You know that you're always welcome here,' Jared said.

Emma glanced at her husband. 'She really is upset and needs looking after. Now go and wash your hands before you eat.'

'I don't need telling,' said Jared mildly, going over to the sink and picking up a bar of Palmolive soap. 'And it's you, love, who needs looking after. I'm not having you rushing around after our Maggie in your condition. You have enough to do with the housework, shopping, chasing around after Owen and worrying about what to do about the cottage if Ally and Hester do decide to emigrate after all.'

Maggie stared at Emma. 'Are you having another baby?'

Her sister-in-law nodded. 'Aye, but don't let that worry you. I'm fine. Your brother is just an ol' fusspot.'

'And I'll carry on being one if I see the need,' said Jared, rinsing his hands under the tap and drying them. 'Owen's at that age where he's a right handful.'

'Deirdre says we should be grateful that he's healthy and full of beans,' Emma said.

'Who's Deirdre?' asked Maggie.

'She used to work with Irene at the home in Blundell Sands, but she's now at the children's home in Formby. She has charge of some handicapped children,' Emma murmured. 'You might get to meet her before Jimmy goes back to sea, because they've gone out together a few times and seem to get on well.'

'D'you mean they're just good friends, or something more?'

Emma shrugged. 'Only time will tell.'

'She's great with Owen,' said Jared. 'I reckon sooner or later she'll want a home and children of her own.'

Maggie decided she had heard enough about Deirdre, and asked after Ally and Hester and the cottage. 'I thought they'd only lived there a couple of years or so.'

'They have, but Ally wanted to emigrate when he finished his National Service. Hester didn't fancy the idea then, though,' Emma said. 'She's changed her mind since Ally suggested trying out Canada instead of Australia. It's closer to home and her father's not getting any younger, and he has a crippled wife to look after.'

'I know, but he does have a married daughter living with them and also a married son living in Liverpool,' said Maggie.

'That's why Hester has decided to let Ally have his way,' said Emma, sitting at table.

'So it could be that you're going to need new tenants,' Maggie said.

'Either that or we sell the cottage,' said Jared. 'I know Emma is reluctant to do that, what with it having belonged to her grandparents before her and her great-grandmother before them.' He changed the subject. 'Anyway, what's been wrong with you, Mags?'

She did not immediately reply because she had just put a forkful of food in her mouth, so it was Emma who told him that his sister had been ill with bronchitis.

'That's nothing new,' he said.

Maggie glanced across at him. 'I was in bed for a fortnight. I collapsed in the street,' she added for good measure.

Her brother sat up at that and frowned. 'Mrs Cooling should have phoned me. I am your guardian.'

'Maggie didn't want you to worry. She has a TB scar on her lung,' said Emma. 'She needs a good long holiday.'

Jared's weather-beaten face stilled a moment and then he said, 'How long?'

Maggie hesitated. 'I'd like to stay at least a couple of months.'

Husband and wife stared at each other.

'I'll pay my way,' Maggie said hastily. 'The doctor said I had to get out of London to a place where there was plenty of fresh air. I've given up smoking and he said I needed to put on weight.'

'I agree with him there,' said Jared, and carried on eating his meal. At last he put his knife and fork neatly together on his plate and looked at her. Maggie waited impatiently for him to speak, knowing that Emma being pregnant was the big factor as to whether her brother would allow her to stay as long as she wanted.

'You generally stay with our Dot,' said Jared.

'I know, and I'm fond of her, but her tongue's sharper than yours and Billy teases me. He calls me a stick insect.'

'If you put on weight he won't be saying that any more,' Jared said.

'There is that, of course,' said Maggie. 'But Emma is a better cook than our Dot and I want her to teach me. As well as that, your house is bigger and the spare room is roomier and I'll get to know Owen better if I'm staying here. And besides, Jimmy puts up there when he's home from sea.'

Jared glanced at Emma. 'What d'you think? You'll have to put up with her more than me.'

'I thought you loved me,' said Maggie mournfully.

Emma looked at her. 'He does. We do. But there'll be no getting up at eleven o'clock and slouching around in a housecoat if you stay here.'

'You're going to have to pull your weight,' said Jared. 'I expect you to help Emma with the housework and shopping and enter-tain Owen. You can take him on walks, which means you'll be getting plenty of fresh air at the same time. Run him into the ground so, after I've read to him at bedtime, he falls asleep as soon as his head touches the pillow. You can take your turn bathing him and even practise his alphabet with him.'

'You don't ask much, do you?' Maggie said. 'Perhaps you'd like me to swing from the chandeliers to entertain him, as well?'

Her brother placed his hands behind his head and grinned. 'Why not? Best to start as you mean to carry on.'

'Take no notice of him,' said Emma, smiling. 'You're not a monkey. Why don't you go and have a bath? You've had a long journey.'

'Don't start spoiling her,' Jared warned. 'Besides, she hasn't finished her dinner yet.'

'I can't eat any more right now. I think my stomach has shrunk over the years. I'm not used to eating large meals,' Maggie said, pushing her half-eaten meal away.

'No wonder there's nothing of you,' responded her brother.

Emma said, 'I've made some scones and I've some of my homemade blackberry and apple jam still. We'll have them with a cuppa in front of the fire in an hour. You can take her holdall up to the spare room when you go and look in on Owen, Jared.'

He nodded, and soon Maggie was following him upstairs. 'Is this all you've brought?' he said, holdall in hand.

'Yes, I came on impulse. I must phone Mrs Cooling and let her know where I am. I'll need the rest of my clothes. I'll reimburse her for the postage, of course,' said Maggie hastily.

He dropped her holdall outside the spare room and made no comment. Maggie followed him into her nephew's bedroom and gazed down at Owen, who had fallen asleep while waiting for his father. One pyjama-clad leg was outside the bedcovers and his right arm rested on the pillow. In his hand he clutched a Dinky taxicab. She thought he looked almost cherubic with his dimpled cheeks and silky eyelashes shielding eyes that were grey. She was reminded of Tim Murphy's son Jerry, and hoped they would get the welcome they deserved when they arrived at Tim's mother's house.

Five

Tommy McGrath stood in the shadows with Jerry by his side, tapping an envelope against his teeth as he gazed across at the house where his brother's van was parked outside. Inside the envelope was a letter addressed to Marty and their sister Peggy which Tommy had written before leaving London that morning. He knew his reluctance to face his brother and sister was not only cowardly but presumptuous as well. But he did not feel up to facing their questions and could not afford to risk them refusing to take responsibility for Jerry. Something that Marty had done from the moment the lad was born, having been married to Bernie at the time, unaware that Tommy and Bernie had married secretly a few months earlier. She had believed Tommy dead as she had heard nothing from him after he had vanished because the police were searching for him. Realising she was pregnant and not wanting to tell her mother of her secret marriage, she had tricked Tommy's elder brother, Marty, into marriage.

Tommy would have taken his son to his mother's house, but he doubted his welcome would be as warm now as it would have been last year. Besides it was situated too close to Bernie's mother's house for comfort. The auld bitch had always hated him, ever since he had licked her youngest son, Dermot, in a fight over a bag of marbles in the school playground. If she got wind that he was back in Liverpool, he could guarantee that she would do her best to see him behind bars.

This, despite Tommy not being to blame for either her youngest son, Dermot, being a snitch, or for the head injury Bernie sustained in a motorcycle crash in Blackpool last summer. Bernie should have worn the crash helmet she had been given, but she had always been more concerned about appearances than was sensible. Nor had it been his idea to scarper with Jerry to London, the way he and Bernie had done last September.

Tommy had been gearing himself up to face the music and confess the truth behind the whole sorry mess he had got himself into, a mess that had caused his family embarrassment and grief, when he had returned to Liverpool just over a year ago. Only then had he discovered Bernie had bigamously married Marty, having discovered she was pregnant with Tommy's child.

Not that he blamed Bernie completely for the situation, but she certainly had liked spending money, and he believed that was the reason why she had seduced Tommy into marrying her on the sly. She had been as cowed by her mother as he was and, once the deed was done, it was too late to go back on it. It was the reason he had turned to crime. If he had been a gentleman, he should have taken Bernie to Australia when he had to get out of Liverpool fast, being in trouble up to his neck. He sighed, telling himself that it was pointless raking over the past – it was much too late now for regrets.

He felt a tug on his trouser leg and glanced down at Jerry. 'When are we going in, Daddy?'

How to tell him? thought Tommy, who had been reticent to

talk about the unusualness of their situation to his son. Instead he had thought 'least said soonest mended' when they arrived in London. Even when Bernie had moaned about needing a bit of peace and quiet, he had not taken the opportunity of trying to explain to Jerry why he had two daddies. So instead Tommy had used the time to get to know the son he had not known existed until he returned to Liverpool from abroad.

He and Jerry had enjoyed visiting Kensington Gardens, where they had kicked a ball around and gazed in fascination at the statue of Peter Pan. Tommy remembered a similar one in Sefton Park, Liverpool. They had visited the flicks, and once Tommy had even taken Jerry to the Natural History Museum.

It was Bernie who had told Jerry he had two dads. God only knew what else she had told their son when he had been out earning a crust. Especially after she started having funny turns, which had frightened the three of them.

'Daddy, are you listening?'

Tommy glanced down at the boy. 'OK, son, I'll tell you what we're going to do. You're to hold this letter tightly and I want you to give it to your other daddy and Auntie Peggy. Now your mam's in Heaven, Auntie Peggy's going to look after you while I'm working hard to earn lots of money.'

Jerry looked doubtful. 'Aren't you coming in?'

'There isn't room for me, but you'll have Josie for company. You remember your sister, don't you? Your mam showed you a photograph of the pair of you together often enough.' Josie was really Jerry's half-sister as she was Marty and Bernie's daughter.

Jerry nodded, but his lower lip jutted out and he clung tightly to Tommy's trouser leg. 'I don't want you to go.'

'Got to, son.'

'Want to go with you.'

Tommy had not foreseen this. He had convinced himself that Jerry would recognize the house and be in a tearing hurry to be reunited with the man who had brought him up as his own son. Tommy reckoned Marty was a much better father than he could ever be. His brother was upright and honest and took his responsibilities seriously. Tommy had been aware of that since they were children. Even when Marty had spoken scathingly to him and almost torn his hair out at Tommy's antics, he had never left him alone to stew in his own juice. Instead, times without number, he had been prepared to take the blame for the brother who had fled the scene of his latest misdemeanour, knowing that if their father knew of it, he would tan Tommy's hide.

'I'll tell you what, son,' said Tommy. 'As soon as I've earned enough money and found a place good enough for both of us to live in, I'll be back for you.'

Jerry was silent a moment and then said, 'Cross your heart?'

'Cross me heart,' Tommy said.

'Want to see you do it.'

Smart lad, thought his father. A chip off the old block. Tommy crossed his heart. 'Now, I'll carry your case across the street and then you've got to rattle the letterbox and knock three times for luck.'

'The magic number,' said Jerry.

'Yeah, that's right: three's the magic number.'

Tommy handed the envelope to him and picked up both suit-cases. He hurried Jerry across the road, glad there was no one about at this time of evening. He placed the smaller suitcase on the step and hugged his son briefly. 'Now you be good for your Auntie Peggy and your other daddy. Don't rattle the letterbox until after you've counted to ten.'

He ruffled the boy's hair and hurried away, only to pause on the corner of the street and look back. It was a relief when the door opened and a woman stood silhouetted in the doorway. From that distance he could not recognize his sister, but if he had been standing closer, he would have seen that she was a blonde not a brunette. He waited no longer but headed for the bus stop, hoping he would not have long to wait before a bus to Liverpool turned up.

Irene Miller was barely able to believe her eyes as she stared down at the boy. 'Jerry! What are you doing here?'

'Yo-you're not Auntie Peggy!' The boy's bottom lip quivered and he would have made a bolt for it if he hadn't blundered into the suitcase his father had left on the step.

Irene seized Jerry by the arm and drew him into the house. 'Marty!' she shouted up the stairs. 'Come quick!'

A fair-haired, well set-up figure appeared at the top of the stairs. 'What is it, love?'

'You're not going to believe this, but it's Jerry!'

For a moment there was silence, and then Marty came running down the stairs. Jerry took one look at him and, wrenching himself out of Irene's grasp, he flung himself at Marty. Irene felt tears prick her eyes as Marty lifted the boy and hugged him.

'Where've you come from?' he asked unsteadily. 'And where's your mam and dad?'

'Other daddy's gone to make lots of money.' Jerry thrust an envelope against Marty's broad chest. 'This is for you.'

Marty and Irene exchanged glances. 'What about your mam?' she asked.

'Mammy's gone to Heaven,' replied Jerry.

For a moment Marty and Irene were speechless. Then she said, 'Tommy must have brought him here. He can't have gone far.'

Marty handed Jerry and the envelope over to her. The boy struggled in her arms. 'Lemme go!' he cried.

But Irene hung on to him as Marty left the house. 'Watch out for the suitcase!' she called.

It was too late and Marty caught his foot on it, causing the suitcase to fall flat on the ground as he tripped over it. He swore beneath his breath as he felt a stinging on the heels of his hands. But he picked himself up and set off down the street in the direction of the library on Linacre Road. What wouldn't he do to his brother when he caught him! he thought.

Marty was not far from the bottom of the street when he saw a bus going in the direction of Liverpool. Even so, he sprinted to the main road so he could have a clear view of the bus stop, but there was no one standing there. Pausing to catch his breath before making his way back to the house, he thought about what Jerry had said about his mother being in Heaven. Marty could do with knowing more about her death and whether his brother had informed Bernie's family. Somehow he doubted it.

A grim-faced Marty entered the house, glad to see the suitcase had been moved from the step. He found Irene and Jerry in the kitchen. The sweetie tin she normally kept in the sideboard cupboard was on the dining table minus its lid, along with an envelope addressed to him and his sister, Peggy. A small case containing toy cars with its lid up was also there.

Jerry was sitting in a chair by the fire, with a red lollipop in one hand and a Dinky car in the other. He attempted to get up from the chair as soon as Marty entered the room, but his uncle told him to stay where he was and picked up the envelope. Gingerly, he slit it open with a finger.

Irene came in from the back kitchen, carrying a steaming jug. She placed it on a cork mat on the table. 'I take it you didn't catch him.'

'I might have if I hadn't fallen over that b— suitcase,' Marty said. 'Get us some hot water, love, and the first-aid box. I've scraped skin off the palms of my hands.'

'You poor love! I hate it when that happens. It really hurts.'

'You can say that again,' he muttered.

Irene was away only a few minutes, keen to know what was in the letter. As she placed a small bowl of water and first-aid box on the table, she watched Marty unfold the sheets of paper. His eyes scanned the lines of writing, but his expression was unreadable, even to her.

'So, what does he say?' she asked, removing cotton wool and a tin of Germolene from the box and placing them on the table.

Marty held out the pages to her. 'Read it for yourself.'

Irene sat down and spread the letter out in front of her. From what she knew of Tommy, she had expected his handwriting to be almost indecipherable, but it was easier to read than her own scrawl because it was not in what they used to call 'joined-up writing' in junior school, but printed out meticulously.

Dear Marty and Peggy,

You have probably guessed by now that Bernie and Jerry went off with me, so you will be as mad as hatters with both of us. But she could see nothing else for it and you know Bernie nearly always gets her way. What you will not know is that we were wed shortly before I had to do my vanishing trick, and she only married you, Marty, because she was already having a baby. Jerry is mine, not yours. Anyway, I am telling you this now because Bernie died a short while ago. We had been living in London. I knew this bloke and he spoke for us and we were able to get a basement flat to rent. Bit of a pig of a place but at least we had a roof over our heads. She started having funny turns and when she caught the flu that finished her off. It blew me to pieces I can tell you. I did not know if I was coming or going for days. Anyway, she is dead and buried and I decided that I needed some help if I was to try and earn an honest living. Do not crack up laughing, I know what you think of me, but I never thought Bernie would die and I feel I should try and go straight because I want to do something right. I think it is lousy for Jerry to be motherless. Poor little sod. So what do you think? Will you both look after him for me until I make my fortune? I can almost hear you laughing at the thought. I know you will be a better father to him than I could ever be. By the way, Bernie told him that he was lucky in having two daddies, you and me. I wonder how my life would have turned out if I had been lucky enough to have had a different dad from the one I had to suffer. But I did have you, big brother. Anyway, do not even think of trying to find me. I will be in London and it is a helluva big place to try and find someone.

Thanks. Tommy

Forgot to ask, will you let Bernie's mother know she's gone? I couldn't face it. I will be in touch when I have some good news. Give my love to Mam.

'He's got a nerve but that's some letter,' said Irene, raising her head and gazing at Marty.

'Isn't it just,' he muttered. 'But at least he's admitted he and Bernie were married before she married me bigamously, so hurrah for that!'

'I find it hard to believe that he actually wrote it. It would have taken him more time printing it out than doing double writing. But he can really string words together and his writing is so neat. Pity he never bothered writing to you when he vanished and you all thought he was dead.'

'Yeah, it makes you wonder, doesn't it? Although, most likely it was because he didn't want to be traced and risk the police getting wind of where he was.'

'What are you going to do?' Irene glanced at Jerry and lowered her voice. 'Or would you rather not discuss this right now? Only, I'll have to be going soon.'

Marty sighed and changed the subject. 'Come and give us a hand here, love.'

While Irene had been reading the letter, he had been attempting to cleanse the grazes on the hand where a flap of skin had lifted off. She suggested he sat down. Immediately Jerry scrambled down from the armchair and came over to them.

'I'm thirsty,' he said, leaning against Marty's chair.

Irene put down the cotton wool and reached for the jug. She poured some cocoa into a small mug and added extra milk and told Jerry to sit at the table. He did so, and as Irene proceeded to deal with Marty's injuries, the boy's eyes kept going from his face to hers. As soon as he had finishing drinking, he said, 'Can I see Josie now?'

'She's asleep,' Irene murmured, closing the first-aid box.

Jerry turned to Marty. 'I want to see Josie. Other daddy said I'd be able to play with her. I promised him I'd be good for you and Auntie Peggy and I have been good so far. But where's Auntie Peggy?'

'She doesn't live here any more,' Marty said. 'This is your Auntie Irene and you're to be good for her, too.'

Jerry looked doubtful. 'Why doesn't Auntie Peggy live here any more?'

'Because she's married and lives with her husband.' Marty frowned at Irene. 'I've just thought – what am I going to do in the morning? Who's going to look after Jerry?'

'Stop worrying,' said Irene. 'I'll explain to Peggy when I see her later. I'm sure she'll be prepared to come with me first thing in the morning. I'll speak to Matron about Jerry and, fingers crossed, she'll agree to him coming along to the nursery with Josie.'

Marty smiled and, leaning forward, kissed her. 'What would I do without you?'

Irene kissed him back. 'You don't have to do without me.' She lowered her voice. 'I've been thinking since reading that letter. Surely, with Bernie dead, we can go ahead with the wedding sooner. Her death should simplify matters with the church.'

'I'll speak to Father Francis and see what he has to say.'

Irene's blue eyes shone. 'He's been such a help to us in discovering your wedding to Bernie was bigamous. I know he's not our parish priest, but I'd like him to take part in the ceremony.'

'I'll try and see him tomorrow on my way home from work. I'm going to have to drop in and see Ma, anyway.'

'Couldn't Peggy do that?' suggested Irene. 'She could take Jerry with her to see your mother.'

His expression brightened. 'That's an idea. See what she thinks when you see her later.'

But Irene was not to see Peggy that evening, because she and Pete had already gone to bed by the time Irene arrived at the Marshall household in Bootle. As she made ready for bed, she thought how it seemed not to have occurred to Marty to refuse to fall in with his brother's plans. She felt a stir of anger. Tommy really was a selfish swine. How dare he shift his responsibility for his son on to Marty and scoot off to London, fancy-free once more! Not only that, but also leaving the job of informing Bernie's mother of her youngest daughter's death was really not on. She could not wait to hear what Peggy thought of it all.

'You're not going to believe this,' said Irene, sitting at the breakfast table across from Peggy the following morning.

Peggy swallowed the last bit of arrowroot biscuit and glanced at her. 'What aren't we going to believe?'

Irene dropped her bombshell. 'Jerry turned up on Marty's doorstep around about eight o'clock last night with his suitcase and a note.'

Peggy's mouth fell open. 'You're joking!'

Irene shook her head. 'Cross my heart and hope to die. It's the gospel truth.'

'Now why doesn't that surprise me?' said Pete. 'We should have guessed that Tommy would never be able to cope with a kid and Bernie going doolally at the same time.'

'Prepare yourself for another shock,' Irene said softly. 'Bernie's dead.'

Peggy reached out a hand to Pete, who laced his fingers through hers and squeezed her hand gently. 'You all right, love?'

She hesitated and then nodded.

Irene reached into a pocket and withdrew an envelope and placed it in front of Peggy on the table. She stared down at it. 'That's our Tommy's writing. Miracles happen. He's actually written us a letter.'

'Open it, Peg, and let's see what he has to say,' Pete urged.

'You can read it with me,' she said.

Pete began to read the letter over his wife's shoulder.

Irene watched their faces as she buttered a slice of toast and then spread jam on it. Her teeth crunched into the toast, breaking the silence.

'Tommy's got a bloody nerve,' said Pete, glancing across at her.

'That's what I said to Marty.' Irene looked at the clock on the mantelpiece. 'He's going to need you to look after Jerry this morning, Peggy. D'you think you can come with me when I leave in a quarter of an hour? He also suggested you might like to take Jerry to visit your mother. She needs to know what her precious blue-eyed boy's done now.'

Before Peggy could answer, Pete's mother came into the kitchen. 'Good, you're still here, Irene. I'll catch the bus with you,' she said.

Pete glanced at his mother, Gertie, a short, plump woman with greying hair. 'Peggy will be going with you. Her nephew has turned up on Marty's doorstep and he needs someone to look after him.' He turned to Irene. 'I must admit your news far outweighs mine.'

'And what's your news?' she asked.

'I met Maggie Gregory on the train when I was coming home from work.'

Irene shrugged. 'I bet she'll be here and gone in a flash. She never stays long.'

'I think she'll be staying a bit longer this time,' said Pete.

'I don't care about Maggie right this moment,' said Peggy impatiently. 'I'm really annoyed with our Tommy, especially the way he takes it for granted that our Marty will shoulder his responsibilities – and expecting him to break the news to Bernie's mother. She'll hit the roof.'

Irene looked at the clock. 'We'll have to be going.'

'Have you told Irene about our Norman?' Gertie Marshall's mouth tightened as she shrugged on her coat.

Irene shot a glance at her. 'What about Norman?'

'He's only gone and got himself engaged to some other girl without telling me.'

'I thought he and Maggie had a thing going,' said Irene.

'So did we,' Pete said, shrugging on his coat. 'Ma's not the only one who's hurt, so is Maggie.'

'Has she come up here because Norman's dumped her and she wants some tea and sympathy from her family?' asked Irene with a touch of sarcasm.

'No, she's had a really bad bout of bronchitis and has come up here to recuperate,' Pete said.

'Ooops, I should have kept my mouth shut,' said Irene. 'But Maggie's cousin Betty always went on about Maggie having been spoilt.'

'Let's forget Maggie for now,' Peggy said impatiently. 'I want to see Jerry and make sure for myself that he's all right. I don't know how our Marty is going to break the news to Bernie's mother.'

'Maybe her mother's best believing Bernie's still alive,' said Gertie. 'From what I've heard about that woman, she just might get violent and shoot the messenger.'

'I know she's never had a good word to say for either of my brothers,' said Peggy. 'And it wasn't our Tommy or Marty who was a bigamist, but her daughter. Bernie knew what she was doing. She tricked our Marty into marrying her because she was pregnant and didn't want to tell anyone she had secretly married our Tommy.'

'Agreed, but let's drop the subject for now,' Pete said. 'It's time I was off to work.'

'And we'll have to get a move on,' said Irene. 'I've work to go to, as well.'

Peggy wasted no more time. The three women were in a sombre mood as they made the journey to Litherland. They parted at the bus stop opposite the sausage factory where Gertie worked. She told them she wouldn't be in for tea as she was going straight to West Derby, so not to expect her until about ten.

The two women hurried to Marty's house, where they found Jerry and four year old Josie, who was the spitting image of Peggy when she was a little girl, sitting opposite him. Both were dressed and eating cornflakes. Immediately Jerry saw Peggy, he shot up and ran to her. She gave him a hug and a kiss before greeting her brother and Josie.

Marty was in the act of placing corned beef and pickle butties into a haversack and darted his sister a relieved look. 'Am I glad to see you? You all right with taking charge of Jerry until later?'

She squeezed her brother's arm. 'He's my nephew too, isn't he? It's our Tommy who's a pain in the neck.'

'No argument there,' said Marty, slinging the haversack over a shoulder. 'Sorry, but I'm going to have to rush.' He kissed Josie and squeezed Jerry's shoulder and then kissed Irene. 'See you later, love.'

He was halfway through the door when she called, 'What are you going to do about seeing Father Francis?'

He hesitated. 'I'll see how I'm fixed for time.'

'What about seeing Bernie's mother?' asked Peggy.

'Same with her. Can't say I'm looking forward to it,' he said. 'Look, I'm going to have to go. I've a couple of big jobs on.'

Irene saw him to the door and waved him off before going back inside the house, where she found Peggy clearing away the empty cereal bowls. 'Me and Josie will have to leave for the nursery in a few minutes,' she said.

'OK!' Peggy paused in the doorway that led to the back kitchen. 'Is there any shopping you'd like me to do for Marty and the kids when I nip along to Mam's with Jerry?'

Aware that the children were most likely listening, Irene nudged Peggy into the back kitchen and took her purse from a pocket. 'Get us an Easter egg for Jerry. I've one already for Josie. I'll also need a fresh loaf and a pound of mince.' She handed over a pound note. 'I hope that's enough.'

'Don't worry about it,' said Peggy. 'You can always give me any extra later.'

'And don't forget to keep your eye on Jerry,' Irene whispered. 'It's not impossible that he'll remember where his other grand-mother's house is, given that it's within walking distance of your mother's.'

'That's a good thought. Monica, Bernie's niece is still living there; she was very fond of the kid and gutted when Bernie and Tommy vanished with him.'

'You're not thinking Monica would snatch him if she knew Jerry had been dumped on Marty – take him to live with Bernie's family, are you?' Irene's blue eyes had widened.

Peggy gasped. 'That never occurred to me.'

'I'm not saying Monica would do such a thing. I like the girl, and she's babysat Josie a few times for Marty and me, but blood is thicker than water and she might think Jerry belongs with them. And would she be far wrong?'

'I might agree if he was an orphan, but he's not,' Peggy said. 'Anyway, knowing our Marty, he wouldn't allow it. In his eyes Jerry is a McGrath, and he took on responsibility for him from the moment Jerry was born.'

'That was when he believed he was his son.'

Peggy agreed. 'Even so, he's still fond of him, and he is our nephew.' She went over to the sink and deposited crockery and cutlery on the draining board. 'But you're making me question whether it's a good idea for me to take him to see Mam and tell her about Tommy. She's not brilliant at keeping secrets, and if she was to tell our Lil—'

'Well, that's up to you,' said Irene, glancing at the clock on the mantelpiece. 'I'm going to have to go.'

Peggy saw her and Josie out and then returned to the kitchen, where Jerry was playing with his cars. He looked up at her. 'Are we going out, Auntie Peggy?'

Peggy came to a decision. 'Yes, later. We'll go to the park and then to the shops, but first I've some housework to do and then I must make a phone call.'

'To my other daddy?' he asked.

She almost asked him which one did he mean, but decided just to smile and say, 'Yes.'

Six

Maggie was struggling to hook Owen's harness on to the ring attached to the pushchair, but her nephew would not keep still. He was as slippery as an eel but she was determined not to give in to him and allow him to walk. Of course, he was old enough not to need a pushchair any longer, but it was at least a mile to the beach and there was no way she was going to risk him tugging his hand out of her grasp and running on to the road and getting himself killed. Why had she volunteered to take him to the beach? That was a daft question. She knew the answer. It was because she wanted to prove, to her brother and his wife, that she was prepared to pull her weight. Crazy! It was only her first full day in Formby and she should be resting.

'Would you like a hand with that?'

For a moment Maggie could not work out where the voice was coming from, and then she lifted her head and gazed in the direction of her sister's house and saw a dark-haired man standing the other side of the fence.

'Who are you?' she said, slightly breathless with bending over. 'What are you doing in my sister's garden?'

'I'm Joshua Colman.' He placed a hand on the top of the railing fence and vaulted over it.

She stared at him in astonishment; in different circumstances she might have admired his athleticism. 'What d'you think you're doing? Where's Jimmy? Are you a friend of his?'

At that moment, Owen wriggled out of her hold and slid out of the pushchair. She made a grab for him but he was too quick for her. Joshua seized hold of him, preventing him from escaping through the open front gate, and handed him over to Maggie.

She muttered her thanks, noticing that his neck and face were weather-beaten, as if he spent a lot of time outdoors. He had eyes the colour of treacle toffee and strong-boned features. He was dressed casually in an open-necked checked shirt and beige corduroy trousers.

She dumped Owen into the pushchair. 'Now keep still or there'll be no treats for you,' she warned.

Owen stuck out his tongue and she was tempted to give him a light smack, but knew Emma did not believe in physical punishment. Instead she bent over and grabbed hold of his tongue. 'Behave yourself or else,' she warned.

He jerked his head backwards and she lost her grip on his tongue. 'I want chocolate and then I'll be good,' he lisped.

'You're far too spoilt, young man. You only have chocolate if you're good in the first place.' She heard a chuckle behind her and whirled round. 'What's so funny?' she demanded.

'If you don't know, then it's a waste of time my telling you,' said Joshua. 'Watch out! He's at it again.'

She whirled round and was just in time to prevent Owen from scrambling from the pushchair. She held him down with a firm hand and called over her shoulder, 'Who are you? And don't tell me your name again because it doesn't mean a thing to me.'

'I know Billy from the army. He told me next time I was in Liverpool to drop by. I've just got back from Cyprus. I didn't know he was going to be away this weekend.'

'You should have telephoned,' Maggie said, struggling to get a clip on Owen's harness through the ring on the pushchair. She managed the first one.

'I telephoned from Liverpool yesterday,' he said.

'What time? Because if you'd phoned early enough, my sister and Billy would have still been here.' She struggled with the second clip and managed to get it done. 'There, that will make you stay put.'

He frowned. 'I thought they'd be at work and, as I wanted Billy's advice on an urgent matter, I decided to catch a train. I hoped I'd find him at home by that time. Unfortunately I'd forgotten the number of the house, so I telephoned from Formby Station and a man answered. He told me he was Billy's step-brother and that Billy and your sister had gone away. He suggested that as I had taken the trouble of coming to Formby, I could phone Billy from the house as they'd left a number where they could be contacted. We got talking and he realized he knew my uncle and suggested we had a drink and something to eat. I ended up staying the night.' His eyes glinted. 'Satisfied?'

She flushed. 'Yes, although you didn't have to tell me the whole story.' She picked up the bag containing a packed lunch, a bottle of lemon and barley drink and beach paraphernalia.

'I haven't. Because I could have mentioned that I was forced to wait outside the telephone box because this girl inside was nattering on and on. Then, when she finally decided to ring off, she pushed the door so hard it not only hit me in the stomach but she then trod all over my feet.'

She felt herself squirming inside as their eyes met. 'Was that you? I did say I was sorry at the time.'

'Yes, but somehow I had the impression that you blamed me for being there.'

'I was tired,' she muttered. 'I'd come up from London and been travelling for hours. Now, if you don't mind, I've got to get going.' Without another word, she made for the gate, hoping he would be gone by the time she returned.

She set off in the direction of the beach. Owen appeared to have settled down, as he was no longer trying to wriggle out of his harness, but was gazing about him as he wheeled his favourite Dinky black taxi backwards and forwards on the blanket covering his legs.

She allowed her mind to drift, thinking of Emma who had looked so pale and drawn earlier that morning after suffering a bout of morning sickness. Maggie had decided she might never have children. There was too much suffering and hard work involved. She had insisted that Emma put her feet up and have a rest. Not that her sister-in-law had agreed straightaway. She had told Maggie that they could make the beds together and tidy downstairs. That done, and having shared coffee and biscuits, Maggie had made some sandwiches and left Emma reading Maggie's copy of *Vogue* with her feet up on a pouffe.

Could she be satisfied with staying at home all day like most married women with young children? Although, according to an article she had read, since the war, increasing numbers of mothers had been finding themselves part-time jobs once their children started school.

Which led her on to wonder: what was she going to do with her life? She thought of what Tim on the train had said about her having a go at being an actress. It was not a new idea, having occurred to her when she had met Dorothy Wilson in Lenny's coffee bar up on Hope Street in Liverpool a few years ago.

The actress had grown up in a back street of Liverpool and worked her way up through the theatre, eventually to become a star of stage and screen. At the moment Maggie had no idea where she was, but knew Lenny would most likely have a contact telephone number and address.

But she did not have to get in touch yet. She needed to build up her strength, put on some weight and continue to resist the urge to nip into the nearest newsagent's or tobacconist's for a packet of cigarettes. She also had to stop thinking about Norm's letter. She heaved a sigh and thought instead of the telephone call she had made to her landlady.

She had apologized for not informing her that she was leaving, and promised to send her a month's rent in lieu of notice and extra money so she could dispatch Maggie's clothes and anything else she had left behind in her suitcase. It would probably come by train, and the sooner the better, as Emma's clothes were too big for her and Maggie liked to look well dressed. She thought of Tim Murphy and their arranged date. Would she go? Would he turn up in a month's time? It could be that he might have completely forgotten about her by then. She decided to make up her mind nearer the time.

It was at that moment she heard her name being called, and instantly she turned round. Her eyes lit up as she caught sight of the well set-up figure of Jimmy Miller, clad in a reefer jacket and navy blue trousers, with a seaman's cap perched on his light brown hair.

'I wondered if I'd get to see you before you went back to sea,' she said. 'What were you thinking of, entertaining a strange man in Billy and Dot's house?'

Jimmy grinned. 'Josh just told me he'd spoken to Dot's sister, so you know the story. He's not a bad bloke. I'd just got out of the bath so that's why I missed you back at the house.'

'He said you knew his uncle.'

'So do you, as it happens. He's Lenny's nephew.'

Maggie could not conceal her surprise. 'Lenny who owns the coffee bar on Hope Street?'

'I don't know any other.'

'He doesn't look a bit like him.'

'Josh might take after his father. It was his mother who was related to Lenny.' He came up alongside her. 'I'm on my way to the children's home so I might as well walk with you.'

'Why are you going there?'

'I'm meeting my girlfriend, Deirdre. She works there.'

Maggie had forgotten about his girlfriend. 'Can't I persuade you to go to the beach with us, instead? I'm not used to entertaining little boys.'

He kicked a pebble. 'No chance. Me and Deirdre have little enough time together.'

'When are you going back to sea?'

'Later today. I'm on the Canadian run, which means I'm only away for about a fortnight, so that's not too bad. But she works shifts, so it takes a bit of juggling to spend any length of time together.' He paused. 'So how are you and Norm getting on? You can't see much of each other.'

'I'm going to see even less of him in the future,' Maggie muttered.

'Why's that?'

'You're bound to find out so I might as well tell you. He's gone and got himself engaged to someone else.'

For a moment Jimmy was silent, and then he said, 'Well, you're best finding out now if the pair of you don't suit, rather than getting married and discovering it afterwards.'

Maggie knew he was right, but Norm's treatment of her still hurt. 'We never got as far as him asking me to marry him. I fooled myself into believing we were heading that way.' Her voice quivered.

Jimmy put an arm around her shoulders. 'Don't get upset, Mags. You're a good-looking girl and there's plenty more fish in the sea. You're bound to meet someone else if it's a husband you're after. I must admit I thought having a modelling career was more important to you.'

She shrugged off his arm. 'Don't you start! Everybody seems to think that having a career prevents a woman from wanting marriage as well. But that's not true in my case.' She paused and then found herself saying, 'As it happened, I've met someone who just might turn out to be the right man for me.'

Jimmy said, 'You're kidding. You can't be talking about Josh, surely?'

'Don't be ridiculous,' she said hastily. 'No, I met this bloke on the train from London yesterday.'

'You mean he just picked you up?'

'No, it wasn't like that,' she said indignantly.

'Is a southerner?'

'No, he's a Liverpudlian who's been living in London.'

'So has he come up here to see his family?'

'He's going to be living with his mother, who's a widow. He's starting a business up here. But don't you go mentioning him to our Dot,' she said swiftly. 'I don't want the third degree from her about him.'

'OK! When will you be seeing him again?'

She sighed heavily. 'Questions, questions. I wish I hadn't mentioned him now.'

'What have you got to hide?'

'I've nothing to hide,' she said, exasperated. 'I'm supposed to be seeing him sometime after Easter.'

'And if he doesn't turn up?'

She hesitated and realized she did not like the thought of Tim Murphy not showing. 'If he doesn't I'll put it down to experience and know he isn't the one. Life has proved that I'm not always a good judge of just who is the right man for me.'

Jimmy stopped outside a pair of wrought-iron gates. 'I hope you've arranged to meet him in a public place?'

'I'm not daft!' She glanced up at the brick wall above which was displayed a sign with the name of the children's home on it in gilded lettering. 'So this is where your girlfriend works?'

There came the sound of running footsteps, and a few moments later a rosy-cheeked young woman appeared the other side of the gates.

'I'm sorry I'm late, Jimmy.' She sounded out of breath as she unlocked the gate. 'I hope I haven't kept you waiting long?' She stepped outside on to the pavement.

'I've only just got here.' Jimmy took her hand. 'Let me introduce you two. Deirdre, this is Maggie Gregory, Billy's wife Dot's younger sister. You must have heard them talking about her.'

'You're the one who lives in London! You're the model.' Deirdre gazed admiringly at Maggie.

'Not any more.' Maggie's voice was tinged with regret. 'I've been ill so I'm staying with Jared and Emma for a while.'

'I wish I was as lovely and slim as you,' said Deirdre as they shook hands.

'Thanks, but I need to put weight on,' Maggie said. 'I believe you and Irene used to work together.'

'Yes, that's how Jimmy and I met. I'm so pleased to meet you. I do like your outfit.'

Maggie almost said 'This old thing', but decided that might sound as if she had tons of even more fantastic clothes in her wardrobe. 'It was my job. I suspect in no time at all I'll be slouching around in any old thing, now I'm no longer modelling. Anyway, I won't keep you. Owen and I are off to the beach. See you again. I hope you have a good trip, Jimmy.'

Maggie hurried away, wondering if Jimmy and Deirdre would get married one day. They could not have known each other long because she had never heard of her until Emma mentioned her yesterday. Last time Maggie had seen Jimmy talking to a girl had been at the Gianellis' house and he was playing guitar. The girl was Lucia, Nellie Gianelli's niece, and she was a good few years younger than Jimmy, but it was clear she'd had a crush on him. What would Lucia make of Jimmy having a girlfriend? Unrequited love could be even more painful at that age, thought Maggie, feeling a familiar ache. It probably made much more sense if one did not bother with love at all.

Seven

It was three weeks later and Maggie had settled in at Jared and Emma's, although there were times when she missed her independence, London and her job.

'Do you want a hand with that?'

Not again, thought Maggie, although this time the voice did not belong to Josh Colman but her sister, who had returned from a weekend in Wales, only to go away again for Easter on a visit to see Ally and Hester at Emma's cottage in Whalley. There was still no date set for when the couple would definitely be leaving for Canada, and Emma was of the opinion that Hester was dithering again about whether to go or not.

'No, I can manage,' called Maggie.

'It takes some doing, I know, and you still don't seem to have the hang of it, despite having taken Owen out for the past three weeks,' said Dot, resting her elbows on the fence dividing her garden from that of Jared and Emma.

Maggie could feel her temper rising, and was tempted to say something bitchy to her sister, who so far had no children, despite having been married the same day as Emma and Jared in a double wedding that had been pure fairy tale. Dot had always gone in for the glamour look and had lots of fellas after her in her younger days. She had worked as a sewing machinist and used to make some of her own clothes. Now she had a part-time job working in a shop in the village, but today was Wednesday and she had the whole day off.

'I just don't like people watching me,' Maggie said, straightening up. 'I've done it now and we'll be off.'

'You going to the beach?' Dot asked. 'I could come with you if you like?'

'You don't have to bother, but thanks for the offer,' Maggie said, determined to ignore the hurt expression in her sister's eyes, knowing what would happen if she agreed. Her sister would somehow take control of the pushchair, and Maggie would be left walking aimlessly by her side and be bombarded with questions about her life in London and what she was going to do in the future and what did she think had gone wrong between her and Norm that he should get himself engaged to someone else. It was not that she was not fond of her sister but, just like their cousin, Betty, Dot thought she had the right to give Maggie orders because she was the eldest. But the real truth was that Maggie had started to enjoy her lone walks with Owen. Her nephew was used to her now and she enjoyed playing with him. She liked reading him stories and teaching him his numbers and letters. She found it a real thrill when he got them right.

'Please yourself. I've loads to do anyway,' said Dot with a shrug. 'You just make sure you don't catch cold and end up with pneumonia. I bet there'll be a real sharp wind coming off the sea.'

'Don't fuss, you sound just like Mam, and I'm not a child any more,' Maggie said, manoeuvring the pushchair out of the gate.

'You'll soon get the hang of that,' said Dot.

'I already have the hang of it,' said Maggie pettishly. 'It's you watching me that's making me clumsy.'

'Don't make me your excuse,' said Dot. 'Anyway, I shouldn't have mentioned going with you. I could be having a visitor today.'

'I hope you have a nice time together,' said Maggie, resisting asking who was her sister's visitor.

'Don't you want to know who it is?' called Dot.

Maggie ignored the question and carried on walking, thinking that most likely she would find out later because Emma would probably spot anyone visiting next door.

But Maggie was to discover the identity of her sister's visitor when she reached the bottom of the avenue. Jimmy's sister, Irene Miller, was coming in her direction. She thought the other girl didn't look her usual lovely self. For a moment Maggie hesitated, because she and Irene had never been bosom chums, due to Irene being her cousin Betty's best friend. She had even visited Betty in California the other year. When the three of them were younger, the two older girls would gang up on Maggie and not invite her to go places with them or let her in on their secrets. Even so, Maggie decided she had better stop and pass the time of day with Irene for a few minutes.

'Hiya, Irene. Are you OK?'

'Better than I was; a cold. I'm over it now but having an extra day off work. I believe you've been bad with bronchitis.'

'I'm a lot better than I was. I'm doing what the doctor ordered and getting plenty of fresh air and have given up the ciggies.'

'Good for you! I know that takes some doing.' She smiled. 'I see you've taken over looking after Owen.'

'Yes, Jared's orders. With Emma pregnant, he wants me taking some of the load off her shoulders.' She ruffled her nephew's light brown hair. 'I think I prefer the opposite sex at this age. In some ways they're so much easier to handle.'

Irene laughed. 'You wouldn't think that if you had a whole gang of them to look after. They can also be little terrors. Have you seen your Dot this morning?'

Maggie nodded. 'She's expecting you, isn't she?'

Irene smiled. 'I'm hoping to persuade her to visit the children's home with me. My friend Deirdre phoned and said they were shorthanded and could do with some volunteers. The home is run by a charity and I thought it might help Dot if she was to spend some time with the handicapped children.'

'What d'you mean, help her?' asked Maggie bluntly.

Irene hesitated. 'I think it would be good for her to be around children. Children like Georgie, for example.'

'Who's Georgie?'

'He was a favourite of mine when I worked at the home in Blundell Sands. His mother died when he was born and his father did not want him when he realized George had a club foot.'

'That's sad,' said Maggie.

Irene agreed. 'I'm hoping your Dot will want to help him – and it could help her at the same time.'

Maggie's brow puckered. 'In what way?'

Irene hesitated. 'Think about it, Maggie. How long have she and Billy been married, and still they have no kids?'

'I've always thought they didn't want kids. They seem to be happy enough without them, and are always going away for weekends.'

'They probably enjoy themselves, but it could be that it helps fill a hole in their lives. If Dot is broody and nothing is happening, imagine how much it must hurt now that Emma's having another baby?'

Maggie nibbled on her lower lip, stuck for something to say. She was thinking her sister had probably had more to do with Owen when Maggie lived away. But Dot did have a job and the house and a husband to look after, so why was Maggie feeling guilty? Jared had told her that he expected her to help out with Owen, so she was only doing what she had been told. It had been a bonus that she was actually beginning to enjoy the times spent with her nephew. Even so, perhaps she could be a bit kinder to her sister.

'I hope she agrees to go with you and see the children,' Maggie said.

Irene nodded. 'So do I.'

There was another silence. Then Maggie remembered something Emma had told her. 'I heard you were getting married. When is the wedding?'

Irene sighed. 'I don't know yet, but when the time's right I'll send you an invitation.'

Maggie had not expected a proper invitation. Maybe one to the evening do, but this sounded as if she would be invited to the service and wedding reception. 'Promise,' she blurted out. 'I'd like to see you married. We've known each other a long time, and what with Betty in California and unlikely to be at your wedding, I could fill her shoes.'

Irene looked taken aback, and that caused Maggie to say hastily, 'Not that I could ever really do that. I was always an outsider where you two were concerned.' She stopped abruptly, thinking she had probably said much too much. 'I'd best go. See you!' She hurried off.

Irene stared after her, wondering whether she and Betty had really treated Maggie as that much of an outsider when they were younger? Did she really want her at her wedding? She felt guilty even asking herself that question. Remembering that in some ways Maggie had suffered as much sadness in her life as she and Betty had.

She pushed the thought to the back of her mind. What was she doing worrying about Maggie? It was not as if she was home-less and had no one. So Norm had dumped her and she had lost her job and had to watch her health, but there were people having a worse time than her in the world.

She went on her way, thinking of Georgie and the other handicapped orphans she hoped to persuade Dot to visit and help with that morning. On the tail of that thought, her mind drifted to Jerry and his dad Tommy. Marty had spoken to Father Francis; he had been as exasperated with Marty's brother as they were. Annoyed that he had not only avoided staying around long enough to talk with his brother and sister, but also had not visited his own mother or his dead wife's mother. The priest had expressed regret at Bernie's death and had also spoken to Marty, convinced that if he could get his hands on Bernie's death certificate, then most likely it would enable him and Irene to get married sooner than they had thought possible.

Irene felt really angry with Tommy. If only he had told them where he was living in London, they could have written to him, but unless he got in touch with them again, they had no means of getting their hands on Bernie's death certificate. Father Francis had mentioned the possibility of writing to the register office for deaths, births and marriages in London, but to do that they really needed to know when and where Bernie had died and her address in London.

The priest had also been shocked by the news that Bernie's family had not been informed of her death, although he had understood why Marty was fighting shy of visiting them and kept putting off the moment when he would have to break the news to her mother. He had offered to have a word with the priest in whose parish Bernie's mother and sisters lived, but Marty had told him that he felt it was his responsibility, and to leave things as they were for the moment. So Irene and Marty were no further on with their marriage plans, which they both found extremely frustrating. She would happily throttle Tommy if she could get her hands on him, but first she needed to get her hands on Bernie's death certificate.

Eight

Tommy unbolted the Judas door in one of the large wooden gates and stepped into the street off Lark Lane in south Liverpool. The lane was an extremely popular shopping centre, having on sale almost everything a housewife and the lone man might need. There was a Lune laundry, several bakeries, grocer's, butcher's and greengrocer's. Within a short walk was the Bluebird fish and chip shop, a decent shoe and boot shop, a draper's, florist, several barbers and hairdressers. There was even a funeral parlour, a doctor's surgery, a Children's Welfare Clinic and a couple of places he could do without, such as another garage and the local nick. The latter having given him quite a start when he'd passed it, but then he had stroked his beard and decided the scuffers wouldn't be expecting to see him in Liverpool, especially after all this time.

He really liked the area, having walked the length of the lane since his arrival. In one direction it ran towards the Mersey, but ended in Aigburth Road some distance before it reached the river. In the other direction it took the traveller to Sefton Park. Tommy had visited the park several times in his youth, and would have visited more often, but it was some distance from his childhood home in the north end and he had been unable to afford the fare.

What he remembered most about the park was its aviary, boating lake, and the statue of Peter Pan which was similar to the one in Kensington Gardens in London. Tommy felt certain his son would enjoy seeing the Liverpool statue one day and, just like he had once done, would have a go at clambering up it, stroking the well-rubbed shiny head of a rabbit on the way. He missed his son, but knew only too well that it would be impossible for him to have Jerry living with him and to give him the attention he needed.

Tommy reached for the packet of cigarettes in the pocket of his navy blue overalls, thinking now of Marty and Peggy. A nerve at the corner of his eye twitched as, yet again, he imagined his brother's reaction to finding Jerry on his doorstep. He felt uncomfortable at the thought and took out a cigarette. He was desperate for a smoke, but he put the cigarettes away, knowing that so close to the garage forecourt it would be stupid to risk any fumes from oil or fuel being set alight.

A woman pushing a pram across the road called out a good morning to him. He returned the greeting before going back inside the yard and unbolting one of the big gates and pushing it wide open, so any would-be customers would know the yard was open. Business was slow to take off, but he had every confidence that it would build up.

Inside the yard was a huge working garage with a pit. Next to the garage was a separately built brick ground-floor office, with a small kitchen to the rear, as well as a cloakroom with a toilet and washbasin. Outside was a flight of steps that led to a room upstairs that had been used for storage but which he had turned into a bedroom.

The lease on the premises and the goodwill had taken the remains of Bernie's life insurance, after the expense of the funeral had been deducted, and most of the money he had managed to accumulate since he had left Liverpool a few years back and travelled to Australia. Oddly enough, the previous leaseholder had decided to up sticks and emigrate with his wife and children to the other side of the world. Tommy had told him that he had lived in Australia for a while, but that he had come home for family reasons, working his passage on a cargo ship docking in Liverpool.

Tommy took a deep breath of air tainted with oil and exhaust fumes and wished that he could turn the clock back, but it was too late now. He just had to be glad that he had managed to avoid being caught for his minor role in a robbery for which he would probably have been sent down for several years. Was he making another mistake in coming back? He thought of the various jobs he had taken on at garages and the occasional lonely homestead in Australia, working on any kind of vehicle that needed fixing. Yet here in Liverpool was where he felt most at home.

He went through the office into the kitchen and put on the kettle. Time for a cup of tea and a bacon sarnie. As he sat in the office enjoying his breakfast, his eyes were fixed on a map of the area that covered Toxteth Park, the Dingle, Aigburth and up as far as Woolton. One thing was for sure, if he studied the map often enough he wouldn't get lost. There were a lot of posh houses this end of Liverpool – so unlike the neighbourhood where he had been brought up – and he was determined to show his family that he could make good. His plan was that one day he would visit and tell them that he had made such a success of everything that now he had a house of his own. It was his intention to be as good a father to his son as Marty had been before him. All Tommy needed for everything to be perfect was a new mother for Jerry.

He glanced at the calendar that had been hanging on the wall when he'd moved in, and not for the first time checked the date that he had pencilled in. It was this coming Saturday he had arranged to meet the woman from the train, Maggie Gregory. Would she turn up at the meeting place? He stroked his beard and wondered whether to shave it off because it made him look older. Then he remembered his purpose in growing the neat goatee.

At that moment he heard the sound of a vehicle being driven into the yard and instantly hurried outside to welcome whoever it was, hoping he, or even she, would become a regular customer.

Nine

'"Many a tear has to fall, but it's all in the game",' hummed Maggie, sitting at the dressing table, applying make-up. The door was ajar and from downstairs she could hear Emma having a conversation on the telephone in the hall. She was talking to Hester in Whalley, and from what Maggie could make out, Emma and Jared were intending to visit Hester and her husband Ally next weekend. The couple had at last made up their minds about emigrating to Canada, but there was a lot to sort out before they were to finally leave the cottage to cross the Atlantic.

Maggie heard Emma say goodbye and the receiver go down. The next moment there was the sound of footsteps on the stairs and then the rap of knuckles on the open door. 'Can I come in?' asked Emma.

'Of course.' Maggie replaced the top on her Yardley's lipstick.

Emma sat on the bed. 'You going somewhere?'

'To Lenny's.' Right at that moment, Maggie had no intention of mentioning her assignation with Tim Murphy.

'It's a while since I've been there. But why are you dollied up? He's not having a party, is he?'

'Not that I know of, but what with all my clothes having arrived at last, I thought it would be good to dress up. Besides, I like to look attractive when I go to the theatre.'

'The theatre?'

'Yes, I've booked a ticket for a matinee as well. *The Merry Widow* is on at the Royal Court. Paul Anka is on at the Empire next week and I'd like to go and see him, too.'

'Who's Paul Anka?' asked Emma.

'Oh, Emma, you are a square, almost as bad as our Jared. He's a pop singer and got a golden disc for "Diana".'

'That's a rather nice name for a girl,' Emma murmured.

'It's OK,' said Maggie. 'If I have time I'll also have a look around the shops and maybe go on somewhere else later in the evening. That's all right with you, isn't it?' she added casually.

'Of course it is. You've stayed close to home since you arrived, it's time you got out and enjoyed yourself. You've been such a good help with Owen and in the garden, although you could do with more practice cooking. Anyway, I was wondering if the Gianellis might be having one of their musical evenings soon? You used to like going there, didn't you?'

'Occasionally, but I haven't heard anything. Besides, I'd rather go into town. I often went to the theatre when I was in London.'

'Do you miss London?' Emma smoothed the ruffled pink candlewick bedspread.

'Sometimes.' Maggie went over to the wardrobe, thinking she could hardly say she really, really missed it on occasion. She took out a jacket of blue and green Italian silk twill that matched the skirt she was wearing. She had been given the suit in lieu of payment last autumn. She put it on and, discovering that it was a bit snug, she pursed her lips. Had she been enjoying Emma's cooking too much? If so, she was going to have to start watching her weight. She didn't want to get fat. What she needed was a good excuse to fast the odd time so it wouldn't rouse comment from Jared and Emma. Unfortunately she could not use Lent as an excuse because that was well past. Soon it would be the Whit weekend.

'That looks lovely on you,' said Emma, sounding envious.

'Thanks. You don't think I've put on weight?'

'Hardly any. You really did need to put on a few pounds, though. You were beginning to look scrawny.'

'Scrawny!' Maggie was hurt. 'You're not serious, are you?'

'Aye, you look much better now.'

Maggie studied herself carefully in the mirror. Perhaps she did look more attractive. Curvaceous. 'I don't want not to be able to get into my clothes,' she murmured. 'I'd like to stay just as I am. Maybe I should give up potatoes and bread?'

'Don't be daft! You need your carbohydrates if you're chasing round after Owen and helping me out with housework and shopping. Anyway, if you do find your clothes getting tighter, you can always ask Lynne Walker to let them out. She's a really good dressmaker. I still have the smocks she made for me when I was having Owen. Honestly, you really do look better for having a bit more flesh on you.'

Convinced, Maggie picked up a pair of turquoise suede gloves and a black shoulder bag. 'I'd better get going or the day will be over before I even get started.'

'Enjoy yourself,' said Emma, smiling. 'I look forward to hearing all about it when you get back.'

Lenny's, on Hope Street, was situated not far from the Anglican Cathedral, opposite which Maggie had lived for a while in a top-floor studio with Betty when she was an art student at the college nearby. Her cousin had also worked part-time in Lenny's coffee bar.

As Maggie opened the door and went inside, she was remembering it was here that Betty had first met her future husband, Scottish-American, Stuart Anderson, which just went to prove that romance could blossom pretty much anywhere. The jukebox was playing Russ Conway's jaunty piano hit, 'Side Saddle' and she looked about her for an empty table, but they all appeared to be taken by teenagers. She decided to skip lunch and just have a word with Lenny. She wormed her way between tables towards the kitchen, only to find the entrance blocked by a waitress.

'Sorry, madam, you can't go in there,' said the girl.

Maggie thought there was something familiar about her. 'Don't I know you?'

The girl looked her up and down and her eyes widened. 'Yes, and I've seen your photo in a magazine. Aren't you Maggie Gregory, Betty's cousin?'

'That's right! I think we met at that party she threw before she went to Italy a few years back.'

'Yes. I'm Bobby. I remember you wanted Mam to make you a suit and a couple of dresses but they never materialized.' She frowned.

'Sorry. If I remember rightly, my sister-in-law's needs came first, and even my cousin said she had first claim on your mother's services.'

'That's right. Your sister-in-law is Emma Gregory.' Bobby paused. 'Mam would love that outfit you're wearing now. It's the bees' knees!'

Maggie chuckled. 'The colours are all wrong for a bee. How is your mother?'

'Oh, she and Sam are fine, they've two kids now. A boy and a girl, and they adopted Nick, who comes in here, as well. I don't know if you ever met him, but he's taken over from Jimmy Miller in Tony Gianellis' music group. You know Jimmy, don't you?'

'Since we were kids. I was wondering who'd be playing in his place.'

'Now you know. Anyhow, what can I do for you?' asked Bobby.

'I was wanting to speak to Lenny?'

'I'm sorry, but he has someone with him and doesn't want to be disturbed.'

'It wouldn't be Dorothy Wilson, would it?' asked Maggie, her face lighting up.

'No, it's his nephew.'

'You mean Joshua Colman?'

'That's him.' Bobby smiled. 'Have you met him?'

'Yes, and I'm not in any rush to meet him again.'

'I'm tempted to ask why but I won't,' said Bobby.

'He didn't do anything too terrible. He just rubbed me up the wrong way when we met in Formby, and I'm a bit embarrassed by the whole thing now. Anyway, you can give Lenny a message for me. I want to speak to Dorothy and I thought he'd know where I can reach her.'

'I can tell you that,' said Bobby. 'She's in America and won't be back until later in the year.'

'Damn,' muttered Maggie.

'Was it urgent?'

'Not life and death.' Maggie shrugged elegant shoulders. 'I'll just have to wait until she gets back. I'll see you around.'

'OK! I'll mention it to Lenny anyway. He's often in touch with her.' Bobby smiled. 'I'd best get back to work. See you.'

Maggie watched her go into the kitchen but did not immediately leave. Instead she rested her aching back against the wall, thinking the pain was probably due to digging over a flowerbed and putting in fresh plants.

Suddenly she realized the jukebox had fallen silent, but the level of noise had risen. It was ages since she had been as carefree as these college kids. In fact she doubted if she had ever been as carefree. Life had been fairly tough and, after the war, what had made it even worse was her father taking ill. Her mother's sister, Lizzie, had come to their rescue by putting money into buying them a big house in which the Gregorys and Lizzie and her daughter Betty had made a home. It was because of her sister's generosity that Maggie's mother had been able to leave her children an inheritance.

'Oh, you're still here, Maggie.'

Maggie looked at Bobby, who was carrying a tray of tasty but extremely fattening fried sausages, bacon, egg and beans on a couple of plates. 'I'm glad you're still here actually,' she said. 'Lenny told me that I should have taken your address and phone number. Perhaps you could write it down – if there's any news from Dorothy he'll be in touch.' She hurried away to a nearby table with the tray, saying she would be back.

Maggie was in the act of writing down her brother's address and phone number when a voice said, 'Hello, Miss Gregory. I wasn't expecting to see you here.'

She glanced up, straight into the lively brown eyes of Lenny's nephew, Josh Colman, who was in army uniform. 'I-I thought you'd left,' she blurted out.

'Couldn't wait to see the back of me, I suppose?' he said mournfully.

Maggie felt colour flood her cheeks. 'Don't put words into my mouth,' she said stiffly. 'Just because we got off on the wrong foot . . .' She stopped abruptly. Josh had raised an eyebrow, and she wondered how he could do that. It had always fascinated her when film stars had done so on the silver screen. Now he was wiggling his eyebrow and a giggle rose in her throat. 'Don't do that!' she spluttered.

'Sorry, I didn't mean to put you off your stride,' he said, straight-faced. 'I'll be going now.'

'Back to barracks?'

He smiled. 'I knew you were clever as well as dishy.'

The smile died in her eyes. 'Are you being sarcastic?'

He looked surprised. 'Why d'you say that?'

'Because . . .' She could not finish. How could she tell him that she couldn't believe someone like Josh Colman could believe that of her? He was several years older and had been out in the world. He must have met more sophisticated women. She didn't feel a bit clever or dishy. If she had been, then Norm wouldn't have dumped her.

She turned abruptly and left the coffee bar, recalling that she had a date with someone with whom she had hit it off right away. She decided that she would have a less fattening ham salad in Lewis's restaurant. It was not until she arrived there that she remembered she had forgotten to give Bobby the scrap of paper with her brother's address and phone number on, although it was possible that Bobby would see it on the table where she had left it.

After her lunch she made her way along Charlotte Row and then took a short cut through St John's Market to the Royal Court in Roe Street. During her walk she found herself thinking about Tim Murphy and his dead wife and whether he was still in love with her. What had she been like? Had she been a blonde like Maggie? She imagined her as good looking and as well dressed as her husband, with wavy blonde hair and an hourglass figure. Maybe a bit like Marilyn Monroe in the film *Gentlemen Prefer Blondes*, which had starred the sexy brunette Jane Russell as well. Perhaps she was more like Jane than Marilyn Monroe, thought Maggie.

Was it true men preferred blondes?

If it was true, then why had Norm thrown her over and got himself engaged to another girl? Why had blondes been pigeon-holed as dumb; it didn't make sense and was as bad as classing all redheads as having fiery tempers.

Maggie decided she was being dumb, thinking such thoughts. Instead she should relax and look forward to her afternoon at the theatre. She had always wanted to see *The Merry Widow*, having been told that the music was great, as were the costumes.

The reports on *The Merry Widow* proved true. The plot was amusing, romantic and full of misunderstandings. A few hours later, Maggie left the theatre humming 'The Merry Widow Waltz'. The operetta had met all her expectations and she wished that she could see it all over again. As it was, she went along to the box office at the Empire and bought two tickets for the concert starring Paul Anka next week.

Imagining herself in the role of the merry widow, Hanna, who had been left a fortune, Maggie set off in the direction of Dale

Street, thinking to treat herself to a long-playing record of the music. She had a feeling there had been a film, years ago, with Jeanette MacDonald playing the leading role. She wondered if it was the kind of music Tim Murphy enjoyed, and looked forward to telling him about it. Of course, he might not be at the meeting place. She would be a bit disappointed if he was not there, but she would wait twenty minutes; if he had not arrived by then, she would catch the train to Formby.

Maggie's pulse was a bit uneven as she approached the black-ened arches of the Exchange Hotel that led to the entrance of the railway station. She could see no sign of Tim, so it looked like she might be catching the train to Formby in half an hour or so after all. Then suddenly a man hove into view from behind one of the pillars. Her heart lifted as she recognized the bearded and smartly dressed figure. He strolled towards her, coming to a halt a foot or so in front of her.

'It is you,' he said, smiling.

Maggie returned his smile. 'I'm glad you recognize me.'

'How could I forget you?' he said, gallantly. 'Jerry said after you left that you reminded him of a princess in a pantomime.'

Her smile grew. 'I wish.'

'I'm not kidding.' His blue eyes were lively. 'You look just as good now as then. That suit is a great colour, and as for the cut . . .' He gave a low whistle.

She gave a twirl. 'Glad you like it. You don't look so bad yourself.'

He grinned and took her hand and drew it through his arm. 'I take it things have worked out for you.'

'Pretty well.' Maggie's heart fluttered like a sparrow's wings hovering over the bird table in her brother's garden as her hand rested on the worsted fabric of his sleeve. 'How about you? Did your mother welcome you and Jerry with open arms? And how is business?'

'Business is going well. I could have worked this evening but I didn't want to let you down.'

'You were so certain I'd come?' she said.

'Why should you agree to meet me if you didn't want to see me again? Wouldn't you have been disappointed if I hadn't turned up?'

'Yes! I was thinking if you didn't come I'd treat myself to some fish and chips on the way back to my brother's house.'

'We could have a fish-and-chip supper here in town later if you'd like?'

'I'd enjoy that. Have you any idea where you'd like to go before then?' Maggie asked.

'You like music, don't you?'

'Do I like music? I've just been to a matinee at the Royal Court. Have you ever seen *The Merry Widow*? It was fabulous!' Her eyes shone.

'Can't say I have, but the word "Merry" in the title and your reaction makes me want to see it,' he said. 'But not now. I was thinking more about jazz.' He cocked an eye in her direction.

'Jazz?' Maggie laughed. 'I should have guessed you were a fan.'

'I thought we'd go the Cavern. Ever been there?'

She shook her head. 'What's it like?'

'It's one of the best venues for jazz in Liverpool. It's situated in a cellar and I had no idea it existed until I came back from Australia.'

She thought it sounded exciting. 'Then let's go! Although, I'm telling you now, I'm more of an Elvis fan than of Chris Barber.'

'You mean ol' jelly hips,' said Tim.

She glanced at him. 'Don't you like Elvis?'

He grinned. 'Did I say I didn't? I can tell you that I admired his guts for saying he wanted to be just an ordinary soldier when he was called up.'

She hugged his arm. 'I did too. He could have enlisted in Special Service, you know, and just entertained the troops.'

'I know. I read it in the newspaper. I hope you'll still enjoy this evening if you're into rock'n'roll and operetta.'

'I like most music. I even enjoy skiffle,' she said.

His eyes lit up.

'I used to go to a club in London with some friends where the musicians played both jazz and skiffle,' said Maggie. 'My friends up here, though, are more into rock'n'roll, and some have formed a group. One of them, Jimmy, has had to drop out because he's gone back to sea. You do know that Tommy Steele used to be a sailor, don't you?'

'No, but I do know he had a hit with "Singing the Blues".'

'That's him. I've seen him in the flesh,' she said with a hint of pride. 'I've been to the Two I's coffee bar where he was discovered. Have you ever thought of learning an instrument or singing with a jazz group?'

He shook his head. 'Nah! My father would never allow us to have a go at a musical instrument. I was told to shut up even if I sang along with a tune on the wireless. He was a right misery.'

There was a silence, which she broke by asking about Jerry and Tim's mother. 'They get on fine,' said Tim.

Maggie glanced at him. 'She's not finding him too much to cope with? I know my nephew can be a holy terror sometimes. I can manage him now, but then I'm not as old as your mother.'

'She has complained now and again that he's running her into the ground, but I remind her that he'll be going to school later in the year and so it won't be forever.'

Maggie nodded. 'It's the same with Owen, but my sister-in-law is having another baby, so it's going to be all go, even when Owen starts school.'

'Mam tells me that I was a little imp like Jerry when I was small, but I grew out of it, so I don't doubt he will too.'

'I never realized what hard work kids are,' Maggie sighed.

'I know what you mean,' he said with feeling. 'I couldn't make up my mind whether it was harder coping with Jerry before Bernie died or afterwards.'

'What d'you mean?'

His brow furrowed. 'There were problems in our marriage but we could never have got divorced.'

She stared at him. 'Are you a Catholic?'

He nodded. 'I think we would have separated eventually. To be frank, I regret her death, because it shouldn't have happened and sometimes I feel to blame.'

'Why?' She stopped abruptly, thinking she might have overstepped the mark. 'I'm being nosy. You'll be wishing you hadn't suggested we meet up.'

'No, I'm not. I've often put my foot in it. I'm glad you're not perfect.'

She laughed. 'Now you've definitely put your foot in it? Didn't you know I am perfect?'

He said, 'Of course you are. But what a topic, hey? Let's drop the subject of death and dying. Anyway, we're nearly there.'

They had arrived at the narrow thoroughfare that was Mathew Street. Maggie gazed up at the buildings on either side, which were tall and dark and seemed to swallow up the air. She took several deep breaths.

'Are you OK?' asked Tim.

'This street reminds me of a horror movie.'

'I like horror movies,' he said, smiling.

'So do I when I'm sitting safely in a cinema seat.'

There was a sound that reminded her of hollow footsteps, and she clung to his arm. 'What was that?'

'Nothing to worry about. Here we are.'

In front of them was a doorway. Maggie offered to pay for her own ticket but Tim told her to keep her money. They went inside and down some steps. Even before they reached the cellar, she wanted to get out of there, but knew there was no way she could tell him how she felt when he believed he was giving her a treat. There were already plenty of people in the cellar, and the atmosphere was fuggy with cigarette smoke. A number of people were leaning against the pillars that held up the arched ceiling while others were seated. All were listening to the music being played by a group performing on a small stage. Tim managed to find Maggie a vacant seat and she sat down. He bent over and whispered, 'I just want to listen to this number, and then I'll fetch you a drink. They have a rule here that they only serve soft drinks, by the way.'

'That's all right with me,' she whispered, easily able to imagine a stampede if a fire broke out due to a dropped cigarette butt by a drunk. She concentrated on listening to the music, so as to shut out the thought of the lack of fresh air in the cellar. The acoustics were pretty good, although she had no idea of the name of the song being played.

It was not until she had downed half a glass of orange juice to ease a throat that felt as dry as dust that she asked about the song. 'Am I right in thinking it's about a man in love with a woman who was that fat he needed to chalk how far he had to reach round her when he hugged her?'

He nodded. 'It's called "Huggin' and Chalkin'". It's been round for a while, came from the States, and was recorded by Hoagy Carmichael.'

'Who?' she asked.

He looked amazed. 'You must have heard of Hoagy Carmichael. He's a musician and composer and has been in films. He wrote the music to "Stardust" and "Georgia on My Mind", as well as loads of other stuff such as "Lazybones",' enthused Tim.

'You mean "Lazybones, sleeping in the sun"?'

'That's the one.'

'But that's not jazz, is it?'

'Hoagy started off in jazz and moved on to ballads and the like.' Tim squeezed her shoulder. 'Now hush! They're about to play again.'

The vocalist launched into 'Mack the Knife', and Maggie found herself comparing the way it was sung to Louis Armstrong's rendition, which she had heard on the radio.

'Why does most jazz come from America?' she asked once the song finished.

'That one didn't. It started off as a song in the German version of *The Threepenny Opera*, about a highwayman,' said Tim.

Maggie was impressed by his knowledge. 'I never knew that.'

Before she could ask any more questions, the group launched into the hit made famous by the king of skiffle, Lonnie Donegan's 'Puttin' on the Style'.

'Come on, let's dance,' said Tim.

'I don't mind if I do,' said Maggie, draining her glass and placing it under her chair.

There was not much room to let oneself go, but they managed a sort of shuffle and jive in an extremely small space. Maggie realized that for the first time in a long time, she was feeling carefree and really enjoying herself. This despite a certain soreness in her throat, due no doubt to the cigarette smoke blending with the body odour generated by the heat of so many people packed into the cellar.

It was to be another hour before she felt compelled to tell him that she would have to go. He did not try to persuade her to stay, but escorted her outside and walked with her in the direction of Exchange Station. She was hoping that he would ask her out again. She was not disappointed, and when he suggested them meeting up again, she said immediately, 'I bought tickets for the Paul Anka concert which is on at the Empire next week. Say you'll come?'

For a moment she thought he was going to refuse, but then he agreed. They arranged a time and place to meet and then he kissed her lightly on the mouth and walked away. She could feel that kiss on her lips all the way to Formby.

It was not until she left the train and was walking past the fish-and-chip shop that she remembered they had not had that supper he had suggested. So she went inside and bought a portion of fish and chips and managed to eat the lot before reaching her brother's house. It had been quite a day, but Maggie had made up her mind not to tell Emma about Tim. She would say she had met an old friend and they had gone to the pictures together.

Ten

'Jared and I are going to the cottage this weekend,' said Emma. 'We thought you might enjoy coming with us. The country air will do you good.'

Maggie could not argue with her sister-in-law's reasoning, although she hardly knew the couple emigrating to Canada. Still, she would have gone if she had not arranged to meet Tim.

'I've made other arrangements,' she said. 'Sorry.'

'What arrangements?' asked her brother, glancing up from his newspaper.

'I've bought tickets for the Paul Anka concert at the Empire.'

'Who are you going with?'

For a moment Maggie would really have much preferred to tell the truth, but it struck her afresh that her brother might not be overjoyed at the idea of his little sister dating a man whom she had only met on the train from London a short while ago. She would have to continue keeping quiet about Tim.

'A girl I know from school. I bumped into her when I was in town last week.'

'All right, I hope you have a good time,' said Jared. 'But I am planning on dropping Emma and Owen off at the cottage in time for the Whit weekend, as she wants to make the tearoom and shop ready for the bank holiday. I'd appreciate it if you come as well and stay with her and Owen to help her out.'

'Will Hester and Ally have vacated the cottage by then?'

'Aye, they're going to spend some time with their families before they leave the country,' said Emma.

'OK, I won't make any arrangements for then,' Maggie promised.

'Good.' Jared smiled at her. 'You're not a bad kid.'

She raised her eyebrows. 'I'm not a kid! I'll be twenty next birthday and I've lived on my own for several years.'

'I'm still your guardian,' he said firmly. 'I have to look out for you until you're twenty-one.'

Maggie rolled her eyes and said no more on the subject, but instead asked if anyone wanted a cup of tea and went and put the kettle on, thinking of her next date with Tim and wondering how his mother was coping with Jerry and if, when the weather improved, he might suggest them taking his son out for the day. She was certain the break from her grandson would do Tim's mother a power of good.

Eleven

Mary McGrath gazed through the kitchen window at her grandson, who was kicking a ball about in Marty's backyard with her granddaughter, Josie. She glanced at Marty. 'I can't believe you still haven't told Bernie's mother that her daughter's dead and Jerry is living with you.'

'It's a difficult thing to tell a mother,' said Irene.

'That I can agree with,' said Mary. 'But it's no excuse. She needs to know. I'm feeling really on edge about it all.'

Marty turned on her. 'Why are you worrying? It's our Tommy who's to blame. I'm bloody annoyed with him!'

'Don't swear, son,' said his mother, clicking her tongue against her teeth. 'It doesn't sound nice.'

'You can't blame him for getting angry, Mam,' said Peggy. 'How would you have felt if Jerry had turned up on your doorstep out of the blue with a note from Tommy asking you to look after his son?'

'He must have been really stuck about what to do,' Mary said.

'You know why he didn't come to you, don't you?' continued Peggy. 'It's because he knew our Lil wouldn't have tolerated having Jerry staying at your house.'

'Her baby is due soon,' said Mary. 'You can't blame her, and our Tommy will have thought about her being pregnant.'

'Tommy doesn't know Lil's having a baby, just like he doesn't know I'm expecting now,' said Peggy hesitantly.

Her mother stared at her. 'That's news! When did this happen?'

Peggy said, 'It'll be here in time for Christmas.'

Mary took a deep breath. 'A Christmas baby.' She smiled. 'Congratulations, love.' She kissed her daughter, but within minutes recommenced talking about Tommy. 'Anyway, Tommy probably gave thought to me no longer being a spring chicken.'

'I suppose there could be something in what you say, but it's more likely he didn't want to face you,' said Peggy, spooning sugar into her tea. 'The least he could have done was to write to Bernie's mother or one of her sisters or brothers, himself. He must have one of their addresses.'

Mary reached in her pocket and took out a handkerchief and blew her nose. 'I know what your father would say if he was here,' she said in a muffled voice.

'Never mind what Dad might have said,' Peggy muttered. 'Our Tommy mightn't have turned out the way he did if it wasn't for the way Dad treated him. It's Marty who has to make the decisions in the family now, so don't you be telling anyone about any of this, Mam.'

Mary's head shot up. 'You don't have to tell me what I should or shouldn't do, our Peggy! I won't go gossiping. We've all suffered in this family because of what Bernie did. Your father was not to blame for that!'

Marty looked up at the ceiling but kept his peace.

'Still, I don't want to speak ill of the dead,' continued his mother. 'As for that family of hers, maybe it's best to let them live in ignorance if that's what you and Marty think is best.'

'It's what Pete's mother thinks,' Peggy said.

'Enough, both of you,' said Marty.

But his mother could not shut up. 'What about Father Francis?' She drummed her fingernails on the table.

'Marty has already spoken to him,' said Irene, who so far had kept out of the discussion.

'Have you, son?'

Marty nodded. 'He's of the opinion that only by my producing the death certificate could we speed things up. Obviously our Tommy gave no thought to providing me with evidence that Bernie really is dead.'

His mother clicked her tongue against her teeth again. 'He doesn't know about you and Irene wanting to get married, does he?'

'No, but he should have thought her mother and sisters might want proof of her death.'

'I've just thought there's another possibility as to why he hasn't given you proof,' said Peggy, her eyes alight. 'Bernie might have left him and Jerry and not be dead after all?'

There was a stunned silence.

Then Irene said, 'But that would mean Tommy's letter was a pack of lies.'

'But it could be the reason why her mother and sisters haven't ever been round here asking if we've heard from our Tommy. Bernie could have been in touch with them and told them a pack of lies,' said Mary.

Before anyone could comment on this latest thought, there was a noise at the back door. A moment later, Josie appeared. 'Jerry's burst the ball on a sticky-out nail,' she said.

Jerry came up behind her. 'It wasn't my fault. It was hers.'

'Who does he sound like?' said Peggy, shaking her head.

Neither her brother nor mother bothered saying 'his father'. 'We have to find Tommy, and the sooner the better,' Marty said firmly.

Jerry gazed up at him. 'You don't have to go looking for my other daddy. He said he'd come back when he's made lots of money. You wait and see, he'll be here.'

'That's just it, sunshine,' said Marty emphatically. 'I don't want to wait and see. If I took you to London, would you be able to find the house where you stayed when you were living there?'

Jerry frowned. 'Dunno. But the lady might know.'

'What lady?' asked his grandmother, looking surprised.

'The lady on the train. She and other daddy talked a lot,' said Jerry.

Mary turned to Marty. 'Has Jerry mentioned this lady before?'

'No.' Marty frowned down at Jerry. 'This lady – did she get on the train with you and your other daddy?'

Jerry shook his head. 'She was sitting in the carriage already.'

'So they didn't know each other?'

Jerry nodded and then shook his head.

'Which d'you mean? Yes or no?' asked Marty, exasperated.

'I fink they'd seen each other before.'

'What makes you say that?'

'She said he'd helped her pick up some cigarettes she dropped and mentioned his beard.'

'Holy Mother of God!' exclaimed Peggy. 'Our Tommy has grown a beard. I bet he thinks he won't be recognized now when he visits Liverpool again.'

'He won't look like my little boy any more,' said Mary dolefully. 'I've never liked beards.'

'He's not a little boy, Mam,' snapped Peggy.

Marty sighed. 'Jerry, d'you remember anything else the lady and your other daddy talked about?'

The boy screwed up his face.

'Think hard, Jerry,' His grandmother said coaxingly. 'And I'll buy you something nice.'

'What?' he asked immediately.

'A Dinky car for your collection,' Peggy suggested. 'And I'll buy you some sweeties.'

'Can I have some sweeties too?' asked Josie.

'Hush, love,' said her grandmother absently.

'Well, Jerry?' asked Marty.

He heaved a sigh. 'She wore a lovely long frock like a princess in a pantomime.'

'Never mind that!' said Marty. 'What did they say to each other?'

'He told her he'd swam in the canal.'

'What would he tell her that for?' asked Peggy, looking surprised.

They all stared at Jerry, who chewed on his lip.

'Is that all?' asked his grandmother.

Jerry blew out a breath and then he smiled. 'He told her that he jumped off a sand hill. Did you know he did that, when he was a little boy like me? I'd like to do that.'

'Now why would he be telling her about stuff he did as a child?' asked Irene.

'With his conceit, he was probably telling her his life story to pass the time,' Peggy suggested sarcastically.

'I don't remember ever taking him anywhere where your father would have allowed him to go jumping off sand hills,' said Mary.

'He could have gone with some of his mates,' Marty muttered.

'I don't see how this is going to help us find him,' said Irene.

'Do I get my Dinky car and sweets?' asked Jerry.

'We'll see,' said his grandmother.

'We can always try that place in London where they keep the records of births, marriages and deaths to get a death certificate,' said Irene, wanting desperately to know for certain whether Bernie was alive or dead. 'We know Bernie's married name and that she was living in London at the time she died, so that's a start.'

'I told the lady that my mummy was in Heaven,' said Jerry.

'She'll be lucky being allowed through the pearly gates,' Mary muttered.

Ignoring that comment, Irene said, 'It would be a real help if Jerry could remember what was happening the day his mummy went to Heaven.'

'He won't remember,' said Peggy. 'He's only a child.'

'I do remember!' cried Jerry. 'I wanted my mummy and I couldn't go and see her 'cos it was foggy outside. Really, really foggy. Other daddy said he couldn't see his hand in front of his face.'

Peggy groaned. 'So what? I bet they have loads of foggy days in London town. There's even a song about it. This isn't getting us anywhere.'

'I wouldn't say that,' said Irene, her eyes alight. 'I bet if we were to get in touch with Maggie Gregory, she'd remember a day that was worse than any other a couple of months or so ago.'

'Maybe, maybe not,' said Peggy.

A silence fell.

'What about my sweeties?' asked Jerry, tugging on Peggy's arm.

She stood up and held out a hand to him. 'Come on, then, let's go to the sweet shop.'

'What about my Dinky car, too?' he asked.

'You're going to have to wait for that,' said his grandmother. 'You carry on thinking, and see if you can remember anything else your other daddy might have said to the lady on the train.'

Marty and Irene exchanged glances which spoke volumes of their belief in their chances of getting married any sooner than they first had hoped.

Twelve

Maggie hurried across Lime Street in the direction of the Empire, hoping that Tim would be on time so they could be in their seats before the curtain went up.

She was pleased to see that he was standing outside the theatre. She thought that was another tick in his favour. His being early at the meeting place last week was not a one off. She liked a man who didn't keep a girl waiting.

'You all right?' he asked, pulling her hand through his arm.

'Yes. How has work been?'

'Still busy, I'm glad to say. It could be that I'll eventually have to hire someone,' he said, heading towards the theatre entrance.

'That's great! I couldn't be more pleased for you. Would you say that the automobile is here to stay then?' she teased as they entered the foyer.

'I'd bet on it. I reckon the day will come when most families will have a car. The government is going to have to build more motorways to cope. One of my customers told me about the Preston by-pass, which opened just before Christmas, and another motorway is being built between London and Leeds. It'll be a while before that's finished, though.'

'My brother has a van and a car,' Maggie said as they joined the queue to show their tickets. 'He has his own building business. He and my sister-in-law and nephew have gone up to their cottage in the country this weekend. I was invited to go with them but I told them I had a date.'

'So did your brother ask who with?'

She hesitated. 'Yes, but I-I didn't say too much. He's my guardian and can be a bit over-protective.'

'Why would you need a guardian?' Tim asked.

'Because I'm under age and my mother left me some money.' She pulled a face. 'My mother didn't trust me to be sensible, so she tied some of it up in a trust fund until I'm twenty-one.'

He gazed at her. 'But the way you look, he doesn't keep you short.'

'He gives me an allowance but he's not over-generous and I did earn enough money while modelling to pay my way and afford the odd treat most of the time.'

'You always look like a million dollars, and I appreciate you treating me this evening.'

She laughed. 'You treated me last week. But I'm soon going to have to be very careful about what I spend until I find another job.'

He bought a programme from an usherette and they followed several people into the auditorium. Their seats were in the mid-stalls and they managed to sit down as the safety curtain went up.

'Just in time,' he whispered in her ear.

Maggie enjoyed the concert as much if not slightly more than *The Merry Widow*, because she was sharing the experience with a companion who appeared to be enjoying the acts that were supporting Paul Anka, who was at the top of the bill. There was an impressionist, a magician, a ventriloquist, a comedian and a singing and dancing double act, as well as the Canadian pop singer, who wowed the audience with his renditions of 'Diana', 'Don't Gamble with Love' and 'All Of a Sudden My Heart Sings'.

Maggie was delighted that not once had Tim said that he would have preferred an evening of jazz at the Cavern to that evening's concert.

'I like a variety show, don't you?' she said as they left the theatre.

'They were all good,' said Tim. 'Shall we go and have an

oyster and champagne supper at Connolly's?' he suggested. 'My treat this time.'

Maggie groaned. 'Oh, I'm sorry. I come out in a rash if I eat shellfish.'

'Hell, that's a shame,' he said.

'Isn't it just! I go all blotchy and I'm not a pretty sight,' she said ruefully.

'Then what would you like to eat?' he asked.

'I love duck the way the Chinese do it.'

'Then let's go to the Cathay on Renshaw Street.' He took her hand and tucked it into his arm. 'I think I'll have a curry.'

'Have you looked up any of your old friends since you've been back?' asked Maggie.

'I've been too preoccupied with work.'

'But you might bump into someone sooner or later,' she said.

He shrugged. 'If I'm honest I'd rather not. Probably you don't remember what it was like here during the war and afterwards. It was all a bit . . . chaotic. Some of us went a bit wild at times and got into mischief. I want to put those times behind me. I want a different kind of life now.'

'You mean now you're a father and have Jerry to consider?'

He nodded.

She would have liked to have known more about the younger Tim, but obviously he didn't want to talk about the old days. 'How is Jerry? Are he and your mother getting used to each other now?'

'As much as they ever will. It will be better for both of them when he starts school.' He changed the subject. 'So this cottage you mentioned belonging to your brother and his wife, where is it?'

'Actually, it belongs to Emma. It's in Whalley, near Clitheroe, and come Whit week I'll be going up there with them. My brother extended the cottage so there's more room for her to cater for hikers and visitors to the ruined abbey nearby.'

'When you say cater . . .?'

'She does lunches and teas for passing trade, and also sells her jams and pickles and knitted garments, such as witch dolls.'

He raised his eyebrows. 'Witch dolls?'

'She doesn't call them that, any more, but you've heard of the Pendle witches, haven't you?'

'No.'

They had reached Lewis's corner and stood a moment under the statue of Sir Jacob Epstein's *Liverpool Resurgent*, unveiled in 1956 to celebrate Lewis's centenary. It was a favourite meeting place for shoppers and courting couples alike, although the nude statue was seldom given its official title by Liverpudlians.

'I'd never heard of them either until Emma came on the scene. She calls them wise women sometimes, and makes up little bags of herbs and recipes to go with them. If you're interested, I'll borrow Emma's book and you can read up about them.'

'No thanks, I have no time to read,' said Tim. 'She must make some money out of them to go to all that trouble.'

'I think she must. We seldom discuss the subject. I suppose if I was to help her with the business, then I'd need to know more about it.'

'D'you think it's likely you'll be getting involved?'

She did not immediately answer because they had arrived at the Cathay, so went inside. Fortunately the restaurant had begun to empty out after the mid-evening rush and they were shown to a table by the window.

After ordering their meals and drinks, they talked about the show they had seen, and naturally that led on to a conversation about their favourite pop music. By the time their meals arrived they were on to films. As they ate, he told her that he watched scarcely any television, as his mother didn't have a set, and neither had there been one in the flat in London. The only programme he said that he regretted not seeing was *The Quatermass Experiment*, because he had heard from one of his customers that it was good and he liked science-fiction.

It was while Tim was ordering more drinks that Maggie glanced out of the window and saw Pete and Peggy Marshall walking on the other side of the road. For a moment she thought of knocking on the window to draw their attention, but then she changed her mind, realizing it was highly likely that they would catch sight of Tim and ask questions. She noticed that they had stopped outside Pollard's, the childwear shop.

'What are you staring at?' asked Tim.

Maggie took her eyes off them for a moment. 'A couple I know.'

'Where are they?'

She went to point them out but they had vanished. 'They've gone now. I've known Pete for years. He's the twin brother of the bloke I used to go out with. He and his wife were married just before Christmas after an on-off relationship that went on for years.'

'You're kidding!'

'No, it was due to religion. Her father was against the match. She's a Catholic like you and he's a Proddy like me.'

'I thought you might be a Proddy when you realized I was a Catholic.'

'You don't have to sound like I come from another planet,' said Maggie, feeling her colour rising.

He flushed. 'I didn't mean to. The last time I went to church was Bernie's funeral, and I can't remember when before that.'

'I didn't go at all while I was in London but since I've been back up here, I sometimes go with Emma and Owen. My brother goes only on high days and holidays.' She sipped her drink. 'I wonder if they've been up to Lenny's place.'

'Who?'

'My friends.'

'Oh. What's this Lenny's place?' he asked.

Maggie told him, adding, 'Lenny is a friend of the actress, Dorothy Wilson. He was one of the first to get a jukebox up that way, but he also has live music now. It could be that my friends have been to a live performance of the group I told you about when we were at the Cavern.'

Maggie took another sip of wine. 'Seeing Pete and his wife outside Pollard's has got me wondering whether they're having a baby. Not long married after a long wait. It's possible.'

'I think it's best not to rush into these things. I certainly wish Bernie and I had waited. Not that I'm not fond of Jerry, but sometimes I definitely think it's best to wait,' he said, downing the rest of his beer before glancing at his watch.

Maggie also glanced at her watch and gasped, 'I'm going to have to go. I don't want to be leaving it to the last train in case I miss it. My brother would have a fit if he knew I was going to be walking up the lane so late. It's going to take me some time getting to Exchange Station.'

'You're making him sound like my br-father,' corrected Tim hastily. 'Surely you can get a train at Central Station that'll connect you to the Southport one?'

She made no reply, busy putting on her jacket. Fortunately the bill had already been paid and they were soon out of the restaurant and heading in the direction of Lewis's.

'D'you want to meet up again?' asked Tim.

'If you like, but I doubt I'll be able to for a couple of weeks. Perhaps you can give me your phone number and I can ring you?'

He hesitated. 'I'm on a waiting list waiting to be connected and I'd rather you didn't ring me at my mother's. What about giving me your brother's phone number?'

Maggie did not immediately reply, thinking her brother would not be too pleased if an unknown man rang up asking for her. 'I can't remember his number off the top of my head,' she lied.

Tim hesitated. 'Give me his address then?'

Maggie knew she could hardly tell him that she couldn't remember that either, so she wrote down Jared's address on a scrap of paper and gave it to him. She wondered if he was expecting a kiss. Then, as if he had read her mind, he leaned towards her. Their lips met, his asserting some pressure, and then they drew apart. She let out a trembling breath. 'See you soon,' she said brightly.

'I'll be in touch.' He watched her as she hurried away before striding off in the direction of Renshaw Street. He had almost reached the bus stop when a couple emerged from The Vines pub on the corner near the Adelphi Hotel. His heart seemed to leap in his chest as he recognized his sister Peggy. She was with a bloke whom he recognized, having seen him for the first time the day of the motorbike accident in Blackpool in which Bernie had suffered her head injury and Tim a broken arm. He had forgotten the bloke's name.

As if sensing his eyes on them, they glanced in his direction. Had they recognized him? He was taking no chances, and turned and ran in the direction of Central Station before doubling back into Renshaw Street by taking a short cut up the alley next to Lewis's. Only when he was convinced he was not being followed did it occur to him that most likely neither of them would recognize him with the beard.

He should never have panicked. Feeling a right fool, he strolled the rest of the way to the nearest bus stop where he could catch a bus to Lark Lane. Once on the bus, he determined to put his sister and the man accompanying her out of his mind. But it proved to be far from easy. What if they had seen him? Might they start looking out for him in earnest?

Thirteen

'You're not going to believe this,' said Peggy, following Marty into the house.

'What aren't I going to believe?' asked her brother, glancing at Pete who was just behind her.

'We think we saw your Tommy,' Pete said.

Marty froze. 'Where?'

'We were coming out of The Vines near the Adelphi and I'd swear it was him, despite the beard,' said Peggy.

Marty's eyes glinted. 'You didn't get to speak to him by the sound of it.'

'Did we heck,' said Pete, removing his jacket and hanging it up. 'He shot off like a rabbit being chased by a weasel.'

'He realized you'd seen him?'

'He must have, from the way he took off,' said Peggy. 'Talk about greased lightning. We were never going to catch him.'

'I'd have had a go if it hadn't been for this damned leg,' said Pete bitterly, rubbing his gammy leg.

'You're absolutely certain it was him?' Marty said, pushing wide the kitchen door and going inside.

'It was him all right, and he was standing at a bus stop,' said Peggy firmly. 'One where you get the bus heading in the direction of Aigburth or Princes Park.'

'Who does he know who lives there?' Marty muttered.

Peggy shrugged. 'Let's be honest. We never knew half his friends, even when he was a kid. Besides, what's he doing up here without getting in touch with us? He's up to something.'

'We're going to have to keep an eye on Jerry,' said Irene, taking them by surprise.

Peggy stared at her. 'I didn't realize you were here.'

Irene wiped her hands on her apron. 'I've been doing some messages and then I took the kids to the park. They're upstairs right now. I heard most of what you've said and, if you don't mind my saying so, you shouldn't talk about this in front of Jerry, or even Josie.'

'Perhaps we shouldn't mention it to Mam either,' said Marty. Peggy nodded.

'What if . . .' Irene stopped abruptly.

The other three stared at her. 'What if what?' asked Marty.

'Nothing! I just had a stupid thought,' said Irene.

'Say it!' he urged.

Irene said hurriedly, 'What if Tommy didn't return to London when he left Jerry here, but only said he did so that you wouldn't go looking for him here in Liverpool.'

Silence.

'Would you say it's the sort of trick he might play on you?' asked Pete.

Marty hesitated. 'Depends what he has to gain by it. He could have mates here whom he could talk into giving him a helping hand.'

'We don't know any of this for sure,' Peggy said. 'The only thing we can take a guess at is that he thinks we might have seen him. Otherwise, he wouldn't have made a run for it. Let's just wait and see if he turns up here or at Mam's.'

They all agreed.

'I'll put the kettle on,' said Irene. 'And while we're on the subject of Tommy, are we going to do anything about finding out if Bernie is really dead?'

'You mean that if he has lied about going back to London, then he could have lied about that, too, and Bernie *is* alive in London?' said Peggy.

'Exactly,' said Irene.

Marty shook his head. 'I have my doubts as to whether our Tommy would lie to Jerry about his mother being dead if she'd just walked out. I know Tommy's gone off the rails a few times, but I just don't think he's that cruel, and I can't see the point of him telling us Bernie's dead if she isn't.'

'Pride,' said Irene, folding her arms across her chest. 'He

wouldn't want you knowing she'd walked out on him. Anyway, I'd still like to get my hands on her death certificate. I'm fed up of waiting on other people to give us the go-ahead to get married.'

'So am I, love,' said Marty. 'But it can't be much longer now. I'll have another word with Father Francis and I'll check out Tommy's old haunts to find out if anyone has seen him.'

Irene was not as convinced as Marty that Tommy would not lie to his son if it would serve his purpose. After all, she had asked herself more than once what kind of man dumped his son on his brother's doorstep without a by-your-leave! Then it had occurred to her that Bernie might just possibly have written to one of her sisters telling her all her troubles. But which sister? And then there was also her niece, Monica, who had often babysat for Marty and Bernie when they had lived in the grandmother's house together. It had been a while since they had seen Monica, but Irene knew she was involved with Tony Gianelli's music group. Apparently she had the kind of voice that Tony deemed worthy of the odd number. So it was possible Irene might find news of her at the Gianellis' house, where the group generally practised and which was only a short distance away across the canal from Marty's house. She decided to pop over there as soon as she had some free time.

As it happened, the following Tuesday evening, the group were in the Gianellis' front parlour, rehearsing for the evening do of a wedding. There had been more changes in the line-up since Irene had last heard them play, and she only recognized Tony Gianelli, who had a heavenly tenor voice, and Nick, Bobby's stepbrother, who played guitar, washboard and the ukulele.

Irene had mixed feelings when she saw that Monica was also there because she might be about to make a big mistake by talking to her about Bernie. She was rather an attractive girl, not pretty exactly, but she had nice eyes and a smiley mouth. Good hair, too.

Still, nothing ventured, nothing gained, and Irene went over to her. 'Monica, you're just the person I want to see,' Irene said brightly.

The girl reached for a glass of water on a stool nearby and downed half of it. 'Does Marty want me to look after Josie while the pair of you have a night out? It's some time since I did that. What with Peggy and her mother being willing.'

'Let's sit down,' said Irene, sinking on to the nearest sofa.

Monica sat on its arm. 'So what is it you want?'

Irene spoke casually, 'I was wondering when did any of your family last hear from your Auntie Bernie?'

Monica shrugged. 'Mam and I haven't heard from her at all. I'm sure Gran hasn't either.'

'Not even at Christmas?'

Monica shook her head. 'The whole family are fed up with her. Gran never stopped going on about Aunt Bernie spoiling Christmas for her. In the end, one of my uncles took Gran to Ireland and she still hasn't come back. She's staying with her brother on his farm near Donard in County Wicklow. We've only had the odd scribbled postcard since she went.'

'No sign at all of her coming back?'

Monica screwed up her face. 'I can't see Gran staying there forever. The farm is in the middle of nowhere, and besides, one of my aunties is having another baby and she wants Gran there. She hasn't said she'll come yet, but it wouldn't surprise me if she's back in Liverpool in time for the birth.'

In a way that news was a relief to Irene. 'When is the baby due?'

'Late summer, I think,' replied Monica. 'I suppose it's a waste of my time asking if Marty's heard from Tommy?'

It was on the tip of Irene's tongue to tell the girl that Tommy had been in touch and dumped Jerry on them because Bernie was dead. But fortunately, at that moment, Nick came over and sat down beside her.

'So how did that number sound to you, Irene?' he asked.

'I thought it sounded fab.'

His face lit up. 'Great.'

Irene stared at him, thinking that he was going to break a few hearts before he was much older. 'How's the family?'

'Everyone's fine, although Dad's not too happy about his sister, my Aunt Hester, and Uncle Ally emigrating to Canada. I am, though. One day I plan on going there myself and it would be useful having family over there.'

Irene was tempted to ask why he wanted to go so badly, but he had not finished talking and her ears pricked up at the mention of Maggie. 'Bobby was telling me that Betty's cousin Maggie called in at Lenny's place not so long ago.'

'Was she on her own?'

'Apparently. Bobby said that she had put on some weight and was wearing this fantastic silk twill suit. She wanted to get in touch with Dorothy Wilson and thought Lenny might be able to help her. As it was, Bobby was able to tell her that she was in America and wouldn't be back over here until autumn.' He added casually, 'I could have told her that much. Dorothy Wilson keeps in touch with our family. You do know that she, Dad and Mam knew each other when they were younger?'

Indeed, Irene did know that Detective Inspector Sam Walker and his wife Lynne had been acquainted with the famous actress since their early teens. Maggie's cousin Betty had provided her with that snippet of information, and lots more besides.

She wondered what Maggie could want with Dorothy Wilson. Just as she wondered how Monica would react if she overheard her whispering to Nick to pass on the word to the inspector that Tommy McGrath was back in town. But only too easily she could imagine Marty's reaction if she took such a step. He might be angry with his brother, but there was a bond between them that was not easy to break. Irene might be utterly fed up of waiting to be Marty's wife, but she knew that she was going to have to leave it to Marty to find his brother and to get at the truth about Bernie.

Fourteen

It was some weeks later and Maggie had returned to Formby, hoping that Tim would be in touch. Jared had driven up to the cottage and so she had decided that it would be a good idea to leave the couple and Owen to enjoy a weekend to themselves now that Ally and Hester had vacated the cottage.

Come Monday, Maggie went shopping in preparation for Jared and Emma's return and arrived back to discover her brother's car in the drive. She wasted no time entering the house and found Emma in the kitchen, sorting out washing.

'So you're back,' Maggie said. 'You're earlier than I thought. The traffic must have been good.'

'Hester phoned yesterday. She wanted to ask whether we'd like to join a party that she and Ally are having in their cabin before the ship sails.'

'I thought they'd have sailed by now.'

'They would have done, only both the Canadian Pacific and Cunard lines had ships damaged in the St Lawrence River. Due to ice, would you believe – at this time of year! Hester and Ally's liner, the *Empress of Britain,* was one of those needing repairs in Gladstone Dock, so that's why they're behind with all their plans. So you're invited to the party too if you want to come. God only knows when we'll get to see them again once they leave,' said Emma.

'At least Canada is much nearer than Australia.' Maggie began to unpack the shopping. 'When is the party?'

'Tomorrow. It's a spur-of-the-moment event.'

'Right-i-o. So will Jared be taking me up to the cottage next weekend?'

'Yes, but Owen and I will go with you again. If the weather is good it could get quite busy.'

'Will there be more day-trippers than when the school summer holidays begin?' Maggie asked.

'If the weather's good there'll be plenty. Even if it isn't sunny and warm, we could still get a good turnout,' said Emma. 'And there'll be visitors to the abbey as well. During bank holidays and the summer months during which I hope you'll feel able to cope alone some of the time. I really do need your help with me being pregnant.'

Maggie thought about the ruins of the fourteenth-century Cistercian building, which had suffered destruction during the dissolution of the monasteries in the reign of Henry VIII. Suddenly she felt nervous just thinking of all that was expected of her once she was left completely on her own, and whether she would come up to scratch. But, of course, she was not going to be on her own yet. Her spirits lifted as she remembered Hester and Ally's farewell party. She must choose something really stunning to wear as, unlike her cousin Betty, Maggie had never been on an ocean liner before.

'It's some ship,' said Maggie, awestruck. 'This cabin is fantastic. In fact it's enormous. It has to be first class.'

Hester's half-sister Jeanette told her, 'Actually, it's a stateroom. Hester was left some money by the Welsh woman she lived with when she was evacuated to Whalley during the war, so she and Ally decided to blow it and enjoy a bit of luxury. He thought it would make her feel better about going. She felt bad enough leaving Liverpool and the job she loved in the police force to live in Whalley.'

'Well, I think it's well worth it,' said Maggie, looking at herself in a mirror.

'What's well worth it?' asked Nick, coming up behind them.

Maggie looked up at him. 'This stateroom! If one has to go by sea, it's definitely the way to travel.'

'It won't be long before the aeroplane supersedes ships like this,' Nick said, plonking himself down on the double bed. 'It stands to reason. They'll get people to their destination much quicker, and that's what a lot of travellers want these days.'

'Irene Miller has flown,' said Jeanette.

'I didn't know she had wings,' Nick said, straight-faced.

Maggie giggled. 'I've always fancied having wings.'

'I bet she and Bobby wished they could have flown to America the other year,' Jeanette put in. 'They had a real rough crossing going to New York and, after reaching there, they still had hundreds of miles to get to California to stay with Betty. Fortunately, Dorothy let them use her hotel suite in New York for the night so they could have a good rest.'

'Lucky them,' said Maggie. 'I haven't seen Betty for ages.'

'She could be coming over next year. Or is it the year after?' murmured Jeanette. 'They're thinking of flying. It'll really save time, with Stuart having relatives in Scotland, as well as wanting to see those in Liverpool.'

'It'll cost them,' said Maggie, wondering if her brother and sister were aware that their cousin and her husband were planning on a trip to Britain. 'I presume they'll be bringing the baby?'

'She's a toddler now,' said Jeanette. 'By the time they come she'll probably be talking.'

Maggie wondered how that would make Dot feel, as there was still no sign of her sister starting a family.

'I'd still travel by liner if I ever get the opportunity to visit Hester and Ally in Canada,' Jeanette said.

'I'd definitely fly,' said Nick.

Maggie remembering that Nick was a police cadet, said, 'I don't suppose you've thought of joining the Canadian Mounties? I can just picture you in a red tunic and riding breeches and a wide-brimmed hat.'

He grinned. 'Why not? Although, I'd have to learn to ride a horse first. But they do say that the Mounties always get their man and that sounds good to me. Now, if you'll excuse me, I want to have a word with Hester and then I'll have to be off.'

Jeanette and Maggie watched him go over to Hester. 'I just hope that one day Nick achieves his aim,' said Jeanette softly.

Maggie agreed, hoping life would turn out well for him. There was something very likeable about Nick.

The party came to an end and farewells were exchanged. Those not sailing left the ship, and Maggie stood with Emma and Jared on the landing stage with Hester and Ally's nearest and dearest, waving as the *Empress of Britain* set sail for Canada. She thought of Tim and how he had travelled to Australia, and wondered how long it would take to fly to the other side of the world. When would she see him again?

Tommy stood, leaning against a tree, thinking he mustn't forget that during the next few hours he was his alter ego Tim Murphy. Fortunately he had not lost the scrap of paper with Maggie's brother's address pencilled on it. So here he was in Formby, hoping to catch sight of Maggie. It was a quarter of an hour since he had got here, and so far there had been no sign of life from the detached house opposite. He made up his mind to wait another ten minutes and, if Maggie did not appear, then he would go over and knock on the front door. He thought dreamily that her brother's house was the kind of house he would love to have himself.

A few moments later the front door opened and a woman appeared. 'Can I help you?' she called across to him.

He decided she must be Maggie's sister-in-law because he remembered being told that she was pregnant. Taking a deep breath, he crossed the road and stopped at the gate. She was standing the other side of it, clutching a rolling pin against the bib of her floral pinny. Obviously she regarded him as a suspicious character. She had a pleasant face but was in no way as good looking as Maggie.

'Have I disturbed you in the middle of your baking, Mrs Gregory?' he asked.

Her eyes widened a fraction. 'How d'you know my name?'

'Maggie mentioned it. I was wondering if I could see her.'

'She's not in.'

Tim thought: *That's a blow.*

'Who are you?' she demanded.

He held out a hand. 'Timothy Murphy. I met Maggie in London.'

She stared at his work-worn hand and then took it and shook it. 'My sister-in-law didn't mention she was expecting anyone. She's taken my son for a walk as far as the shops. She shouldn't be much longer.'

He flashed that smile that had charmed many a woman. 'I'll wait. You couldn't let me have drink, could you? Only I'm parched and it was a bit of a journey getting here.'

Emma hesitated and then said, 'If you don't mind waiting in the garden, I'll bring you a cup of tea.'

'Thanks.'

She walked back to the house and closed the door.

Tim respected her common sense in not inviting a stranger into her home. He opened the gate and went over to a bench beneath a bay window. He took out a cigarette and lit up, hoping that Maggie would soon be here. He sat, enjoying his smoke and looking at the flowers and listening to the birds. He thought that Maggie might have been born in Bootle, but it was obvious that the family had risen in the world. He thought of his own background and that of his brother and sisters. His mother had done her best to bring them up respectable. He knew he had let her down, but he was now doing his best to make up for his mistakes. He could not pretend it was going to be easy keeping his nose clean. He wasn't like his brother, who had always seemed to find it easy living the righteous life. Except for that one mistake when he had allowed Bernie to seduce him, of course.

Tim glanced behind him at the house and thought about his mother scrubbing the front step – every day of her married life, excepting Sundays. She would polish the brasses on the front door, and at least once a fortnight she would wash the net curtains. Mary McGrath had always liked everything just so. She would have loved this place, with its shiny front door and decent locks, which were clearly designed to keep out the likes of his erstwhile crooked companions.

It was a comfort to know those who had led him astray were in prison, and likely to stay there a few years longer, he thought. They could no longer twist his arm and punch him in the gut to persuade him to do stuff he knew he would regret later. He wondered if Maggie's sister-in-law had suspected him of casing the joint when she saw him loitering across the way.

'Tim?'

He started and then smiled at Maggie, who had a little boy by the hand. Slowly, he rose to his feet, thinking the lad reminded him of his son, and he experienced a pang of guilt. 'Hi, Maggie!'

'You came!' she said, her eyes alight.

'I thought I'd better had if I didn't want to leave it a month or more before seeing you again. You look really cool in that shirtwaister dress,' he said, his eyes full of admiration.

Her smile grew. 'Thanks for the compliment.'

Owen tugged his hand out of Maggie's and ran off round the side of the house. 'You don't look so bad yourself,' she said, peering closer. 'Is that shirt shantung silk?'

'Aye, I bought it in Singapore a few years back.' He dug his hands into his pockets. 'I've been up to my eyes, but it was such a lovely day, I thought I'd drop by and see if you'd like to go to the beach.'

She stared at him for several moments. 'Maybe. If you wait here I'll take the shopping in and have a word with Emma.'

Even as Maggie spoke, her sister-in-law appeared from round the side of the house, carrying a cup and saucer. 'So, you've found each other,' she said.

'Yes, we've found each other,' said Maggie. 'Is the cup of tea for Tim?'

'Yes. Do you want one? He told me that you met in London.' Emma handed the cup and saucer to him. 'But he's not from London, is he? He's from up here. I can tell from the way he talks.'

'Just like your accent tells me you're a woolly-back, if you don't mind me saying,' said Tim. 'Thanks for the tea, Mrs Gregory. Much appreciated.'

'I've been called a woolly-back before, but I was born in Liverpool,' she said.

Maggie interrupted their conversation. 'He helped me when I fainted in the street. Then we met on the train coming to Liverpool.'

Emma's glance flickered over Maggie, and then the man for whom she had just made a cup of tea. 'I don't know why you haven't told us this before, Maggie. I think Jared would say it puts a different complexion on things.'

'What things?' asked Maggie.

Emma did not answer.

Maggie wondered if her sister-in-law was thinking that she might have taken a shine to Tim on the rebound after being dropped by Norm. 'We both like music. Isn't that true, Tim?' she asked. 'We're just good friends.'

He hesitated, but there was a look in Maggie's eyes that told him that she wanted him to agree. 'Yeah, just good friends,' he said.

'We thought we'd take a walk to the beach,' said Maggie. 'I know it's a bit late in the day, but perhaps I could make some sandwiches so we could have a picnic?'

Emma hesitated and then nodded. 'You do that, lovey.'

The two women went into the kitchen, leaving Tim to enjoy his cup of tea in peace.

'So what does he do for a living, this good Samaritan of yours?' asked Emma.

'He's a motor mechanic and is setting up his own business here in Liverpool,' said Maggie, dumping the shopping on the kitchen table.

'Surely he could have done that in London? Unless he was only there on a visit?'

Maggie was reluctant to tell Emma that Tim was a widower with a son, the death of his wife being the deciding factor in returning to Liverpool. If she did tell Emma, then she was bound to tell Jared, and no doubt he would say that she was too young to be getting involved with a widower with a child.

'He lived in London but his mother was widowed and so, as he's her only son, he decided to return to Liverpool.'

'I see,' murmured Emma. 'I have to admire him for making the decision to move back north after beginning to make a new life for himself in the south.'

Maggie agreed it was very thoughtful of him.

The back door opened and Owen burst in saying he wanted the toilet. Glad of the interruption, Maggie set about making meat-paste sandwiches. It did not take her long, and after filling a flask with coffee, she went outside, almost colliding with Tim, who was returning the cup and saucer. She took them from him and washed them in the sink, before leaving them on the draining board to dry and picking up the shopping bag with a towel and their picnic inside.

'See you later, Emma,' she called.

As the couple set off for the beach, Maggie said, 'I'm surprised you didn't bring your son with you.'

'I decided I wanted you to myself. I thought that I'm going to miss you if you're going to be spending most of the summer up Lancashire.'

'I'll miss you, too. Although probably next time we meet I'll have improved my baking skills and should be able to make a decent hotpot.' Gazing at him, Maggie thought his face looked thinner and he had slimmed down. 'You must come up and visit me at the cottage. There will be times when I'm up there on my own and I could cook for you.' She paused. 'I think I've mentioned there's some lovely scenery round about. I really can't understand Hester and Ally emigrating.'

'Is that the couple who were living in the cottage?'

'Yes, they sailed the other day. They held a party on the ship and had this fabulous stateroom.'

'Would you ever consider emigrating?'

Maggie shrugged. 'I've never given it much thought. I did hear that Hester wasn't keen on going. She found it difficult enough marrying and moving to Whalley, because she had to quit the job she loved in the Liverpool police force.'

His hand tightened on hers. 'She was a policewoman?'

'Yes! And would you believe that her father was in the force, too, as well as her brother. He's Detective Inspector Sam Walker.

You might have heard of him. His photograph has appeared in the *Echo* on several occasions.'

'Bloody hell!' exclaimed Tim, recognizing the name. 'Pardon my French,' he added hastily. 'But . . . but three coppers in the same family! Imagine living amongst them or even next door. You'd be scared stiff of putting a foot wrong.'

'The father's retired now and lives on the Wirral, but I did hear that DI Walker's adopted son, Nick Rogers, has joined the police cadets.'

Tim blew out a breath. 'Wow! What a family!'

'They're not all in the police force. Jeanette, who used to work in the Cunard Building, wasn't tall enough, and is married now with a baby.'

He hesitated. 'Not to a copper, I hope?'

Maggie smiled. 'No, a sailor.'

'How did your family get to know the Walker family?'

'It's a long story, but to make it short . . . Hester was evacuated during the war to Whalley and attended the village school, where she met Emma. After Hester returned to Liverpool, they didn't see each other for years. Then, purely by accident, some friends and I went into the cafe where Jeanette had a Saturday job and afterwards Emma and Hester met up again.'

'Your sister-in-law said that she was born in Liverpool.'

Maggie nodded. 'Her mother was from Whalley, but she ran away because she wanted to go on the stage. She met Emma's father, who was an artist in Liverpool.'

Tim smiled and shook his head. 'Simple as that. It never fails to amaze me how many Liverpudlians go into show business. You only have to think about the comedian Arthur Askey and the actor John Gregson.'

'There's also the pop singer Marty Wilde and our Dorothy Wilson, of course,' added Maggie. 'I've even thought of going on the stage.'

He stopped and stared at her. 'I can just see you on the stage. Can you sing? You've a nice talking voice. Go on, give us a song? I bet you can hold a note.'

Maggie felt her cheeks go hot. 'You're teasing me. I should have kept my mouth shut.'

'Why? There's nothing wrong with being ambitious,' he said,

swinging her hand. 'There's money to be had. Just look at Lita Roza and Alma Cogan. I bet they're worth a bob or two.'

'I was thinking more of being an actress. One day becoming a television and film star, perhaps.'

'It wouldn't happen overnight,' said Tim. 'Whereas these pop stars seem to come out of nowhere and the next moment they're top of the pops. I wouldn't even say a good singing voice is necessary to get a record into the top twenty.'

'Well, if you think it's that easy, why don't you have a go yourself?' Maggie suggested.

He laughed.

Then they both fell silent and remained so for a while as they walked past the graveyard belonging to St Luke's Church. Some of the tombstones were dappled with sunlight as the sun's rays slanted down through the swaying branches of the trees.

In no time at all they had reached the pinewoods. Maggie breathed deeply of the scent of pine that mingled with the fresh saltiness of the sea air. 'I love that smell,' she said.

Tim gazed sidelong at her rapt profile. 'Beats engine oil,' he said.

She turned her head and smiled at him and he drew her close and kissed her on the lips. It was the sound of someone approaching that caused her to pull away. Then she saw the red squirrel with its tufted twitchy ears, bright eyes and bushy tail, squatting in the leaf litter a few yards away. She put a finger to her lips. Tim turned slowly and the squirrel scampered away.

'I love squirrels,' she said.

'I never thought of you as being an animal lover,' he said.

She was surprised. 'Why?'

He rubbed his nose. 'It's probably wrong of me, but I can't see models and animals mixing. Mustn't get hairs on clothes, that sort of thing.'

'I can see why you might think that,' she said, strolling between the trees. 'But I do like cats.'

'I always wanted a dog,' he said.

'And never the twain shall meet,' said Maggie.

'What d'you mean by that?'

'You're a dog lover and I'm a cat lover. They say you can't be both.'

They walked on.

'There's the car park ahead,' she said.

They gazed into the near distance, beyond which could be seen an expanse of gleaming water. 'You aren't planning on having a swim?' he asked.

'Were you?'

'I haven't brought my trunks.'

'Is that a "no" then?'

'If the beach was deserted I'd have a go – I'm hot with walking all this way. You called me nesh last time we talked about swimming in the sea. When we were kids, we went in the water in our underpants if we didn't have trunks.'

'There's some smashing men's underwear these days being modelled for catalogues,' said Maggie. 'Boxers and the like, in all colours, patterns and fabrics.'

'I suppose it's you having been a model that made you study the subject?' said Tim.

'You could say that. The truth is that I knew a Yankee designer and I read a book he wrote about changes in men's underwear during the twentieth century. Did you know that the T-shirt was regarded as underwear until recently? And it was during the war that white lost its popularity with soldiers? Their underpants were dyed khaki because the enemy would shoot at white ones hung out to dry in the desert. So if you want to swim in your underwear, don't let me stop you,' said Maggie, hiding a smile. 'I'm not going to even paddle.'

He took her hand. 'I don't mind you swimming in your underwear if you feel like a swim.'

'No thanks, I'm not ready for you to see me in my underwear yet,' she said cheerfully. 'Especially when I'm not wearing my best. Anyway, we don't really know each other well enough, and I've already been hurt by one man.'

He toyed with her fingers. 'I'm not going to hurt you. I'll pass on the swim. Let's go and have our picnic and walk along the beach.'

She nodded and, hand in hand, they headed for the beach. It was not until they halted with one accord on a decent, smooth stretch of sand that Maggie took out a large beach towel and spread it out. 'If we were in Australia now, would you go swimming?'

'That would depend on if there were any sharks about,' he replied.

She took out the picnic. 'There could be jellyfish washed up on the beach, and weevers in the sea here.'

'Weevers?'

'Fish,' she said, sitting on the towel and unwrapping the sandwiches from their greaseproof paper. 'Our Jared warned me about them. They bury themselves in the sand in shallow water, but leave their eyes and a fin sticking up that can give you a nasty sting. Worse than a jellyfish.'

He sat down beside her and took a sandwich. 'Thanks for the warning.'

'If it ever happens to you, wash the part where you've been stung in very hot water and that will help get rid of the poison.' She bit into bread and meat paste, chewed, swallowed. 'I believe the pain can last for ages. The most sensible thing to do is to wear beach pumps and watch where you put your feet when you go into the water.' She finished her sandwich and reached for another and offered him one too. 'Actually the sea's quite scary when you think of all the creatures that live in it.'

Tim grinned. 'I don't suppose you'll be doing any sailing on ships anytime soon?'

Maggie shrugged. 'There are places I'd like to go. Did you ever see *Doctor at Sea* with Dirk Bogarde and Brigitte Bardot?'

'Can't say I did.'

'It was a few years ago. You might have been in Australia. The ship supposedly went all the way to South America and he met Brigitte there. She was a nightclub singer. I was still at school and I really fancied going to South America. Then I looked up the distance in my atlas, and it was thousands of miles away. I thought, "blinking heck, that's a lot of water to cover", and so I changed my mind.'

'I remember my sister saying all Liverpudlians had sea-water in their veins.'

Maggie shot him a look. 'Your sister? I thought you were an only . . .'

He hesitated. 'I am now. She was killed in a motorcycle crash a few years ago.'

'Oh, I am sorry.' She reached out and touched his arm. 'How old was she?'

'Only in her twenties.'

'You've had it tough, haven't you?' she said softly. 'Losing two women in your life so young. I thought losing my parents was bad enough, but at least they were quite old.'

'Yeah, life can be a bugger, but it has to go on,' he said in a flat voice.

She leaned towards him and kissed him.

The kiss was sweet and lasted a long time. Then they drew slowly apart without a word and ate another sandwich. She wondered whether it was a fluke that his kisses made her feel good.

He took out the flask. 'Is it tea or coffee?' he asked.

'Coffee,' Maggie answered. 'White coffee. I've even put sugar in it. I hope that's OK with you.'

He smiled. 'You think of everything.'

'My family wouldn't say that. Spoilt, that's what they think of me.' She was aware of the hushing of the waves as they lapped the shore in the background, and was reminded of the passionate love scene on the beach between Burt Lancaster and Deborah Kerr in *From Here to Eternity*.

'We all need a bit of spoiling at times,' said Tim, pouring out the coffee and handing her a cup.

'I agree, because sooner or later it comes to an end. When Mam died, that was it for me. It was as if my brother and sister and cousin believed I'd turn into someone who thought everyone should dance to my tune. Whereas, being the youngest in a family, mostly you get bossed about.'

'I can see where you're coming from,' said Tim, and blew on his coffee.

'It'll soon cool down,' Maggie said.

He nodded. 'What about the war?'

'What about it?'

'It had its effect on those of us who were born just before it started.'

'And those who were war babies like me. Were you evacuated?' she asked.

'No, but when the Blitz got really bad, Mam would start out in the afternoon with some other mothers and us kids and head for the countryside out Aintree way. We'd stay there sleeping in the fields and trudge back home the next day, not knowing if our house would be there or not.' He took a mouthful of coffee.

She gazed out to sea where there was a ship on the horizon. 'I don't remember the Blitz. What I do remember are parts of houses looking like they'd been sliced by a giant knife, with torn wallpaper and the remains of fireplaces still visible. It made me feel sad because they'd once been someone's home. There were plenty of open spaces littered with bricks, slates and chunks of plaster. We'd play at houses with the bricks, and chalk out hopscotch squares with plaster and use slate for counters.'

'You'd be living in Bootle then?'

She nodded. 'It was later we moved to a house in Litherland.'

He shot her a glance. 'Where in Litherland?'

'The other side of the Leeds–Liverpool canal, where the houses have big gardens.'

'So . . . so nowhere near the library? It's just that I had a mate living close to there.'

'No, and my brother sold the house after Mam died, and I moved in for a while with my cousin. She had a flat in Liverpool, up by the Anglican cathedral. But I wasn't there long because we got on each other's nerves. I lived here in Formby for a while and then went to London.'

'So, are you still feeling glad to be back up here?'

'I feel better physically, although I worry about putting on too much weight.'

He smiled. 'I wouldn't. You look great.'

'Thanks. I'll feel even better once this summer is over, and hopefully I'll know something about what the future holds for me.'

'Well, don't go rushing into things. You're only young, so don't be worrying. You never know what's round the corner. Something great could happen.'

'I hope so.'

They finished their picnic and tidied up after them. He took the bag from her and they set off along the beach. They talked idly of this and that, enjoying their surroundings and each other's company. Eventually they made their way back to Formby village.

'I won't come to the house,' he said when they reached the corner of the avenue. 'But I'll be in touch.' He kissed her quickly and then sauntered away.

Maggie stood, waving until he was out of sight and wondering when she would see him again. She thought about Jerry and his mother, as well as his wife and sister who had died so young. She so wanted to make him happy.

Fifteen

Tommy finished servicing the Austin Mini and sighed with relief. It was Saturday, and he could now take the rest of the day off. He was tempted to use the car for his own purposes, as he had done in the past with vehicles he had worked on, but that was what had got him into trouble in the first place. What if he was stopped by the police? He only had his old driving licence with him, and none of the paperwork relevant to this car. Still . . .

He sighed. It was a while since he had been in touch with Maggie and he wanted to see her. Aside from her physical charms, he'd enjoyed their conversation and was keen to get to know her better. Whit had come and gone and he was hoping she would be back in Formby now. If he wanted to carry on seeing her, then he had to get over the fright of seeing his sister and her bloke outside The Vines pub. He excused his cowardice by telling himself his nerves were on edge due to pressure of work.

Tommy was aware that his brother and sisters believed he lacked a conscience, but they were wrong; his conscience had been bothering him on and off since he had come back north. Whatever they thought about him, he did feel bad about not getting in touch with his mother, and also about the promise he had made to his son which he was determined to keep. He had to admit that in the past he hadn't been in the habit of worrying too much about broken promises, believing that all grown-ups broke promises to their children. But Bernie's illness and death had made him realize the error of his ways and his obligation to his family.

Perhaps it was time to risk getting in touch to reassure his mother that he was doing all right. How likely was it that just this one time he would be seen by any of Bernie's family? He decided first that he would ring the owner of the Austin Mini after he had cleaned his hands.

He went over to a shelf and took down a container of Swarfega. He was just wiping his hands on a cloth when he heard a noise. It was a kind of snuffling, whimpering sound and his heart seemed to flip over. He had caught sight of a rat the other day and it had caused a shiver to run down his spine. He hated rats. At least the sight of the vermin had convinced him that he had done right by not bringing Jerry here to live with him.

The noise came again and he crept over to his workbench and picked up the wrench lying there. The noise had stopped, and for a moment he remained motionless, ears pricked. Then the sound came once more. This time he thought he had managed to pinpoint the noise so, gathering up his courage, he wasted no time in tiptoeing in its direction. He caught sight of something moving and threw the wrench with all his might.

The resulting yelp was ear-splitting, and definitely did not belong to a rat. He raced across the floor and fell to his knees beside the dog. It was the scruffiest-looking mongrel he had ever seen, and the expression in its brown eyes smote him to the heart and filled him with guilt when he noticed the blood on its flank. He decided he was going to have to do something about the poor creature before he did anything else.

Holding the dog gently, Tommy wiped away the blood. Fortunately it proved to be only a flesh wound; he left the dog curled up on an old sack. He provided it with a drink of water and the bones from the mutton chops he'd had for his supper last night. The mongrel pounced on them as if he was half-starved. Leaving the dog downstairs, Tommy ran lightly up the stone steps to his bedroom and changed into his best suit. He combed his hair and beard, put a pair of sunglasses in his pocket, dabbed on a touch of Old Spice and then went down to the yard. He picked up the car keys and immediately the dog got up from its makeshift bed and followed him over to the car.

'Where d'you think you're going?' he asked.

The dog woofed.

Tommy hesitated. Then, on impulse, he fetched the sack, opened the front passenger door and put the sack in the well. He ushered the dog inside; after a moment's hesitation, it jumped on to the sack and curled up. Tommy climbed into the driving seat and, taking a deep breath, put the key in the ignition and donned the sunglasses.

He made just a couple of stops and purchased some sweets, chocolates and dog biscuits at the far end of Lark Lane before heading for his mother's house, parking a few streets up on the opposite side of Scotland Road. He opened the packet of dog biscuits and dropped a couple in front of the mongrel, which it immediately wolfed down. He dropped a couple more on the sack and told it to stay and that he wouldn't be long.

Then he wasted no time taking a short-cut past the pub on the corner of the street where he had grown up, and walked up the back jigger. He came to a backyard door, which he would have gone past if the house number had not been written on the newly painted door in bold black numerals.

He tried the latch, but it did not yield, so he did what he had done many times as a boy, and with the box of chocolates and two bags of mixed sweets tucked inside his jacket, he climbed up the door and over the wall into the yard. The door to the back kitchen was unlocked but when he tried to push it wide open, it became obvious that someone had their shoulder to it, because he could hear breathing.

'Is that you, Mam?' he called.

There was a murmur of voices and the door was flung open. His mother stood there with the poker in her hand. Looming in the background was his extremely pregnant youngest sister Lily.

'It is you!' gasped Mary.

Tommy felt a rush of emotion, which caused his voice to sound harsh. 'Yeah, it's me, Mam. But I can't stop. I just want you to do me a favour.'

Lily's eyes flew wide. 'You've got a nerve!' she cried. 'You go off without a word to anyone, and didn't even make the effort to see Mam when you were here a few months ago. Now you think we're going to open our arms to you as if you were the prodigal son. Do us a favour and leave!'

'I love you, too, Lil,' drawled Tommy. 'Now, will you shut up? I was talking to Mam.'

'Who said she wanted to talk to you?' demanded Lily. 'You're a disgrace to the family.'

'Be quiet, Lily,' said Mary. 'I can speak for myself.'

'Of course, you can, Mam,' said Tommy. 'Now that Dad's not around. You never could get a word in with him here.'

Mary clutched the poker more tightly. 'Now keep your dad out of this or I might lose my temper. What is it you want?'

He removed the box of chocolates from beneath his jacket. 'This is for you, Mam.'

'You polished sod,' muttered Lily. 'Trying to get round her.'

Mary hushed her daughter and handed the poker to her. 'I knew you weren't all bad,' she said, taking the box from him. 'Are you going to come in for a cup of tea and tell us how poor Bernie died?'

'That's if she is dead, and not run off with another man,' put in Lily.

Tommy started back. 'What the hell d'you mean by that? She's dead all right. Poor Bernie. It came as a shock, I can tell you.'

Mary signalled to him to come into the house.

'No, Mam, I can't. I've something else I have to do.'

'Is it work, son? Is it honest work?' she asked.

He looked injured. 'If our Marty showed you me letter, then you'd know I'm doing me best to go straight.' Reaching beneath his jacket again, he produced the two bags of sweets. 'Could you give these to Jerry and Josie? Now I have to go, Mam.' He leaned forward and kissed her cheek before turning away.

'Wait, wait,' cried his mother, waving the box of chocolates. 'I need you to do something for us if I've to do something for you.'

'Yeah, and you won't think twice about it if you've a decent bone in your body,' Lily said.

Tommy gave her an impatient look. 'I'd forgotten just how much of a nag you were. What is it, Mam?'

'Well, it's really for our Marty. He needs Bernie's death

certificate,' Mary said. 'He wants to get married, you see. He has a very nice young woman. A good Catholic girl. But, as you can imagine, the situation is what Father Francis says is unusual. What with Bernie having wed you secretly and then Marty bigamously.' She sighed heavily. 'When I think about my poor grandson believing he has two fathers. The poor lad is completely confused. This mess needs sorting out.'

'I know I'm to blame for some of it, Mam, but—'

'Some of it!' exploded Lily. 'Most of it.'

He turned on her. 'I didn't know Bernie would get pregnant and trick our Marty into marrying her, did I?'

'He wouldn't have done so if you hadn't been such a sneaky coward,' said Lily, resting her arms on her bump.

'Shush, Lily,' ordered her mother. 'Anyway, Tommy, Father Francis reckons it can all be sorted out in no time if Marty could produce Bernie's death certificate.'

Tommy hesitated. 'I suppose it's the least I can do for Marty. I've got a spare, so I'll pop it into the post. I've got to go now.'

Again he tried to leave, but his mother stayed him with a hand. 'Bernie's family still don't know she's dead. Her mother's gone off to Ireland to escape from all the upset, but you can bet she'll be back. So you're best not coming round here again, because when she does learn the truth she's bound to have it in for you.'

Tommy swore beneath his breath. His mother slapped him on the arm. 'Less of that. Now go, but keep in touch.'

'Sorry, Mam. Thanks for everything. I'll see that Marty gets the death certificate. Now I really do have to go.' He wasted no more time but left in a hurry, determined to see Maggie and let the dog have a run on the beach at Formby if it felt up to it.

Maggie put down the teapot, sank on to a chair and gazed across the kitchen table at Emma. 'I can't believe you're serious?'

'Of course I'm serious! You enjoyed your time at the cottage, didn't you, especially when the weather was so lovely?'

'Yes, but living up there on my own for the whole of the summer and being in charge of the tearoom and shop. I think that it might be beyond me.'

'You won't be managing on your own the whole of the time.

I'll be going backwards and forwards until just before the baby's
due.'

'But I can't bake and cook the way you can,' Maggie protested.

'You're not completely hopeless,' said Jared. 'You've done your
bit in the short time you've been living with us. Emma will carry
on showing you how to go about things, as well as teaching you
other stuff, before leaving you alone to cope. That won't be until
the second half of July.'

Maggie rubbed the back of her neck, thinking of Tim. A sigh
escaped her and she wondered if this was a way of getting her
out of his reach. It was true that Jared had not said a word about
him, but that could be because Emma had told him not to do
so, wanting to keep the peace between them.

'I'm not as convinced as you, Jared. Emma has a real light
touch with pastry, and when she's making soup or hotpot she
doesn't even use a cookery book, but has everything in her head.'

'I can write the other recipes down for you and you'll soon
get the hang of it,' Emma said persuasively. 'It'll be such a help
to me. If you don't agree, it means I'll probably have to give up
the business and maybe even end up having to sell the cottage
– and I'd hate to do that.'

'You could find another tenant,' suggested Maggie.

'It's not as easy to do that as you might think,' Emma murmured.

'I suppose not, but I'll be away from family and friends.'

'You were away from us and them when you were living in
London,' Jared pointed out.

Emma glanced at him. 'Tell her she'll be staying rent free and
she'll earn a share of the profits.'

He smiled at his sister. 'Did you hear that, Maggie? You'll be
financially better off . . . and you'll still be able to spend some
time here when we go up there the odd weekend.'

'Having said that, you'll have to be up at the cottage with us
every weekend when it gets really busy in summer,' Emma added
hastily. 'Anyway, it'll be good for your health, spending more
time in the proper countryside.'

Maggie suddenly realized that Emma, who had grown up in
the Lancashire fells, did not regard Formby as proper countryside.
A thought occurred to her. 'I'm not giving you a definite "yes"
right now, but I'll let you know by next weekend.'

Jared looked at Emma who nodded. 'All right. That sounds fair enough,' he said.

With that settled, Maggie could only hope that Tim would get in touch before then. So it came as a pleasant surprise when he arrived on the doorstep later that day with what she could only regard as a scruffy mongrel. As Emma had gone shopping and Jared had returned to work, leaving Owen with Maggie, she invited him into the kitchen, but suggested he leave the dog tied up in the back garden.

'Not only might the cat go for it if you bring it inside, but Emma is a bit house proud and definitely won't want dog hairs on the furniture,' she said, aware that Owen was eyeing the dog with interest. 'It doesn't bite, does it?' she added uneasily.

'I hope he does. I'm thinking of using it as a guard dog,' said Tim.

'Owen, don't go near it,' warned Maggie.

'He'll be all right once I introduce them to each other,' said Tim.

Maggie was not convinced. 'Where did you get it from?'

'He turned up earlier today.'

'You mean he's a stray?'

He nodded, deciding to keep quiet about taking the dog for a rat and throwing a wrench at it. 'I felt sorry for it.'

Looking at the disreputable creature, Maggie said, 'I can see why, but I think you're daft. A dog ties you down in a way a cat doesn't. What does your mother think?'

'He'll be living at the yard. I told you I'm going to keep him as a guard dog. Mam won't have anything to do with him.'

Owen asked, 'Won't he get lonely?'

Tim looked down at the lad. 'He's a stray and is used to being on his own. He'll be that made up having regular food and a warm place to sleep that the only worry he'll have is if any burglars try and break in.'

Maggie hid a smile. 'He doesn't look what I'd call ferocious. You should have got yourself an Alsatian.'

'No, Fang will do me.'

'Fang!' She laughed and put on the kettle. 'I bet you got that name out of a comic.'

He nodded. 'An old one. Anyway, what's wrong with comics?

There weren't any books in our house when I was a kid, but Mam would buy me the odd comic. I loved the *Dandy* and *Beano*, as well as the *Hotspur*, which I used to pinch from my . . . friend.'

'My brother used to read the *Eagle*,' Maggie said, pouring milk into cups.

'That was more for the posh lads than us.'

'We weren't posh. Although maybe Emma's father was, because I'm sure Jared mentioned once that it was he who started him off reading the *Eagle*. I think I might have told you that he was an artist and had money.'

'So your brother married a rich wife.'

She shot him a glance. 'Not rich, rich, and she didn't realize he'd left her money because he died during the war when she was a little girl. The cottage belonged to her mother's parents. Did you have a good Whit bank holiday, by the way?'

'I was busy working. What about you? How did your time up at the cottage go?'

'Fine! So you didn't take your son out?'

She thought that for a moment he looked uncomfortable. Then he said, 'Only to the park to kick a ball around.' He changed the subject. 'How are you for next Saturday?'

Her spirits soared and then sank. 'I don't know. I'll have to speak to Emma. Why, what's happening?'

'I've tickets for a jazz concert in the afternoon. It's in the open air, so I'm praying it doesn't rain.'

Maggie smiled as she spooned coffee into mugs. 'I should be all right.' She hesitated. 'There is something I feel you need to know.' She proceeded to tell him about Emma and Jared's plans for her weekends and during the summer.

It was gratifying that he looked dismayed. 'Does this mean we'll see hardly anything of each other during the summer?'

'If I agree to their plan, yes.'

He frowned. 'You'd be crazy to turn them down. You'll be living rent free, with no one watching your every move – and getting paid as well.'

'That's true, but there'll be times when I'll be lonely because I know hardly anyone up there. But if you—'

'If I what?'

She hesitated, took a deep breath, and burst out, 'You're your own boss, so you could come and visit me and I'd have something to look forward to. As I've told you, it's lovely countryside up there. Your dog would enjoy it and so would Jerry. As long as you don't let Fang roam free and chase sheep, because he could get shot if he did.'

A slow smile lifted the corners of Tim's mouth. 'I'd like that. When would be the best time to come?'

'A weekday, and you can do the journey there and back easily in a day if you can borrow or hire a car. Otherwise it means changing trains. If you can come you can phone me. I'll give you the number.'

He frowned and then his brow cleared. 'All right! Let's talk about it next Saturday. That's if you can make it?'

'Where's the concert taking place?'

'Sefton Park. You know where that is, don't you?'

She frowned. 'I can't remember ever going there, but I know it's the other side of Liverpool.'

He paused. 'Shall we go for a walk after we've had our coffee while I work out the best place for us to meet?'

She agreed, and over coffee he suggested they meet beneath the clock in Lime Street Station at twelve o'clock.

'And if I'm not there by twelve thirty, you'll know I'm not coming.' She added hastily as his face fell. 'But I'll definitely try to be there.'

Soon after, they set off with Owen and Fang for the beach. Tim had parked the car round the corner and decided not to mention it, knowing he would have to return it to its owner later that day. He didn't want Maggie asking him about it if he didn't arrive in it another time.

Maggie asked Tim whether he had been doing anything other than fixing cars and going to the park with Jerry. He shook his head and talked about the motors he had fixed and the people who had moved in next to the garage. She listened while keeping her eye on Owen. He was running along the sand with the dog, which appeared to be limping.

They parted on the corner of the avenue, near Emma and Jared's house. 'Hopefully I'll see you soon,' said Maggie.

He nodded, kissed her, and walked away with the dog on a length of rope.

Maggie and Owen arrived back at the house to find Emma and Dot talking on the front step. Owen ran up to his mother and tugged on her skirt. 'I want a doggie,' he said.

Emma shook her head and glanced in Maggie's direction. 'What's this about a dog?'

'We've been to the beach with Tim.'

Owen said, 'He has a dog to guard his garage from burglars.'

Dot raised her eyebrows interrogatively. 'Where does he live?'

'In Liverpool.'

'So why didn't he see you home?' asked Dot. 'I'd have liked a look at him.'

'He had to get back to Liverpool.' Maggie glanced at Emma. 'He's asked me to go with him to a jazz concert next Saturday afternoon.'

'Well, that puts the kibosh on our plan, Emma,' said Dot.

'What d'you mean?' asked Maggie.

'We thought Billy could take the three of us up to the cottage with Owen, and we thought of also taking Georgie from the children's home as well,' Dot informed her.

'There's nothing stopping you all going without me,' Maggie said. 'Why don't you take Deirdre and Irene and some of the other kids as well? I presume Emma has told you her plans for me?'

'Yes, and I told her she must be crackers trusting you,' said Dot frankly. 'Your suggestion about the kids isn't a bad idea, though. Although we'd have to persuade either our Jared or Marty to come as well as we'd need extra transport.'

'I'm glad you think I'm good for something.'

Emma said hastily, 'She's only kidding you about being crackers. She really thinks it'll be good for you having some responsibility.'

'It'll certainly stop you feeling sorry for yourself,' said Dot.

Maggie said sweetly, 'Why should I feel sorry for myself when I have my family sorting my life out for me? Anyway, if I'm going to be working at the cottage for most of the summer, I'm going to need some workaday clothes, so I might as well get them next Saturday when I go into town to meet Tim.' On those words she hurried into the house, determined to make the most of her day out next week.

Sixteen

Irene hurried across the bridge holding Jerry and Josie by the hand. She should not have dropped in at Nellie Gianelli's, but she had received a letter from Betty and so had wanted to tell the older woman the latest news from California. They had got talking about other matters, such as the phone call she had received from Dot asking if she, Marty and the children would like to go up to Whalley on Saturday. The time had passed so swiftly that it was half past five before Irene realized it. If she didn't get a move on, there would be no meal on the table for Marty when he arrived home from work.

How she wished they would hear from Tommy, as it would make such a difference to their lives. She would be living with Marty and would not have to be going backwards and forwards from the Marshalls' house in Bootle to Litherland. Where the hell was he? It just wasn't blinking fair, leaving them to look after Jerry when he was really Tommy's responsibility. It was no good thinking, like Pete's mother, that maybe his casual attitude to Jerry was due to Tommy being unaware that he had a son until eighteen months ago. He was just irresponsible; unlike Marty who, despite having doubts about his being Jerry's father, had treated the boy as if he were his son.

'Irene!'

At the sound of her name, and recognizing that voice, Irene looked in the direction of Marty's works van as it drew up outside the Red Lion.

'Were you looking for us, love?' she asked. 'Sorry, I haven't got the dinner on yet, but there was a letter from Betty and so I took the kids and went to visit Nellie.'

'Never mind that, we can go to the chippy.' He grinned at her as he climbed down from the van. 'I've some good news.'

'Tommy!' she cried.

'Mam rang me at work. He dropped by at her house with a box of chocs for her and sweets for the kids.'

'Did she ask him about Bernie's death certificate?'

'Yes! He said that he'll post it.'

'Well, that's a turn-up for the books,' said Irene, smiling.

'You know what this means?' he said, seizing her by the waist and kissing her.

She released the children's hands and returned his kiss. When they drew apart she said, 'I can't believe it's going to happen at last.'

'I reckon we could be married in a couple of months' time. We can go on honeymoon. I'm sure Peg or Mam would look after the kids.'

'I'm sure they would. We'll have to book the church. There's a hundred and one things that need to be done,' Irene said excitedly.

'Come on, let's get home,' said Marty, grabbing her by the hand. 'We can talk better there.'

Jerry tugged on Marty's jacket. 'What about the chippy?'

Marty smiled down at the boy. 'We'll go to the chippy. Don't you be worrying, and I've some sweeties for you from your other daddy.'

'What about me?' asked Josie, her attractive little face turned up to his.

'There's some for you too,' Marty said, giving her a hug.

'Your Tommy's generous all of a sudden,' murmured Irene, tempted to be catty and ask whether he had stolen them. But what was she thinking of? That would upset the children.

'Where is my other daddy?' asked Jerry.

'I don't know, but I'm sure he'll be in touch again,' Marty said.

'D'you think we're going to see more of him now?' Irene asked as she ushered Jerry and Josie into the van.

Marty dropped his voice. 'He didn't tell Mam where he was living, but apparently he is working.'

'Perhaps we shouldn't be counting our chickens until we have the death certificate in our hands,' Irene said, her mood changing. 'I'm not going to make any plans until we do.'

'Don't start looking on the dark side again,' Marty said, frowning. 'He hasn't anything to lose by letting us have the certificate. In fact, he has more to gain.'

Irene could not see how that could be, but kept quiet. She

would believe Marty's brother had turned over a new leaf when he took responsibility for his child and she and Marty were man and wife at last.

Two days later an envelope plopped through the letterbox and was picked up by Irene when she arrived home from the nursery with the children. It was addressed to Marty but, convinced that he would not mind her opening it, she slit it with the butter knife and took out the two enclosed sheets of paper. One was the death certificate, and the other was an official form detailing where and when Bernie's body had been interred.

Instantly Irene wished she had left the envelope for Marty to open, because seeing the details of Bernie's death in stark black and white made her wonder if they might cause Marty grief. After all, he had once been in love with her, and he and Bernie had lived as man and wife for four years, much longer than he and Irene had known each other. Irene had only met Marty about eighteen months ago. She had been going into town on the train with her brother Jimmy and Peggy had got on the same train with her father and Marty.

Slowly she replaced the forms in the envelope and placed it behind the clock before setting about peeling vegetables and frying mince. When Marty came in she told him about opening the envelope and apologized.

'That's all right, love,' he said, putting an arm around her. 'I can understand you being impatient. I'll take the certificate to show Father Francis on the way home from work tomorrow.'

She noticed he did not pick up the envelope straightaway, but went and washed and changed before doing so whilst she dished out their evening meal.

'Sad, isn't it?' he said, after reading the contents of the envelope and putting it back behind the clock, before sitting at the dining table.

'Yes!' Irene was relieved that he was prepared to talk about how he felt. 'She wasn't much older than me. I was sad when Mam died, but at least she had lived almost twice as long as Bernie.'

'The sad thing is that it needn't have happened. If only she and Tommy had been honest from the beginning about getting married. Even when he disappeared a few months after their secret marriage, she could have told the truth instead of tricking me into marrying her because she was pregnant. The whole thing was crazy.'

Irene agreed, adding, 'But you wouldn't have Josie if he had told the truth, and you wouldn't want to be without her, would you?'

He smiled. 'No. Even so, I still believe honesty is the best policy, and I'll tell my brother that when I get to see him again. In the meantime, at least we can start planning our wedding instead of just dreaming about it.'

'What about Saturday?' she asked. 'Can you get time off for us to go up to Whalley? It would be great to have a day out with the kids and some of my family and friends. Jimmy's going to be home, so he'll be able to come too.'

'I'll do my best,' said Marty.

Maggie was humming to herself as she walked hand in hand with Tim beside the lake in Sefton Park. She had never thought she would feel so happy when it was only a few months since she had received the letter from Norm. She was beginning to believe that she had never really loved him after all. Her feelings for Tim were so much stronger, and she so wanted to be with him.

'You're humming out of tune,' said Tim, grinning. 'But I'm glad you enjoyed the concert.'

After the concert, they had been to see the peacocks and other birds in the aviary, as well as the statue of Peter Pan. He had told Maggie how he had swarmed up it when he was a kid, and how he planned to bring Jerry here when he had time. Now they were making for the nearest exit to St Michael's Railway Station.

She smiled at him. 'Jazz musicians often seem to play out of tune to me, but you're right, I enjoyed the concert, and I'm glad I came and it didn't rain. I'd have hated getting this outfit wet.'

He gazed at her in her peach-coloured slacks, beige and orange-flowered blouse and peach jacket. 'I don't blame you. Some women look terrible in trousers, but you look really peachy.'

'Thanks!' Maggie took a deep breath. 'It's great being out in the fresh air listening to music. Much better than a smoky old cellar.'

'Are you saying you don't like the Cavern?' he said, sounding disappointed.

'Only because it affects my chest,' said Maggie hastily. 'I'm really pleased with myself for managing to quit smoking.'

'You've done well.'

'I know. I've surprised myself,' she said with a giggle.

He squeezed her hand and they walked on in silence until they arrived at the train station.

'If you don't mind, I'll have to say tarrah here,' said Tim, sounding regretful.

Maggie looked at him in dismay. 'Have you had enough of me already? I thought you'd be coming into town with me.'

'Don't be daft! I could never have enough of you. It's just that the owner of the car I'm working on lives nearby and I want to have a word with him.'

'Oh, I see.' She sighed. 'I suppose work has to come first.'

'Of course it does, because I have to make a success of the garage.'

'D'you think you'll be able to come to the cottage during the summer?'

Tim hesitated. 'I hope so. I can't promise, but I'll do my best. I'm going to have to work really hard. But if I can make it, I want you to promise me that there won't be any of your family there, so we'll be able to spend time on our own,' he said, drawing her close.

Maggie understood how he felt. 'They generally only pop up at the weekends,' she said, rubbing her cheek against his beard.

He turned his head so his mouth was against hers and murmured. 'Good. You'd better write down the cottage's particulars, and any other information I might need.' Their lips met briefly.

She moved slightly away from him and opened her handbag and took out a pencil and paper and wrote down directions to the cottage. 'Don't forget to ring me and let me know when you're coming. Although, hopefully, we'll be able to see each other before then.'

'Will do.' He kissed her again and then hurried away.

Seventeen

Irene rang the bell again and waited impatiently. She was bursting with news, but still nobody came. Neither was there any sign of life coming from next door. It was a Wednesday afternoon in late July 1959, so it could be that Dot had gone out for the afternoon into town on a shopping spree, and Jared and Emma might be up at the cottage with Maggie and Owen.

Irene sighed. Her news was going to have to wait. Still, she could drop by later on the way back from visiting the children's home, where she needed to speak to Deirdre without delay. As she walked briskly down the lane to the home, she thought how great it was to be free. She had left Josie and Jerry with Peggy and Pete's mothers, who were taking the two children on the ferry to New Brighton. The sun was shining and there was only the lightest of breezes, so it was a perfect day to be out in the fresh air.

Irene was made welcome at the children's home but, before she could tell Deirdre her news, her friend volunteered her to help get the children ready for an outing. 'I thought a nice picnic and a nature walk,' said Deirdre, fastening up a child's cardigan.

'It sounds just the ticket,' Irene said. 'But you must let me—'

'By the way, you're not the only volunteer here,' Deirdre interrupted. 'Dot's here. She's helping with the babies for a change.'

Irene was delighted. 'I called at the house but got no answer. I must have a word with her before we go.'

'You can have a word with her later. She's busy now.'

'I thought she had taken a liking to Georgie,' said Irene, dropping her voice. 'Didn't she take him up to Whalley that time I couldn't go?'

'Yes, but I'm not sure about how Billy feels. Anyway, today she's helping out with the babies.'

Irene stilled. 'Has she ever said anything to you about adoption?'

'No.' Deirdre patted the shoulder of the child in front of her and straightened up. 'Why? Has she mentioned it to you?'

'No, but if she's coming here regularly, it could be that it has occurred to her that adopting a child is a fine thing to do.'

Deirdre looked thoughtful. 'She does have a soft spot for Georgie but that doesn't mean Billy would be in favour of adopting him. He's the sort of man who would want a son he could teach the tougher sort of games to play. Don't you think?'

'You're probably right,' Irene murmured, watching the lovable little boy who had been a favourite with her at the former children's home where she and Deirdre had worked. 'Anyway, I could be completely wrong about Billy and Dot not being able to have children. They might just have chosen not to do so in this day and age. It's not as if they were Catholics like you and me.'

'Are you suggesting she could have visited the family planning clinic?' asked Deirdre. 'Perhaps you could ask her.'

Irene thought it would be better if Dot brought up the subject first. She could object to being asked such a personal question. Besides, Irene had a much more important topic to discuss with Dot and Deirdre.

She waited until she and Deirdre and the small group of handicapped children had left the home behind. Both had children by the hand who preferred keeping close to a grown-up. Georgie was one such child; he clung to Irene's hand as he gazed about him happily.

'I've some good news,' Irene burst out, not taking her eyes from two of the girls who were skipping ahead amongst the trees.

Deirdre smiled. 'You've set the date for your wedding.'

'I should have known you'd guess right away,' said Irene wryly. 'When is it to be?'

'The twenty-sixth of September, the Saturday before Michaelmass Day. I want you to be my chief bridesmaid. What d'you say?'

'I'd be made up!' Deirdre's plump cheeks were rosier than ever. 'What colour frock will I have? And will there be other bridesmaids?'

'Josie, of course. And I think I'll have my stepsisters, Daisy and Rosie, as well. The daughters of Mam's third husband. Marty's mother thinks we should have Jerry for a pageboy.'

'I don't see why not. He's a nice-looking little lad and you don't want him to feel out of things.'

Irene could think of nothing to say to that which wouldn't sound unkind, so remained silent.

'We'll be able to have chrysanthemums in our bouquets,' Deirdre said happily. 'I love those creamy big-headed ones! I only wish Jimmy and me were getting married as well.'

'Have the pair of you discussed it?'

'Yes, but it won't be for ages. We're thinking the year after next, because we'll need to save up, not only for the wedding, but we'd like to be able to put a deposit down to buy our own house.' Deirdre paused. 'Actually, I'd prefer to get married earlier and carry on working after we're married. It's not as if Jimmy is going to be coming home from work every day, and I'd have to be there for him.'

'But what if you started a baby?' asked Irene.

Deirdre was silent a moment and then she said, 'There are ways and means of preventing a pregnancy.'

Irene took her eyes from the two little girls a moment. 'But you're Catholic, and if you're talking about the rhythm method then I wouldn't trust it. From what I've read, it's not completely reliable.'

'Am I to believe that you and Marty haven't tried it?' Deirdre said quietly.

Irene stared at her. 'Marty and I haven't been sleeping together, if that's what you think. He has two kids to support, without risking bringing another one into the world right now.'

Deirdre flushed. 'It was Jimmy who . . .' Her voice trailed off.

'What did my brother say to you?' Irene asked indignantly.

'He thought you and Marty would be making the most of your opportunities. What with the pair of you spending so much time together in the house during the evening, even if you do go off to the Marshalls' house every night. If you're not, then all he said was the pair of you must have the willpower of saints.'

Irene chuckled. 'I'm no saint, and neither is Marty.'

Deirdre stared at her, perplexed. 'I don't know what to make of that.'

'Make of it what you will. All I know is that, come the twenty-sixth of September, I'll probably go a little crazy.'

'Will you be giving up work?'

'I don't know yet. The wedding is still a couple of months off. I'll think about it more seriously nearer the time.'

It was on that note that they were disturbed by piercing screams, and both shot off in the direction of the noise. After they had stopped the fight between two of the girls over a large fir cone, Deirdre said breathlessly, 'I often wonder how little girls are able to scream so loud. I hope I have boys when I have children. I'm just glad Matron's not around, or I could be getting the sack for negligence.'

'Rubbish,' Irene said robustly. 'You're a very conscientious nurse. These things happen and I don't see a need to mention it, do you?' She smiled. 'Now, where's the food for the picnic?'

Later that afternoon, Irene left the children's home with Dot. As they walked along the lane, they discussed the forthcoming wedding and who was going to give Irene away.

'Marty was talking about asking Jimmy to be his best man. He thought Billy might not mind giving me away,' said Irene.

'I'm sure he'll be happy to give you away,' said Dot.

'And he's known me as long as Jimmy, with us having grown up in the same street.'

'Anyway, you and Marty are best waiting until Jimmy gets home before mentioning this to Billy. Whichever task Jimmy takes on, he's going to have to make a speech.'

'I know.' Irene pulled a face. 'I think I'd prefer listening to what Billy has to say about me rather than have my brother chuntering on, making jokes at my expense.'

'He wouldn't,' said Dot, smiling.

'Oh, wouldn't he?' groaned Irene.

She changed the subject. 'Anyway, will you tell Billy we've set a date? And Emma, Jared and Maggie? I'm presuming they're up at the cottage. I'll be sending proper invitations out, of course.'

Dot nodded her blonde head. 'Maggie's going to be at the cottage most of the summer. All that fresh air will be good for her chest. Did you know she discovered she has a TB scar on her lung?'

'Poor ol' Maggie.'

'Oh, she'll survive. She's tougher than she looks. And now she's given up smoking and has put on a bit of weight and has herself a new boyfriend, I'm sure she'll come on in leaps and bounds.'

'She already has another boyfriend! She hasn't been home five minutes,' Irene joked. 'What's his name?'

'Timothy Murphy.'

'Sounds Irish.'

'He's a Scouser, although she met him in London. Anyway, Emma told me that he has his own business.'

'Emma's met him?'

'Yes. Apparently he's not bad looking, despite the beard. I must admit, after hearing that Norm had dropped her, I was worried she might take up with someone completely unsuitable on the rebound. But it sounds like she has more common sense than I credited her with.'

'What about her modelling? What about London? Will she ever go back?'

'Who's to say? You know Maggie.'

Irene frowned. 'I was always closer to Betty. Although Maggie and I used to go to school together sometimes, we were never the best of friends, and what with her going off to London, I haven't seen much of her. D'you think I should include the boyfriend on the invitation?'

'Perhaps you could invite him just to the evening do. That's if you are having one?'

'We haven't made up our minds yet. Marty and I would like to go away for a few days on our own, and that will cost money.'

'I'd wait and see how things go. After all, if she and the boyfriend see scarcely anything of each other during the summer, it could be that their relationship will die a death.'

Eighteen

Maggie was taking scones out of the oven when the telephone rang. She almost dropped the tray, and only just managed to save most of the scones from sliding to the floor. As it was, two landed on the tiles.

'Damn!' she muttered, dashing to pick up the receiver, hoping it might be Tim. To her delight it was; as soon as their brief conversation was over, she wasted no time in making preparations for his visit.

She could not wait to see him as they had not met for several weeks, and she was especially pleased that he was able to come that day, because not only was she was on her own, but the sun was shining. He had mentioned staying in the village overnight, having decided to leave Fang for a neighbour to feed and walk, and his mother was happy to look after Jerry. So Maggie whizzed round to the local pub to see if they had a vacancy and to do some shopping while she was out. She would have liked to have offered the spare room, only she knew that tongues would wag, and that meant Emma and Jared would get to know of it when they came here for the bank holiday weekend.

Fortunately the Spotted Dog had a room available for that night, although she was told they were fully booked for the coming weekend, so she booked a room and then visited the shops and bought some locally produced lamb, extra vegetables, butter and cream, as well as a couple of freshly baked crusty loaves, before hurrying back to the cottage. She had already made a pan of soup and set about preparing a Lancashire hotpot just as Emma had taught her. The two ruined scones she threw out to the birds.

Once the hotpot was in the oven, she made another dozen scones and a coffee and walnut cake, thinking they should satisfy Tim – and any customers who called, although she doubted she would be overwhelmed by tourists until Saturday. She would have to make a huge hotpot and more scones for then. She would leave it to Emma to make such Lancashire culinary delights as Chorley and Eccles cakes, as she was the expert, but she knew that she was going to have to perfect her own attempts sooner rather than later.

By the time Tim's van drew up outside, later than she had expected, Maggie had dealt with six customers, bathed, changed, put on make-up and redone her hair several times. She was on pins, in case he thought her cooking was rubbish. She prayed that they wouldn't be disturbed by a sudden rush of visitors to the abbey.

Her heart lifted as he climbed out of the van and smiled at her.

'So you managed to find me,' Maggie said, taking a couple of steps across the pavement towards him.

'I'm here, aren't I?' he said, seizing both her hands. 'You look good enough to eat.'

She laughed. 'I thought you'd be hungry by the time you got here, so I've made a hotpot and baked a cake and some scones.'

His eyes lit up. 'Sounds just what the doctor ordered. I'm starving. I'm not much of a cook and I've noticed lately that the waist of my trousers was getting looser.'

'I wish I could say the same about my waistband,' Maggie grimaced. 'If not many customers drop in, I end up eating the food before it either goes off or stale.'

'You still look good to me,' he said.

'Flatterer.' She tugged on his hands. 'Come inside. You can have something to eat and then I'll show you the village.'

'Don't you have to stay here in case of customers?'

'I'll put the "Closed" sign in the window now you've arrived, so we can relax,' she said, leading the way through the front room, which was set out with tables and chairs and a Welsh dresser on which was a display of goods for sale.

Tim gazed about him. 'Nice!'

'I'm glad you approve,' Maggie said as he followed her into the kitchen.

He let out a low whistle. 'This is a great kitchen. You wouldn't believe from the front of the cottage that it was this big.'

'It's been extended. There was a huge back garden, because in Emma's great-grandmother's day she grew all her own vegetables and kept hens. We don't bother with hens any more. On a warm day, customers can eat outside, because the garden is still a fair size.'

She opened a door off the kitchen into a small square, the other side of which was another door. 'This is the downstairs lavatory and there's another one outside. And upstairs Jared has built a proper bathroom over the extension.'

'He's clever is your brother?' said Tim.

'I suppose he is. I probably take him for granted.'

'You shouldn't.'

Maggie glanced at him and thought he looked serious. She slipped her hand through his arm. 'I suppose we all take our families for granted. Especially big brothers who have always done things for us.' She drew him over to the table. 'Another time I'd like you to meet Jared, but right now you're to sit down and relax while I dish out the hotpot.'

Soon they were seated across from each other, and between mouthfuls of lamb and vegetables, they talked about what they had been doing. After they had finished eating and washed up, she suggested they went to the inn first, before she showed him the rest of the village.

'Let's do that later,' he said, drawing her into his arms.

There was an expression in his eyes that caused her heart to race; she did not argue, but surrendered to his embrace.

They tumbled on to the sofa and kissed passionately. It seemed a natural progression from there to going further. Yet when his hands began to fumble with her clothing and his fingers undo buttons, alarm bells rang in her head. This was generally the point where Maggie called a halt, and this moment was no different.

'Better not,' she said unsteadily, managing to worm her hands between their bodies. 'Please!' she gasped.

'Please do or please don't?' His breathing was rapid and uneven.

A giggle rose in her throat. 'Don't tempt me!' She pushed against his chest with both hands.

'I thought it was what you wanted,' he said, shifting to the end of the sofa and frowning.

Maggie buttoned up her blouse. 'I'm not saying it isn't, but I can't see the sense in taking risks,' she said unhappily.

He stared at her for several moments. 'Come here,' he said abruptly, stretching out a hand.

She hesitated, and then slowly slid along the sofa towards him. He put an arm about her shoulders. 'I want you, Maggie. And what with being alone and it feeling so fantastic us being together, I was tempted.'

'I'm sorry if you think I led you on. But a girl has to be careful.'

'So does a bloke.'

'I just don't want to get into trouble. It happened to someone I know and she ended up having to have an abortion. It was horrible.'

'Wouldn't the bloke marry her?'

'Good God, she hated him. He was a married man and he raped her!' She shuddered. 'Just the thought of him makes me feel sick.'

'Not all men are like that.'

'I know that!'

'If you were to get pregnant, I'd marry you. I could do with a wife.'

Maggie's emotions were in confusion. 'You're not asking me to marry you, are you?'

'If I were, would you say yes?'

'I don't know.' She stood up. 'Shall we go and have that walk?'

'All right!' He got to his feet and said in a tight voice, 'You'd best show me where this inn is, seeing as how you've booked me in.'

Maggie went and slipped on a cardigan. 'You're annoyed with me, aren't you?'

He shrugged. 'What's the point of me being annoyed? I hate it when people try and make me do things I don't want to do. I understand how you feel. But when you feel ready, just let me know and I'll come running. I still fancy you like mad.'

Maggie felt a warm glow inside her. After being rejected by Norm, it felt good that Tim still wanted her despite her making him wait for sex. 'I'm glad you feel like that, because I still fancy you, too.' Even as she spoke, she realized that she more than fancied him, she was probably in love with him.

They left the house and drove to the Spotted Dog, which was next to St Mary's churchyard. He parked the van outside the inn and they went inside, where he signed the register and was shown his room. When he came back down, she asked him was he ready for a walk, or did he want to have a drink in the pub?

'Later, let's go and have that walk.'

She slipped her hand in his and said, 'I thought you might like to see the garage that Ally rented when he and Hester lived in the cottage.'

'You mean the couple that emigrated to Canada?'

'That's right. He was a motor mechanic like you. There's a "To Let" sign still up.'

They set off, and Maggie felt much more relaxed now he had

signed the register at the inn. For a moment earlier she had thought he was going to change his mind about staying overnight, but she had been wrong, and she was happy to know she would be able to enjoy his company for the rest of the evening and tomorrow morning at least.

When they reached the garage he stood for several minutes gazing at the building with its couple of fuel pumps outside. 'I wonder how much business he did,' he murmured.

'I don't know. Emma and Jared might have some idea. I could ask if you're interested.'

He shrugged. 'If he had been doing well, surely he wouldn't have emigrated.'

'I think he had it in mind to emigrate when he finished his national service but then he met Hester and she wasn't keen on leaving England because of family. I think I told you.'

'She was the policewoman?'

Maggie nodded. 'Have you seen enough?'

'Yeah.' He looked about him. 'What else is there to do here in the evenings, besides go for walks?'

'There's an amateur dramatic club and the men play cricket and bowls. There's church activities. We could go and have that drink at the pub, or we could drive into Clitheroe and see a film.'

'There's no cinema here?'

'I know they used to show films on the first floor above the Co-op,' said Maggie. 'I don't know if they still do.'

'Then let's go into Clitheroe,' he said.

So they went to see a film starring Debbie Reynolds and Bing Crosby, and afterwards had a drink at the pub before he walked her home. He kissed her good night but did not come inside the cottage.

She did not sleep well that night, and wished he was in bed beside her, but the gossips would have a field day if she had risked inviting him to stay the night. He had mentioned needing a wife, so perhaps he was prepared to wait a while longer for her. After all, it was not that long since his first wife had died.

He arrived around nine o'clock the following morning and they went for a drive through the winding country lanes to Pendle Hill, where they had only a short walk because he didn't have the proper footwear, but he promised to come again because – as Maggie had said – it was beautiful countryside round about.

She felt a bit lonely after he had gone, but the very next day, Jared arrived early in the evening with Emma and Owen. Over a supper of scrambled eggs and potato scallops and peas, they brought each other up to date with their news. Maggie thought it best to mention that Tim had been up for a visit and had stayed at the Spotted Dog, while Emma regaled her with the news that Irene had set the date for her wedding and they were to expect a proper invitation.

'When is it to be?' Maggie asked.

'The last Saturday in September.' Emma patted her large bump. 'The baby should have arrived by then, and pray God I'll be up and about and able to attend the wedding.'

'And will it have quietened down up here by then?' asked Maggie.

'Aye, you can come back to Formby the week before.'

'You don't want me there for when the baby's due?'

'No, Dot said she'll be on hand to help me after the birth, and Jared will be taking some time off.'

That suited Maggie, and she thought it should give her plenty of time to go into Liverpool and buy a new frock.

'But you've plenty of lovely frocks,' said Emma, stifling a yawn. 'I've asked Lynne Walker to make me a new outfit and, by the way, she told me that Dorothy Wilson is due back at the end of September.'

Maggie was glad to hear the news, but she wondered what Tim would make of her plan to consult the actress about maybe trying out a career on the stage. She decided to keep quiet about it until after the wedding, when she would pop into Lenny's.

The wedding invitations duly arrived at the cottage a fortnight later while Emma was there. The bank holiday weekend had been extremely busy because the weather had been fine, and she and Owen had stayed on while Jared returned home. Emma was thrilled when they heard the news that the Queen was to have another child in the New Year.

'She said that she always wanted more children,' said Emma. 'I'd like at least another one too.'

All Maggie wanted right then was to hear from Tim, because on the invitation card Irene had included Maggie's boyfriend and she wanted to tell Tim about it.

But the days went by and still he did not get in touch. She told herself not to worry, that he must be busy, and there was still plenty of time for her to hear from him before the wedding. But how she wished he had thought to provide her with an address or a phone number where she could get in touch with him.

Maybe the truth of the matter was that he'd realized that he had acted precipitously in mentioning marriage. Maggie also thought about the mother, hovering in the background, who just might resent him taking up with another woman so soon after returning to Liverpool.

It was the beginning of September, and Maggie was wiping over the garden chairs and tables after a downpour when the telephone rang. Immediately she rushed into the house, only to find that it was Jared. Even so, she was pleased when he told her that the baby had come early and he was the proud father of a daughter. Both mother and baby were well. They had not decided on names yet, but one of them would be Mary after Emma's mother.

It was to be another week before she heard from Tim. Her spirits soared when she recognized his voice. He apologized for not being in touch and told her that he'd had an accident, news that immediately worried her. He reassured her that it was not life threatening. He had been working on a car when he had cut his hand so badly that he needed to go to hospital and have a tetanus jab and stitches.

She expressed sympathy, and suggested he might like to have a break and come up to the cottage. He told her that driving was too painful, so he would wait and see her when she returned to Formby. She suggested that – instead of him coming all the way to Formby – they should meet in Liverpool. Lenny's coffee bar on Hope Street would be a convenient meeting place. She went there often when she visited Liverpool.

She told him about Irene Miller and Marty McGrath's wedding invitation. She was just about to add that they had both been invited when the pips went and she realized he must be phoning from a telephone box. The phone went dead and she put the receiver down and stayed near the phone, hoping he would find some coins and ring again. But he did not do so. She felt at a loss, not knowing what steps to take next to try and get in touch with him. She would just have to hope he would ring her again before the wedding.

Nineteen

'Aren't you ready yet, Maggie?' Jared's voice floated up the stairs.

She did not bother replying because she was putting the finishing touches to her make-up and was nearly ready. She shrugged on the matching bolero to the dress she had bought in Du Barry's on Lime Street, gave one last look at her reflection, then pulled on her gloves. She picked up her handbag and the wedding present for the happy couple and left the bedroom.

As Maggie hurried downstairs she could hear the baby grizzling, and hoped she would fall asleep and stay that way during the service. There was no doubt that her niece Diana Mary was a lovely baby, with lots of curly dark brown hair, but she had kept her awake a couple of nights since her return to Formby.

'About time too,' said her brother.

'You do look nice,' said Emma, who was wearing a dark pink jersey suit with a white frilly blouse and wide-brimmed pale pink straw hat trimmed with daisies.

'You look nice, too,' Maggie said, wishing Tim was there to see her, but she still had not heard from him and was worried. What if he had caught blood poisoning from that cut, despite the tetanus jab, and died?

'Enough of the mutual admiration, ladies,' said Jared.

'Sorry to keep you waiting.' Maggie reached up and kissed her brother's cheek. 'But I have a reputation to keep up, having once been a model.'

He opened the front door and led the way, signalling to Maggie to sit in the front as Emma was going in the back with the baby and Owen.

Maggie said. 'I've yet to meet the groom. What's he like?'

'Jimmy seems to think a lot of him,' Jared said. 'I've only met him briefly and he was friendly enough.'

'He's had a lot on his plate this past year, according to Billy,' said Emma.

'Is he good looking?' asked Maggie.

Jared let in the clutch. 'You'll be seeing him soon enough, so you can make your own judgement.'

Maggie sighed. 'OK, I'll be patient. One question . . . if Jimmy's best man, who's giving Irene away?'

'Billy,' said Emma. 'And Deirdre is her maid of honour, so he and Dot and Deirdre left early for Pete's mother's house.'

'So now you know everything, stop nattering and let me concentrate on my driving,' said Jared.

Maggie sank back into the car seat and was silent for most of the journey, thinking of Tim and wondering if she would ever see him again.

Half an hour later, the car drew up outside English Martyrs Church in Litherland and they went inside. Maggie recognized many of the faces. Jeanette and her husband, Davy, the Gianellis, including their cousin, Lucia, and Sam and Lynne Walker. She noticed Jimmy and another man talking to a priest she recognized as Father Francis. Presumably the other man was the groom, Marty. He was fair haired, unlike his sister Peggy, who was a brunette. She was sitting in the second row from the front, next to her husband, Norm's twin brother Pete.

'Is Father Francis taking the service?' whispered Maggie.

'No, the parish priest will be officiating,' said Emma. 'Father Francis will be taking part. Apparently he's known Marty since he was a little boy. He grew up in his parish near Scotland Road and is still the family's parish priest.' She paused. 'Here's the priest who's taking the service.'

A priest in elaborate cream-embroidered robes came into view and began to converse with the groom and Father Francis. Then she noticed Pete's mother, coming down the aisle with a middle-aged man and a boy who looked to be about ten. They sat in the pew next to Pete and Peggy.

'Who are the man and the boy?' Maggie whispered.

'Irene and Jimmy's latest stepfather and his son, Patrick,' whispered Emma.

'Fancy having had two stepfathers and two stepbrothers, Billy and this boy, Patrick,' Maggie murmured.

'Some relationships are even more complicated,' said Emma.

Before Maggie could ask her what she meant by that, the groom and the best man took up their positions and so did the priests. She was aware of a slight commotion at the back of the church, and the next moment the organist launched into Wagner's bridal music from *Lohengrin*.

Maggie turned to get a look at Irene as she proceeded down the aisle on Billy's arm. She had always been a 'looker', thought Maggie, but now she looked stunning, utterly radiant. She seemed completely unaware of the people in the pews as her gaze was fixed firmly on her future husband, who had turned slightly and was smiling at his bride.

Maggie's heart seemed to jerk inside her breast because there was something familiar and heart-warming about the groom's smile. Maybe it was due to a facial likeness between him and Peggy? Then Maggie became aware of Deirdre glancing at her with a smile. She was followed by three younger bridesmaids and a pageboy. The girls were strangers to her, but with a sense of shock she recognized the pageboy.

At least she thought she recognized him, but perhaps she was mistaken. It was true that he had a definite look of Tim's son, Jerry. But if he was Jerry, then surely Tim should be here, too? Yet she had seen no sign of him.

The boy was gazing about him as if looking for someone. Was he looking for his father? Then suddenly his eyes met Maggie's. For a moment he looked puzzled, and then his face lit up. The smallest bridesmaid seized his blue satin sleeve and tugged on it.

Maggie's mind was in a whirl. The boy *was* Jerry! She remembered the first time she had seen him asleep in the basement room in London, and then in the railway carriage with his father. The way the boy had smiled at her surely meant he had recognized her too. What was he doing here in the role of a pageboy? She longed to ask someone, but already the priest was speaking.

Maggie did her best to concentrate on the age-old words of the marriage service, but the questions kept coming, although she realized that she was going to have to wait for answers until the ceremony was over. The service seemed to go on forever as it included a nuptial mass. At last it was over and the congregation streamed out of the church in the wake of the bride and groom.

Maggie seized her sister's arm as they came out into the sunlight. 'Who's the pageboy?'

'Ouch! You pinched me.' Dot rubbed her arm and gave Maggie a sharp look. 'Why d'you want to know?'

'Just curiosity,' she said hastily.

'Come off it. I've never known you to be that interested in kids before.'

'He reminds me of someone.'

'He's Marty and Peggy's nephew,' Dot said.

Maggie was so stunned by her sister's reply that for a moment she was dumbstruck. Then she found her voice. 'If you'll excuse me. I just want a word with Pete and Peggy.' She hurried away before Dot could question her further.

'Hi, you two!' She pinned on a smile as she joined the couple. 'Lovely wedding.'

'Lovely,' said Peggy. 'And not before time, too.'

'Why d'you say that?'

'It's too complicated to explain,' Peggy murmured.

Maggie was reminded of Emma's earlier comment about some relationships being more complicated than others. 'The pageboy is adorable,' she said.

Peggy rolled her eyes. 'Don't let Jerry hear you say that! We had a real job persuading him to dress up in blue satin. He said it was for cissies.'

Jerry! Maggie plunged in. 'He's your nephew, I believe, Peggy.'

'That's right. My other brother's son.'

Maggie's mouth went dry. 'I don't think I've ever met your other brother,' she said huskily.

'No, you wouldn't have,' muttered Peggy. 'He's been away a lot.'

'Is he here now?' Maggie asked.

'We don't have his address, so we couldn't get in touch.' She stiffened. 'Hell, look who's here!'

Before either Pete or Maggie could ask who she was talking about, Peggy rushed away.

'Who's she seen?' asked Maggie.

Pete did not answer because he was watching his wife's progress through the crowd. 'You'll have to excuse her,' he said. 'Peg's pregnant and she gets a bit over-excited now and again. We thought this day would never come; now it has, Peg doesn't want anyone spoiling it.'

'So who's this person who might spoil it?'

Pete did not answer because he was watching his wife. 'Damn!' he muttered. 'You'll have to excuse me, Maggie.' He limped off in Peggy's wake.

Maggie was about to go after him when she spotted Jerry, who was dragging an elderly woman by the hand. They were heading towards Peggy, who was talking to a young woman whom Maggie had a feeling she had seen before, but whose name she could not remember. Maggie was beginning to feel really queer. Her breath seemed to be shivering through her whole body and she felt angry and scared at the same time. She wanted out of there, but at that moment Jerry suddenly seemed to notice her. Their eyes met and he smiled.

She was just thinking of going over to him, when a group of people walked in front of her and cut Jerry off from her sight. By the time the laughing and talking crowd had passed, Maggie could see that the woman and Jerry had met up with Peggy and the young woman, and Pete had joined them as well. They appeared to be arguing, then suddenly they all looked in Maggie's direction. Her heart began to race and she had a sense of impending disaster. She had to get away.

She wasted no time heading for the gates and, despite wearing high heels that made it difficult for her to run, she managed to get halfway to the main road without anyone catching up with her. She felt so out of breath that she had to slow down and rest against a garden wall. It proved a mistake, because the next moment she felt a tap on her shoulder. She turned slowly and stared up at Pete.

'Where are you off to?' he panted.

'Why did you have to follow me?' she gasped.

'I think you know. You're the lady on the London–Liverpool train Jerry told us about.'

'So he did recognize me,' she whispered.

'Yes! Where's Tommy, Maggie?'

'Tommy! I-I don't know any Tommy.'

Pete looked disbelieving. 'Don't lie! You spoke to him on the train. You were in the same carriage with him and Jerry on the way back from London.'

Maggie felt sick. 'The man I spoke to told me that his name was Timothy Murphy,' she croaked.

'You're kidding me!'

'No, I'm not!'

Pete swore beneath his breath. 'I'm so sorry, Maggie. It's him who's the liar. His real name is Tommy McGrath and he's the black sheep of the family. Do you know where he's living?'

'No,' she whispered, sagging against the wall. 'He told me he and Jerry were living with his mother.'

'Another lie,' Pete said grimly. 'Jerry has been living with Marty and his little girl, Josie. Peggy and Irene have been helping to take care of him.'

'But why should he lie to me?' she cried. 'We were getting on so well.'

Pete sighed heavily. 'Oh, my God! He turned the charm on and you fell for him. You know what he did? He left Jerry on Marty's front step with a note asking him to take care of his son because he couldn't.'

Maggie did not want to believe what Pete was saying, but she sensed there was no denying the man she knew as Timothy Murphy was Tommy McGrath, and that he had told her a pack of lies.

'I can't understand why he lied to me,' she said in a bewildered voice.

'What else did he tell you?' asked Pete.

'He told me his mother was possessive and jealous of any woman who came into his life. I could understand that being reason enough for him to be reluctant to take me home to meet her.' She paused. 'If he's not living with her and Jerry, then he must be living at the garage.'

'Where is this garage?'

'I don't know! In Liverpool somewhere! He told me he's been working hard to build up a car-repair business. I'm sure he . . .

he's fond of Jerry. I could tell from the way he was with him on the train, and the boy seemed fond of him, too,' babbled Maggie.

'Maybe! But not so fond of him that he would take responsibility for his motherless son. The only person Tommy really cares about is himself. You have no idea of the pain and worry he's caused his family,' Pete said bitterly. 'I bet he never told you that he's wanted by the police.'

The colour drained from Maggie's face and she felt as if she was about to faint. 'Why d'you have to tell me that?' she whispered. 'Haven't I been hurt enough already? First by your brother and now by . . .' She swayed.

Pete hastened to prop her up. 'I'm sorry, Maggie, but everything I say is true. None of the family knew it at the time, but Tommy had married his wife Bernie secretly, only to leave her in the lurch when he was wanted by the police. He left the country, but no one knew where he'd gone until he turned up again last year. They believed he might be dead before that. To cap it all, he then borrowed a motorbike and went off with Bernie to Blackpool, where they had an accident in which she received a head injury. The owner, her cousin, reported him to the police for having stolen it. If you know how we can get in touch with him, then tell me.'

Maggie was horrified by Pete's revelations. Was it true? She did not want to believe it could be. 'He-he never gave me an address or phone number!' she cried, her voice breaking. 'He-he only ever phoned me at Jared's house, and we met in town or Formby.'

'Now why should he do that,' said Pete, 'if he didn't have something to hide?'

Maggie shook her head dumbly.

At that moment a young woman approached and tapped Pete on the shoulder. He turned and looked at here. 'Why couldn't you leave this to me, Monica?' He sounded exasperated.

'Because it's just as much my business as it is yours, Pete,' said Monica. Her face was flushed and now she was staring at Maggie. 'So this is the lady on the train who Tommy was chatting up?' She looked enquiringly at Pete.

'Who are you?' Maggie asked.

Pete answered her. 'Monica is Bernie's niece. She only learnt today that her aunt is dead. Neither Tommy nor Marty could bring themselves to tell Bernie's family.'

Maggie took a deep breath. 'The day I first met him he was on his way to the hospital to visit Bernie. The woman who was looking after Jerry told me that she was in a bad way. Jerry was asleep on the sofa and looked like he had been crying. I was very ill myself at the time, and I didn't see either of them after that until weeks later. It was the day we caught the same train to Liverpool. It was then that Jerry told me his mother had gone to Heaven. Tim . . . Tommy and I got talking, and when we reached Liverpool, we arranged to meet up in town a month later. We've been out a few times to the beach, a couple of concerts and the Cavern. He said his marriage was a mistake and most likely they would have separated sooner or later.' Her voice shook. 'Now I'd like to leave.'

'Where will you go?' Monica demanded. 'To him?'

Maggie looked at her scornfully. 'How can I go to him when I don't know where he is? I've had a terrible shock and I want to be left alone! I've told you everything I know.'

Maggie wasted no time putting some distance between herself and them. Her spiky heels hammered on the pavement as she hurried along. She came to an abrupt halt, teetering on the edge of the pavement on the main road as buses, cars, and even bicycles whizzed past. Her heart ached, and for a beat she thought of plunging into the traffic with reckless abandon. Then she thought: *how stupid is that?*

The next moment she felt a nudge in the ribs. 'I can't believe you don't know where he is,' said Monica. 'I'm coming with you. I've more than one bone to pick with him.'

Maggie gazed at her wearily. 'You can believe what you like.'

There was a lull in the traffic, and Maggie took off across the road at a run. Monica followed her; on reaching the other side, she grabbed Maggie's arm.

'I'm not going to give up,' Monica said. 'I'm going to stick with you.'

Maggie glared at her. 'Don't be stupid! You won't gain anything by it. Now let me go! You'll have people staring at us.'

'So what? I want you to know that I believe you now.'

Maggie stared at her suspiciously. 'What exactly do you believe?'

'That he hasn't told you where he lives, or anything much about his previous life. Because from what I know of Tommy, it's the kind of thing he would keep quiet about. He plays his cards close to his chest. Auntie Bernie was a bit that way too. You might know by now from Pete that the pair of them got married and didn't let either family know anything about it. And as Pete probably told you, none of us knew where Tommy was until last year. We thought he was dead. Little did we know that it was he who was Jerry's father. Aunt Bernie tricked Marty into marrying her and kept it secret that she had married Tommy before he disappeared, and that she was pregnant. She was a bit of a sexy piece before she let herself go. She had a helluva temper, and I know from having lived in the same house as Marty and Bernie and Gran that Marty regretted ever marrying her. I can believe Tommy felt the same way later.'

Although Maggie had been told most of this information only a short while ago, it sounded different coming from Monica. She let it sink in as she walked aimlessly along the pavement with Monica by her side.

After a few minutes she said, 'I take it that it's true what Pete said about Tommy being wanted by the police?'

'He borrowed a car from the garage where he worked and it was used in a robbery. He drove the car. That's how he managed to escape when the robbers were caught.'

Maggie gasped.

'My gran hates him. She blames him for the accident that caused Auntie Bernie's head injury, and for her marrying him in secret. Both of them knew that Gran would have been utterly against a marriage between them, because Tommy and my Uncle Dermot were always at daggers drawn when they were kids. She blames Tommy for every other mortal sin that Auntie Bernie committed, including her being a bigamist.'

'He never told me any of this,' Maggie muttered, deeply hurt as well as enraged by the extent of Tommy's duplicity.

'Obviously he couldn't face the truth and is pretending to himself it all happened differently.' Monica took a deep breath. 'Anyway, I don't know how I'm going to tell Gran and the rest of the family that Aunt Bernie's dead.'

'I'm sorry, but there isn't anything I can do about that,' said

Maggie. 'At least now I know why he lied to me. He felt he had to keep all this from me because he was ashamed.'

'Ashamed! I don't know if he's capable of shame.' Monica shook her head. 'So what are you going to do? If you understand his reasoning and still love him, then all I can say is that I feel sorry for you.'

'Did I say I loved him?' Maggie's eyes glinted like drowned sapphires. 'I don't need your pity. I've had to cope with worse than this.'

'So *what* are you going to do?'

'That's none of your business.'

Monica looked annoyed. 'You're as bad as Marty and Peggy for not telling me that Jerry was back with them. I've known Jerry since he was a baby and I often looked after him. I was really upset when Auntie Bernie and Tommy took him away.'

Maggie felt a twinge of pity for the girl as well as herself. 'Surely you can understand Marty and Peggy's reasoning if they didn't want their brother arrested?'

'Sure, but it's no excuse. We had a right to know that Auntie Bernie had died. Tommy should have told us at the time and we could have all gone to the funeral,' said Monica. 'I understand why he didn't. He knew Gran would have the police on him like a ton of bricks.'

And that could still happen if they were to trace his whereabouts, thought Maggie.

'So what are you going to do?' Monica asked again.

Maggie said vexedly, 'You don't take no for an answer, do you?'

'No, so are you going to tell me?'

'I'm still thinking about it. Now, if you don't mind. I have somewhere to go,' Maggie said, heading for the bus stop that would take her into Liverpool.

Monica followed her.

Maggie was glad to find scarcely anyone in the coffee bar. Lenny himself took her order. She was surprised by how hungry she felt, until she realized she had not eaten since breakfast and all she'd had then was a bowl of cereal. 'Where's Bobby?' she asked.

'Teacher-training college,' he replied. 'Although art is her thing, she reckons she's not good enough to make money out of it, so is having a go at what her mother wants her to do.'

'I hope she'll enjoy it. Anyway, it was you I wanted a word with.'

'I remember last time you wanted to have a word it was about Dorothy. Is that why you're all dolled up? Hoping to make an impression on her?' he teased.

She hesitated. 'I'm . . . I'm supposed to be at a wedding.'

'Then what are you doing here?'

She wondered whether to tell him the truth, but experienced one of those painful pangs just thinking about what she had discovered at the wedding. She wondered whether she should be feeling guilty about running away without a word of apology to the bride and groom; although no doubt Peggy and Pete would explain why she had left. Maggie just did not want to see the worry and horror on the faces of those who cared about her if she had stayed. She realized that Lenny was still standing by the table, waiting for her reply.

She swallowed the tightness in her throat. 'There was someone there I didn't want to meet.'

'It wouldn't be Pete's twin, would it? Name of Norm.'

Lenny's suggestion startled her, but she saw a way out of telling him the truth. 'You heard about him dumping me?'

'Lousy way to treat you.'

She agreed and changed the subject. 'I remember last time I came, your nephew was here. He was about to return to his regiment.'

Lenny smiled. 'That's right. He's here now.'

'Oh! Is he in the kitchen?' She hoped Josh would stay there if he was.

'That's right. He's a good lad is Josh. The army's been his family for a while, but he'll be getting demobbed in the not too distant future, which will fit in with my plans nicely.'

Maggie almost asked what his plans were, but decided it was really none of her business. Besides, it was Dorothy Wilson she was interested in.

'I heard Miss Wilson is back in Liverpool.'

'Yes, right now she's in rehearsals at the Royal Court. She's appearing in a play. An old-fashioned one, unlike these kitchen-sink dramas that appear to be all the rage right now.'

'They're not my kind of thing,' said Maggie dismissively. 'Although I did go and see *Look Back in Anger* at the flicks, but only because Richard Burton was in it and I love his voice.'

'Dorothy says it's him being Welsh, there's music in every word he speaks.'

'I'd agree with that.' Maggie rested her elbows on the Formica-topped table and forced herself to concentrate on the conversation. 'I've never heard him sing, though.'

'We can't all be singers,' Lenny said. 'I'd better go and see to your order.' He vanished into the kitchen.

Maggie crossed her fingers, hoping he wouldn't mention her name to Josh. If he came out and spoke to her, she was not sure how she would cope. She gazed about her, not wanting to think about their last exchange and the way she had reacted to his compliment. Instead she thought about Betty having worked here part-time and found herself wishing that her cousin was here now. Betty knew what suffering was and, despite them not always seeing eye to eye, she would have liked to have talked to her about Tim – or Tommy, as she now had to think of him.

'So what have you come here for?' asked Monica, sitting down on the chair across from Maggie.

Maggie put her face in her hands. 'Do you have to follow me?' she asked in a muffled voice.

'Yes,' Monica said, 'I'm still feeling hurt that I wasn't invited to the wedding, even though I now know the reason why.'

'You could always take my place,' said Maggie, glancing at her.

'I would if you'd swap clothes with me. That outfit you're wearing is real snazzy.'

'No dice.'

'Pity. I reckon I could knock the fellas dead if I could afford to dress like you do. Aren't you a model?'

'I used to be.'

'Why aren't you now?'

'I have my reasons. Why, are you interested in modelling? You're not bad looking, but you could do with being skinnier.'

'You're not skinny. Anyway, I don't want to be a model. I want to be a pop star. Did I hear you say that Tommy took you to the Cavern?'

'Yes. Have you been there?'

Monica nodded. 'I'm hoping to sing there one day.'

'Good luck to you.'

'Thanks!' Monica hesitated. 'You really don't want to talk about Tommy, do you? D'you think that's sensible? Wouldn't it be better if you got rid of all that anger inside you?'

Maggie stared at the other girl and longed for a cigarette. She reached for her handbag, only to remember she no longer smoked. She found herself thinking of that morning when Tommy had lit her cigarette for her, and felt tears well up inside her.

Monica said, 'Did you ever meet him here?'

'I wish you'd shut up.'

At that moment Josh came over to the table and placed a plate in front of Maggie. She glanced up at him, and then just as swiftly dropped her gaze to the plate of egg, bacon, beans and chips, and remembered the time when she had eaten barely enough to keep a sparrow alive. 'I shouldn't really be having this,' she said unsteadily. 'I'm . . . I'm getting fat.'

'Rubbish,' said Josh. 'Even though you don't care for my compliments, you've a nice figure. You don't want to look like a stick insect again.'

'You've been listening to Billy.' She cleared her throat. 'He used to call me a stick insect.'

'Shows how much you've changed,' said Josh.

'Yes, but I don't want to look like Humpty Dumpty either.'

'I'll help you eat it if you like?' suggested Monica, her eyes going from one to the other.

Josh glanced at her and smiled. 'You here again.' He gave his attention to Maggie once more. 'Most men like a woman with a bit of meat on her, kid. You want to hear Uncle Lenny rave about Shirley Bassey!'

'Who says I'm after pleasing a man?' Maggie picked up a fork and dug it into a chip. 'Does Miss Wilson know Lenny has a pash on Shirley Bassey?'

He grinned. 'She knows she's the only one for him. I know you don't like compliments. Maybe that's down to what that bloke Norm did to you? But I'm just letting you know that there's no need for you to be worrying about your figure. You're OK, kid.'

'Thanks,' said Maggie, seeing no need to explain that Lenny had got the wrong end of the stick, thinking she was still upset over Norm. She was aware that Monica was looking at her askance and willed the other girl not to mention Tommy.

Fortunately, Monica made no comment, only asking for a strawberry milkshake. Although, she did add, 'By the way, Maggie, Josh's only being nice to you so you'll come in here more often and order big meals to help his uncle get rich.'

'I don't blame him. I know what it's like being in Lenny's shoes,' she said. 'I've been running a tearoom up in Whalley all summer.'

'Have you now?' Josh looked at her with fresh interest. 'Well, if you're ever stuck for a job, just say the word to Uncle Lenny and you can help out here with the cooking.'

'No thanks,' Maggie said. 'My feet and back need a rest. What I do want is to have a go at acting. I'm hoping Miss Wilson will give me some advice.'

Josh rubbed his nose. 'I've heard her say that it's hard work and not as glamorous as you might think.'

'The same goes for modelling.'

'I daresay it does. Could be that Dorothy'll turn up before you go. I'll tell Uncle Lenny that you think you have what it takes to be a star of stage and screen. He can pass the message on.'

Maggie's colour rose. 'Do I sound that confident to you?'

'You need confidence,' Josh said. 'Anyway, you'll never know unless you give it a go. Enjoy your meal.' He placed the bill on the table and went to make Monica's milkshake.

'So you want to be an actress,' said Monica, reaching out and pinching a chip from Maggie's plate.

Maggie hit her hand with the back of the fork. 'D'you mind?'

'I'm hungry.'

'That's no excuse.' Maggie glared at Monica, and was taken aback when tears welled in the other girl's eyes. 'What's up with you? You've nothing to cry about. It's me whose heart is broken. You can have three chips,' Maggie shoved three to the side of the plate, 'and no more.'

Monica's tears vanished and she smiled. 'Thanks. You're not a bad skin. I hope you become rich and famous. It would be one in the eye for Tommy.' She munched on a chip. 'I bet you want to get back at him.'

'If you don't shut up about him, I'll stab you with this fork for real the next time,' Maggie muttered. 'Let me eat in peace.'

'OK! Don't get your knickers in a twist. I was going to ask what Josh meant when he mentioned Norm, but I'll mind my own business.'

'Good!' said Maggie.

Peace reigned, but Maggie could not get Tommy out of her mind. She ate everything on the plate. When Lenny returned he told her, 'It looks like you're out of luck. Dorothy just rang and said that she's going to be late, but that if you give me a phone number, she'll ring you later this evening.'

Maggie thanked him and wrote the Formby phone number down on a scrap of paper and handed it to him. 'I really appreciate this. Could you do me another favour? If a bearded man of about twenty-five, smartly dressed, comes in here any time this coming week looking for me, could you tell him I don't want ever to see him again.'

Lenny raised his eyebrows. 'That doesn't sound like Norm.'

'It isn't. But will you do what I ask?'

'OK! What's this one done to you? I don't like playing messenger boy.'

Monica said coaxingly, 'Do this for her, Lenny? She has a good reason for not wanting to face him, but she's too much of a lady to tell you why.'

'Does this bloke have a name?' asked Lenny.

Maggie hesitated and then tilted her chin. 'He has two actually. Tommy McGrath and Timothy Murphy. But who's to say that he mightn't give you a different one altogether.'

'He's an actor, is he?'

Maggie thought back to their times together, and said with a tremor in her voice, 'Yes, he definitely is.'

Twenty

The living room door burst open and Jared, Dot and Billy, followed by Emma with the children, entered the room. 'Thank God, you're here,' said Jared.

Maggie looked up from the *Stage* newspaper and said, 'I'm sorry if you were worried.'

'Are you all right?' asked Dot anxiously.

Emma said, 'Of course she's not all right. Otherwise she wouldn't have run away. I must admit I almost exploded when I heard that the boyfriend, Tim, was Tommy, Marty's brother.'

'If only that was all there was to know, it wouldn't be so bad,' said Billy. 'A lot of families have skeletons in their cupboards.'

'I'd like to get him by the neck,' said Jared quietly, 'and shake him until his teeth rattle with fear.'

'Didn't you hear what Pete said . . . that what Tommy is good at is avoiding getting hurt?' Dot flopped down on the sofa next to her sister. 'So did you come straight back here, Mags?'

'No, I went and had something to eat at Lenny's place,' Maggie said, folding the *Stage* and wishing Tommy was big and brave instead of such a coward.

'Good for you,' said Jared.

Owen ran over and climbed on Maggie's knee and snuggled up against her. She felt touched and soothed by the warmth and softness of his body against hers. 'I was hungry and I wanted to talk to Dorothy Wilson. I'd heard that she was back and I thought I might find her there.'

'But why did you want to talk to her?' asked Dot.

'I'm thinking about becoming an actress.'

'An actress!' Jared ran a hand through his thick brown hair. 'I think I'll have a whisky.'

Maggie watched her brother go over to the cocktail cabinet. 'It's not unusual for a model to go into acting.'

'What does *she* think of the idea?' asked Emma, sitting the other side of Maggie, with the baby in her arms.

'If you mean Dorothy, she was in rehearsals at the Royal Court, but she rang me here later.' Maggie paused with a hand to her mouth.

'And?' Her sister prodded her in the side.

Maggie blinked and cleared her throat. 'She invited me to watch her and the cast in rehearsal on Monday morning. I'm to meet her for breakfast at Lenny's, so-so we can have a ch-chat beforehand.'

'Well, that should take your mind off things,' Dot said, getting up and asking Emma if it was all right to make a pot of tea.

'Of course,' said Emma before turning to Maggie. 'Does this mean you'll be leaving us?'

Maggie stroked Owen's hair back from his forehead with an unsteady hand. 'I don't know anything for certain yet.'

'It's likely, though, isn't it?' said Billy, accepting a whisky from Jared. 'By the way, something you should do is write an apology to Irene and Marty.'

Maggie nodded, thinking she would find the task difficult, but she wanted to be seen to be doing the right thing in everyone's eyes.

'What if it means living in London again?' Emma asked.

'And what about the cottage?' said Jared. 'Although at least summer's over and the tearoom and shop won't be doing much business until next Easter.'

'I could still go up there occasionally.' Maggie felt more nervous than she had felt since she had learnt of Tim's deception. 'I could be rubbish at acting.'

'True, you might,' said Dot, standing in the doorway holding the tea caddy. 'On the other hand, you can always try singing and dancing and end up in the chorus line. You've a pretty face, so your looks will stand you in good stead.'

'Thanks a lot, sis,' muttered Maggie, thinking that to be in the chorus line was the last thing she wanted.

Maggie need not have worried. At least not as far as the chorus line was concerned. Although she was possibly more worried that Tommy might just feel brave enough to seek her out at Lenny's, but the fact that he had not telephoned her had now convinced her that he had no intention of seeing her again. As soon as she had mentioned the wedding invitation over the phone, he had realized that he would be unmasked and so had decided to stay out of trouble. After all, running away from tricky situations was what he was good at. She had to put him out of her mind and look to the future.

Come Monday morning, Maggie was awake while it was still dark, preparing for her meeting with the famous actress. By the time she arrived at the coffee bar, she was trembling with nerves and excitement at the thought of the next few hours, and could remember only half of what she had planned to ask Dorothy Wilson.

Again, she need not have worried, because Dorothy had plenty to talk about as they breakfasted with Lenny. Not only was there the gossip from the theatre for Maggie to take in, but also plenty of Hollywood gossip about film stars Maggie had only ever thought of seeing on the silver screen.

There were also photographs of Dorothy on set to view, posing with her various co-stars in her latest film. Dorothy showed her sketches of the costumes she would be wearing for the play she was rehearsing.

'I thought the clothes would interest you, what with you having been a model,' she said.

Of course, she was interested! Wouldn't most women be? thought Maggie.

Once at the theatre, Maggie found herself being introduced to the stage manager, the producer, the general wardrobe mistress and the props and runner, as well as Dorothy's leading man. Then she sat in the stalls to watch the rehearsal. Parts of it were enjoyable, while others were worrying, especially when the director yelled at one of the young actors for forgetting his lines.

She was aware of a sinking feeling, remembering the difficulty she had found even remembering how to spell words out aloud in spelling tests at school. As for learning poetry, she had been rubbish. Why had she ever believed she could be an actress when she had such a terrible memory? She said as much to Dorothy after the rehearsal was over.

'It's true that not being able to remember lines is definitely a setback but that doesn't mean you should despair. Learning lines needs practice and isn't insurmountable,' said Dorothy. 'What you really need to ask yourself is: is it the dream of becoming a top-notch actress that attracts you, or is it something extra-special that draws you to a way of life you've seen just a little of here in this theatre?'

For a moment Maggie was lost for words, and then she said carefully, 'If I'm honest I'd have to say that I thought of being an actress as something I would be able to do if I ever had to give up modelling, and that's what has happened. I've always enjoyed dressing up and being the centre of attention, and you have to admit that in a way that's what being up on that stage is all about.'

'It's about more than that, Maggie!' Dorothy said with a mixture of amusement and annoyance. 'Although you're not the only hopeful who has thought like that.'

'Then it's about escaping into another world. Not being yourself, but making believe that you're someone else far more interesting, and getting paid lots of dosh for doing so,' suggested Maggie.

'There is that.' Dorothy laughed and patted Maggie's hand. 'But you're in for a rude awakening if you're expecting lots of dosh at the beginning of a career. In comparison with all those who enter the profession, lots drop out within a short time and get what's known as a "proper job" because they just can't live on what they earn. It took me years to earn a decent wage, and even longer to make the big bucks.'

Maggie was disappointed. 'But surely it's easier to become famous these days? What with television?'

Dorothy smiled. 'One's face can become so familiar that one becomes a household name, but also people can get bored with seeing the same person too often. Television is also completely different to stage work. Just as the stage is not the same as film-making. Sorry if I'm disillusioning you,' she added.

'I'm sorry too,' Maggie said mournfully. 'I'd fixed my mind on working with you in repertory theatre. Getting away from home, going from place to place where I'd meet different people.'

Dorothy fixed her with a thoughtful stare. 'Well, if that's what you want, then there's nothing stopping you from working behind the scenes. With your interest and knowledge of clothes, you could be my personal dresser. I should imagine, too, you're quite an expert when it comes to make-up. I generally do my own when working in the theatre, but I'd be happy to give you a try-out. You won't get paid much, but you won't find me too demanding and just might find it fun.'

Maggie's expression brightened. 'How long would you want me in that role?'

'It depends. It's possible the play will get to London and if it does . . . who knows how long it might run. One thing is for certain, I'd have to leave it next spring; I'm doing a musical in

New York next year and I've a contract for another two films, so I'll be going to Hollywood.'

Maggie said enviously, 'You do have an exciting life.'

'It's not all excitement, sweetie.' Dorothy's expression was world-weary. 'It's damned hard work and there're those one misses when one's away so much.' She looked wistful. Then she straightened her shoulders and added, 'Still, mustn't complain. Have to make hay while the sun shines, because one never knows when it might suddenly come to an end.'

'I hope it won't be for years and years. You're such a good actress,' Maggie said sincerely.

Dorothy chuckled. 'Depends on how well I wear, sweetie. Now you'd best be off. Speak to your brother about what I've said, and let me know in a day or two whether you want to come with me as my dresser and general helper. You can always do a bit of walk-on work, too.'

Maggie thanked her and, with a tarrah, went off to catch the train. Her life was about to take a different path from the one she envisaged a year ago when Norm was still in her life. But she was over him now and, although she knew it would be some time before she could honestly say she felt nothing for the man she had known as Tim Murphy, surely one day that time would come, too?

Twenty-One

Monica lifted the knocker and banged it three times. When nobody came, she banged again even harder.

'All right, I'm coming. No need to knock the door down,' said a female voice.

The door opened and Monica recognized Pete's mother. 'Are Pete and Peggy in?'

'No, they're at Marty's. What is it you want?'

Monica's face fell. 'To talk to them. I'll go there.' She turned away, 'Hang on. I thought someone said that the newlyweds had gone away for a few days,'

'They have and won't be back just yet. Pete and Peggy are staying at their house. Is this about Marty's brother?'

'I'd rather talk to Pete and Peggy, if you don't mind, Mrs Marshall.'

'I don't mind, luv, but you do know that Peggy's having a baby and we don't want her getting upset.'

Monica stared into the concerned eyes in the wrinkled face framed by iron-grey frizzy hair and said, 'I think Peggy is tougher than you and Pete credit her for. Still, I don't mind talking to you. I'd have had to walk there as I haven't the coppers to spare for the fare, and I'm blinking tired. I've heard there's no flies on you, so I think you'll give me a sensible answer. Can I come in?'

'Well, I'm not going to keep you standing on the step if it's a private matter,' said Gertie with a faint smile.

Monica stepped over the threshold and followed the older woman up the lobby and into the kitchen. 'Sit down,' Gertie said. 'Cup of tea?'

'No, it's OK. I don't want to be too long. Mam will be wondering where I am and Gran is due home this evening. One of my aunts has had a baby.' Monica perched on the arm of the sofa. 'I presume your Pete told you what happened at the wedding?'

'He and Peggy told me that Maggie has been going out with Peggy's younger brother without realizing it, and that he'd lied his socks off to her,' said Gertie, lowering herself into an armchair drawn up in front of the fire. 'He thought I'd have an interest because Maggie had been seeing Pete's twin while she was in London.'

'I didn't know that.' Monica looked thoughtful.

'Sorry as I am to admit it, he dropped her for another girl who we've yet to meet.' Gertie sniffed. 'Apparently they're engaged. I'm just hoping the pair of them don't turn up and tell me they've already been married in a registry office and didn't want any fuss, so didn't invite us.'

'You've given me an answer to something I've been wondering about,' said Monica. 'Maggie doesn't seem to do well with men, despite her being so good looking.'

'That's how it is with some people.' Gertie leaned forward.

'You're not so bad looking yourself. Anyway, what have you to tell me, luv?'

'I know where Tommy is and I thought Pete would know the best thing to do with the information, with Marty away on his honeymoon.'

Gertie drew in a breath, but before she could speak there was the sound of a key in the front door. A few moments later her eldest son, Dougie, entered the kitchen. 'Hello, Ma!' he said. 'I've just come to see if you can babysit for us tomorrow evening.'

Her face lit up. 'Hello, son. You're just the person we need.'

'No,' said Monica, staring at the man in police uniform and getting to her feet. 'I can't tell him!'

'What can't you tell me?' asked Dougie. 'Speak up, girl!'

Monica shook her head and hurried out of the house.

Dougie stared at his mother. 'What was that all about?'

She sighed. 'I can't tell you.'

He frowned. 'Just tell me, Ma. I think I know that girl. She has some link with Peggy's family.'

'I don't know all of it,' Gertie said hesitantly. 'But you'll know that Peggy's brother, Tommy, got himself mixed up with a bad lot and drove the getaway car in a robbery.'

'Yes, I know that. He disappeared and the others were caught.' Dougie's pale blue eyes were intent on his mother's face. 'Has he been spotted, because you do know he's still wanted for that crime?'

She nodded.

'Well?' asked Dougie, after a minute or so had passed and his mother was still silent.

She sighed. 'Monica has just told me she knows where he is.'

He frowned. 'So why did she come here, instead of reporting it at the police station?'

'She came to tell Peggy and our Pete.'

Dougie's frown deepened. 'Does she think they'll help him to get away?'

'I don't know what was going on in her mind, although I wouldn't have thought so.' She shook her head.

'He's broken the law and needs to come to trial. Where does the girl live?'

'I don't know all the ins and outs of it. I do know Tommy's father was an old sod and told the lad never to darken his door again.'

'That's beside the point. Where does the girl live?' he repeated.

Gertie pressed her lips together and did not speak for several moments. Then she said, 'His mother loves him, and I'm not going to be responsible for Tommy being put behind bars by you.'

Dougie groaned. 'Come on, Ma. If you didn't want me to do something, you shouldn't have told me any of this. Spill the beans. I don't want to arrest you for obstructing the course of justice.'

She gasped and folded her arms across her chest. 'Your father would turn in his grave if he heard you threaten me. I've always been proud of you, but what kind of son is it who threatens his poor ol' mother with imprisonment?'

Dougie flushed to the roots of his flaxen hair. 'And what kind of mother is it who takes the side of a criminal?' he said gruffly, turning away. 'I'm going.'

'Where are you going?'

'Two can play at this game, Ma,' he muttered, and left.

Monica ran as if she was being chased by a banshee. Her grandmother had frightened her with tales of these unearthly Irish female spirits when she was a little girl. Was she making a mistake thinking that Pete and Peggy were the right people to speak to about Tommy? Maybe she should have confronted Tommy herself and told him just what she thought of him hurting so many people by his behaviour? She had rejected the thought of hurrying home and telling her mother Cissie, who was one of Bernie's elder sisters, of his whereabouts, because she would have told her brothers, and Monica – having told them of their youngest sister's death – did not like to think about what they would do to Tommy if they got their hands on him.

At last the library was in sight. She turned the corner and went up the street where Marty and Irene's house was situated. She banged on the door. It opened that quickly, she thought Pete must have been in the parlour and seen her coming.

'What are you doing here, Monica?' he asked.

'I've something to tell you. Can I come in?' she gasped, stumbling over the threshold.

Pete grabbed her arm to prevent her from falling. Then he helped her up the lobby and into the kitchen. 'Look who's here, Peg.'

Peggy set the lemon-coloured matinee coat she was knitting aside and stared at Monica. 'What's up?'

'It's your Tommy,' Monica said breathlessly. 'I know where his garage is.'

Both Peggy and Pete went very still.

Then Peggy asked, 'Where?'

Pete said, 'Have you told anyone else?'

'I spoke to your mam, but then your big brother had to come in, didn't he! So I beat it. Can I have a drink? I'm parched.'

Peggy said, 'I'll make a cup of tea.' She hurried out into the back kitchen but was back in moments. 'So what did Dougie have to say?'

'Pete's mam thought he was just the person we needed, but I didn't.'

Pete and Peggy exchanged glances. 'D'you think your mam will have told him what I said to her?' Monica asked.

Pete sat down and stretched out his damaged leg. 'Depends on what he said to her.'

'I didn't tell your mam where Tommy is,' said Monica swiftly. 'I wanted to tell you two first. I thought you'd know what to do.'

For a moment Pete looked at her blankly, and then Peggy said, 'You surprise me, Monica. I thought after what happened with your Aunt Bernie, you'd want Tommy punished.'

Monica sat down on the sofa. 'That's how most of the family feel, but in my opinion there's worse people around who get away with murder. I've had time to think. Aunt Bernie was as much to blame for what happened to her as he was. In fact, I bet she was behind it all.'

'So what d'you want me to do?' asked Pete, puzzled.

'Warn him he should get out of Liverpool before it's too late.'

'Surely you could have done that?' asked Peggy.

Monica rolled her eyes. 'Are you mad? Gran would kill me if it got out I'd thought of helping him. Pete's got to do it. He has a car so he can drive into the garage and speak to him there. But watch out for the dog.'

'Tommy's got a dog?' exclaimed Peggy.

Monica nodded.

Pete was staring at her, as if he could not take his eyes off her. 'After all you said the day of the wedding, I feel I have to ask you: do you actually like Tommy?'

She flushed. 'I don't hate him. The one I can't stand is my Uncle Dermot. He's a creep. And he'd love it if my uncles could get their hands on Tommy, beat him up and see him behind bars. I know Tommy's broken the law and he's a lying so-and-so, but he didn't physically hurt that jeweller, did he?'

Pete was silent.

'None of us are perfect,' said Peggy, placing the teapot on a cork mat on the table and staring at Pete.

'All right!' said Pete. 'I know I'm no angel, and it could have been me in a juvenile court a few years ago if it hadn't been our Dougie who found me when I fell off that windowsill. It could be that he'll need reminding of that if he goes looking for Tommy.'

Monica stared at him from beneath drooping eyelids. 'So what are you going to do?'

'Tell me where Tommy is. How did you manage to trace him?'

She told them how she had seen Tommy enter Lenny's coffee bar and had followed him when he left. She made no mention of how sick and worried he had looked at the time.

Pete said, 'OK! I'll see what I can do.'

Relieved, Monica said, 'I'd best be going. Mam will be wondering where I am.'

'I'll give you a lift to the corner of your street,' said Pete.

Tommy was working late. He found it helped to keep his mind occupied, as he hated to think that it was definitely all over between him and Maggie. He had called in at Lenny's coffee bar on the Monday after Marty's wedding and asked after her. The owner's response had been enough to convince Tommy that his son had been at the wedding for certain, and that someone had told Maggie all about Jerry's father.

A few weeks ago, when she had mentioned on the telephone about having an invitation to his brother's wedding, he had felt sick to the stomach. It had been a relief when the pips went. He had been at a loss what to do, unable to face telling her the truth about his past. He had told himself that it was best not to get in touch with her again.

But, after a few days, he had begun to toy with the idea of writing to her, but his injured hand had made that difficult. Still, he had made several attempts at putting pen to paper, but the truth put him in such a bad light that he had given up. Instead he had decided that it was better for both of them if he called it a day and stayed away from her.

It was only on the evening of Marty's actual wedding day, when Tommy had gone out and got drunk, did it occur to him that Maggie might not actually have attended the wedding. Since the phone call, he had been expecting her to discover the facts about his past at his brother's wedding, knowing there was a strong possibility of Jerry being there and Maggie recognizing him. He should have caught a train then and visited her and told her the truth – or at least some of it.

Too late now. Her brother would know all about him, so Tommy didn't dare show his face in Formby. Jared would want to beat him into pulp for hurting his sister. Perhaps the best place would be at the cottage? Presumably she would be returning there in the near future. She was a reasonable woman; she could have calmed down and might be prepared to listen to his side of the story. Although, whichever way he looked at it, Tommy knew he had acted like a louse and he would not blame her if she told him to get lost. There was no way he could redeem himself in her eyes.

He finished the job, eased his shoulders and stretched before beginning to put his tools away. Suddenly Fang began to bark and Tommy could hear the sound of an engine. Thinking it could be a late customer, he hurried outside and opened the Judas gate and stepped on to the pavement.

Some older lads were kicking a ball around, there were girls playing hopscotch, and several smaller boys were playing marbles in the gutter. A car had parked on the other side of the road and, as he watched, the driver's door opened and a man eased himself out with the help of a walking stick. Tommy recognized him almost immediately and his heart began to thud. He thought of going back into the yard and locking the gate, but decided he needed information, so he crossed the road.

'How the hell did you find me?' he asked.

Pete stared at him, unable to disguise his irritation with his wife's youngest brother. 'I thought that might be the first thing you'd say. I tell you now, I wouldn't be here if it weren't for Peggy and Monica.'

'Monica!' Tommy scrubbed his beard with a hand that shook slightly. 'What's she got to do with this?'

'She followed you from Lenny's. She wanted to warn you to get out of Liverpool but did not want to do it herself. Her uncles are after your hide, now they know Bernie's dead, and would have your guts for garters if they get their hands on you.'

Tommy's stomach took a nosedive. 'I'm not scared of them,' he muttered, thrusting his thumbs in the pockets of his overalls. 'I'm doing well here and I've no plans to leave. Anyway, I find her grandmother much more terrifying.'

'I don't blame you, because she really hates you,' said Pete, his eyes glinting. 'Even so, if I were you, I'd seriously consider moving on. The police are bound to get to know that you're back sooner or later.'

Tommy paled. 'You haven't told your brother about me or Inspector Walker?'

'No, I bloody haven't,' snapped Pete. 'But Monica visited Ma's and my brother turned up. He knows Monica knows where you are. He could have her in for obstructing the course of justice for not telling him your whereabouts, and she could end up in jail. Is that what you want?'

Tommy cleared his throat. 'What d'you think I am? She's a good skin, is Monica. What about our Marty? Does he know where to find me?'

'He's still on his honeymoon. Peggy and I are looking after Josie and Jerry.'

A muscle quivered in Tommy's cheek and he mumbled, 'That's good of you.'

'If you're interested, all this happened because Jerry and Maggie recognized each other at Marty's wedding. A pity you couldn't have been there. He remembers her as the lady on the train. He thought she would be able to tell us where you were, only you were too bloody crafty to give her an address or a phone number, or even your real name. So much for trusting the woman you've been dating. You've hurt her, you know? And you've brought nothing but shame on your family.'

Tommy flinched. 'Don't hold back, will you!'

'I could say a bloody sight more, but I've said what I came to say.' Pete turned away.

Tommy stared after him a moment, and then slowly crossed the road towards the garage. He was about to go through the Judas gate when he heard the roar of an engine. He looked over his shoulder and saw a car turn the corner from Lark Lane. The boys playing football made no move to get out of the way, but the car did not slow down so they suddenly had to scatter. The boys playing marbles in the gutter did not move quickly enough, though, and one tripped over the kerb, right into the path of the approaching vehicle. Tommy barely hesitated; he tore across the pavement and pushed the boy out of the way. The car hit Tommy and he was flung through the air and crashed into the yard gates. The vehicle did not stop but carried on.

'Bloody hell!' cried one of the girls, staring after the car, while another girl helped up the little boy Tommy had saved. A couple of the lads playing football exchanged looks and ran off, while another grabbed the hand of another little lad who had grazed his knees and was crying.

Pete had managed to note the licence plate of the car; his heart was thudding in his chest as he limped over to where Tommy now lay, sprawled on the ground. A dog was licking his face. Those children who had remained gathered around Tommy, as Pete, with difficulty, managed to get down on one knee. He pushed the mongrel away.

'Is he dead, mister?' asked one of the girls.

Pete fumbled for Tommy's pulse. At first he had difficulty finding it, and then it was there beneath his fingers. 'No, he's still alive. Can you go and dial 999, love?'

Both girls left with a skip and a jump, and then broke into a run in the direction of Lark Lane.

Pete had given no thought to the possibility of the police turning up on the scene, but a policeman came a few minutes before the ambulance arrived. He didn't even want to make a guess at the injuries Tommy might have sustained. In fact, he would have liked nothing better than to have climbed into his car and driven off, but he knew he was going to be the main witness at this hit-and-run scenario, so he had to stay. He was not looking forward to telling Peggy, especially given her condition, about what had happened to her brother. For all Tommy was the scallywag of the family, he knew that blood was thicker than water where the McGrath family were concerned.

Several hours later, Pete was tucking into homemade minced steak pie, chips and peas. 'It could have been worse,' he said.

'Tell Mam that,' Peggy said, resting her elbows on the table. 'A concussion and fractured pelvis and torn shoulder ligaments. She'll have a fit. And whatever you do, don't go mentioning the police questioning Tommy when we go and see her.'

'Fortunately the bobby from Lark Lane Police Station didn't recognize him. It was one of the kids who told him that his name was Timothy Murphy, and pointed out it was painted on the garage door.'

'Well, let's hope they don't discover he's actually Tommy McGrath.' Peggy sighed. 'I wish we knew what your Dougie was up to.'

'You don't think I'm going to tell him about today, do you? And he doesn't know where Monica lives, or what her surname is,' said Pete. 'If he comes here we tell him that we haven't seen her.'

'Are we going to be looking after the dog until he gets out of hospital?' asked Peggy.

Pete glanced through the window into the yard, where Fang was curled up on an old bit of blanket inside a cut-down cardboard box. It had scoffed some mince and broken dog biscuits in gravy, and was now sleeping with one eye open. 'I suppose we could have left him in the garage to guard the place, but it would have meant arranging someone to feed it every day, and who do we trust? The only other option was that I visit the place every day, and I don't fancy that. Anyway, Marty will be home tomorrow, he can make the decisions.'

'The kids are going to miss the dog when it goes.'

Pete shrugged. 'Tough luck.'

There was a silence.

'You should drop in at your mother's and let her know what's happened,' Peggy suggested.

'It can wait.'

'What about Monica?'

'I'm leaving her to Marty. There's no way I'm going round to the grandmother's house.'

Peggy sighed yet again. 'What about Maggie? Do we let her know what's happened?'

'She's finished with him for being such a lying sod. Let her get on with her life.'

Peggy stood up. 'She might hear about it from someone else. News gets around. If Irene was to tell Jimmy and he told Deirdre or Billy—'

Pete said soothingly, 'Don't be getting ahead of yourself, love. Think of the baby. Even if Billy told Dot and she told Jared and Emma, it doesn't say that they'll tell Maggie. If she was my sister, I wouldn't mention Tommy in her company.'

'All right, you seem to have all the answers,' Peggy said tartly.

Pete could have told her that there was something that was worrying him and there wasn't anything he could do about it. Tommy risking his life by saving the life of a little boy, and getting injured in the process, was the kind of local-interest story that appealed to journalists. If they found out about it and they printed a photo of Tommy, who knew what might happen.

Twenty-Two

'You should see this in the *Echo*, Marty?' Irene shoved the newspaper that she had bought from a vendor in Southport Railway Station under her husband's nose. They were on their way home from Blackpool.

'Hang on! You're holding it too close.' Marty grabbed the open newspaper and placed it on his knee.

Irene poked her finger at a photograph. 'I'm sure that's your Tommy!' she whispered, shooting a glance at the two women in the railway compartment to see if they were listening. 'Who d'you think is responsible for putting his photo in the *Echo*?'

Marty frowned. 'Give us a chance to read the article beneath it.'

She fell silent, watching his expression as he read. When he lifted his head, she said, 'Well?'

'You never know the minute when something completely unexpected is going to happen.' Marty's expression was one of reluctant admiration. 'He saved some kid from being hit by a car and was injured himself. He's in Smithdown Road Hospital.' He folded the newspaper and handed it back to her.

'Do they give his name?'

'Timothy Murphy,' he answered in a low voice.

Irene stared at her husband and mouthed, 'What are we going to do?'

Marty made no reply. She realized that, most likely, she would not know what he'd decided until they left the train. But he did not leave the train along with her when they reached Seaforth and Litherland Station, but told her he would take a bus to the hospital when he reached Liverpool. She had no choice but to fall in with his plans.

When Irene arrived at the house, it was to find Peggy preparing a meal for their homecoming and the children playing ball in the back yard. Without delay, Irene showed her the newspaper. 'Do you know anything about this?' she asked.

Peggy nodded. 'Where's Marty?'

'He's gone straight to the hospital. Is Pete coming here to pick you up?'

'Yes.' Peggy wiped her hands on her apron. 'But sit down and I'll make a cuppa and tell you everything I know.'

It did not take Peggy long to unburden herself, because Irene did not interrupt her with questions. Peggy had only just finished talking when Pete arrived. He had the *Echo* with him and, after greeting Irene and being told where Marty had gone, he said, 'This is what I feared. Despite the beard, I bet someone recognizes Tommy.'

Peggy stood up. 'I'll have to go to Mam's.'

Pete put his arm around her. 'I thought you'd want to do that, but maybe you should have something to eat first. Think of the baby.'

Peggy hesitated and then nodded. The children were summoned inside, following by Fang. They greeted Irene with cries of delight and hugs. She looked at the dog askance, rolling her eyes when she was told it belonged to Tommy. The children asked whether she had brought them anything, and where was Daddy? Irene told them they would have to wait until after dinner for their presents. Words that ensured they sat at the table without delay and ate their dinner without any fuss.

Peggy and Pete left soon after, and Irene produced a jigsaw and a toy tram as well as sticks of Blackpool rock. She told them they could only have a small piece each before cleaning their teeth and getting ready for bed.

'But we want to see Daddy,' said Josie, jumping up and down.

Irene promised that, as soon as he arrived, he'd be up the stairs to read them a story, but if they went to bed in half an hour like good children, she would read them a story then.

Irene settled down to await Marty's return. By nine o'clock he had still not arrived home, and she was just considering phoning his mother's house when the telephone rang. She picked up the receiver and recognized Dot's voice.

'Hi, Dot!'

'You arrived back safely then,' said Dot.

'Yes, what can I do for you?'

'Nothing! I was just ringing to see that you'd got back all right and to ask if everything's okay.'

Irene hesitated, wondering what Dot and Billy knew, although Peggy had not mentioned having spoken to them. 'Have you seen this evening's *Echo*?'

'No, we only get the *Formby Times*. Why, is there something interesting in it?'

Irene cleared her throat and read out the article over the phone. Dot gave a low whistle. 'Wow! Who'd have believed it!'

'My thoughts exactly.' Irene told her that Marty had gone to the hospital, and of his fears. 'If someone does snitch on Tommy, then you can bet it'll be leaked and be in all the newspapers tomorrow.' Irene ad-libbed: '*Hero who saves child's life is man wanted by the police in connection with driving the getaway car in a robbery five years ago.*'

'You're not thinking that Maggie would shop him because he's lied his head off to her?' said Dot.

'No, I wasn't thinking that at all,' she said. 'But I'm hoping she doesn't read the *Echo*. Don't you think it would be best for her if she doesn't start feeling sorry for him? At the moment there are those who really do think he's a hero.'

'You mean she's better forgetting all about him?'

'Don't you? I know I've never really had a good word to say about Tommy in the past, and I don't believe him doing one good deed wipes away all the selfish stuff he's done but . . .'

'I won't mention any of this to our Maggie. If she finds out herself, that's different. As it is, she's starting a new life.'

'Doing what?' Irene asked.

'As Dorothy Wilson's dresser and assistant. Maggie's brilliant with clothes, style and make-up. She might even get to do some acting. They'll be travelling in some play around the country and will probably end up in London. After that, who knows? Maggie has told me that Dorothy is going to Hollywood next year. Who's to say she mightn't end up going with her? Give our best to Marty,' added Dot, and rang off.

Marty was not having a good time of it that evening. His first port of call had been to the hospital in the hope of seeing Tommy, only to be told that visiting hours were over and a policeman was with his brother. That information was enough to send Marty to his mother's house. He arrived to find his youngest sister feeding her baby, and was told not to worry about their mother as Lily would take care of her. Peggy and Pete had been there already and had told them what had happened with Tommy.

'Me and Mam and the baby are going to have a nice little holiday in Ireland, away from the gossip, with some old friend of Mam's. By the time we get back, hopefully it will all have blown over,' said Lil. 'It's not as if we've been sheltering him and have broken the law.'

Marty could see his younger sister's point of view, but did not think his mother would cast aside her younger son as quickly as his sister was prepared to do. He left and went to visit Father Francis, who had already seen the article in the newspaper and had planned to call on Tommy in hospital, as well as visit his mother.

'If someone does identify our Tommy from that photograph, I'd like to know who it is,' said Marty, grim-faced.

'Have you any ideas who might do so?' asked Father Francis.

'I did wonder about Maggie Gregory. Apparently Pete said she was knocked sideways when she discovered that he had lied about his name and a lot of other stuff.'

The priest frowned. 'I know Maggie. She's one of those young people who used to visit my sister's house for their musical evenings. I wouldn't have thought she'd get involved with the police. Anyone else?'

'Bernie's family. Especially her mother and brothers. They would be cock-a-hoop if he was arrested and sent to prison.'

Father Francis sighed. 'Of course, there are others who would be pleased to see your brother behind bars. The crooks who were jailed, for instance.'

'But they're still in prison.'

'They have family, no doubt, who just might want revenge,' Father Francis said heavily, getting to his feet. 'Anyway, Marty, I'll have to see you out. I have a sick parishioner I must visit. Keep in touch.'

Marty thanked him and left.

He paused outside the presbytery, wondering whether to get in touch with Inspector Walker, who knew Tommy's background. If his brother was arrested, Sam Walker was the person most likely to know what would happen to him next. Might he be moved to a prison hospital, or would they leave him where he was and keep an eye on him until his case came to trial? And what kind of prison sentence was he likely to be given? Marty wished he was back in Blackpool on his honeymoon. Then he squared his shoulders and decided to visit Sam Walker tomorrow.

Irene had his supper on the table within minutes of Marty entering the house. 'How did things go?' she asked.

He told her.

She went over to the sideboard and took out a bottle and poured a glass of port apiece. 'I wonder how many years inside Tommy is looking at if he is arrested.'

'I wonder.' Marty downed the contents of the glass in one go. 'By the way, don't talk about this in front of the kids. I don't want Jerry getting upset.'

Irene said indignantly, 'As if I would, love. I do know some-thing about kids, you know. I think the poor lad has been through enough already.'

'I'm sorry! I know you're great with kids.' Marty covered her hand with his. 'I just wish Tommy had stayed in London and not brought his problems here. I feel sorry, too, for young Maggie.'

Irene's fingers laced through her husband's. 'Dot phoned me. She told me that Maggie has got herself a whole new life already, working for Dorothy Wilson. You know, the actress?'

'Of course I know who she is.'

'Maggie's going to be travelling around the country with her and the rest of the theatre group, with some play that will most likely end up in London. Then our famous actress is off to Hollywood in the spring and, who knows, Maggie just might go with her. So don't be worrying about her. She'll get over it.'

Twenty-Three

London: November 1959

Maggie experienced stirrings of apprehension mixed with pleasure as she and Dorothy stepped out of a taxi and climbed the steps to the front door of Mrs Cooling's lodging house. She recalled the thrill of those first months in London, when everything was new and exciting. But those happy memories were tinged with sadness and disappointment that things hadn't entirely worked out the way she would have liked. She also found herself thinking of Tommy, remembering how he had helped her when she'd collapsed in the smog, and then again outside the corner shop when he had lit her cigarette, and that fateful meeting on the train to Liverpool.

She sighed inwardly, thinking she had done a good job of putting him out of her mind while on her travels, despite Lenny mentioning an article in the *Echo* about Tommy before she had left Liverpool. She had thought of asking her family if any of them had seen it, only then decided to see if they would mention it to her. But nobody had, and she could only believe that was because they thought she had been hurt enough by Tommy. She wondered, not for the first time, who had recognized him and reported him to the police. Could it have been Monica? The thought made her feel uncomfortable, but she told herself that he had taken the risk of being recognized when he returned to Liverpool, and she was not going to blame herself or the other girl for his arrest. He had caused her enough pain as it was; she had to continue focusing on what she was doing now.

It had occurred to Maggie earlier, when the train pulled into Paddington, that she was most likely going to pay a price for returning to London. November was not the best time to arrive in the Big Smoke. The play had been a success in Liverpool, Manchester, Doncaster, Birmingham, Coventry and Oxford. In fact, wherever it had played, Dorothy had received standing ovations for her performance. It was possible the play might run and run through winter.

Maggie was not only worrying about her own health, but feeling more than a little concerned about that of her employer. Having worked closely with her, she was aware just how much of herself Dorothy gave to each performance. She would not admit it, but Maggie could recognize the signs of strain and weariness, and guessed that the actress was in need of a damn good rest. The difficulty about Dorothy taking time out was that, although her understudy knew her stuff, those who had bought tickets for the play in advance wanted to watch Dorothy Wilson in the starring role. Maggie guessed there was going to be no easy solution to the problem if it arose.

Mrs Cooling welcomed them both with obvious pleasure. 'You look as lovely as ever, Dorothy. As for you, Maggie, I'm glad to see you've filled out.' Immediately Maggie felt as if she had blown up like a balloon. 'Now come and have afternoon tea with me,' added their landlady. 'And you can tell me all your news.'

It was not until after a good natter over tea and buttered toasted teacakes that they were able to escape to their rooms and relax. Dorothy said they would visit the theatre tomorrow morning, so Maggie had the rest of the day off today. Opening night was in three days' time. Maggie knew a few changes had been made to the script, especially for the London audiences, but nothing that altered the theme of the play. Their landlady would be coming to the first performance, and to the party afterwards. Fingers crossed, thought Maggie, all would go well, and the London critics would love it as much as those in the provinces had done.

She decided to make the most of this leisure time and go and visit some of her old haunts. She made her way to Soho and the 2 I's coffee bar on Old Compton Street, humming the hit song 'Singing the Blues'.

She was enjoying an espresso, as well as reliving the experience of being in the very place where Tommy Steele had first been spotted, when she suddenly noticed a familiar face outside the window. Her heart began to thud and she half rose in her seat. For a moment she felt quite dizzy, so she sat down quickly. Norm. Did she really want to speak to him after all the hurt he had caused? On the other hand, she had moved on, and they had been friends a long time, so perhaps she should be magnanimous and forgive him.

She finished her espresso and left the coffee bar, having noticed Norm heading in the direction of Dean Street. She was curious to see if he was meeting anyone. Perhaps the woman for whom he had ditched her. He was still in sight, and she watched him cross into Shaftsbury Avenue, home of the wonderful Edwardian Apollo Theatre. This area was a magnet for theatregoers, she thought with a thrill of excitement. If Norm had gone in a different direction, he would have eventually come to the colourful Covent Garden. As it was, she had a shrewd idea he was heading for Leicester Square.

Good guess, she thought a few minutes later, watching as he gazed at the stills of the film showing at the Odeon. Perhaps he was meeting his lady love, planning on taking her to the cinema. Maggie had stopped a few yards away, prepared to wait a short while to see if his date arrived.

Suddenly he turned; as his eyes scanned the faces of the people milling about the square, his gaze suddenly fixed on Maggie.

Knowing she had been spotted, she walked slowly towards him. 'I thought I recognized you, Norm,' she said.

He screwed up his face. 'Is it really you, Maggie?'

'Of course it's me,' she replied, exasperated. 'I know it's a while since we've seen each other, but I haven't changed that much.'

'You've filled out.'

She felt like sinking through the ground, wondering why that was the first thing people noticed about her these days? 'I'm no longer modelling,' she said.

He looked astonished. 'I thought you had your heart set on having your face and figure on the front page of *Vogue*.'

'I did, but times change. Anyway, there are those who think my being this shape suits me.'

'You do look good.'

'Thanks a bunch for your charming compliment,' she said sweetly. 'Anyway, what are you doing here? Meeting someone important?'

He reddened and blurted out, 'I'm sorry for my last letter. I eventually received yours and it made me feel a bit of a rotter.'

'At least you now realize that it was a lousy way to finish with me.'

'Yes, I should have thought a bit more about what I scribbled down.'

'I found it cruel.'

He nodded. 'I didn't mean to be cruel.'

'I don't suppose you did.' She took a deep breath. 'Anyway, it was better to find out that we don't suit before we did anything stupid, such as getting married.'

'Yeah, you're right,' he said in a low voice.

She waited for him to tell her about his fiancée, but all he said was, 'So, what are you doing now you're no longer modelling?'

'You haven't been in touch with your mother or Pete?'

He hesitated. 'No.'

She looked at him in disgust. 'You ought to be ashamed of yourself.'

He frowned. 'Never mind me. You haven't answered my question.'

She said quietly, 'And you haven't answered mine! As it happens, I've only just come back to London. I had to leave on health grounds. I've been living at Emma and Jared's cottage, working in the tearoom and shop during the summer.' She paused. 'So, how is married life?'

'It didn't work out,' he said shortly.

Yippee! She felt a tremendous sense of satisfaction, but adopted a sympathetic expression. 'Oh, I am sorry. What happened? Assuming you want to talk about it?'

He shrugged. 'She wasn't the person I thought she was.'

'That must have been a big disappointment to you.'

'You can say that again. Women!' He shook his head.

She felt another twinge of annoyance. 'Well, it takes two, Norm, but you are probably better off without us. I feel like that about some men, truth be told. It rather puts you off having anything to do with any of them.'

He looked taken aback by her seeming challenge. 'Are you blaming me for putting you off men?'

'Well, if the cap fits . . . But, as it happens, I also met someone else after you but I dropped him when I discovered he'd been lying to me. So, yes, I'm right off men. I'm happy being single and doing exactly what I want.'

'You mean working in the tearoom and shop up north?' There was a derisive note in his voice that really got on her nerves.

'No. At the moment I'm working in the theatre. Do you remember Dorothy Wilson?'

He nodded. 'She's a Liverpudlian actress who's made it big.'

'That's right. She's really famous. Although not so famous that she's not prepared to give a fellow Liverpudlian a helping hand up the ladder.'

He stared at her in astonishment. 'You're not telling me you've gone on the stage and are appearing in a play with her?'

'We spend a lot of time working together. The play is really proving popular. It's been performed in theatres all round the country and now it's going to be showing in London.'

'Wow! I'd like to see it,' he said, smiling. 'I'm really impressed.'

She said softly, 'You'd never get a ticket. It's completely sold out.'

He looked disappointed. 'Couldn't you get me a freebie for tonight? My ship sails tomorrow.'

'Sorry, there's no performance this evening.' She sounded regretful but was in truth relieved.

He frowned. 'What a bloody shame! I'd have loved to have seen you up on the stage with Dorothy Wilson. You're really going up in the world. Modelling, what's that compared to being on the stage and in films?'

She decided to ignore that slur on the career she had once set her heart on. 'I'd better get going. I thought I might go and see a film and then have something to eat.'

He surprised her by saying, 'How d'you feel about going to the matinee here at the Odeon? Afterwards we could have a meal. My treat.'

Maggie considered throwing his invitation in his face, but those two words 'My treat' caused her to change her mind. 'All right! For old time's sake.'

'Then let's go.' He offered her his arm and she slipped her hand through his, and they went inside the Odeon.

It was not until a few hours later when they were sitting at a table in the restaurant in Chinatown that Maggie said, 'I heard Pete and Peggy have a daughter.'

'Have they? That's quick.' He looked slightly put out.

'And a car,' she murmured, reaching for her glass of wine as he perused the menu. 'I remember you saying that's what Pete needed, and you talked about the car you'd like when you finish with the sea I don't suppose that's on the cards, is it?'

He glanced at her over the menu 'I'm surprised at you asking that, Maggie. You know the sea is my life. You were always so understanding about my being away so much in the past.'

'I thought you might have been prepared to give it up for *her.*'

Norm appeared not to have heard and was gazing down at the menu again. 'I presume you're having your favourite duck, or special chow mein?'

'Yes, please.' Suddenly she was reminded of Tommy and of the time he had taken her to the Cathay on Renshaw Street. A tide of emotion swept over her. She forced down the lump in her throat and reminded herself that he was a deceiving, no-good rat.

Norm ordered and then took a deep draught of his beer. 'She wanted me to give it up,' he said gruffly. 'I suppose I can understand her point of view a bit better now, but at the time I felt really mad with her because I'd told her the sea was my life. When I repeated that conversation to her, you should have seen her face. She looked like she was sucking a sherbet lemon, all sour.'

'So did she give you an ultimatum?'

He nodded. 'I felt like I'd been punched in the stomach when she said that she didn't want to see me any more.'

'I can imagine. It's really painful getting tossed aside like an old piece of rag,' Maggie said lightly.

He stared at her. 'I really didn't want to hurt you, Maggie. I was hoping that by now you would have forgiven me.'

'Oh, I have! But at the time, would you believe me if I told you I was tempted to make a little stuffed mannequin and stick pins in it?' she said cheerfully. 'You do remember that we sell witch dolls up at the shop in Whalley?'

He looked uneasy. 'You're giving me the creeps, Maggie. When you said that you had to leave London on health grounds, what was wrong with you?'

'If you're thinking I had a nervous breakdown and went a bit nutty because you ditched me, you're mistaken.'

'The thought had occurred to me.'

'You really do flatter yourself, Norm,' she said, reaching for her wineglass again. 'Have you forgotten I have a chest?'

He stared at her bosom. 'You didn't used to have much of a one.'

'You've obviously forgotten I used to suffer from bronchitis a lot in winter. The doctor told me I needed to give up the ciggies, as well as get out of London, so I moved in with our Jared and Emma and their little boy in Formby at first. They now have a daughter as well. I'm hoping to get back up there for Christmas. It would be lovely being home for a family Christmas.'

'What about the play?'

'I'm sure the understudy will manage,' she said casually.

'You have an understudy?'

She nodded and changed the subject, asking him about the places he had visited since last they had been in touch. Eventually they rose from the table and left. He accompanied her to the nearest Tube station. 'Perhaps I'll get to see you in Liverpool sometime,' he said.

'Maybe. You really should keep in touch with your family.'

He frowned. 'I work hard, you know? I have little free time.'

'I wouldn't argue. But, like me, you weren't around when your mother wrote to Irene in California, telling her that her mother was very ill. She died before Irene had time to get home and see her,' said Maggie bluntly.

'That's not going to happen to Ma. She's as strong as an ox.'

'Well, if you think like that, then you'd better start praying she carries on being as strong as an ox, because she not only has a day job still, she babysits for your brothers' kids and also visits Irene's stepfather, Alfred. You might have forgotten, but her mother and your mother were best friends, and she's taken pity on the poor widower and his children.'

He scowled. 'Thanks for letting me know. I'll have to go. I have to get back to the Isle of Grain tonight.'

'See you again sometime and have a safe voyage,' said Maggie.

'Thanks. I hope the play's a smash hit here in London. See you.' He bent his head and made to kiss her, but she averted her face. His scowl deepened and he turned away and strode off.

Maggie grinned. No doubt she wouldn't be seeing him in Liverpool, although he just might get in touch with his family. She was surprised that he had even made the attempt to kiss her. Despite his apology, she thought that he still had a nerve thinking she would want his kisses.

Later that evening, Maggie told Dorothy about having met an old flame, whom she had known since she was at school, but who had dropped her after meeting someone else. But who in turn had been dropped and now seemed to want to make up with her.

The older woman put down the sheet music she was reading and looked at Maggie pensively. 'You think there's a story there. Is it that you want to get together again?'

'No. I told him I'd had it with men after the way he treated me – and having met someone else I fell in love with, which didn't work out either.'

'Would you try again with the other bloke if you were to see him again and discovered that he wasn't all bad?'

Maggie hesitated. 'Did Lenny mention Tommy to you?'

'Yes.'

'I suppose he showed you the article about him having been involved in a robbery?'

'Yes.' Her eyes met Maggie. 'Did you ever read it?'

She shook her head. 'I didn't want to because I knew it would upset me.'

Dorothy frowned. 'I suppose it would be painful knowing he could play the part of a hero while at the same time being an old-fashioned cad.'

'What d'you mean, a hero?'

Dorothy told her about Tommy saving the life of a child at the risk of his own.

Maggie was flabbergasted. Why had nobody told her?

'Well?' asked Dorothy eventually. 'Do you feel any better about him now?'

'I never did believe he was completely bad or without feelings. But he told me so many lies, and that I find hard to forgive.' She reached for the sewing basket that had been her mother's. Dorothy had caught a heel in the hem of a skirt and it needed repairing.

'I remember fancying someone when I was just a few years younger than you,' Dorothy said. 'He was in love with a friend of mine, but she was killed in the Blitz. He was dead attractive. Later I met up with him again and we went out together and talked about getting married. But all the time I was keeping something back from him. I didn't exactly lie to him, but I omitted to tell the truth. In other words, I lived a lie by deceiving him. Then he met someone else and, although I felt really mad with him for preferring her to me, I knew they'd be better for each other. She knew my secret, and eventually it came out. They married. Although I was a bit hurt, I was pleased for them, eventually. Anyway, I felt something for this other bloke, who some might have thought wasn't a patch on the first one. He'd been a bit of a lad in his day and I hadn't seen him for years. He'd been away in the army and I was to find that it was in his company I was able to relax, be myself and have fun. Love comes in different guises,' she murmured.

She fell silent.

Maggie waited, wondering if the bloke she could relax with was Lenny. 'So how is that supposed to help me?' she asked casually.

Dorothy gave a twisted smile. 'Now you're asking! I'm sure I had something in mind when I started.'

'You mean your mind drifted off and you lost the thread?'

'Exactly.' Dorothy yawned.

'The thing is,' said Maggie impulsively. 'I don't know if it was something I said that caused him to be arrested.'

'I shouldn't think so. There was a photograph of him in the *Echo* a day or two before he was arrested. Someone must have seen it, recognized him and informed the police.' Dorothy stifled another yawn. 'I'm tired. I'm off to bed. Goodnight.'

'Sleep tight. Don't let the bugs bite.'

'Better not let our landlady hear you mention bugs.'

Maggie smiled faintly and carried on sewing, thinking she had enough in her life at the moment without worrying about their landlady and bugs. But she would now like to read both articles that had appeared in the *Echo*. She could not help wondering whether – if Dorothy knew about Tommy – Josh knew about him, too.

Twenty-Four

'"What a friend we have in Jesus, all our sins and griefs to bear. What a privilege it is to carry everything to God in prayer",' warbled Gertie.

'Why aren't you singing a carol instead of a hymn?' asked Pete, stretching to press a drawing pin through the loop on a garland of colourful paper chains and anchoring it to the picture rail. 'It's almost Christmas, after all.' He was perched precariously on a stepladder.

'I learnt that hymn when I went to Christian Endeavour meetings. It's surprising what comes back to you years later, without you even having to think about it.' His mother glanced up from packing presents into her holdall. 'You be careful, lad. You should have left that until Peggy gets back from her mother's.'

'You're at it again, fussing. I can manage this. I wanted to get it done while peace reigns.'

Gertie's face softened. 'I know she cries a bit, but she's a lovely baby and some babies teethe earlier than others. I remember my cousin's baby was born with a tooth. Anyway I'm going now, so you be careful.'

'I don't know why you insist on going by bus. I could have run you to West Derby in the car if you'd waited.'

'I don't want to wait.' She made for the door, only to pause. 'I've just remembered. There's a letter behind the clock that came at lunchtime. It'll tell you that Maggie is supposedly coming up for Christmas, so the theatre must be closed for a few days.'

'Is she now?' Pete murmured. 'It's nice of her to write and tell us.'

'She hasn't done anything of the sort. The letter's from our Norm. They bumped into each other in London, went to the pictures and had a meal together. What d'you think of that?' she said smugly.

'What about his fiancée?'

'He makes no mention of her. Maybe he changed his mind about her.'

'You're thinking he and Maggie might get together again?'

'I'm not saying anything except tarrah and see yer later.' And on those words, Gertie left.

Instantly Pete climbed down from the ladder and found his twin's letter and read it before finishing his task. Not long after, he heard the front door key in the latch, and a few moments later the kitchen door opened and his wife appeared, carrying the baby who was knuckling her eyes.

'Oh, it does look all nice and festive,' Peggy said, glancing around before placing the baby on the sofa. 'Where's your mam?'

'She's gone to Alfred's. I'm hoping you've brought something in for tea.'

Peggy smiled. 'So we've the place to ourselves. I wish your mam would marry Alfred.' She sat on the sofa and began to remove the baby's bonnet.

'So do I, but I can't see it happening. She might like helping him out with the kids, but living with them, I'm not so sure. By the way, there's a letter from our Norm. He saw Maggie in London and she's supposedly coming north for Christmas.'

'No mention of a fiancée?'

'No.'

'D'you think he and Maggie will get together again? You know your twin better than anyone.'

'I wish people would stop saying that. I no longer know which way the wind blows with him, now our lives have gone separate ways. Anyway, if you were Maggie, would you have him back?'

'No, but she was devastated, wasn't she, when she learnt the truth about our Tommy? She could be desperate for a bit of loving.'

Pete frowned. 'She might have found someone in the repertory theatre. Anyway, how do we even know if she's aware that your Tommy's in prison?'

'We don't.' Peggy lifted the baby from her fleecy all-in-one. 'I'm not going to say anything about him if I see her.'

'Her sister might tell her as she sees a fair bit of Irene.'

'I wonder how he's surviving.' Peggy sighed and finished seeing to the baby's needs, before fetching the shopping bag that she had left in the pushchair.

Pete said, 'So, what's there to eat? I bet it'll be better than whatever Tommy's having in prison.'

'A bacon shank from the cooked-meat shop on Bridge Road. If you can peel and slice some potatoes, I'll make some potato scallops to go with it and open a tin of peas.'

'Sounds good to me.' He grinned. 'Ma's complimentary about your cooking – that's why she's landed you with cooking Christmas dinner. I thought she might be going to Dougie's or Alfred's, but she said she wants to be home for the baby's first Christmas.' He kissed Peggy on the cheek on his way into the back kitchen.

Peggy sighed, thinking it would have been nice to have just her and Pete and the baby for Christmas, but she was not going to complain. Her mother-in-law had her good points. But hopefully Pete was wrong and his mother would marry Alfred. It would be a step up for her, moving into his semi-detached, and it would mean Peggy and Pete would have the house completely to themselves. Still, having to put up with his mother was better than being in prison like Tommy.

Peggy found over the next day or so that she could not get her brother out of her mind. She mentioned it when Gertie and Pete came home from work the following day. 'I can't believe it's almost Christmas. I keep thinking of our Tommy spending it behind bars.'

Gertie sat at the table. 'You haven't thought of visiting him?'

Peggy hesitated and shot a glance at Pete. 'What do you think?'

'I'd speak to your Marty about it.'

'If you remember when he enquired about seeing Tommy after he was arrested, he didn't want to see any of us.'

Gertie said, 'Embarrassed, that's why. He's full of shame for letting his family down.'

'Shame! Our Lil would say Tommy hasn't an ounce of shame,' said Peggy, placing the casserole dish in the middle of the table.

'And what do you say?' asked Gertie.

Peggy paused in the act of removing the casserole lid. 'I just wish he'd stayed in London.'

Gertie tapped the table with her knife. 'Someone should go and see him, for your mother's sake. She'll be thinking about him. He might have wandered from the right path, but he was trying to go straight, wasn't he? Hadn't he started his own business?' She glanced at Pete who nodded. 'Now is the time he could do with a helping hand to drag him back on to the straight and narrow,' said Gertie. 'Remember the woman caught in adultery in the Bible, and what Jesus said about he who is without sin casting the first stone?'

'I think you've caught religion from Alfred, Ma,' Pete said.

'And what's wrong with being religious?' Gertie said sharply. 'You might think that I didn't know what you were up to when you had your accident years ago, but I did and kept my mouth shut. I thought at the time you were already paying the price for your foolishness, and it broke my heart to see you suffering. We all make mistakes and deserve a second chance. I think someone in the family should try and see Tommy. From what I've gathered, Peggy, your father was hard on the lad.' She sniffed. 'Anyway, I've said my piece and I'll shut up now and let you dish out the dinner. I'm hungry.'

'You should have thought of that before you started this conversation,' Peggy said tartly.

'Enough said, Peg,' muttered Pete.

Despite her annoyance with Gertie, Peggy did not forget what her mother-in-law had said about Tommy. The next morning she left the baby, Katherine Mary Gertrude, with Pete, and caught the bus to Litherland, intending going to Mass at the church where Irene and Marty worshipped.

Both showed surprise when they saw her sitting in a pew. 'What's wrong with your own church?' joked Marty.

'I wanted a word with you,' Peggy said.

'Well, let it wait until after the service,' he responded.

She nodded, and during the service tried her best not to be distracted by Josie and Jerry whispering together. As soon as the service was over, she hurried outside, not wanting to be drawn into conversation with those she knew who attended the church.

'You should have waited inside,' said Marty, approaching her. 'You look freezing. Let's go to our house and have a cup of tea,' he suggested.

'No, I have to get back home and I don't want Jerry to hear what I have to say. I won't keep you long.'

'Is it about Tommy?'

She nodded. 'Pete's mother thinks one of us should visit him in prison, seeing as how it's almost Christmas. Families coming together, and all that.'

'You're worked up about this, aren't you?' said Marty, putting an arm about her shoulders and hugging her. 'And you're cold. Change your mind and come back to ours and I'll run you home in the van afterwards.'

'No, Irene will be wanting to get your dinner on the table. Just tell me what you think? Do we carry on being completely fed up with him for being a selfish sod, upsetting Mam, dumping his child on you and embarrassing the life out of us all, or what? After all, he saved that little boy's life and bought Mam chocolates and the kids sweets, so we know there's some good in him?'

'I'm prepared to forgive him, and Mam has probably already forgiven him, even if our Lily will never do so,' said Marty. 'And if you remember, I did try to see him but he didn't want to see me. He even refused to see Father Francis.'

'I know but—'

'I'll tell you what I'll do . . . I'll write to him.'

Peggy sagged against Marty. 'Thanks. What'll you say?'

'I'll tell him that we're thinking of him and that Jerry is getting on all right at school. That I'd like to visit him as I think there's matters we need to discuss.'

'Such as that garage of his,' said Peggy. 'What's happening to it? Are all his tools still there?'

Marty frowned. 'I don't know, but I suppose I should find out. Anything else?'

'What about putting a photo of Jerry in the envelope, with a Christmas card from Jerry. He mightn't be able to write much, but you could help him with his name and he can put some kisses on it.'

'You think that's a good idea? He doesn't know Tommy's in prison.'

'But he knows he's somewhere trying to make his fortune, and surely would be made up to be in touch with him. Besides, it might make Tommy think more about what you've taken on – being a father to his son again.' She clutched his arm. 'You could also suggest that he sends Jerry a Christmas message.' She hesitated. 'I suppose you'll have to tell Irene what you're doing?'

'Of course, I'll tell her. Do I mention Maggie Gregory in the letter? Jerry has spoken of her once or twice. He remembers seeing her in the church at our wedding and still calls her the lady on the train and thinks she might know where he is. I'm wondering if I should tell him that Tommy's in hospital and show him the photo and article in the *Echo* that speaks of him being a hero.'

'I suppose it wouldn't do any harm. Although, I don't know if you should mention Maggie to Tommy. Maybe you could write almost casually that she's back in London? If he feels anything for her still, he's best believing she's completely out of his reach. She saw Norm in London, and for all we know they might get back together again.' She relaxed her hold on his arm. 'I'd better get cracking. I can't trust Pete's mother not to burn the potatoes, and Pete was taking Katherine for a walk in the park.'

'OK! I'll let you know if I hear back from Tommy,' Marty said.

'Thanks.' With a clearer conscience, Peggy hurried off home.

Twenty-Five

Maggie stepped down from the train in Lime Street Station and drew in a painful breath. She had hoped never to suffer from bronchitis again, but her chest was feeling tight. Perhaps she would feel better once she was back in Formby. As she walked along the platform, she was praying that Jared had received her message and would be outside waiting for her with the van. She felt she just could not cope with sitting in another crowded train with people coughing and spluttering all over her.

To her disappointment, her brother's work van was nowhere to be seen. Still, he might be late; with it being almost Christmas, the traffic was bad. She waited for ten minutes then decided she had no choice but to catch the Southport train before she froze to death. She had just started walking when she heard her name being called. She turned her head and saw a car pull up at the kerb and recognized the driver as her brother-in-law, Billy.

'Get in and I'll take you to Formby,' he said.

'Thanks. You're a sight for sore eyes,' she gasped, opening the front passenger door. She climbed inside and managed to heave her holdall in with her and drop it on to the back seat before settling herself comfortably.

'Good journey?' he asked.

'The train was crowded, as is to be expected this time of year. I'll be glad to flop out when I get home.'

'Is that how you think of Jared's and Emma's house now?'

'Until I get a place of my own, I suppose it is,' Maggie answered. 'Although I enjoy staying at the cottage if I'm feeling in need of a bit of peace and quiet.'

'You're not likely to get complete peace and quiet this spring. Apparently, Betty's coming over with her bloke and little girl, and she said to Emma how she'd enjoy staying up there for a couple of weeks to do some painting.'

'I thought they weren't coming until the year after?'

'Change of plan.'

Maggie was aware of mixed emotions, and realized that part of her had begun to consider the cottage her domain for most of the year. 'What does she want to paint for when she has a husband to support her?'

Billy glanced at her. 'You're not still jealous of her, are you?'

'I've never been jealous of her!' Bright flags of pink flared in her cheeks.

'I don't think that's quite true, but if you want to kid yourself, that's your problem.'

The colour in her cheeks burned. 'Why are you being so rude to me?'

'Am I being rude? I thought we were just having a conversation. I don't get a chance to talk to you alone that often.'

Maggie glanced at him. 'If we're being honest, I often felt you didn't want to talk to me at all. I've always thought you didn't like me and, as we don't have much in common, that suited me.'

'We share feelings for your sister, so we have that in common. But there have been times when I've thought you don't appreciate her enough, and that annoys me.'

The colour that had begun to fade in Maggie's cheeks flared up again. 'What is this? Get-at-Maggie day?'

'No, but Dot would appreciate your company at our house sometimes. Life hasn't turned out the way she'd have liked, but she just keeps on going. Whereas you always seem to expect the family to rally round when your heart's near to breaking.'

His words almost took her breath away and, for a moment, she could not speak. Then she managed to say in a low voice, 'Are you saying our Dot's heart is near to breaking?'

He nodded. 'I know you've suffered in different ways, but she'd love a child of her own. It just hasn't happened, though. I don't mind for myself, but she does, and now Deirdre is having a baby—'

'Deirdre's pregnant!' Maggie was shocked; could scarcely believe it. She had believed Deirdre had more sense than to get herself into trouble. 'But she's not married!'

'It's not obligatory to be married, but as it happens she and Jimmy were married last week.'

'Why didn't anyone let me know? I'd have sent a card.'

'We thought you'd get to know soon enough. Anyway, Dot is going to feel even worse than when Emma gave birth to her second little one. Christmas is a particularly difficult time for Dot. It would be great if you asked her if you could have Christmas dinner with us. I know you prefer having it at Jared and Emma's, but—'

'I'll have Christmas dinner at your house if that's what she would like,' Maggie interrupted. 'Although I don't see why we can't all have Christmas dinner together. She could watch Owen opening his presents and . . .' She stopped abruptly. 'I'm not thinking, am I? Will she find that painful too?'

'You're getting the idea.'

Maggie said no more, but remembered Irene telling her about asking Dot to visit the children's home with her. Surely Billy knew about that, and of her fondness for the handicapped boy, Georgie? Why didn't they consider adoption? Unless Dot knew that her big, strong, ex-army husband would never countenance such a thing. She realized it took a special kind of person to take on someone else's child. She found herself thinking of Irene and Marty, and wondered how they were coping with Jerry. What, if anything, had they told him about his father being in prison?

She felt that aching sadness, remembering watching Tommy and his son talking in the railway carriage, and how Jerry had wanted to play with his cars. She sighed and told herself to stop thinking of them. Her sister was more important. She had no problem believing Dot could cope with someone else's child, but could the man next to her?

Maggie glanced at Billy and realized how little she knew about her brother-in-law. That he was perceptive where his wife was concerned was obvious, up to a point, but it seemed to her that both of them needed to get together and have a good discussion about what steps they could take if Dot was desperate to have a child to love that she could call her own.

'"Christmas comes but once a year. When it comes it brings good cheer",' sang Emma, stirring the bowl of punch.

Maggie dropped in another slice of orange. 'You don't mind my spending Christmas day with our Dot and Billy?'

'Of course not. You shouldn't have to ask. Besides, I've other visitors coming.'

'Who?'

'My old friend, Lila, her husband, Dougie, Pete's brother, their two kids and her dad. I'm really pleased about it. Lila and I used to see a lot of each other when we lived in Whalley, and I'm fond of her father. But since we married and moved, we don't see each other as much as we would like. So when she phoned to say that she had broken her arm, I immediately thought, why not invite them here?'

'Won't you need help?' asked Maggie.

Emma shook her head. 'Don't be daft. You're forgetting I used to run the tearoom singlehanded. Cooking Christmas dinner for five adults and three little ones, not counting the baby, will be a doddle.'

'I'll peel all the vegetables for you before I go, as well as set the table,' said Maggie, dropping a couple of sticks of cinnamon into the punch.

Emma smiled. 'You really have changed, and I must say I appreciate all the help you've given me since you gave up modelling and came back north. Anyway, you won't be on your own with Dot and Billy. I heard her telling Jared that she's invited Jimmy and Deirdre.' She hesitated. 'You do know Deirdre's pregnant?'

Maggie nodded. 'That's why I'm surprised Dot's asked them to dinner.'

Emma frowned. 'Why?'

'Another person we know having a baby and our Dot shows no signs of getting pregnant. She must feel it.'

'Of course, she does, but I didn't think you'd give it any thought. Anyway, apparently Dot's asked them because her parents are far from pleased about the situation and didn't even attend the wedding. Jimmy's name is mud in that household.'

'Poor Deirdre and Jimmy.'

'I wouldn't worry too much about it. Her parents could change their attitude once their grandchild arrives. It'll be their first,' said Emma.

'Anyway, they'll be staying the night next door, too. Deirdre was on duty over Christmas and Boxing Day last year, so she's off this year. It'll be good for the newlyweds to have two days together and not have to worry about facing her parents.'

Maggie did feel sympathy for Deirdre, and could understand her not wanting her Christmas spoilt by having to run the gauntlet of her mother's disapproval. Maggie knew that her own mother would have been horrified if she'd got pregnant out of wedlock. But she was going to feel a right gooseberry tomorrow, sitting with two couples at the dinner table. Still, she would make an effort and dress up and put on her best face, and at least she would have plenty to talk about to cover any awkward moments. After all, she had spent a couple of months on tour with a famous actress, finishing up in the West End of London.

Her brow puckered as she thought about Lenny having turned up in London to spend Christmas with Dorothy. It had come as a surprise to Maggie, who had been packing for her trip to Liverpool, and she'd had time only to exchange greetings with Lenny. She had wondered what she would do next if Dorothy decided to leave the play to have a well-deserved break in the New Year. Maggie did not fancy staying on in the theatre in London. Although she had enjoyed her time in rep, she had soon realized that it was not really the life for her.

Neither did she want to remain here in Formby, just helping Emma with the children and housework until Eastertide, when the tearoom and shop would open again. What she needed was to find something else to fill her time.

Twenty-Six

'That is a fab dress,' said Deirdre wistfully, gazing at Maggie and absently accepting a Babycham from Dot. 'It must have cost you a bob or two.'

'Not a penny,' said Maggie, twirling round. 'It was a gift.'

'A hand-me-down from the other Dorothy,' whispered Dot audibly in Deirdre's ear.

Maggie pulled a face at her sister. 'Do you have to tell everyone my secrets? I was going to pretend that I once modelled for Dior and he sends me a special gift of his latest creation every now and again because he has never forgotten me.'

Deirdre said, 'I suppose, if that was true, you could almost call him your sugar daddy.'

'I wish,' said Maggie, smiling faintly. 'I haven't had any luck with younger men, so perhaps I should try an older one. There was a photographer, Charlie, who was at least forty – he fancied me. Maybe I should have taken him up on his offer to go to the Costa Blanca with him.'

'What about Norm?' Jimmy had been listening, and now sat beside Deirdre on the sofa with his arm across her shoulders. 'Peggy mentioned him when she called at Irene's and Marty's yesterday. Apparently they heard from him and he said he'd seen you in London.'

'He's yesterday's news,' said Maggie firmly. 'He might think we can get together again, but he's mistaken.'

At that moment the front doorbell sounded. 'Could you go and answer that for me, Mags?' asked Dot.

'OK.' She wondered whether her sister was expecting someone else.

'Hello, Maggie,' said Josh, standing on the step, holding a bottle of champagne and a parcel wrapped in Christmas paper.

'What are you doing here?' she blurted out. 'How did you get here?'

'I was invited and I came by car. A new acquisition.' He raised that mobile eyebrow of his. 'May I come in?'

She stepped aside, wondering why Dot had not mentioned to her that she had invited Josh to Christmas dinner.

'Is that Josh?' called Billy, poking his head out of the living-room door.

'Yes,' replied Maggie. 'Let me take your overcoat, Josh.'

He placed the champagne and parcel on the hall table, unbuttoned his tweed overcoat and handed it to her, before removing his trilby and giving that to her, too.

Then he bent his dark head and – to her astonishment – kissed her smack on the lips. His lips were cold and firm and slightly moist, and the kiss was definitely not unpleasant. But should it be happening? It was not so long ago that she had believed her heart was broken, thought Maggie. Yet here she was, enjoying being kissed. She told herself that there was nothing she could have done to prevent Josh from kissing her, what with her hands full of overcoat and hat, but she should be putting a stop to it right now. She did just that by taking a step backwards.

She gazed up at him and realized that his breathing was flurried and there was an expression in his brown eyes that confused her. She could feel her bosom heaving, and was glad that it was concealed by his overcoat.

Then he glanced up and her eyes followed his and she saw the mistletoe hanging from the hall light. 'Happy Christmas, Maggie,' he said, his eyes twinkling.

She managed a smile. 'The same to you. Now, if you'll excuse me.' She carried his outdoor clothes upstairs and placed them on the bed in the spare room. Then she sat beside them and thought further about that kiss. Should she have said something? But what? She had come to the conclusion that she just might have been set up by Dot who had decided to do a bit of matchmaking. She felt annoyed that her sister should be interfering in her life. Although, Dot could not have arranged for that kiss to happen. Surely that was down to Josh, who had taken advantage of her standing beneath the mistletoe. He might even have thought she had stood there deliberately. She groaned.

'Are you going to be up there long?' shouted Dot. 'Only I'll be dishing up dinner any minute now!'

'Coming!' Maggie stood up and hurried downstairs.

She entered the living room just as Josh was opening the bottle of champagne. It made a satisfactory popping noise and, as if to the manner born, he swiftly began to pour the foaming wine into glasses.

Dot glanced at Maggie. 'Josh was going to be spending Christmas all on his own at a time when he has something to celebrate.'

'So you asked him here,' Maggie murmured. 'That was really thoughtful of you, sis.'

Dot gave her a sharp look and then glanced at her husband. 'Actually, it was Billy's idea.'

Maggie supposed that could be true, and said no more about it. She accepted a glass of champagne from Josh with a word of thanks. 'So, what are we celebrating?' she asked.

'Me being demobbed and moving into Uncle Lenny's flat. I'm going to be working at the coffee bar.'

'Oh!' Maggie supposed she shouldn't have been surprised. 'You can cook then?'

Billy laughed. 'Of course he can cook. That was Josh's job in the army. He was a chef and has cooked for hundreds of soldiers in his time, finishing up organizing special dinners for the officers.'

Maggie flushed. 'Nobody told me. I presumed because you were tanned when we first met that you were just an ordinary soldier and spent a lot of time outdoors.'

'I'd just returned from sunny Cyprus,' said Josh, smiling.

'Well, now you know,' Dot said, raising her glass of champagne. 'Here's to Josh and his new venture. That it will be a success.'

Maggie echoed her words and raised her glass to Josh, thinking it looked as if they had more in common than she had thought.

Dot drained her glass and said, 'Anyway, I'm ready to dish up, so take your seats at the table, folks. I don't know about the rest of you, but I'm starving.'

They all trooped into the dining room and sat down, helping themselves from the tureens of vegetables in the middle of the table. Slices of turkey and ham along with stuffing were already on plates. For the next quarter of an hour, the conversation was desultory, and Maggie just listened as she ate, thinking it strange that Jimmy didn't mention Tommy, as apparently he had been at his sister's and Marty's house yesterday. After all, Christmas was a time when families were inclined to reminisce about past Christmases. There was no way she was going to ask him about Tommy, though.

When the meal was over and the washing-up done, they listened to the Queen's speech. Then glasses were refilled and they gathered around the log fire.

'So are you going to tell us about being on tour with Dorothy Wilson, Mags?' asked Jimmy. 'I've never forgotten the first time I caught sight of her at Lenny's. She looked really glamorous.'

'I can tell you she never wears anything cheap. Not even when she's relaxing. It's as if she can never forget that she's a star, or that once she was just a common Scouser,' Maggie said.

'She remembers my mother,' said Josh.

'How?' Maggie asked, recalling that his name had barely cropped up in conversations between her and her employer whilst they were away.

'Mam was Uncle Lenny's sister and the two families lived close by.'

'What about your dad?'

'His parents had the corner shop, and Dad used to help out there. He and Mam met when she used to go in there for messages. They were both killed when a building collapsed near the end of the war. I was kicking a ball and had gone on ahead. It happened so unexpectedly. I heard this roar behind me and I looked back . . .' Josh grimaced. 'But enough about sad, faraway things.'

'But it must be of some comfort to you having someone else other than your Uncle Lenny who remembers your parents and can talk about them,' said Maggie earnestly.

Josh agreed. 'At least Dorothy used to play with Mam, and can bring her alive in a different way when I hear her and Uncle Lenny talk about when they were kids. Girls played different games, so Dorothy has different memories of Mam. Ones that never fail to make me laugh.'

'So you like Dorothy?' said Maggie.

'Yes.'

'Don't you like her?' asked Deirdre.

Maggie glanced at her and smiled. 'Of course I like her. I've got to understand her little ways and she seems to understand what I'm about. Just like I thought . . .' She stopped abruptly.

Her sister stared at her. 'Go on. I'd like to know who else understands you, because I've a feeling you weren't going to say me or our Jared.'

Maggie said, 'No, I wasn't. Perhaps that was a mistake.'

'Trouble with families is that they take each other for granted,' said Billy. 'With outsiders, most of us are on our best behaviour, especially when we first meet them. Although there are some people we can never relax with and be ourselves.'

'Don't you think that it's natural to put on your best side with people, because most of us want to be liked?' Josh took a handful of salted peanuts from the dish on the coffee table.

'Even children do it, and they generally show their emotions more easily than adults do,' said Deirdre. 'Hiding our feelings is something we learn as we get older. Sometimes we find out too late that there are people we just shouldn't have trusted.'

'Just like Tommy,' murmured Maggie, and smiled brightly at Jimmy. 'So what's the gossip from the McGrath household?'

'Forget him, Maggie,' he said. 'I met him before you did, and wouldn't have trusted him as far as I could throw him. If you hadn't known what he was like before he was arrested, you'd have found out about it after it was all over the front page of the *Echo*.'

'I never saw the articles,' Maggie said, 'but Lenny and Dorothy told me some of what was written about him. I know he saved a child's life. I've been thinking that I must go to the Central Library some time and look them up.'

They all stared at her.

Dot said, 'Now you've brought Tommy into the conversation, I can only say you showed sense when you finished with him after discovering the kind of bloke he really was. When you went off with Dorothy, we all thought it was for the best. We didn't want you behaving out of character and going all soft on us by feeling sorry for him. That's why we didn't mention it.'

'I can understand why you kept quiet but . . .' Maggie was aware that Josh was listening, and wondered what he knew about her relationship with Tommy.

'We were told he was a charmer,' said Dot. 'But he was also a criminal. Most likely he would have had every penny off you if you didn't already keep a tight grip on your purse and Jared a proper eye on your trust fund.'

'Are you saying I'm mean?' said Maggie indignantly.

'No, just one of those people who often used to say, "What's mine is mine and what's yours is yours",' said Dot.

Maggie was dumbstruck, knowing she could not deny the truth of her sister's accusation. Obviously Dot knew only too well the kind of person she used to be. 'I'm not like that any more, and I can tell you something: Tim − or Tommy, should I say − never asked me for money.'

'Shall we change the subject?' Billy said hastily, glancing at

Josh. 'Maggie, you were going to tell us what life on the boards was like with Dorothy Wilson?'

Her sister refilled Maggie's glass. 'I still love you, despite your faults. Now take a deep breath and tell us some anecdotes.'

'Let her have a drink first,' said Jimmy.

I wonder . . .' said Maggie, then took a mouthful of Babycham and thought it tasted very different from the real stuff.

'What do you wonder?' asked Dot.

Maggie hesitated and stared at Josh. 'I shouldn't say. I could be mistaken.'

Dot said, 'What is it?'

'Say it, Maggie,' said Josh lightly. 'I think we can trust those at this table to keep a secret.'

She cleared her throat. 'It could be that Lenny's thinking of retiring.'

'He's not that old,' said Dot.

'But he is getting on,' Deirdre put in.

'Early forties, I reckon. That's not old,' said Dot.

'What do you know, Maggie?' asked Jimmy.

'Not much,' said Maggie cautiously. 'I know Dorothy is waiting for the date to be finalized for when filming starts in Hollywood, but before then she's going to be in a musical in New York. Now I know about Josh, I've been thinking that Lenny might have decided to accompany her and leave Josh to look after the business.' She looked at Josh, who remained silent.

'I don't know why the pair of them don't get married,' said Dot, taking a chocolate from a cut-glass dish. 'What d'you say, Josh?'

He just raised an eyebrow.

'Maybe it's because she knows her fans would prefer her to remain single?' said Deirdre.

Jimmy said, 'You do know that Dorothy Wilson is Nick's mother?'

They all stared at him in disbelief, thinking about DI Walker's adopted son.

'You'd better be careful what you say, Jimmy,' warned Billy.

Jimmy took a long drink of his Guinness. 'I'm not kidding. Our Irene told me, and it was Betty who told her. She had it from Bobby who had it from her mum Lynne. Apparently Lynne and Dorothy were in the same home for unmarried

mothers during the war. Bobby's father was killed when his
boat was torpedoed, and Lynne was able to keep her baby with
the help of her grandmother. Dorothy Wilson had hers adopted.'
He said softly, 'What have you to say to that, Mags? I even
know who the father is. At the time he had no idea she was
pregnant. She didn't tell him because she was so hellbent on
being an actress.'

All the time Jimmy had been talking, Maggie had been
remembering what Dorothy had told her the day she had seen
Norm in London. 'So she had him adopted,' murmured Maggie.
'Anyway, Nick has turned out all right. He's in the police cadets
now.'

'The couple who adopted him as a baby are both dead,' said
Deirdre. 'The mother died when he was a young teenager and
then the father was murdered by his own brother, who managed
to escape to Canada.'

'Bloody hell!' exclaimed Billy, getting up and fetching himself
a bottle of Guinness. 'Do you want one, Josh?'

'No, better not.' He was frowning.

'Anyway, getting back to Nick. The brother was another just
like Tommy,' said Jimmy. 'It was all about money, and the brother
didn't care who he hurt. When things went wrong he made a
run for it.'

Maggie was shocked by his comment. 'No, Tim wouldn't kill
anyone!'

'I think that's enough, Jimmy,' said Dot, glancing at her sister's
face. 'You can't compare murdering your brother with driving a
getaway car.'

Jimmy reddened. 'OK! I take back what I said.'

Deirdre burst out. 'Nick was fortunate to be adopted by
decent people. When I think of the handicapped children I
care for. At this time of year it breaks my heart that they're
not part of a proper family. I doubt they'll ever be as fortunate
as Nick.'

'And some of them are such affectionate kids, too,' said Dot,
a slight choke in her voice.

Billy changed the subject. 'So what d'you have to say, Josh,
about the chances of your uncle and Dorothy getting married?'

Josh smiled faintly and stood up. 'I think it's time I was going. With Uncle Lenny away, I have a lot of organizing to do. Thanks for the dinner, Dot. Drop by at the coffee bar anytime and I'll cook you a free special.'

She smiled at him. 'Will do. I'll bring my sister, too.'

'I'll go and get your overcoat,' said Maggie hurriedly, wishing Dot had not said that. He might think her sister was trying to push her into his arms. She rose and left the living room.

Josh was talking to Billy in the hall when she came downstairs, and she overheard mention of Cyprus and Archbishop Makarios. They broke off their conversation, and Billy left them as she handed Josh's hat and coat to him.

'It was nice seeing you,' she said.

'Same here.' He shrugged on his overcoat.

'You didn't think I said anything out of place about your Uncle Lenny and Dorothy?'

He smiled faintly. 'I could have stopped you if I'd wanted. Anyway, the news will soon get round that there's a new face in the kitchen at the coffee bar. I'm more concerned about what Jimmy said about Dorothy having had an illegitimate child and that getting out. It mightn't do her career any good.'

'I thought you were going to say that you were worried about Lenny finding out, because I'm pretty sure she'll have told him.'

He nodded. 'I know they're close.'

'Marriage on the cards, you think?'

He smiled and opened the front door. 'Goodnight, Maggie. Take care.'

'You, too.'

She watched him walk down the path, wondering how old he had been when his parents had been killed. He was younger than Billy. It could be that Josh was the same age as Tommy, and yet Josh seemed more mature. She supposed that was not surprising, considering he had seen his parents die and had no siblings to stand by him. As well as having been in sunny Cyprus where there had been terrorism and British soldiers killed. He stopped at the gate and waved. She waved back and then closed the door.

Twenty-Seven

Maggie picked up the envelope from the doormat and went into the kitchen. Recognizing the handwriting, she took a knife from a drawer and slit open the envelope. She took out the single sheet of Basildon Bond blue notepaper and went to the window overlooking the garden. As she had thought, the letter was from Norman. He hoped to be home sometime in March or April and looked forward to seeing her. Obviously he wanted to pick up where they had left off in London.

Well, he could keep on wanting! She gazed out over the dreary garden with its scrawny lawn and flowerbeds that showed a number of daffodil and narcissi shoots. She hoped it wouldn't snow. Her nephew might love it, but she was going into Liverpool that evening and would rather not have to contend with slushy pavements. She'd had a rotten cold which she had passed on to Emma. Thank goodness, she was over it now, but she could not wait for the weather to warm up. The only real sign of spring, besides the shooting bulbs, was a single purple crocus under the apple tree.

Dorothy and Lenny had provided their friends and customers with a surprise last week by announcing in the local press that they were man and wife, having tied the knot at Caxton Hall register office in Westminster on New Year's Day. They had managed to keep it quiet for weeks, but soon they would be leaving for America. All day today, Lenny's customers would be welcome to a free celebratory coffee, milkshake, or glass of wine, and a slice of wedding cake. Then this evening their special friends were invited to a buffet, with drinks and live music. No doubt Josh would have organized the buffet while Maggie was still dithering over what to wear. Both Emma and Dot had told her they didn't know what she was worrying about because she would look lovely in whatever she wore. While that was nice to know, it did not help to solve her dilemma.

Eventually she settled on a lime green shot-silk top with a

scooped neckline that was trimmed with gold lace, and a green flared skirt splashed with red poppies. She placed in a shoe bag a pair of gold leather high-heeled shoes to change into when she arrived at Lenny's. *Or should she be calling it 'Josh's place' now?* she mused. Having no wish to catch a heel in the cracks in the pavement, she put on a pair of flatties.

She brushed her long blonde hair back over her shoulders, keeping it in place with a silky gold-coloured crocheted Alice band. She applied make-up and finally put in the jade earrings she had treated herself to at Christmas, and the matching neat little jade cross on a gold chain.

She took a last look at herself in the mirror before reaching for her tweed winter coat trimmed with fur at the neck and cuffs. She picked up her handbag and shoe bag and went downstairs with the coat over her arm. The newlyweds had stipulated no wedding presents, so she was unencumbered by such, and was glad of it because the shoe bag kept bumping against her thigh.

'Well!' Her brother gazed at her with a ghost of a smile. 'They'll see you coming all right in that lime green blouse.'

Maggie wrinkled her nose. 'You think it's too bright?'

'No, it's fine.' Emma darted a warning glance at her husband. 'You look lovely, Maggie. Young and fresh.'

'There's certainly a hint of spring about you,' Jared said. 'D'you want me to give you a lift to the station?'

'Thanks, that would be jolly.'

'Jolly?' He looked at her askance. 'Well, I hope you have a jolly time, but come home sober and in one piece.'

'You don't have to worry about me. I'll be on the last but one train, so if you don't mind meeting me then, big brother?' Maggie asked as she skipped to the front door ahead of him.

'Of course he will,' said Emma, who had followed them out. 'Enjoy yourself, lovey!'

Maggie had every intention of doing so, because she did not doubt there would be people there she knew, including some members of the music group. She was looking forward to hearing them and wished she could play a musical instrument. All the way on the train into town, she was thinking about a variety of things that she would have liked to have learnt when she was younger, but at least she could cook now and was looking forward to tasting what Josh had chosen to serve for the buffet. She was also able to knit and sew, and that had come in handy on several occasions. She was hoping it would prove useful again in the weeks to come.

'Maggie, is that you?' At the sound of that voice Maggie paused, gazing across the street towards the Philharmonic pub.

'It can't be!' she cried in astonishment.

'It is,' said her cousin, freeing her arm from that of the man at her side and almost skipping across the road towards Maggie.

'But I thought you weren't coming over until after Easter, Betty,' said Maggie.

'Change of plan. I'm having another baby, so we decided to bring the holiday forward.'

'Congratulations.'

'Thanks.' Betty slipped her arm through Maggie's. 'You're looking well. Better than I thought you would after hearing all your woes from Emma and Irene.'

'Don't remind me.'

Betty scrutinized Maggie's face. 'OK! Enough said. But you know what you've got to do, don't you?'

'Yes,' and Maggie sang the words of a famous Frank Sinatra song.

'You always did have a lousy singing voice,' Betty chuckled.

'No, I did not!' protested Maggie. 'I remember me and Mam coming back from shopping in town and you and I ended up having a singing competition and I won.'

'Rubbish,' Betty said firmly. 'My rendering of Frankie Laine's "Ghost Riders in the Sky" was definitely the best.'

'You have to be joking! Mario Lanza could knock the socks off Frankie Laine. I remember how Mam and I loved his singing.' Maggie sighed. 'Happy days!'

'Sometimes they were and sometimes they weren't,' said Betty quietly.

For a moment they were both silent, remembering the past.

'So this is Maggie.'

Maggie looked up at the owner of the voice. 'You must be Stuart,' she said, stretching out a hand.

'That's right!' He solemnly shook hands with her. 'It's good to meet you, Cousin Maggie.'

'Good to meet you, too.' Maggie was thinking that Betty had done well for herself. Not only was her cousin's husband not bad looking, with a very nice American accent, but he had a decent job as an architect and lived in a very nice part of San Jose in California, if the photographs she had sent to Emma were anything to go by.

'I think we'd better get a move on,' he said, freeing her hand. 'Dorothy and Lenny will be waiting for us.'

'You're going to the party?' She was surprised.

'My stepsister, Lynne, told us about it, so we rang Lenny and asked if we could join them,' said Stuart.

'And, of course, he said yes, because Betty worked for Lenny a few years back,' said Maggie.

'And I stayed at the same hotel on Mount Pleasant as Dorothy when I was over here so we got to know each other,' said Stuart.

'Yeah, you're not the only one who can say "I know a famous actress", Mags.' Betty chuckled.

'Is that where you're staying, at the same hotel?' Maggie asked.

Betty nodded. 'There really isn't the room at Lynne and Sam's, with their little ones as well as Nick and Bobby. They're going to be at the party, too, because she's helping out with the catering and Nick's in the band.'

'What about your little girl?' asked Maggie.

'She's far too young to enjoy an adult party, so the proprietor of the hotel is keeping an eye on her for us,' Betty said.

The three of them began to walk along Hope Street. Even before they reached the coffee bar, they could hear the sound of music and voices. There was a man on the door who asked their names and ticked them off on a list before allowing them in.

Betty exchanged glances with Maggie. 'I didn't expect security.'

'Maybe it's because Dorothy is famous,' said Stuart.

Maggie had been expecting the party to take place downstairs with the tables and chairs pushed back against the wall so there would be room for dancing, but they had been directed upstairs. She sat on the bottom stair and changed into her high heels before following Betty and Stuart up to the flat.

The main living room was much larger than she had thought it would be, and there were already a number of familiar faces to be seen. Amongst them were Monica and Nick. Maggie thought about having been told he was Dorothy's son. Was he aware of it? She noticed that Betty and Stuart had found their hosts and were busy chatting to Lenny and Dorothy. There was no sign of Josh, and Maggie decided that he could be in the kitchen.

At that moment she saw Irene approaching with a young lad. 'Hi, Maggie! Let me introduce you to my younger stepbrother Patrick. Patrick, this is Miss Gregory.'

He smiled at Maggie. 'I've heard your name mentioned. You're the lady on the train.'

His words caused a slight shock to shiver down her spine. 'Jerry still calls me that?'

'Yes,' said Irene.

'Let me take your coat and shoe bag and I'll put them in the guest bedroom,' said Patrick.

She handed them over without a word, wondering how the mention of her being the lady on the train had come up in conversation, but decided not to ask. Instead she said, 'Looks like it's going to be a good party.'

Irene agreed. 'I hope you don't mind me bringing this up, but what with Patrick mentioning you being the lady on the train, I thought I'd tell you that Jerry has never forgotten you.'

Maggie flushed. 'I don't know why he hasn't. I've only seen him once since then, and that was at your wedding.'

'He said you looked like a princess when he first saw you on the train. If he could see you now, he might think the same. That's a lovely outfit you're wearing.'

'Thanks. You look nice too.' Maggie was uncertain what to make of Irene's words. She had never been one for paying her compliments in the past. She now felt unsettled, having started to believe that she was putting what had happened between her and Tommy behind her. Yet she could not resist asking after Jerry. 'How is Jerry? He'll be at school now, won't he?'

'Yes, and loving it. With a bit of help he made a Christmas card for his father, which Marty enclosed with a letter to Tommy.'

'You . . . you've been in touch with him?'

'Yes, although I can guess what you're thinking,' Irene said.

Instinctively Maggie dropped her voice. 'Does Jerry know that his father is in prison?'

'Would you tell him if you were in our shoes?'

Maggie moistened her lips. 'I honestly don't know.'

'We decided to leave it to Tommy to make that decision if he responded to the card that was sent.'

'And did he?'

'Yes.'

Before Irene could expand on what she had said, they were interrupted by Lenny and Dorothy, who appeared at her shoulder along with Josh.

Josh smiled down at Maggie. 'Hello, stranger. I hope you're feeling better now.'

'So Dot told you I'd had a rotten cold that went to my chest?'

'Yes, she said that otherwise you'd have come with her to the coffee bar for food,' Josh said. 'You're looking well now. In fact, really stunning.'

'Thanks!' She could feel her cheeks warming. 'You're looking pretty good yourself.' He was wearing dark trousers with a maroon waistcoat over a blue shirt. His tie was also maroon coloured, and fastened in a neat Windsor knot. She suddenly felt as frivolous as a butterfly in the lime green top and bright floral skirt, and was aware that Dorothy appeared distracted and was looking about her. As for Irene, she had drifted away in Betty's direction. 'I like what you're wearing,' Maggie said. 'Maroon is one of my favourite colours, and goes so well with blue or green.'

'So speaks the ex-model with excellent taste in clothes and style,' said Lenny.

'I suppose Dorothy said that,' Maggie said, smiling.

Hearing her name, Dorothy looked at Maggie. 'It's true. I hope you never lose it, despite working in kitchens.'

'I reckon it's something I'll never lose,' said Maggie. 'I'll be going up to the cottage soon.'

Dorothy frowned. 'I thought you might have been staying on with Jared and Emma, and in that case you could have given Josh a hand in the kitchen here.'

For a moment Maggie could think of nothing to say in response to that and, before she could find the words, Dorothy had slipped a hand through Lenny's arm. 'Now how about a glass of champagne, folks?' she called out.

Josh said, 'I'll catch you later, Maggie. I must see to the champagne.' He hurried off.

'Now all I need is someone to hand round the hors d'oeuvres,' said Dorothy.

'I can do that if you like?' offered Maggie.

'No, you're a guest.'

Maggie said, 'I was going to tell you that I've another idea how to make money in order to support myself. One that I'm sure you'll approve of.'

'And what's that?'

'Dolls' clothes. Except I thought of making historical costumes. I just so loved those ones you wore in the play.'

There was a sudden popping sound and someone gave a cheer.

'The champagne,' said Dorothy brightly. 'If you'll excuse us, Maggie.'

'Of course.'

Maggie watched her go, wondering if Dorothy had actually heard what she had said. She supposed it was understandable, her being distracted at her own party. She watched the couple cross the room to where Josh was pouring champagne into glasses on a long table covered by a pristine white cloth. There was a beautiful flower arrangement of spring flowers in the middle, which could only have been imported from the Channel Isles, she thought.

She wandered over to where the musicians had settled themselves in a corner. She recognized 'Love Me Tender', which had been a hit for Elvis in 1956. She had even seen the film. Tony Gianelli was doing the vocals and Nick was on guitar. Then she noticed Monica join him at the microphone. She might not have as good a voice technically as Tony's, but she certainly could sing.

'Champagne?' said a voice in Maggie's ear.

She glanced up at Josh and took a glass from a tray. 'Thanks.'

'What d'you think of the group?'

'I think they're great, but then I would say that. I've known a couple of them for years,' Maggie murmured, taking a sip of champagne. The bubbles tickled her nose and she put up a finger and held back a sneeze.

'How long have you known Monica?' asked Josh.

'I met her that day I came into the coffee bar and she followed me in. The day you brought me the meal I'd ordered from Lenny.'

'I remember. You were upset over a bloke called Norm.'

'Actually, I wasn't. Your uncle got it wrong. I was over Norm but I let Lenny think what he did.'

'So was it the other bloke, Tommy, you were upset about?'

'You make me sound pathetic,' muttered Maggie. 'Like I'm a real wet.'

'I don't think that. I've been serious about a few girls myself. But none of the relationships worked out and I'm glad now.'

'It's different for men. They seem to like playing the field.'

'That's a bit of a sweeping statement,' Josh said.

'Maybe it is.' She bit her lower lip. 'Sorry. Tell me why you think they didn't work out for you?' She really wanted to know.

'Could be because I'd signed on to stay in the army after doing my national service. Not every woman fancies living in army married quarters.' He raised an eyebrow. 'Or it could have simply been that their feelings for me weren't strong enough when it came to the test.'

'Test?'

'If something is going to last, it needs to be strong enough to survive when difficulties arise.'

'I've never thought about that,' said Maggie.

'Look at your sister and Billy and her wanting kids.'

Maggie was taken aback. 'He's spoken to you about that!'

Josh nodded. 'Despite him being a few years older and above me in the ranks, we hit it off. I felt able to go to him if I had problems, and I like to think he respects my opinion enough to discuss the difficult stuff with me.'

'And what do you think? Because I guess he doesn't want children as much as she does.'

'Only because he enjoys married life with just the two of them. So it's a testing time. If you love someone you should be prepared to make sacrifices, and it doesn't come easy. Especially in their case.'

Maggie could see what he meant and sighed. 'I'd like my sister to be happy.'

He smiled. 'Naturally.'

She changed the subject. 'Anyway, why did you ask me about Monica?'

'I like her. She often comes into the coffee bar and I worry about her. Same with Lucia; she's even asked if she can have a job here.'

'Why do you worry about them?'

He glanced about him. 'I'll tell you later. I'm going to have to go.' He moved away.

Maggie watched him as he continued to hand out champagne; he was more of a deep thinker than she would have believed. Then she looked to where Lucia, Tony's cousin by marriage was seated. She remembered how the younger girl had once had a crush on Jimmy. No doubt, now he was married, she would turn her attention to someone else in the group. Maybe Nick? She thought about what Jimmy had said about Nick being Dorothy's son, and of how his other adoptive father had been murdered by his brother. How was it that some young people turned out so well with all that baggage to carry with them in life? Was he aware that Dorothy was his mother? Did she know he was her son?

'Plate.'

Maggie glanced at Patrick, who was going to be another heartbreaker by the look of it. She smiled. 'Thanks.'

'Bobby and my sister Rosie will be around in a few minutes with the hors d'oeuvres.' He moved away.

'Love Me Tender' had come to an end, and Maggie watched as Josh handed a glass of champagne apiece to Monica and Tony. Nick and the drummer refused the bubbly, and a few minutes later he brought them glasses of beer. Maggie became aware that her cousin had sat in the chair next to her, but before they could exchange a word, Bobby and Rosie approached with trays of hors d'oeuvres.

'Wow, this is a real feast,' said Maggie, gazing with a caterer's interest at the variety of food on offer. There were strips of smoked mackerel on fingers of toast, small chunks of ham and pineapple, chicken liver pâté on toast, small portions of diced potato and green pea salad in mayonnaise, and potted shrimps garnished with lemon.

'Did you make these, Bobby?' asked Betty.

'Rosie and I did the ham and pineapple and mixed the potato with the green peas and mayonnaise,' answered Bobby. 'Rosie wants to work in the catering business. She also did the potted shrimps garnished with lemon and made a trifle. Josh did everything else.'

'Josh told me that I should join the WRAC if I'm really interested in catering, because I could get to travel as well,' said Rosie excitedly. 'I'm going to mention it to Dad. I know I'm too young yet, but the sooner I put the idea into his head, the better. Aunt Gertie told me that's what you need to do with some men when you want to get your own way.'

At that moment there was a commotion in the doorway and heads turned. Betty's face lit up and she stood up and hurried over to the newcomers.

Maggie bit into a finger of toast and smoked mackerel and stared at Pete and Peggy. She wondered if she might learn something more about Jerry and Tommy from them, because Irene seemed to have forgotten she had been about to tell her something further. She sighed, thinking she would be better off not thinking of them.

'So what do you think of the smoked mackerel?' asked Josh, appearing in front of her. 'I was tempted by some smoked eel, but decided it isn't to everyone's taste.'

'I love smoked mackerel. Perhaps it's something I should think of having at the tearoom,' said Maggie, her eyes alight. 'I reckon it would go well with a salad and crusty bread in summer; a change from Lancashire hotpot if we were to have a heat wave.'

His lips twitched. 'How likely d'you think that would be?'

'One never knows,' Maggie replied, managing to balance her glass and plate with dexterity.

'D'you remember the summer of forty-seven?' asked Josh.

Maggie counted back to how old she would have been then. 'Just about. It was so hot that tar melted between the cobbles. It had been really cold at the beginning of the year and the snow had seemed to last for ages.'

'There were power cuts and we had to have candles,' said Josh. 'I reckon we're due another heat wave. If you'll excuse me, Maggie,' he added, and left her sitting alone before she could ask him why he worried about the girls.

But she was not left alone for long, because Peggy and Pete came over with Betty. 'Hello, you two. Long time, no see.'

'You look nice, Maggie,' said Peggy, drawing up a chair. 'I'm dead jealous of that green number you're wearing. It's fabulous. I reckon Norm's eyes would be out on stalks if he saw you now.' She glanced up at Pete, who was standing behind her with his hands resting on her shoulders. 'What d'you think, love?'

'I don't think Maggie cares what he thinks. He's history.'

Maggie agreed. She was more interested in the music. Nick had begun to play the introduction to 'The Twelfth of Never'. Monica moved over to the microphone and began to sing.

'I love Johnny Mathis singing this song,' whispered Peggy. 'It's so romantic.'

Maggie could not have agreed more. To have someone to really need you as well as love you to the end of time was surely what everyone wanted? And when Tony joined Monica at the microphone, a tingle went right down Maggie's spine. The girl's voice added an extra dimension to the rendering of the song. How could she have forgotten that Monica wanted to be a pop star? Maybe if a recording agent spotted her, she might just get her wish. How would the girl's grandmother and the rest of the family respond to that? Thinking of them, she wondered how they had reacted to Tommy's arrest and imprisonment after hearing of Bernie's death. Did she dare ask? Did she really need to know? Then she saw Marty go over to Monica, and decided that perhaps it was best to leave things as they were. After all, what had she to do with Monica's family? She should just enjoy the party.

There was more food, and Maggie had to admit that Josh and his helpers had made a good job of the catering. The bacon ribs were really tasty and the slices of chicken and roast beef were tender and moist and melted in the mouth. There were crispy fried potatoes and buttered carrot batons. By the time dessert had been consumed, which was a choice between trifle, fruit salad and cream and homemade chocolate Swiss roll, Maggie knew that she might have to let her waistband out.

Champagne glasses were recharged and Lenny thanked everyone for coming. He revealed that he and Dorothy would be leaving Liverpool for America in a few days' time. They would be making their home there for good. A collective gasp filled the room because most there had believed the couple would be returning to Liverpool later in the year.

'Did you know about this?' Maggie asked Josh, who happened to be standing nearby, clutching a half-empty champagne bottle.

He nodded. 'But I was sworn to secrecy.'

'So you're going to be the new owner of the coffee bar, not just an employee?' she asked. 'It is something I have thought possible when I guessed Dorothy and your uncle were likely to marry and him accompany her to America.'

He nodded. 'I'm going to give it a go, at least until the lease runs out, which will be in a couple of years' time.'

'It'll be very different to your life in the army,' said Peggy, who was sitting nearby.

'It's risk that makes life interesting. I've done the travelling and now I'm ready to settle down.'

'You're lucky,' said Pete, glancing across at him. 'I wanted to go to sea but I had an accident and that put an end to it. But what you said about change . . . I've been considering having a go at something completely different.'

Peggy nudged Maggie. 'I've heard this. I'm going to the toilet. D'you want to come?'

Maggie decided she might as well go with her. The room was becoming smoky and a bit too hot.

The toilet was occupied so they waited outside.

'Lenny's nephew seems a nice bloke,' said Peggy.

'Mmmm!' murmured Maggie.

Peggy cocked her head to one side. 'You're not struck?'

'I didn't say that. I like him.'

'What if he asked you out?'

'I'd consider saying yes.'

'Only consider? You are being cautious. I suppose that's because of what happened with Norm and Tommy,' said Peggy. 'My brother's not all bad, you know. Ask Pete.'

'I know that.'

The lavatory door opened and Betty emerged. 'I'd go for the nephew. You'd never have to cook a meal for him, Mags.'

'I said I'd consider saying yes,' repeated Maggie to shut them both up.

Peggy slipped inside the toilet and left the cousins alone.

'So what was this Tommy really like, Mags?' asked Betty. 'I don't remember ever meeting him.'

Maggie sighed. 'I really don't want to talk about him. You'd be better asking Peggy. Or ask Irene, I'm sure she'll have a different opinion of him. After all, she's been stuck with his son.'

'I don't think family are always the best judge. They think they know you back, front and inside out. The same with parents, who only see what they want to see. So I'm asking you. There must have been something about him that hit the spot, because you're a fussy so-and-so and not easily pleased.'

'Am I?' Maggie folded her arms in a defensive gesture across her breasts. 'Maybe that's because of Dad. He was the best, kindest, most generous and courageous man I've ever known, so most others fall short in comparison.'

Betty's face softened. 'I know. Uncle Owen was a lovely man, but nobody's perfect, Maggie. I suppose what it boils down to in the end is whether you love someone enough to tolerate their faults.'

Maggie's eyes flashed with annoyance. 'Tommy lied to me. He didn't even trust me with his real name.'

'Maybe he was trying to be the person he wanted to be with you and found it easier to suppress the truth than to admit to all his imperfections,' said Betty.

Maggie guessed that could be true, but she doubted she would ever know for certain, even if he confessed to it and that seemed extremely unlikely. 'I don't want to talk about him any more.'

'All right, I'm sorry. I'll say no more about him. Instead why don't you take my advice and go for Lenny's nephew? He's available, and I'm sure he thinks you're dishy. You could make it your business to drop by at the coffee bar at least once a week and get to know him better. After all, the pair of you have something in common. You're both involved in cooking and catering.'

Maggie sighed. 'How can I drop by at the coffee bar every week if I'm up in Whalley?'

'Surely Emma will give you a break sometimes?'

'Yes, but . . . oh, I wish people would leave me alone to go my own way,' cried Maggie, hugging herself and leaning against the wall.

'And what way is that, Maggie?' asked Peggy, coming out of the toilet. 'We don't want you to end up an old maid living in the cottage with a couple of cats for company.'

Maggie drew in her breath with a hiss and went into the toilet, slamming the door behind her.

Betty and Peggy stared at each other. 'I think we've annoyed her,' said Peggy.

'She can be really stubborn. It could be that she'll be better off living alone in the cottage with a couple of cats and listening to recordings of Mario Lanza than having a real man?'

'I can hear the pair of you!' called Maggie. 'And I'm not the only one who can be stubborn. Anyway, what's wrong with Mario Lanza? And I like cats! That kind of life will suit me down to the ground. I'm fed up with people telling me what to do. I can understand how Greta Garbo felt when she said, *I vant to be alone!*'

Twenty-Eight

'You do realize that if you go to the cottage now you're not going to be alone and you'd have to share a bed or sleep on the sofa?' said Emma.

It was a fortnight after the party, and Maggie felt a need to get away. 'I thought Betty and Stuart were going up to Scotland to see his relatives before going to the cottage?'

'No, Betty decided she couldn't cope with the long journey, so Stuart's gone up with their daughter while Betty is at the cottage with Irene.'

Maggie frowned. 'With Irene! I thought Betty wanted to do some painting. Has Irene taken the kids with her?'

'Just Josie.'

'Who's looking after Jerry?'

'He's at school most of the day; the Gianelli kids take him home to their house and Marty fetches him from there.' Emma sat down opposite Maggie at the kitchen table. 'Why don't you go into town?' she said persuasively. 'You can pop into George Henry Lee's and see if you can find a couple of buttons to match the ones on my red cardigan.'

'All right,' said Maggie.

Emma smiled and went into the living room.

Maggie followed her and watched as her sister-in-law opened her sewing box and took out a red button with a metallic centre. 'I couldn't find any to match in the local haberdashery,' said Emma. 'You should have more luck in town.'

Maggie agreed and left to catch the train. Once in town, and having had no luck in matching Emma's button at George Henry Lee's, she went to Lewis's. Again she was unlucky, so she decided to buy a set of attractive red buttons that had caught her eye, thinking it would be easier to replace the lot on Emma's cardigan rather than trying to find two to match the remaining ones.

After doing so, she wandered around the haberdashery department, looking at the different fabrics, especially remnants that were cheap, and imagining what dolls' clothes she could make from this or that pattern. Then, not fancying returning to Formby yet, she decided to visit the coffee bar. As she walked up Renshaw Street, she was thinking of her last conversation with Josh. She was so busy thinking that she was not watching where she was going, and collided into someone.

'Sorry, I didn't see you there.' Aware of a steadying hand on her arm, she looked up into eyes the same blue as Tommy's.

'It's Maggie, isn't it?' said Marty.

'Yes.' She could not think what else to say because she was struck afresh by that vague facial likeness to Tommy.

'How are you?'

'Fine,' she said brightly. 'I-I believe Irene and Josie are up at the cottage with Betty.'

'That's right.'

'Is . . . is Jerry all right?' she blurted out. 'I suppose he would have liked to have gone with them if he weren't at school?'

'He was all right about it once he realized the Gianelli kids would be taking him home with them. They have a slide and a swing and all manner of playthings in their garden.' He gazed at her intently. 'He remembers you, you know!'

Maggie flushed, wishing now that she had not mentioned Jerry. Why was it she took such an interest in him when she scarcely knew him? It was not as if the boy needed her in his life. Tommy might have mentioned needing a wife once but—

'You're welcome to pop in and see him any time,'

The invitation so surprised Maggie that she blurted out, 'Any news of your brother?' Then, realizing what she said, she gasped, 'Forget I asked!'

She hurried away. What had made her say that? She must be a fool to still feel something for Tommy, but it was proving increasingly difficult to quash her memories of him. Their conversations and the fun they had, and yet it had all been spoilt by his lack of trust in her. She carried on walking, thinking instead of Josh and how strong and talented he was, and just how much they had in common. She walked up Lycee Street, past the bombed church and as far as the Philharmonic Hall, before turning into Hope Street and dawdling along the pavement until she came to the coffee bar.

Pushing open the door she went inside. She had arrived at a time when most of the students who frequented the coffee bar were otherwise engaged. Only two other tables were occupied, and there was no sign of a waitress.

She sat down. The jukebox was silent, the couples were conversing in low voices, and she was content to sit there, waiting for a while and looking about her. It was then she noticed something different about the place. There were photographs on the walls, and some she recognized as being those that Dorothy had shown her of America. They weren't just enlarged photographs of Hollywood, but some were of San Francisco and San Jose, where Betty lived.

Maggie stood up and went to have a closer look at several of them, and was just considering whether she should go over to the counter and press the bell for service when Josh emerged from the kitchen.

He smiled when he caught sight of her. 'Hello, Maggie. What can I get you?'

She returned his smile. 'An espresso and a cake, please?'

'What kind of cake? Buttercream and jam, fruit cake, chocolate Swiss roll or plain Madeira?'

She gazed at him and decided that he really was worth a second or third, even a fourth glance, and if he were to ask her out then she would say yes.

'Well?' he asked.

'Do you make them all yourself?'

'I still employ the woman that Uncle Lenny hired to make the fruit cake and Madeira. She's been here almost since he opened up. I'm thinking of making my own custard tarts and seeing how they go.'

She was interested. 'I've never made them myself.'

'Then come and try one next week.'

She hesitated. 'I'll probably be up at Whalley, but when I get back to Formby I'll drop in and give them a go. Right now I'll try the buttercream and jam.'

He nodded and was back in what seemed no time at all with her order. She forked a decent bite-sized piece of cake and spooned it into her mouth. He hovered. She kept him waiting until she had eaten half the cake before saying, 'It's as good as Emma's.'

'Emma is your sister-in-law?'

'That's right. She owns the cottage and tearoom in Whalley. That's where I'll be spending most weekends heading up to summer, when I'll be there most of the time. She makes lovely Eccles and Chorley cakes. I've tried my hand at them and I think mine are improving, but they're not up to her standard yet.'

'You'll get there,' said Josh. 'I'd like to give them a try.'

She was delighted with his remark. 'I'll bring you some next time. It's a pity you couldn't come and visit. But, of course, now you're in charge here you're no longer a free man.'

He looked pleased. 'Thanks for the invitation, anyway. How's the coffee?'

She took several mouthfuls and said, 'As good as any I tasted in London.' She finished her cake. 'So, where are your waitresses?'

'Bobby's back at college and Lucia will be in later. I also have two sixth-formers who come in at lunch time and round about four o'clock when school lets out.'

'It must take some getting used to working here after cooking meals for hundreds of soldiers.'

'You can say that again.' He hesitated. 'I'll leave you to finish your coffee.'

She was not long in doing so, and took the bill and the money to the counter and rang the bell. He appeared almost straightaway. 'I'll definitely recommend you to those I know,' she said.

'Thanks, love.' He smiled as he took her money. 'Don't forget to call in again and try my custard tarts!'

She thought it was silly of her to feel warmed by his calling her 'love'. 'I won't. And I won't forget to bring some Eccles cakes for you to try out.' She paused. 'By the way, whose idea was it to put the photographs up on the walls?'

'Dorothy mentioned that there used to be paintings up on the walls at one time. I think she said the artist was your cousin, Betty. One of the photographs is of her house.'

'I know I've seen most of them before, but they were a much smaller size. They look great enlarged.'

'Thanks.'

She hesitated.

'Was there something else you wanted to ask me?'

She nodded. 'You said at the party you were worried about the girls. Why?'

'Because you get some peculiar types hanging around outside at times. I've even thought they might have followed the girls here.'

She frowned. 'There are some real creeps around. Maybe you should have a word with the beat bobby to keep his eyes open for any suspicious-looking blokes.'

He nodded. 'I just might do that. Are you sure you'll be all right on your own?'

She smiled. 'It's broad daylight and I carry a hatpin with me.'

'Wise girl.'

He saw her out and she set off along Hope Street towards the Anglican cathedral, thinking she might go inside and look around. It had been a few years since she had been in there, not since she'd shared a flat with Betty in one of the houses in Gambier Terrace across the road to the rear of the building. She thought of her cousin and Irene up at the cottage, and was glad she was not there with them. Most probably it would be like when she was a kid and they did stuff together and she was left on the outside.

Maggie had scarcely set foot in the house when Emma told her that there had been a phone call for her. 'Who was it?' she asked.

'I couldn't hear him properly. There was that much noise in the background. It was a man, and I suppose he could have been in a railway station.'

Maggie shrugged off her coat and hung it up before taking the paper bag with the buttons from her handbag and placing it on the hall table. 'It could have been Norm. If it was, then he was probably letting me know he was back in England and was at Euston and would be catching the train to Liverpool.'

'In that case you could probably check by phoning his mother,' Emma suggested. 'He's bound to let her know. D'you have her number?'

'It's in the address book. D'you want to have a look at these buttons and tell me what you think? I couldn't match the others, so I thought a new set would be best.'

Emma said they would do and asked if Maggie had enjoyed her trip to town. She told her about the lovely fabrics in George Henry Lee's and showed her some of the remnants she had bought with the idea of making dolls' clothes. 'I might also go back there and buy some fabric to make myself a new dress.'

'Haven't you enough clothes?' Emma asked her.

Maggie shrugged, not wanting to admit that some of her dresses were a bit tight. 'I just feel like something new.' She left the kitchen and went upstairs before Emma could ask her any more questions.

It was not until their evening meal was over that Maggie decided to ring the Marshalls', despite having made up her mind she was not going to get involved with Norm again. Still, she wanted to know if it had been him who had phoned.

Peggy answered the phone. 'Hi, Maggie. What can I do for you?'

Maggie told her.

'Pete's mam is out; as far as I know, Norm hasn't phoned here.'

'Then it might not have been him,' said Maggie, frowning.

She was about to put the phone down when Peggy said, 'I believe you saw Marty today.'

Maggie thought that news got round quickly. 'I was going to Lenny's. I wanted to try the place out now Josh is in charge.'

'How did you get on? Was he friendly?'

'Of course he was friendly. Why shouldn't he be?' There was an edge to Maggie's voice. 'I'm a customer and I'll be going back there because he wants me to try out his custard tarts. And he's going to taste my Eccles cakes. Satisfied?'

'You don't have to get your knickers in a twist, Maggie. It sounds as if it's a waste of time my asking whether he asked you out.'

'I wish people would stop trying to pair me off with someone,' she said crossly.

'Keep your hair on. Anyway, I was going to ask – did you know Irene's having a baby?'

'What!' Maggie could only think: *Poor Dot!*

'I said Irene's having a baby. You can imagine that she and Marty are thrilled to bits. It's what Irene wanted. A baby of her own.'

'Well, all I can say is that I'm glad I'm not up at the cottage with her and Betty, because the talk will be all pregnancy and babies.'

'I can understand you feeling like that,' said Peggy. 'It's more expense, of course. Especially now that Jerry is at school and growing by the day.'

'I know that from watching my nephew Owen. Poor Marty, he'll be having to work extra hours.'

'Well, you'd be wrong,' said Peggy.

'Why am I wrong?'

'Because our Tommy is handing over money for Jerry's keep.'

Maggie was stunned. 'How? Where's he getting the money from if he's in prison?'

'That surprises you, doesn't it, Maggie? It surprised us, too. Bye!' The phone went down.

Maggie was flabbergasted. She felt like ringing back and demanding an answer to her question. Except she had a feeling that Peggy was teasing her and would not tell her. 'What am I to make of it?' she muttered.

'What did you say?' asked Emma, who was on her way to put the baby to bed.

Maggie hesitated. 'Did you know that Irene's having a baby?'

'No, who told you that?'

'Peggy. And, by the way, they haven't heard from Norm, so it might not have been him.'

'It still could have been; perhaps he's planning on surprising his mother by just turning up on the front step.'

'Or it could have been a wrong number.'

'But he asked for Maggie,' Emma said.

'It's a common enough name.'

'All right, so it wasn't him.'

Maggie decided to forget about Norm. As it was, her mind was buzzing. Where could Tommy have got the money from to give to Marty?

She decided to skip going up to the cottage until after Betty had left for America. She and Stuart would be returning home in a few days. In the meantime she would make some Eccles cakes and pay another visit to the coffee bar.

She was baking a couple of days later, when Betty came into the kitchen. Stuart had taken their daughter to see the squirrels. Emma made coffee and she and Betty sat in the kitchen, talking and watching Maggie at work.

'Who are all these Eccles cakes for?' asked Betty.

'Some are for us, Dot and Billy, and some I'm taking to the coffee bar,' Maggie replied.

'You mean Lenny's place?' said Betty.

'No, Josh's place. I'm going to try out his custard tarts and he's seeing what my Eccles cakes taste like.' Maggie opened the oven door and placed a tray in the oven. 'Have you seen the photographs he has up in the coffee bar? There's one of your house and several of San Francisco and Hollywood. They look really good enlarged. Dorothy gave them to him.'

'I must take a look at them. It sounds as if the pair of you are getting nice and friendly,' said Betty.

Maggie darted her a glance. 'I thought you'd approve. How did you and Irene get on at the cottage? Did you get any painting done?'

'A bit. We did more talking and walking than anything else.'

'I suppose it was all about pregnancy and babies?' Maggie said. 'I'd have felt out of it.'

'No, I think you might have been interested. We were talking about Tommy. Irene's feeling better about him. There was a time when she only felt like throttling him. Probably just like you did.'

Maggie had just turned on the tap to wash her hands, but immediately she stopped what she was doing. 'Is that because he's coughed up some money for Jerry's keep?'

Betty stared at her. 'How do you know about that?'

'Peggy mentioned it when I rang her about something.'

Emma turned to Betty. 'Maggie had a phone call from a man, but I couldn't make out who it was and we thought it could have been Norm.'

'You're not going to go out with him again, are you, Mags?' said Betty. 'You'd be a fool to do so.'

'Am I heck?' said Maggie. 'He might think I'm a pushover, but I'm not. So did Irene say where Tommy got the money from?'

'No. Don't forget you've Eccles cakes in the oven.'

Maggie frowned. 'Is it that you don't want to tell me about the money, or that you don't know?'

'Honestly, the kids were with us and I got distracted. Besides, I thought you were no longer interested in him,' said Betty.

Maggie felt anger rising up inside her. 'You're a pig! A few moments ago you told me you thought I'd be interested in what you were talking about. You used to tease me like this when we were kids.'

'I'm being honest,' protested Betty.

'Calm down, Maggie,' said Emma.

'Yes, there's no need to get yourself in a twist. If you're so interested, why don't you drop in at Quiggins on Renshaw Street on your way to the coffee bar and have a word with Marty? If he thinks you've a right to know, then he'll tell you,' said Betty.

As Maggie washed her hands, she thought about her cousin's words and could not make up her mind whether or not to take up her suggestion. What had Marty thought when she had rushed off without waiting for his answer to her question about Tommy? That she was a right idiot, most probably!

Maggie had still not decided what to do when she went to town. She had bought a dress pattern, material and a Dinky car for Owen, and a rattle for the baby, and she was now walking up Renshaw Street. It was as she passed the Cathay Chinese restaurant that she came to a decision. Unfortunately, when she arrived at Quiggins, she was told Marty was out on a job.

'D'you want to leave a message, love?' asked the man behind the counter. 'He shouldn't be long.'

'If you could just tell him that Maggie Gregory would like a word with him. If he can spare the time, I'll be at Josh's coffee bar for the next hour or so.' He wrote down the message. She thanked him and left.

When Maggie arrived at the coffee bar, she was surprised to see Monica sitting alone at a table. She appeared lost in thought, so Maggie hesitated to join her and instead sat at another table that was partially concealed behind an enormous rubber plant. From the jukebox came the strains of Anthony Newley's 'Do You Mind?', which had knocked Lonnie Donegan's 'My Old Man's A Dustman' off the top spot in the charts. She hummed the tune to herself as she waited to be served, wondering whether the waitress was in the kitchen and how long she might be.

Shortly after the record came to an end, Maggie became aware of a commotion. She peered round the rubber plant to see what was going on. A man was leaning over the table where Monica was seated and poking her in the chest. 'Come on, don't you be pretending to me, girl, that you aren't meeting a man here?'

'It's none of your business, Uncle Dermot. Will you go away! You're making a show of me,' she hissed, brushing away her uncle's hand.

'Ha! So you are meeting someone.' He made to poke his niece in the chest again, but she folded her arms, so preventing him from doing so. 'Don't you touch me!' she said. 'Or I'll have the law on you.'

He slapped her face. 'Don't you speak to me like that! Your gran would have a fit if she heard you.'

Monica gasped and put a hand to her cheek.

Maggie rose to her feet and came out from behind the rubber plant. At the same time Josh emerged from the kitchen. 'What's going on here?' he asked.

'Keep out of this, you!' warned Dermot. 'Or I'll smack you across the gob. You're allowing soliciting in this hole.'

Josh frowned. 'Get out of here before I throw you out.'

Monica said, 'Yeah, get out, Uncle Dermot. I'm a good Catholic girl, I am, and this is a respectable coffee bar.'

'You're coming with me, girl!' Dermot seized hold of her arm and dragged her out of the chair.

Maggie gave Josh a shove. 'He hit her a few moments ago. Do something!'

'I'm going, woman!' Josh strode over to the struggling uncle and niece. 'Do as I say and get out of here before I call the police. You're disturbing my customers and I won't have it.'

'You just try and make me,' snarled Dermot.

Josh, his eyes dark with anger, seized Dermot by the back of his collar and dragged him away from Monica. 'Now out!' He propelled him out of the coffee bar and, closing the door behind him, shot the bolt.

There came a hammering on the door, but Josh ignored it and returned to the kitchen. Maggie and Monica stared at each other. 'Are you all right?' asked Maggie.

Monica nodded. 'I didn't see you come in.'

'You seemed in a dream, so I didn't like to disturb you.' Maggie thought the girl looked pale, except where the fading red imprint of her uncle's hand stood out on her cheek. 'Are you sure you're all right?'

Monica nodded. 'I was meeting an agent but he hasn't turned up.' She sighed.

'An agent!'

'Yeah, he'd heard me sing and thought I might have some talent. He wanted to talk to me about recording contracts and stuff.'

Maggie's eyes lit up. 'That would be great. But what does he mean, "you might have some talent"? You *do* have talent.'

Monica grinned. 'Thanks. That makes me feel a lot better.'

They were silent a moment and could hear Josh talking on the telephone. Monica went over to the outside door and shouted, 'You'd better scarper, Uncle Dermot, he's telephoning the scuffers.'

The banging continued for a few moments and then stopped altogether, and they heard voices and then a scuffle outside.

'That's Marty's voice,' said Monica, hurrying over to the door and unbolting it.

Josh suddenly appeared. 'Where's Monica gone? What's the door doing open?'

'Marty's outside. I think we'd better see what's going on.' Maggie did not wait for his reply but hurried outside.

Marty and Dermot were wrestling with each other. Dermot was turning the air blue with foul language and, even as they watched, he kicked Marty savagely in the shin with his hobnailed boot. Marty's leg buckled. Immediately Dermot shoved him to the ground and continued his assault.

Monica jumped on his back and Maggie shouted for Josh, but he was already there and dragging Monica away from her uncle. He got Dermot in a headlock and heaved him away from Marty. Dermot was gasping for breath and was clawing at Josh's hands.

Josh released him abruptly. 'Now bloody get out of here or I'll have the law on you,' he said.

Dermot got to his feet. 'I'll have you for this,' he said hoarsely. 'And as for you, Marty, you'd better keep a good eye on your kids.'

He staggered off along Hope Street, in the direction of the Philharmonic Hall. Maggie took her eyes off him and turned to see that Josh was helping Marty to his feet. He rested against the wall with his eyes closed.

'Are you all right, Marty?' asked Monica.

'I think he's bloody broke my leg,' Marty said through gritted teeth.

Maggie was gazing at Josh with shining eyes. 'That was fantastic the way you handled Monica's uncle. But I didn't like the way he threatened you and Marty.'

Josh shrugged self-deprecatingly. 'He's just a big blow.' He turned to Marty. 'Come on, mate. Let's get you inside.'

Maggie could not help but admire Josh's strength as he half-carried Marty indoors. 'Shouldn't the police be here by now?' she asked.

At the mention of the police, the other customers hurried outside.

'I was bluffing,' Josh said. 'Hopefully he has the bloody sense to have learnt his lesson.' He paused. 'Anyhow, I'm going to dial 999 now. We need an ambulance. Marty will have to have that leg X-rayed.' He looked at the other man. 'I'll call the police, too, if you like.'

Marty shook his head. 'I'll deal with this my own way. I'll go and visit his mother.'

Monica stared at him and slowly smiled. 'Let me know when you're going and I'll come with you.'

'Why, aren't you going home?' asked Marty.

'Not today – and not tomorrow, either. In fact I might leave it a week before I go home. I tried to keep it secret that an agent has shown interest in my singing because I knew Gran wouldn't approve. I think she's been having me followed. She thinks jazz and rock 'n' roll is the devil's music.'

'That's silly,' said Maggie.

'I wouldn't argue,' Monica said. 'But she and Mam are happy with me doing shift work in the biscuit factory, and don't want me trying to better myself.'

'I made a mistake in believing Bernie's brothers were satisfied with Tommy behind bars, but the way he went for me . . .' Marty shook his head.

'So where are you going to stay, Monica?' asked Maggie. 'You can come and stay with me at the cottage if you like?'

Monica shook her head. 'Thanks, but I've somewhere in mind.'

'Where?' asked Maggie.

'The Gianellis. I'm sure they'll put me up for a few days until everything calms down.'

'I'd better go and phone for an ambulance to take Marty to the hospital,' Josh said.

'I don't need an ambulance,' insisted Marty. 'Just let me use your phone and I'll speak to my boss. He'll send someone in the van to pick me up and take me there.'

Josh gave in and everything was done as Marty wanted. It was not until after he left that Maggie realized she had not had a chance to talk to him about Tommy. It was going to have to wait until another time.

Now all was quiet again, Maggie found herself relaxing. Josh made cups of coffee for her and Monica, so she took the opportunity of asking him if she could have one of his custard tarts.

He shook his head. 'You're out of luck, kid. They've all gone like the proverbial hot cakes. Although I do—'

Her face fell. 'But I came here especially. I even brought you some of my Eccles cakes in fair exchange.'

He smiled. 'I was about to say that I'll let you have the one I was saving to have with my cuppa.'

'What about me?' asked Monica eagerly.

'You had one earlier,' he said. 'Besides, I want Maggie's opinion. She's the professional baker.'

Maggie laughed. 'I wish.'

'Don't be modest,' said Josh, grinning. 'I'd value your opinion.'

'All right. I'll sit here at Monica's table.'

'Where were you before?'

She told him. 'That rubber plant is a good screen. I left my tin of Eccles cakes on one of the chairs.'

'I'll fetch it,' said Monica.

She came back with the tin. Its lid was off. 'These look scrummy,' she said. 'Can I have one?'

'Of course you can.'

'I'll get some plates.' Josh handed one to Monica and set a plate with a custard tart on the table in front of Maggie. 'Will Miss let me know what she thinks of it?' he asked her.

'Miss will. And she'll decide how many gold stars it's worth,' said Maggie, her eyes twinkling.

'Just go easy on me, Miss.'

She giggled. 'Don't be making me laugh! You get eating and let me know what you think of my Eccles cakes. You'll soon be having other customers in here wanting a coffee and something to eat.'

'I put the latch on. I thought we needed half an hour to ourselves. I'm staying right here because I want to watch your expression, so I'll know your true thoughts about my custard tart.'

Maggie gave in and ate the custard tart to the last crumb, while she watched his and Monica's expressions as they ate their Eccles cakes. 'Pity you haven't any more custards, Josh,' she said.

He grinned. 'I take it you think it's worth five gold stars. I rate this Eccles cake six.'

'I'd give it ten out of ten,' said Monica.

Maggie smiled, thinking that this was fun after all the kerfuffle earlier. 'Thanks.'

'What about the rest in the tin?' asked Monica. 'Can I have them? I'll pay for them. I'm sure the Gianellis will enjoy them.'

Maggie did not hesitate. 'You have them.'

Josh gazed at her. 'Are you doing anything this Sunday? I was thinking of having a day out in Chester. It's years since I've been there.'

'Say yes, Maggie,' said Monica, sounding pleased.

'As much as I'd like to do so,' said Maggie regretfully, 'I'm off to Whalley for the weekend.'

He looked disappointed. 'I was forgetting. Can't be helped. Work must come first. Another time.'

'Yes, another time would be great.' She offered to pay for the coffee and custard tart, but Josh waved her away and said the Eccles cake was fair exchange. He unbolted the shop door and she and Monica left together.

'What about the agent you were waiting to see?' asked Maggie as they walked along Hope Street.

Monica sighed. 'If he thinks I'm any good, he'll be back.'

'I'd get in touch with him again if I were you. Just like modelling, the entertainment world is very competitive.'

'Perhaps I will,' said Monica.

As they walked into the city centre together, they were silent. It was not until they were about to part in Lime Street that Monica suddenly said, 'Why had you arranged to meet Marty at the coffee bar?'

Maggie hesitated.

'You haven't a pash on him, have you? I know he looks a bit like Tommy, but—'

'Don't be daft! He's a married man and his wife's a friend of mine. Besides, I didn't intend talking to him at the coffee bar. I dropped by at his workplace because I wanted to ask him something, but he wasn't there, so I left a message.'

'Did you want to ask about Tommy?'

'Yes, but I can't imagine you'd know the answer.'

'Try me,' said Monica.

'Peggy told me that Tommy is sending money to Marty and Irene to help with the expense of them looking after Jerry.'

'You're right,' said Monica. 'I know nothing about that, but I can tell you something. From what I've heard, he could be out of prison by the end of next year. His defence lawyer made the most out of Tommy's heroism in saving the little boy's life at the risk of his own. Tommy was badly injured.'

'I didn't know he was badly injured.'

'Oh, he's OK now. Don't you be worrying about him. His injuries stood him in good stead when it came to the trial. There was also the fact that he was newly widowed with a young son and was trying to go straight. It all went down well with the jury. There were also a couple of character witnesses who spoke up about the way his father treated him when he was just a lad,' said Monica softly.

'He told me he hated his father,' said Maggie, thinking Tommy might need help when he came out of prison, despite what Monica thought, but she hadn't finished talking. 'Yes, Mr McGrath put him in hospital once. He also threw him out of the house. I read in a newspaper recently that there's often one in a family that gets picked on more than any of the others.'

'That's so sad.'

Monica nodded, and then she leaned forward and unexpectedly kissed Maggie's cheek. 'Thanks for inviting me up to the cottage, but I've things to do here. See you around.'

Maggie watched her cross the road. When she reached the pavement in front of the Cenotaph outside St George's Hall, Monica turned and waved. Maggie waved back, thinking that perhaps she would go straight to the cottage now. She needed some time alone to think over all that she had discovered that day. She checked for her bank book in her handbag, but it was not there. She counted the money in her purse but there was not enough for a ticket to Whalley. She would have to return to Formby and stick to her plan to go to the cottage at the weekend.

Twenty-Nine

The baby was asleep in her pram in the front garden where Emma was doing some weeding when Maggie arrived. For a moment she leaned on the garden gate, watching her sister-in-law, then Maggie lifted the latch and pushed open the gate. 'Time for you to have a break,' she said. 'I'll put the kettle on.'

Emma glanced up and then scrambled to her feet and removed her gardening gloves. 'I've something interesting to tell you. I'll come with you now.'

'What is it?' Maggie followed her indoors.

'I had a phone call after you went.' Emma began to wash her hands under the kitchen tap.

'Who from?'

'Nellie Gianelli. Her brother wants to talk to you and he'll be visiting her this evening.'

'Her brother? You mean Father Francis?'

'That's the one. Apparently it was him who phoned wanting to speak to you that time I thought it was Norman.'

Maggie was flabbergasted. 'You're joking!'

'Why would I joke?' asked Emma, drying her hands. 'And put the kettle on now, instead of just standing there. Dot will be back soon with Owen and Georgie.'

Maggie was momentarily distracted from her own affairs. 'Georgie!'

'Yes!' Emma smiled. 'She and Billy are trying their hand at fostering.'

At last something else that was positive to celebrate, thought Maggie, her eyes shining. She wondered what Josh would say when he heard about it. 'I'm sure it's the right thing for both of them.'

Emma smiled. 'Yes, and by the way, I've mentioned to Jared that you might need a lift to the Gianellis' house this evening.'

'Thanks,' said Maggie. 'But I haven't said I'll go yet. Did Nellie say what her brother wanted to see me about?'

Emma hesitated. 'Apparently he visits Tommy McGrath in prison.'

Maggie's heart began to thud and she felt for a chair and sat down.

As Emma put the kettle on and set the tea tray, she kept glancing at Maggie. 'Are you all right? Would you like a scone with cream and jam?'

Maggie nodded. 'It's not the only shock I've had today.'

'Why, what else has happened?'

Maggie told her. Emma looked suitably surprised.

'I can't believe this should all happen today,' Maggie said, taking a huge bite out of the cream and jam scone.

'It's happening all right, but you don't have to go and see the priest if you don't want to. I mean, do you really need to know anything more than you do already about Tommy? Don't you think you need to draw a line under your involvement with him? Just think how much he hurt you?'

'Don't you think I've spent enough time thinking about doing just that?' said Maggie, reaching for another scone. 'I've listened to what other people have said about Tommy. Perhaps I need to hear the truth from him now.' Emma was silent as she refilled their teacups. 'I can't say I'm keen on speaking to the priest,' continued Maggie. 'When have I had anything to do with Catholic priests? I've had little enough to do with vicars in my own church.'

'But you've met Father Francis at Nellie's house when you went there with Betty and Irene.'

'That was different. I hardly ever spoke to him.'

At that moment the kitchen door opened, and Owen appeared in the doorway. 'We're here!' he cried.

Dot loomed up behind him with Georgie by the hand. His face was pressed against her skirt as she helped him up the step. 'You're back then, Mags,' she said. 'This is Georgie.'

Maggie thought it was a while since she had seen her sister looking so happy. 'Hello, Georgie!' Maggie hoped her voice sounded normal, because she was not feeling a bit like her normal self.

Owen skipped over to Maggie and rested an arm on her knee. 'Have you brought me anything nice from town?'

'Owen, you don't ask,' rebuked his mother.

'Auntie Maggie doesn't mind my asking if I give her a kiss.' He smiled up at Maggie.

Despite her emotions being in turmoil, she could not prevent a smile and, putting an arm around her nephew, she bent over him and kissed his cheek. 'You'll have to wait and see,' she said.

'Now go and get changed,' said his mother. 'Then you and Georgie can watch television for half an hour.'

Owen said, 'Auntie Maggie will be Georgie's auntie as well, won't she?'

'She will,' said Emma.

Georgie lifted his head and smiled shyly at Maggie, and she realized that next time she went into town she was going to have to buy two Dinky cars.

As soon as Maggie saw Jared, she could tell that he was not convinced that it was in Maggie's best interest to see the priest.

'Do you really want to find out what he has to say about a man who deceived you, or are you being pressurized into it?'

'If I don't go I'll always wonder if I should have done.'

'OK, I'll take you there and pop in and see Marty and Irene at the same time. When you've finished, you can come round to theirs.'

She thought that suited her down to the ground.

Maggie had always enjoyed visiting the Gianellis' house in the past because there was such a welcoming feel about the place, but as she stepped over the threshold that evening, her pulse was racing. She was shown into the front room. To her relief, Nellie's brother did not look like a priest, but was dressed in dark blue corduroy trousers and a pale blue shirt, open at the neck. He looked much less intimidating in his casual clothes. He was helping one of the Gianelli children to do a jigsaw. Nellie told Maggie to sit down, beckoned her daughter out of the room and closed the door behind them.

Francis smiled at her. 'It's good to see you again, Maggie. You're looking well.' He reached into the pocket of the jacket hanging on the back of his chair and took out an envelope. 'Tommy wanted me to give you this.'

Maggie gazed at the envelope and saw that her name and address were typewritten. 'Why didn't he just have it posted?' she asked.

'He wanted to make sure that you would definitely get it. It seems he has more faith in God than the Royal Mail.'

She glanced at him. 'God? Tommy never gave me the impression that he was religious.'

Francis said gravely, 'A near-death experience affects people in different ways.'

At the mention of near death, Maggie felt a sinking in the pit of her stomach at the thought of Tommy's injuries. 'Monica said that he was OK.'

'He is, but it's doubtful whether Tommy will ever be able to work as a motor mechanic again due to the damage to his pelvis.'

She turned the envelope over between her hands. 'So what will he do?'

'Read the letter. I think its contents will surprise you. I can leave you alone to read it now if you wish. You might want to give me a message to pass on to him.'

'Thank you. I'll do that.'

Francis stood up and left the room.

Maggie took a deep breath and slit the envelope open with a finger and removed several sheets of paper. The fact that they were typewritten surprised her. She placed them on the table next to the jigsaw puzzle and flattened them out and began to read.

Dear Maggie,

I know this letter is a long time coming but I honestly believed that you would never want to hear from me again. (Honestly! Maggie thought. Did he really know what 'honesty' meant?) *Lately, though, I've had the impression from a couple of people that you might actually be prepared to read something that I have written. I'm hoping you will forgive me for my lack of communication and for a load of other stuff as well. Mainly for not being honest with you. If you'd had a father like mine, then you might have become a habitual liar like me.* (Blaming someone else for something he should have controlled.) *From the moment I broke a gas mantle when I was four years old and owned up to it and was whacked for my honesty, I thought twice about admitting to anything that seemed likely to result in punishment. Sometimes it was ignorance that got me into trouble, but other times I was just reckless and greedy. I've always run away when trouble stared me in the face and when stuck I've lied my way out of a fix. I'm a coward, and the only brave thing I've ever done was save little Johnny Schofield's life. There are still times when I can't believe that I actually risked my life for someone else.*

Anyway, I didn't intend to deceive you as much as I did. (Then you shouldn't have done so, she thought crossly.) *The name Timothy Murphy I adopted because I liked it, and believed if any of my enemies came looking for me they'd be trying to find me under the name Tommy McGrath. So I'd already reinvented myself before we met. As for the rest, I fancied you when we met on the train, so I wanted to impress you. When we got talking, I began to think that here was a girl out of the ordinary whom I was getting on with and I'd like to see again. I never intended it to get serious, but it did, and that was when I realized what a hole I had got myself into because sooner or later you'd want to see Jerry and meet my mother.* (Too true, and you should have thought of that from the beginning.)

I told you that Jerry and I were going to stay with Mam because I did not doubt that if I told you the truth – that I was planning to dump him on my brother and sister – you would consider me a right selfish sod. Which I am. Even if I'd explained why I thought I was doing the right thing at the time, you probably wouldn't have agreed with me. As for the truth about Bernie, that was so complicated, I couldn't even begin to explain the ins and outs of it all to you.

The same with my getting involved with a gang of thieves. The truth about that was, when I was an apprentice on very little money, some of which I had to hand over to my father, my pockets were always to let. I liked to have money in my pocket to impress the girls, and so I was easily led astray. My having money impressed Bernie all right, and before I knew it we were married.

A big mistake. And now I come to my getting involved in borrowing cars. I would occasionally use one I had repaired, but return it to the garage in time for it to be collected by its owner the following day. Not long after Bernie and I were secretly married, I borrowed a car too many, and if I had not left Liverpool in a hurry, I would have ended up in prison sooner than I did for driving the getaway car in a robbery. So I escaped to Ireland and then went on to Australia.

I just didn't have the guts to tell you about my past and being wanted by the police because I didn't want you to know what a louse I was. At least you and I had some good times together. I would have liked them to last longer, but our Marty's wedding put an end to that. I don't blame you for not wanting anything to do with me after hearing the truth from those who know me best. I should have told you the truth myself. I'm sorry I hurt you.

She paused at this point and took several deep breaths before continuing reading.

Prison could be a lot worse. I'm reading more books than I've ever done and have learnt to type because some reporter said I'd had an interesting life, so I'm having a go at writing my adventures down with her help.

The judge took into consideration some of the time I spent in the prison hospital as part of my sentence. I was also given a shorter sentence than is normally meted out for my crime, and that means I'll be out of here by Christmas 1961. The reason why he did so was due to certain mitigating circumstances, such as my bravery in saving little Johnny at the risk to my own life, as well as my having recently lost my wife and being left with a motherless little boy. I'd shaved off my beard and was wearing my best cherubic expression. The thought of spending years in prison frightened me to death, so I was hoping to rouse sympathy in the breasts of the women in the jury.

Maggie gave a twisted smile, easily able to imagine him doing so. He was incorrigible.

So, Maggie, I've been thinking a lot about what to do with the rest of my life, and I have this idea it should have something to do with music and writing. If I could work from home, I won't need much help with Jerry now he's at school. What with Marty's wife Irene having a baby, I can't be expecting her and my brother to continue taking care of Jerry. Besides which, the poor little sod wants to live with me. Marty showed him the newspaper cutting saying I was a hero. Jerry likes the thought of his dad being a hero. He knows I was injured and can't do all that I used to, and wants to look after me. Kids, they can always surprise you.

Maggie smiled grimly, thinking she could agree with that all right. Knowing she must surely be nearing the end of the letter, she read on swiftly. So far there had been no mention of his having loved her and that he had once said that he would marry her.

This next piece of news will surprise you and I hope you'll be pleased for me. Due to our Peggy's husband Pete managing to remember the licence-plate number of the hit-and-run car, the bobbies traced the driver who, as it turned out, had been drinking. Anyway, his insurance company has paid me a large sum of money because of my injuries, which means Jerry and I should be all right for dosh for a while when I get out of prison. Who knows, maybe I'll be able to write a bestseller. I've also thought of writing music reviews for the newspapers. And I am planning to have my name changed by deed poll – it will be a clean slate for this Timothy Murphy!

I wouldn't mind seeing you again, Maggie, if that's not asking too much? I still have feelings for you.

Tim

Maggie folded the letter with trembling fingers and placed the sheets of paper in the envelope. No mention of love, only that he wouldn't mind seeing her again and that he still had feelings for her.

She left the room, guessing that she would find Father Francis in the kitchen, so she went in that direction. He was sitting at the table with his sister and her husband, drinking sherry.

'Would you like a glass, Maggie?' Nellie asked.

'No, thanks. Jared is waiting for me at Marty and Irene's and I know he likes to spend some time with Owen at bedtime.'

'I'll see you out, Maggie,' said Francis, getting up.

He accompanied her to the front door. 'Is there any message you'd like me to pass on to Tommy?' he asked.

'Thank him for his letter, and tell him I need to think over what he has said before I reply to it.'

Francis nodded. 'I'll tell him that. Is there anything more you'd like to ask me?'

'No thank you.' She walked off down the drive and took out Tommy's letter and reread it as she made her way to the Leeds–Liverpool canal and across the bridge. By the time she reached the library, her eyes were sparkling as she read snippets of it for the third time, trying to imagine what he had really been thinking when he had written certain passages. This reporter who apparently was going to help him write his book, was she another woman he had charmed?

Irene opened the front door to her. 'Everything all right?' she asked, sounding as if she really cared.

Maggie did not answer. 'How's Marty?'

Irene led the way up the lobby. 'You can see for yourself how he is. I could kill that Dermot.'

'I don't blame you for feeling like that,' said Maggie.

Irene ushered her into the kitchen. Jared looked at Maggie. 'Are you all right?'

She nodded and glanced at Marty, who had his leg up, his foot resting on a pouffe. 'How is your leg?'

Marty shrugged. 'Fortunately it isn't broken, but he chipped the bone with his great big hobnailed boot and my leg is swollen. But I'll survive.'

'I'm glad to hear it. He was horrible. I'm glad that Josh almost choked the life out of him.'

'Sit down, Maggie,' said Irene. 'You're looking done in.'

Maggie sank on to the sofa. 'It's been a bit of a day.'

'Would you like a sherry?' Irene asked.

'Thanks.'

'What did the priest have to say?' asked Jared.

'You don't have to talk about it in front of us if you'd rather keep it to yourself,' Marty said swiftly.

'He didn't say much, just gave me a letter from Tommy, although he signed it Tim.' She took a deep breath. 'He's changing his name to Timothy Murphy by deed poll. Also, the letter was typed. Did you know he could use a typewriter, Marty?'

'I knew he was learning to type.'

Irene handed a glass of sherry to her.

Maggie downed the sherry in one go. 'There was a lot in his letter. Did you know he's writing a book?'

'No!' Irene stared at Marty in astonishment. 'Did you know? Peggy hasn't mentioned it.'

'He hasn't mentioned it to me either,' Marty said, shaking his head. 'Did he say what it was about, Maggie?'

'His life so far. Apparently some woman reporter told him he'd had an interesting one.' Maggie toyed with the sherry glass.

'Sounds just like Tommy. Full of himself,' said Irene. 'More sherry, Maggie?'

Maggie held out her glass. 'He did go half across the world to Australia when he was on the run from the police, and admits that he was led astray by a desire for money because the girls like a bloke who had money to spend,' she said softly. 'Then, of course, he could have women readers reaching for their hankies because his wife died young, leaving him with a child to care for. Then, on top of all that, he hit the headlines saving a little boy's life at the risk of his own and suffered injuries and, because of that, he ended up in hospital and prison.' She sipped the sherry that Irene had poured into her glass.

The two men glanced at each other and raised their eyebrows.

Irene said, 'You sound sorry for him.'

'Do I?' Maggie shrugged.

'Where do Marty and I come in this book he's writing?' asked Irene.

'He didn't say, but I'm sure you will come into it,' said Maggie. 'Maybe I will, too. Of course, he'll probably fictionalize parts of it, but it sounds like it could be a warts-and-all story because most likely he believes nobody wants to read about a goody two-shoes.'

'You've got it all worked out,' said Jared, staring at his sister as if seeing her for the first time.

'Have I?' She was not so sure. In fact, her emotions were in turmoil.

'Did he say he was sorry for lying to you and hurting you? That to me is the most important thing he should have said in his letter.'

'Yes, he did. He made excuses for his behaviour, but I expected that, and don't we all make excuses when we've done wrong?' said Maggie, draining the sherry glass.

'I hate to admit it, but I can't help but admire his having a go at something completely different,' said Marty. 'He's not going to be able to fix cars again, and the money he's been awarded for his injuries won't last forever.'

'You can't admire him!' cried Irene. 'After all the trouble and embarrassment he's caused you and the family!'

Marty shrugged. 'There have been times when I'd like to throttle him, but then I'm no saint.'

There was silence.

Jared said, 'Time we went, Mags, if I'm to read Owen a story before he goes to sleep.'

Maggie stood up. 'Thanks for the sherry. I hope your leg gets better soon, Marty.'

'Don't be a stranger, Maggie,' he said, reaching out to her.

They shook hands.

On the way home, her brother said to Maggie, 'I hope you

can draw a line under this whole thing to do with Marty's brother now, Mags.'

Maggie rested her head against the back of the car seat. 'Shall we drop it for now? As I said earlier, it's been a bit of a day.'

Jared glanced at her. 'You aren't feeling sorry for him, are you?'

She glanced at him. 'What d'you think?'

'I don't know what to think. I mean, Marty admitting that he can't help admiring his brother – after all he's done – took me by surprise! He needs his bumps feeling.'

Maggie yawned. 'I'm tired.'

'You need a holiday. We've forgotten you originally came home from London because you were ill. I mean, what were you thinking of, making Eccles cakes for all and sundry?'

'I enjoy baking. It's soothing. I'll enjoy getting away to the cottage this weekend, so don't fuss.'

'OK, as long as you take note of what I've said and don't have anything more to do with Tommy McGrath,' he said. 'After all, he's not the only pebble on the beach now, is he?'

Thirty

Maggie was rolling out pastry when she heard the telephone ringing. She had been at the cottage a fortnight and, although she had been kept busy at the weekends, weekdays were quieter, giving her plenty of time to think about Tommy's letter, which she had yet to answer. The questions she kept asking herself were: Did one good deed make up for a number of bad ones? And was the writer of the letter the real Tommy McGrath or the make-believe Timothy Murphy? Soon she was going to have to come to a decision as to whether she needed to visit him or not.

She thought of Josh and the conversations they'd had, especially the one at Lenny and Dorothy's party. If, after he'd called her at the cottage and she'd told him about the wedding invitation, Tommy had confessed to her in a letter, might she have seen it as a test of her love for Tim and forgiven him? What a difference it would have made if he had plucked up his courage. They could have gone to the wedding together and played happy families. Obviously Tommy had not trusted her enough to put their relationship to the test.

She wiped her floury hands on a cloth and hurried into the front room. She gave the number and a voice came over the crackling line.

'Maggie, is that you?'

Recognizing the voice, she was in two minds whether to pretend she was someone else, but that probably would not work. 'Yes, it's me, Norm. What d'you want?'

'What are you doing up there?' he asked. 'I thought you'd be here. When Emma told me you were at the cottage, I was disappointed.'

'I have a living to earn.'

'If you married me, you wouldn't have to earn a living,' he said. 'I'll come up to Whalley tomorrow and I'll have a ring with me.'

'Marry you!' She was not only astonished but furious. 'Don't be ridiculous. Anything we had is long dead.'

'Don't be like that, Maggie. Give me a second chance. Everyone is entitled to a second chance.'

'So I've heard. But I don't think it applies in this instance. If you come up here, I'll be tempted to push you in the river, so be warned,' she snapped, and slammed the phone down.

She could feel herself trembling and, in an attempt to calm herself, she went into the garden and wandered slowly from shrub to shrub, breathing deeply of the early roses before returning to her pastry-making. Norm's words, 'Everyone is entitled to a second chance,' echoed in her mind. Perhaps it was time to reply to the letter and have a couple of days away from the cottage. There were a few people she wanted to see. And if Norm was to have a wasted journey tomorrow, he only had himself to blame.

Pete had been listening to his twin's side of the phone call. 'I think you're an idiot. You're wasting your time. Maggie's not going to give you a second chance and I don't blame her.'

Norm thrust out his bottom lip. 'Why d'you have to say that?'

'Use your brain. You treated her lousy and you've lost your chance with her.'

Norm grunted moodily, taking out his cigarette case and lighter. 'She agreed to go out with me in London. Once she sees the ring, she'll change her mind.' He lit a cigarette.

'I wouldn't bank on it. Besides, you're not the only fish in the sea.'

Norm stared at his twin through a veil of cigarette smoke. 'You don't mean that bloke who made up to her on the train?'

'Peggy's brother. He's written to her and, according to Marty, she was impressed with what he had to say.'

'You're not going to tell me he'll be out of prison soon and is trying to get her back?' asked Norm in astonishment.

'Not yet, but . . .' Pete let the words hang.

'That's OK then.' Norm visibly relaxed.

'I wouldn't be so sure.'

'Why, what's he got to offer her?'

'More than you think. Anyway, there's Josh as well.'

Norm almost burnt himself on his cigarette. 'Who the hell is Josh?'

'Lenny's nephew; he's taken over the coffee bar. He's a great chef.'

Norm scowled. 'Is he good looking?'

'Why don't you go and see for yourself? I've got things to do.'

Norm decided that he just might do that, and wasted no time heading for the city centre. He strolled leisurely along Renshaw Street, pausing to gaze at the motorbikes on sale, then continued up to Leece Street, thinking of Maggie and what he could do to persuade her that they could still make a go of things. Seeing his twin settled and with a baby had roused longings inside him. He wanted to have someone to come home to and his own place by the time he next set sail.

The first thing he noticed on reaching the coffee bar was that the name was just the same. Could be that this Josh bloke had not made up his mind to definitely stay on here? He pushed open the door and went inside. His ears were immediately blasted by the noise from the jukebox.

He looked round and spotted an empty table and headed over to it. Only when he sat down and a waitress approached him with a smile and addressed him as Pete did it occur to him that he could so easily be mistaken for his twin.

'I'm not Pete, love,' he said, thinking she had a nice smile.

'Oh! Then you must be Norman.'

'That's right.'

'I'm Lucia,' she said, stretching out a hand. 'We've met before at my Aunt Nellie's in Litherland.'

Norm just about remembered her, but she had been much younger the last time he had seen her, and chubby with it. Now she had slimmed down and had a shapely figure and appeared grown up. How old was she? He reckoned about eighteen. 'Pleased to see you again,' he said.

'Same here.' She beamed at him. 'I can't get over how like Pete you are. Anyway, what can I get you?'

'My brother was telling me the new owner is something of a chef.'

Lucia nodded vigorously. 'He's fab. He does a mean Welsh Rarebit and a lip-smacking steak and kidney pie with chips and peas. If you've a sweet tooth, we have some really nice cakes, as well as his homemade custard tarts, and treacle pudding with custard, and Rosie's trifle.'

'Sounds the gear. I'll have a coffee and the steak and kidney pie, and if I'm still hungry, I'll decide on afters then,' Norm said.

She went away with his order and he took from his inside pocket the newspaper he had bought outside Central Station. He wondered what excuse he could make to get a look inside the kitchen, so he could get a butcher's at the chef.

Norm need not have worried, because when he had eaten every delicious morsel of the steak and kidney pie, Josh left the kitchen and came over to his table to ask whether he had enjoyed his meal.

'I cannot tell a lie,' said Norm, giving Josh a swift perusal and decided that the competition might be more serious than he had thought. 'It was the best steak and kidney pie I've ever tasted. Almost as good as my fiancée, Maggie Gregory, makes.'

Josh's smile faded. 'Your fiancée?'

'That's right. I've just got back from sea and we'll be tying the knot as soon as possible.'

'I don't get it. She told me a while ago that she had finished with you.'

For a moment Norman was dumbfounded, and then he found

his voice. 'All couples have their disagreements. We're back together again now.'

Josh did not know whether to believe him or not, but could hardly call him a liar. He'd need to speak to Maggie, but that would mean admitting that her answer really mattered to him. And there was that other bloody bloke who had messed her about to take into consideration as well.

'Anyway, I'd like a pudding. Something light,' said Norman.

Josh pulled himself together. 'Trifle?'

Norm nodded.

Josh signalled Lucia and told her to bring a portion of trifle to Mr Marshall and then vanished into the kitchen.

Norm gazed about him and noticed a girl sitting at a table over by the window. She looked stunning, dressed as she was in a bright green top and yellow slacks. He thought she looked vaguely familiar.'

'That's Monica,' said Lucia, placing a bowl of trifle on the table in front of Norm. 'She sings with Tony Gianelli's group. No doubt you'll have heard of them?'

Norm nodded and turned his attention to the girl in the green top and yellow slacks once more. She was gazing out of the window, so there was little chance of attracting her notice. He went back to reading his newspaper while eating his trifle.

A moment later a man entered and went straight over to the table where Monica was seated. Her face lit up. Norm felt disappointed as he watched the man sit down opposite her and they began to talk. After a while they stood up and, with a wave of the hand in Lucia's direction, Monica and the man left.

Norm decided to forgo coffee and, picking up the bill, took it and the money to the counter. 'You can keep the change, love,' he said.

'Thanks,' said Lucia. 'It looks like Monica might be getting an agent at last.'

'Agent?'

'Yes, she's hoping when he hears her sing this evening, he'll want to get her signed up for a recording contract.' Lucia smiled into his eyes. 'Wouldn't you just love to go to the Cavern and hear the group play? I've heard them practise at my Aunt Nellie's house. They're really good.'

Norm nodded slowly. 'I wouldn't mind hearing them.'

'I've a couple of tickets,' said Lucia.

Norm smiled. 'You're suggesting I come with you?'

She shook her head. 'No, I'm suggested you might like to buy one from me. We're always short of money in our house. What with all the kids, and Mam being pregnant again. I wish Dad would tie a knot in it.'

Norm could not help admiring her nerve. He laughed and took out his wallet. 'How much?'

'Two quid.'

He gave a low whistle but handed over two crisp pound notes. 'I can see you being rich one day.'

Lucia smiled. 'That's my plan.' And she hurried into the kitchen, singing.

'Will you stop that noise?' said Josh, frowning.

She stared at him. 'Sorry, but I'm feeling happy. I just wish I had a date, but all the lads who come in here are too young.'

'I would have thought they were about the right age for you.'

She shook her head. 'I prefer someone more mature.'

'Has *he* gone?'

'D'you mean Pete's twin or the agent? Because they both have,' said Lucia. 'They're going to the Cavern. I wish I had someone to go to the Cavern with, but I only have one ticket and I never feel safe in town on my own, so I think I'll go to the local picture house instead. After all, I can hear Monica and the group practising at Aunt Nellie's anytime.' She stared at him. 'You look like you could do with cheering up. Why don't you buy my ticket for the Cavern?'

Josh hesitated and decided he didn't have anything better to do. 'All right! How much d'you want for it?'

She told him. 'It'll help put food on the family table.' She held out her hand. He raised an eyebrow, but did not argue with her, and handed over the money.

She pocketed the two pounds, thinking that if only he looked at her in the way he looked at Maggie Gregory, she would have given it to him for half price.

Maggie arrived in Lime Street in the late afternoon and immediately went to catch a bus to Litherland. As the bus went along

Stanley Road, she was remembering how, after her father had died, she and her mother used to regularly make this journey after one of their shopping sprees in Liverpool on a Saturday. She gnawed on her lip, thinking of her dad and the warmth and kindness and honesty he had shown to so many people, although that generosity of spirit had blinded him to their faults sometimes.

Nellie was in the kitchen, about to dish out the family's evening meal of spaghetti Bolognese, when Maggie arrived at The Chestnuts in Litherland Park. Getting no answer at the front door, she had gone round the back and knocked there.

'I'm not stopping,' said Maggie. 'I just wanted to ask you to do me a favour and give this letter for Tommy McGrath to your brother to deliver for me. I don't have either of their addresses.'

'Of course,' said Nellie, taking the envelope and placing it in the pocket of her pinny.

'I also wanted to ask if Monica is still staying with you?'

'At the moment she's in town, having gone in early to meet someone. The group is playing at the Cavern this evening.'

Maggie remembered the last time she had been at the Cavern. It had been with Tommy; the place had been smoky and crowded but the music had been good. She made up her mind to go into town and see if she could get in to hear Monica sing. There were bound to be people there she would know, but she had better give her sister a ring and tell her she was going to be late.

It was a fine evening and Josh was enjoying the walk across the city centre. It did not take him long, for he was in a hurry, having left the coffee bar later than planned. He had only just turned into Mathew Street when he felt a blow on the back of the head and his legs gave way beneath him.

If it had not been for a group of young people on the way to the Cavern, then his assailant might have managed to get in a second blow. As it was, he barely managed to escape before they arrived at the spot where Josh was slumped on the ground.

'Did you see that bloke?' cried one of the girls. 'Go after him, you two!' she told the two youths accompanying them. 'See if you can catch him.'

'He might have a knife,' said one of them.

'It wasn't a knife he used but what looked like a cosh,' said one of the other girls. 'Don't be such cowards. Just follow him and see where he goes if you don't want to get too close to him.'

The youths stalled no longer but took off after the man, while the girls bent over the figure lying face down on the ground. 'His head's bleeding,' said the one who had taken command.

'Poor bloke. I suppose we should find a phone and dial 999,' said her friend.

One of the girls gently shook Josh's shoulder. 'Are you OK, luv?' she asked.

'Are you daft? He can't hear you. He's unconscious,' said the first girl.

'What's happened here?' asked a voice behind them.

One of the girls glanced up at the stylishly dressed woman. 'Someone hit him on the head and then ran off. I'll go to the Cavern and tell them what's happened and ask them to dial 999,' she added.

'Well, go on then!' cried her mate. 'And be quick about it. We don't want him dying on us.'

'All right, keep yer hair on,' she said, and click-clacked off in her high heels.

'D'you think we should turn his head sideways to make sure he can breathe?' said one of the girls.

'Do it gently,' said the newcomer, taking the place of the girl who had gone off to the Cavern.

Maggie gazed down at Josh's profile. Her heart seemed to slam against her ribs so that, for a moment, she felt as if she could not breathe. Then she pulled herself together. 'We should put something under his head,' she said, taking off her jacket.

She folded it and knelt on the ground while two of the girls lifted Josh's head, so she could slip the jacket beneath it. As his head was gently lowered on to the jacket, he groaned.

'That's a relief! He's coming round,' said one of the girls.

Josh's eyelids slowly opened and he gazed, bleary-eyed, up at them. Then his eyelids drooped again.

'Hey, none of that,' said Maggie, a tremor in her voice. 'You have to stay awake. Tell me your name?'

'Maggie?' he muttered.

'OK, thank goodness you recognize me. Now open your eyes. I want to see what colour they are.'

'Yours are blue,' whispered Josh.

'That's right,' said Maggie, relieved.

His brow knitted and he winced. 'What am I doing lying on the ground?'

'Some bloke coshed you and then ran off when he saw us coming,' said one of the girls. 'A couple of the lads have gone after him.'

Josh attempted to sit up.

Maggie placed her hands on his shoulders and forced him down. 'Now listen to me and do as you're told, lie down and keep still. You're best staying where you are until the ambulance arrives.'

'Ambulance! Bloody hell, Maggie, I don't want an ambulance.'

'Don't be daft, Josh! You can't ignore being knocked unconscious.'

'I've done it!' A girl's voice interrupted them. 'An ambulance and a bobby are on the way. The bobby will probably get here first.'

She was right.

Within minutes a policeman who had been in the vicinity arrived on the scene, and the girls wasted no time telling him what they had seen. The two youths returned just as the ringing of the ambulance bell was heard, and said that they had lost the attacker but *this* had dropped out of his pocket. It appeared to be a blunt instrument made of wood and, apparently having remembered all the crime films they had ever seen, they had picked it up with a handkerchief in case there were fingerprints on it.

The ambulance drew up at the end of the alley. The policeman managed to exchange a few words with Josh, who protested about being taken to the Royal Infirmary, saying he had baking to do and the coffee bar to open in the morning.

'Don't be worrying about that, Josh,' said Maggie, gazing down into his drawn face, aware that the girls were listening to every word that was said. 'If you give me your keys, I'll see to everything.'

'You know each other?' said the constable.

'Yes,' said Maggie softly. 'But we didn't know we were both going to be here this evening. Perhaps if we had come together, this wouldn't have happened. Do you think this was an isolated incident, constable? Or have there been other attacks on people in this vicinity? Because it's possible I might know who did this.'

The constable said, 'None that I'm aware of, miss. Maybe you should tell me who you suspect?'

She told him what had happened at the coffee bar just over a fortnight ago.

He nodded thoughtfully. 'If it is him, we'll catch him, don't you worry. Now, if I can just take your details and then leave the gentleman with you until the ambulance arrives, I'd be grateful.'

She nodded. 'I'd best give you both our names and addresses.'

Josh opened his eyes and dug into an inside pocket; he produced a key ring with a number of keys on it and handed them to her. 'Thanks, Maggie. But there's things you need to know in case I'm not back by morning.'

She smiled. 'Don't worry about anything. I'm sure I'll be able to work things out. You just rest.'

'What about the tearoom?'

'I'll telephone Emma and explain what's happened. Everything will work out, I promise.'

'Thanks.' He reached out and squeezed her hand and closed his eyes.

She watched as he was carried on a stretcher to the ambulance. When the doors closed behind him, she felt suddenly very anxious. What if his injuries proved serious, even fatal? As the ambulance drove off, she wished she could have gone with him, but it was too late now and, besides, she had made him a promise and had a job to do.

Thirty-One

Maggie stifled a yawn as she unbolted the door, having heard the milk delivery man outside. The last few hours had been busy ones, and she did not doubt that the coming day was going to be even busier. Even if Josh was allowed home, someone was going to have to make sure he did not overdo things.

She carried in the crate of milk and placed the bottles in the fridge. She had checked its contents earlier and looked in the freezer and removed some frozen sausages and bacon. She was just about to make herself a cup of tea when she heard a van draw up outside. She guessed it would be a bread delivery, and hurried outside. She exchanged greetings with the driver and explained what had happened. He made suitable noises as he carried in a tray of bread, rolls, barm cakes, buns and teacakes, before leaving his bill and driving off.

Maggie decided to make a chocolate cake to go with the Eccles cakes she had already baked. She had just placed it in the oven when the door opened and Lucia, Monica, Bobby and Nick walked in, all looking slightly anxious.

'You still here. Isn't he back yet?' asked Nick.

'You knew I'd be here?' said Maggie, surprised.

'We were in the Cavern when these girls came in saying someone had been attacked in Mathew Street. Apparently, they were full of it. Then your name and Josh's came up,' he said.

'It was a shock, I can tell you,' said Monica.

'I only heard about it after Monica told Aunt Nellie, who phoned me to let me know,' said Lucia. 'I felt terrible because it was me who sold him the ticket. I had no idea you were going to be there as well.'

'Why should you?' said Maggie. 'Are you all right to put in a few more hours here today? I've no idea when Josh will be back. I was going to phone the hospital soon. Hopefully they'll tell me how he is, because they don't always if you're not family.'

'But he has no family,' said Bobby, putting on an apron. 'Only Lenny and Dorothy, and they're in America.'

'It must be lonely having no mam and dad or brothers or sisters,' said Lucia. 'I know I moan about our lot sometimes but, thinking about it, I wouldn't be without them. He doesn't even have any cousins.'

Maggie thought about what Jimmy had said on Christmas Day about Nick being Dorothy Wilson's son. If that was so, then Josh did have a cousin by marriage, which was something. But right now, it was not enough. Josh undoubtedly needed her. That thought gave her a warm feeling inside.

'Have you any idea who it might have been, Maggie?' asked Nick.

She looked at Monica.

'I know what you're going to say,' said Monica. 'You thought it might be Uncle Dermot because he threatened Josh. He also threatened Marty, saying he should keep an eye on the kids. I don't have any qualms this time about him being reported to the police. Besides, he snitched on Tommy to the police. I know our family and the McGraths haven't always seen eye to eye, but Gran would go mad if she knew Uncle Dermot had gone for Josh and was thinking of snaffling Jerry and Josie. Marty's made a fab job of taking care of them.'

'Right,' said Nick. 'I'm going to phone Dad.'

The girls looked at Maggie as he went over to the telephone.

'Shall I carry on as usual?' asked Lucia.

'Yes, and you can tell me what usual is, and which is the key to the safe because we're going to need a float?' Maggie held up Josh's keys.

Lucia had no idea which was the safe key, but she knew what some of the keys were for so it was easy enough to work out.

'You're wasting your time there,' said Bobby. 'It's a combination safe. As it happens, I know the combination.'

Maggie left sorting out the money to Bobby, while she took her cake from the oven. Fortunately it was not burnt.

'It looks nice and smells lovely,' said Monica, sniffing the chocolate cake. 'Are you going to put butter icing on it?'

Maggie had noticed that there was a bottle of Camp chicory and coffee essence in the cupboard. 'I'll do coffee butter icing once it cools down.' She would have been enjoying herself if it were not that she was concerned about Josh. What if he died? The thought caused a chill to trickle right down her spine. She told herself not to look on the dark side. She liked it that the girls were prepared to muck in and help her. After working mainly on her own up at the tearoom in Whalley, it was good to have company, although Nick seemed to have disappeared.

She was just icing the cake when Josh walked in. 'You're all right!' said Maggie, unable to conceal her delight. Already she was looking forward to spending the day in his company. 'I was just thinking of phoning the Royal to see how you were.'

'Are we pleased to see you,' said Lucia, grinning.

'What are you all doing here?' he asked, sitting down on the nearest chair.

Maggie thought he still looked pale. 'Are you sure you're all right? You haven't gone and discharged yourself?'

'I'm fine.' He squared his shoulders and cleared his throat. 'Thanks for all you've done, Maggie, but I can manage from now on.'

Her face fell. 'Don't be silly! You can't possibly be doing all the cooking yourself after being knocked on the head. What if you fainted and fell on the stove and burnt to death?'

He gave a twisted smile. 'My, you've a vivid imagination. That's not going to happen.' He hesitated. 'I don't want to keep you, Maggie. I'm sure you've lots to do. After all, you've just got engaged, so your fiancé told me yesterday.'

'Fiancé! What fiancé? Who on earth told you that?' said Maggie.

Josh's expression altered. 'Norm Marshall.'

Maggie was astounded. 'Norm Marshall! I told him I'd push him in the river if he came bothering me again. What a damn cheek!'

'But he said you'd be getting hitched soon. He was quite clear about it.' Josh needed to be absolutely sure he was getting what she had said absolutely right.

'Over my dead body! You wait till I see him.'

'Well, I'm glad to have that cleared up.' He grinned, stood up, and rubbed his hands together. Then he frowned. 'There's nobody else you'd rather be with, is there?'

'If you've seen Billy and he's mentioned a certain letter I received from Marty's brother, I can tell you now that I have no plans to make up with someone who admits to being a habitual liar and a coward. A woman has to be able to trust her man to have faith in her. Although a leopard might change its spots, it no longer concerns me if Tommy or Timmy is spotted or striped.'

He grinned. 'Right! Now, what's there to do?'

Maggie looked at him, her beautiful blue eyes shining in a way that made Josh believe his feelings for her might just be reciprocated.

'Right now?' She dabbed him on the tip of his nose with the icing palette knife and then licked it off and kissed him. His arms went round her and he returned her kiss. If she'd had any doubts about whether he was really the right one for her, they vanished in that moment like morning mist in the rising sun.

The girls clapped and cheered and there was a wolf whistle. 'What's going on?'

Maggie and Josh drew apart and stared at Nick and Inspector Sam Walker standing in the doorway. 'Did you get him?' asked Josh.

Sam nodded. 'As Maggie suggested to our man last night, we went looking for him. And would you believe, we caught Dermot lurking outside the Red Lion in Litherland. He'd been drinking and he tried to persuade the barman there to swear he'd been there all evening.'

'He's crazy,' said Monica. 'He'd have had better luck if he'd stuck to the Throstle's Nest on Scottie Road. They know him there.'

Nick said, 'Maybe, but apparently he's been dropping in at the Red Lion off and on for the past fortnight, and not just in the evenings. He obviously was thinking of snatching Jerry and Josie if he had the chance.'

Monica shook her head in disgust.

'Anyway, his alibi wouldn't have stuck,' said Sam. 'His finger-prints were all over the weapon those lads found. Monica, I've spoken to Marty and he wants you to drop by at his house sometime today before you go home to your mam and gran. He's going to go with you and take Josie and Jerry. He wants to sort out this division between your families for the kids' sakes.'

'Sounds sensible to me,' said Monica. 'And hopefully Gran will be pleased that an agent has taken me on and I'll be doing what I really want to do, and that's sing.'

'Well done, kid.' Josh bent over and kissed her cheek.

'Congratulations,' said Maggie, beaming at her. 'Who's to say that Tommy just might be interviewing you for the showbiz newspapers one day.'

'Why d'you say that?' asked Monica.

'Apparently he sees his future in writing, not only about the music scene but he's writing a book about his life.'

'Blinking heck! Who'd have believed it!' Monica paused. 'I wonder how he and Uncle Dermot will get on if they meet up in gaol. All hell could break loose.'

'All grist to the mill of a writer, I should imagine,' said Nick.

'However good a scene it would make in a book, it's not going to happen,' said Sam firmly. 'Sorry to disappoint anyone.'

'Now, let's forget about the pair of them. Tommy especially is yesterday's news,' said Maggie, her eyes meeting Josh's. 'We'll have to open up soon and we've a lot to think about.'

He agreed and kissed her once more and her spirits soared.

'I'd best be going and leave you lovebirds to get on with things,' said Sam.

Everyone said tarrah.

Josh wasted no time in seeing him out.

There were smiles all around. 'So, folks, d'you want to know what I'm thinking?' asked Monica.

'What?' said Maggie, smiling.

'I think we should have a party as there's lots to celebrate.'

Epilogue

There was to be more than one party, but the larger one took place two months later in the apartment above the coffee bar on Hope Street. All Maggie and Josh's friends and most of their extended family were there, and although Jared might have expressed the odd qualm about his sister's health in moving into a flat at the heart of Liverpool, despite Maggie reminding him that the benefits of the Clean Air Act were starting to kick in, he had to be satisfied with the thought that at least she and Josh would be spending part of the year running the tearoom in the clean air of the Lancashire countryside, while Lucia, ably assisted by Rosie and a sixth-former, and under the auspices of Bobby or Emma, ran the coffee bar during its least busy period, when the university and colleges were closed for the summer holidays.

Downstairs, Lucia was feeling in need of a break. Everybody upstairs now seemed to have had enough to eat and drink, and the noise level was probably louder than it had been in the Cavern the last time there. Maggie and Josh had announced their engagement and had been toasted in champagne – or beers for those who had no taste for the fizzy stuff. Monica and Tony, who had also been taken on by the same agent, were singing Anthony Newley's hit song 'Do You Mind?' in beautiful harmony.

'If I say I love you,' sang Lucia softly to herself.

She sighed. Jimmy, her first big crush, was upstairs, too, although he was on his own, because his wife had given birth to twins, a boy and a girl, and was staying at her parents' home. All had been forgiven since the arrival of the grandchildren.

Lucia had felt a little sad at the thought, but that was all behind her now. Right at this moment, she was starving, having hardly eaten anything because along with Rosie, Bobby, Nick and Patrick, she had been fetching and carrying food and drinks. The others having served themselves had now joined the party upstairs.

But Lucia had just discovered a tin on a chair behind the rubber plant, and recognizing it as belonging to Maggie, she opened it and found, as she expected, some Eccles cakes inside. Lucia really enjoyed an Eccles cake. So, despite knowing she would leave a trail of delicious puff-pastry crumbs on the floor, she did something that she had been meaning to do for a while, and began to walk round the coffee bar to scrutinize the photographs there with more care. She had looked at them before and thought she had seen a man in the crowd on one of the Hollywood ones before, but could not remember which one. She had a feeling she had seen him here on Hope Street, hanging around outside the coffee bar not so long ago, but she did not know his name. How strange if the two men were one and the same.

Lucia was on her second Eccles cake when she heard the clatter of the letterbox. She saw an envelope being pushed through and hurried to pick it up. She expected to see Josh and Maggie's names written there, but it was addressed to Dorothy Wilson. Perhaps it was a fan letter, and the person wanted it to be forwarded to her address in America. She opened the door and was just in time to see a youth vanishing around the corner in the direction of the cathedral.

She shrugged and closed the door, thinking there had been lots of cards for Josh and Maggie from various places in the country and abroad, as well as several telephone calls all the way from London and America during the past week, as well as a card from one of Her Majesty's prisons. She had noticed Maggie give a twisted smile when she had read that one.

Of course, Lucia had known it was from Marty and Peggy's brother. She remembered him coming into the coffee bar once, and also of seeing his photograph in the *Echo*. She had really liked the look of him. And according to what she had overheard, he had been awarded a lump sum for the injuries he had sustained when he had saved that little boy. Not only that, he was going to write the story of his life so far, and she would bet a pound to a penny that it would be a bestseller. Maybe he would have a signing session here in the coffee bar. After all, so many of them at the party upstairs were related in some way or other to him. She remembered hearing Maggie telling Josh that – once they were married – he would have a whole host of relatives. He had winked at Maggie and said, 'One big happy family!'

As Lucia carried the envelope addressed to Dorothy Wilson upstairs, she was humming to herself, looking forward to the day when she would meet the notorious author, Timothy Murphy.